Drama Queen Saga

Drama Queen Saga

La Jill Hunt

www.urbanbooks.net

Urban Books, LLC
97 N18th Street
Wyandanch, NY 11798

ISBN 13: 978-1-62286-721-9
ISBN 10: 1-62286-721-1

First Trade Paperback Printing October 2015
Printed in the United States of America

10 9 8 7 6 5 4 3 2 1

This is a work of fiction. Any references or similarities to actual events, real people, living or dead, or to real locales are intended to give the novel a sense of reality. Any similarity in other names, characters, places, and incidents is entirely coincidental.

Distributed by Kensington Publishing Corp.
Submit Orders to:
Customer Service
400 Hahn Road
Westminster, MD 21157-4627
Phone: 1-800-733-3000
Fax: 1-800-659-2436

Prologue

Kayla drove home, slightly buzzed from the mixture of alcohol and the contact smoke from her girls who were smoking weed while they put together favors at the house of one of her bridesmaids. As Ice Cube put it, today had definitely been a good day. Hell, it had been a good year. She and Geno, the love of her life, her boo, her sweetheart for the past two years, her best friend and the best lover she had ever been with, to say the least, were getting married in two weeks. She smiled at the thought of being his wife.

She met him her junior year of college. They were both transfer students and both majored in English, which meant they were in a lot of the same classes. They hit it off instantly. She was attracted to his rugged body and intellectual mind, a ruthless combination in her book. He was funny and kept her laughing, and she loved being around him. He called her his pro-bono tutor and they did homework together. Study sessions turned into dates and dates turned into overnight rendezvous, and senior year she moved into his small apartment. After graduation, she began teaching and he began working at the local radio station, and they got a bigger place. It was inevitable that they would be married, she knew it. Geno was her soul mate, and everything was looking up for them. Life was good.

She pulled into the driveway and decided to leave the wedding favors that she and her bridesmaids had finished in the trunk of her car. She was too sleepy to even bother with them. She fumbled with her keys and unlocked the door, giggling to herself as she stumbled into the dark apartment. Geno was probably passed out in a hotel room somewhere. His bachelor party was tonight and she had the entire place to herself.

As she made her way past the kitchen, she thought she heard a noise and stopped, listening closer. It was coming from the bedroom. She inched her way to the room she and her fiancé shared and stood in the doorway, amazed at what was going on. The room was completely dark, but she could make out two shadows in their bed, illuminated by the glow of the streetlight coming through the window. The first shadow, was without a doubt a female. Her body was rocking back and forth, breasts bouncing, hair flowing as her head rolled in ecstasy, riding as if she was on one of those mechanical bulls Kayla had seen in commercials for country western bars. The dick must have been good, because whoever she was, she could barely moan. Every time she tried to catch a breath, the second shadow would put it to her with quickness, causing her to gasp again. But Kayla knew the dick was good because it had been thrown to her on a regular basis. She knew what the girl was feeling because she had felt the exact same way that very morning. The second shadow was Geno's. She could tell from the moans and the way he was gripping the headboard with his thick fingers. He liked to grip it when she rode, because he said he could get more leverage that way.

She stood for a few moments, too shocked to move. She had heard stories of men sleeping with the strippers from their bachelor party, but this took the cake. *I know this nigga ain't bring home one of those tricks from his party and fucking her in our house, in our bed. This nigga must be high on crack,* Kayla thought to herself. She got her thoughts together and ran into the kitchen. Making sure she was extra quiet, she pulled a big pot from under the cabinet and filled it with scalding water. When it was full, she struggled back into the bedroom and closed her eyes. Her grandmother had once told her about two dogs that were screwing in her front yard and got stuck together. The only way they got them unstuck was to toss hot water on them. Well, Kayla was about to get two bitches out of her bed. She groaned as she lifted the heavy pot and tossed the hot water on the two shadows.

"Sssshhhit!" the female screamed as the water hit her on the back. Geno was dazed by what was happening until the liquid hit his arms and upper torso.

"What the fuck?" he screamed in pain as the girl rolled from on top of him onto the floor, writhing in pain.

Satisfied with her handiwork, Kayla finally flicked the light switch. Everyone squinted as their eyes adjusted.

"You bastard! You brought a trick home and did her in my bed? Our bed? What kind of shit is that?" Kayla screamed and jumped on the bed, swinging at him.

"Kayla, what the hell is wrong with you? What are you talking about?" he said, looking at his burnt skin.

"Don't play crazy, bitch! How could you do this to me?" She clawed at his face and he grabbed her arms, still looking confused.

"Kayla, calm the fuck down!" he warned. They had never gotten physical in all the time they had been together. It was Geno's rule never to push each other to that limit. He had seen his parents fight his entire life, and told Kayla that would never be him. But he had gone beyond the limit this time, and she didn't care what the rule was; she was out for blood.

"Calm the fuck down? Calm the fuck down? I know you ain't in here fucking another bitch and you telling me to calm the fuck down! Where are you at, bitch? I ain't forgot about your ass, either!" Kayla yanked away from Geno and jumped onto the floor, standing over the still whining woman. The woman whimpered as Kayla yanked her by the hair so she could look into her face. A combination of nausea, betrayal, and pain came over her as she realized who was looking back at her.

"Kay . . ." the woman began. She could not finish because Kayla slapped her so hard that she fell back onto the floor.

"What the fuck is going on?" Geno sat up and looked at the crumpled body next to his bed. He shook his head as sobriety set in and it became apparent that it wasn't his fiancée he had been making love to as he thought, but another woman.

"I can't believe you would do this to me, Geno. Her, I could, but you?" She looked at him with hate in her eyes. Never in a million years would Kayla have thought that Geno would cheat on her. It was the one thing she told him from day one that she wouldn't stand for, and he assured her he'd never do.

"Kayla, I swear. I don't know how this happened. I was drunk and I thought it was you. She was in the bed when I got here." He tried to explain.

"You thought she was me. My God, Geno, then your perception of me ain't that great, is it?" She looked over at the woman and shook her head. "I'm not surprised by you. I just thought you would have pulled something like this after me and him got married."

"He came onto me. I was in here 'sleep and he seduced me!" the woman cried.

"Bitch, what the hell were you doing in my bed? Why the hell were you even in my house? You know what? It don't even matter. You fucked him, you marry him, you slut. At least the same parents will have paid for the motherfucking wedding," Kayla told her. She wiped the tears forming in her eyes before they had a chance to fall.

"Kayla, don't do this. Wait a minute." Geno scrambled for his sweats as he got up. His head was throbbing and his arm began to blister, but he paid it no mind as he tried to get Kayla to listen to him.

"Let her go, G. She better be glad I don't call the police on her for assault. Look at my back. Payback is a bitch, you'd better believe that!" Kayla's sister pointed at her red, swollen back. Kayla ignored her and began to snatch clothes out of the closet and stuff them into her duffel bag. She knew she could not stay in that house another moment.

"Get dressed and get out, Anjelica!" Geno yelled, "Kayla, listen to me. Don't throw this away. I love you and I wanna marry you. This is all just a big misunderstanding."

Geno tried to take the bag from her but she slapped him.

"I advise you to stop talking. The more you try to explain, the worse you make this already fucked up situation. She doesn't have to get out. Y'all can pick up right where you left off after I get my shit!"

"Where're you going, Kay?" he pleaded. He knew he had messed up big time and Kayla was gonna need some time to think. But he wanted her to understand that what happened was not his fault. He needed to know she would still marry him.

"None of your fucking business! I'll get the rest of my stuff later, when neither of you is here! But good luck to you both." She took off the engagement ring she had been wearing with pride for the past year, and threw it at Anjelica. "You can have this and him!"

She stormed out of the house with Geno calling after her and Anjelica still whining about her back. The stupid bitch still didn't have the sense to apologize. Kayla checked into a hotel, not wanting to face her family or friends.

In the two weeks leading up to Kayla's wedding date, she moved into her own place and sent out cancellation announcements, telling everyone that she and Geno decided they just weren't ready. On the day they were supposed to wed, Kayla boarded a plane to Jamaica, their honeymoon destination, by herself. She called Geno from the plane, telling him that she would never forget how he hurt her. He told her that she was totally overreacting and he still wanted to marry her. That they could get through this. She told him she didn't want to get through it because she was already over it. She had decided to go on with her life and so should he. She hung the phone up, vowing to never again trust another man.

1

Whoever said it's better to have loved and lost than never loved at all was a ign'ant ass, Kayla thought as she checked herself in her rearview mirror. It had been a year since her breakup with Geno and she still felt like shit. She had tried to throw herself into teaching and becoming a better person, but even that wasn't helping to mend her broken heart. Her girls had discovered this new sports bar called State Street's and actually convinced her to come. She wasn't all that enthused, but hell, maybe a night out was what they all needed.

All of Kayla's girls were single with no kids. They were hard working, smart, educated black women who were attractive both inside and out. Any man would have been blessed to be with one of them, but they found themselves manless at the present. Kayla had affectionately named them the Lonely Hearts Club and they had fun, nonetheless, just hanging out, living the single life. Their group consisted of Roni and Tia, two of Kayla's college buddies, and Kayla's coworker, Yvonne.

The club was not overcrowded, but there were quite a few people. Kayla had just arrived and was looking for Yvonne when she felt someone grab her hand, startling her. When she turned around, she had to do a double take. For a moment, she thought it was Geno, but it wasn't. Although they had the same caramel complexion and similar features, this guy had a bald head, where Geno kept his thick curls cut close. He wore a mustache and goatee, as did Geno, and they had the same athletic build.

"Oops, my bad," he said when he saw the confused look on her face. "I thought you were someone else."

He checked out Kayla with her cocoa brown skin, dimpled smile, curvaceous figure and short-cropped hair cut. It was no doubt he liked what he saw.

"Oh, no problem." Kayla finally found her voice. "Excuse me."

"At least let me buy you a drink. I know you wanted to slap me for grabbing you like that." He smiled at her and extended his hand. "Craig."

"Kayla, and you don't have to do that, really, it's okay," she answered, shaking it. She quickly turned and spotted Yvonne and Roni coming toward her. She maneuvered past him and shook her head, forcing herself not to turn back around.

"Who is that, Geno's cousin or something?" Roni asked.

"I don't know. He accidentally grabbed me, thought I was someone else or something. His name is Craig." Kayla shrugged.

"He looks just like Geno, except he got a bald head and he got the thug thing going on. Better watch out," Yvonne said. Yvonne thought all hard looking guys were criminals, and she and Roni always had comments about drug dealers and jailbirds.

They found a table near the dance floor and were having a ball drinking and laughing. Soon, Roni and Tia were on the dance floor as Kayla and Yvonne watched. The deejay was spinning old school jams they had not heard in years. Kayla could not stop rocking to the beat. Then, as if on cue, Craig pulled her out of her chair and onto the floor. He had some moves. She could not help but laugh and demonstrate moves of her own. For the first time in a long lime, she was enjoying herself.

"How about that drink?" he asked when the deejay decided to slow it down. She didn't think twice as she followed him to the bar. He seemed like a nice guy and they vibed for the remainder of the evening. She was surprised when she looked at her watch and realized it was after midnight.

"I gotta go," she told him reluctantly.

"The club doesn't close until three. What's the rush?" he asked. "You got a man at home waiting for you?"

"No. If I had a man, do you think I would have let you up in my face all night?" She laughed.

"Oh, I was all in your face, huh? That's how it is? Well, if that's the case, can I at least get your number so I can stay up in your pretty face?" He looked at her with such intensity she felt a chill down her spine.

"Let me get your number and I'll think about it," she said. He asked a passing waitress to borrow her pen then grabbed a napkin off her tray, writing his number on it.

"Well, you do that. But at least call and let me know you made it home safely." He placed the napkin in her hand.

"Won't you still be here until three?" Kayla put the paper in her pocket without looking at it.

"I put my pager number on the top. Call and put in code o-o-one. I'll know it's you."

"Oh, no. I pick my own code. And you'll know it's me. I don't want some code you probably give to all your club chicks." Kayla gave him a quick hug and went back to the table to bid good-bye to her girls.

"I thought you and him went to get a room or something," Tia joked.

"Girl, please. I just met him. I didn't even give him my number." Kayla smirked.

"But I bet you got his," Yvonne threw at her. "I guess you won't be going home pining away for Geno tonight, huh?"

"Why? She met the next best thing tonight. He looks just like him," Roni said. "I ain't mad at you, though. You know my motto. The best way to get over a nigga is to get under another one."

"All of y'all are sick. I'm out," Kayla said and headed out of the club. As she turned to leave, a familiar face in a crowd of females caught her attention.

"Kayla, isn't that—"

"Yeah, that's her." She cut Roni off before she could finish her question. She wanted to walk by and pretend she didn't recognize her, but the pretty woman waved and headed in her direction.

"Kayla! Didn't think I'd run into you!" She smiled.

"Anjelica. I should say the same thing." Kayla didn't even try to fake a smile.

"Well, some friends and I drove up this afternoon. It *is* my birthday."

"Happy birthday, Anjelica." Roni raised her eyebrow at what could be Kayla's twin.

"Thank you, Roni. At least you can acknowledge it, unlike some people. But what can I expect from someone who blames me for every nigga that did her wrong?"

"Whatever, Anjelica. If I were you, I'd get outta my face, you jealous trick. Green was never a good color on you." Kayla turned to leave.

"Geno thought I looked good in green." Anjelica smiled wickedly. She knew that would get a rise out of her sister.

"Don't play with me. I already owe you an ass whooping. And I have no problem giving it to you on your birthday," Kayla growled as she stepped into Anjelica's face. She knew that although her sister talked a good game, she was weak and would never fight her.

"Whoa! Hold up, ladies. I think you two need to separate." Kayla felt a hand on her arm and looked up. It was Craig. He led her out to the parking lot and walked her to her car. She let her girlfriends know she was okay as they stood and talked for a few more minutes.

"Who was that?" he asked.

"That was my sister, the bitch." She smiled at him. She felt so safe next to him; it was somewhat arousing.

"Damn, I thought y'all was about to throw down in there." He laughed. "That was your sister?"

"Yep and today's her birthday. I shoulda gave her ass some licks. That is the tradition, isn't it?"

"I like you. You got spunk. I think that is so damn sexy." He leaned near Kayla.

"I'll call you and let you know I made it home." She winked at him as she got in her car and drove off, leaving him standing in the parking lot.

She thought about Craig all the way home. After all the crap Geno had put her through, maybe she deserved a little uncommitted fun. Maybe Craig was just what she needed. While sitting on the side of her bed, Kayla looked at the piece of paper Craig had given her, wondering if she really should call. Her eyes fell on the picture she still had on the dresser. She and Geno had taken it the day they graduated from City College. Although she hated to admit it, she still loved him. Probably always would. But he had moved on and so should she. Reaching on the nightstand, she grabbed the cordless phone from the charger. She dialed the pager number and after the series of beeps, she entered her cell number along with the numbers six and eight. Smiling, she climbed under her covers and went to sleep.

2

The next morning, she had a message waiting for her. "I'm happy you made it home safe, and even happier that you called me. I really want to get together later. If you're interested, give me a call." Craig's voice sounded so sexy on the phone.

"Call him, girl," Roni advised her. "He was cute and you can have some fun. Don't be all serious. He can be your rebound man."

Kayla should have known not to ask Roni, but she had popped up at the music store to meet Kayla for lunch and she couldn't resist telling her about the message.

"What do I say?" Kayla asked her. Out of all her friends, Roni was considered the wild one. She always had a trail of guys who she had on call, so if there was an event she wanted to attend that required an escort, she had an abundance of men to choose from. She never got too serious or "caught up" and always said she would never get married.

Because of this, Kayla thought, she had never had her heart broken.

"Come on, Kay. Say you're interested. Go out. Have fun. Get some. Girl, you are young and free. Enjoy it," she said between bites.

"I don't know, Ron."

"I know you ain't still dwelling on that nigga Geno. Kayla, he's had no problem getting footloose and fancy-free. I know you heard about his new girl. You better get real. How long has it been? A year?"

"A year and some change. But you're right. I do need to get on with my life." Kayla nodded. She didn't dare tell Roni that she had hooked up with Geno last month on a whim. They had talked occasionally and run into each other at the music store.

"Get out and get some, Kayla. Call him. Go out. What's the worst that can happen?" Ron reached for the check. "It's on me, girl."

"Which one of your suitors hooked you up this weekend?"

"Trey. He got his income tax check and he won't be here next weekend for Valentine's. He feels bad." Roni laughed. "I guess I'll have to go out with Darren so *I* won't feel bad, huh?"

"You are crazy. You give the word player a whole new definition. I can't wait for the day you fall in love."

"Never that, sweetheart. I got too much game."

"Okay, game. Let's go before I get fired," Kayla said and rose to leave.

"So, when are you gonna call?"

"After I get off."

"Handle your business, girlfriend. And let me know how it goes." The two women parted ways and Kayla went back to work. She decided to return Craig's call during her last break. She found the paper that she put in her pocket before she left for work and again paged him with her cell number and the code sixty-eight. She hoped he would call back as soon as she paged him because her break was only fifteen minutes long.

I can't believe I'm doing this. The vibration of her phone startled her to the point that Kayla nearly jumped out of her skin. She looked at the caller ID and recognized the other number Craig had written on the piece of paper. She took a deep breath and let the phone ring twice more. *Don't want him to think I'm sweating him.*

"Hello," she answered.

"So what's with the sixty-eight, beautiful?" Craig asked in his deep voice.

"I'll always leave you wanting more. What's up with you?" She was trying to sound nonchalant.

"I'm doing better now that I've talked to you. You sleep a'ight?"

She could hear him stretching and wondered if he had just gotten up. *Maybe I should have called later.* "I slept fine. Thanks for asking. You busy?"

"No. I'm 'bout to hit the gym and then grab me some food. Would you care to join me?" he asked. She didn't know if he meant the gym or dinner.

"No, I have to work until four. As a matter of fact, my break is almost over. I did want to return your call, though."

"Well, can I take you out later? After you get off? I mean, that's still early. We can catch a movie or something." He seemed really interested in her and she was flattered.

"Okay. What if I call you around seven and we can meet somewhere?"

"A'ight. I'll talk to you then. Bye, Beautiful."

"Bye." Kayla couldn't help smiling as she put her phone back in her pocket.

They met for drinks and a movie that night. Kayla had to catch her breath when she saw him for the second time. The resemblance to Geno was still noticeable; there was no denying the boy was fine. But Craig had a hardness about him that Geno didn't have. He told her he was a chef at a local hotel. He took much pride in his cooking skills and offered to demonstrate them the following weekend, which was of course, one Kayla was dreading. It was Valentine's Day.

"I have to think about it and let you know," she told him as he walked her to her car. She looked at him and still could not deny the attraction she held for him. It wasn't that he looked like Geno. Craig had that same sparkle in his personality that made her laugh, something she hadn't done in a while.

"What's there to think about? You already got plans? I know it's the day for lovers, but it can be for friends, too." He grabbed her hand and held it for a moment as he looked into her eyes. She immediately felt self-conscious and looked away. "Do you know how beautiful you are?" he said.

This totally took Kayla by surprise. She'd been told before how attractive she was. She had even been called beautiful before, but Craig said it with such intensity that it stunned her. She looked up at him and as if on cue in a romance film, he pulled her to him. He kissed her so passionately that time seemed to stand still.

That kiss stayed on her mind for days. It was on her mind Monday when she woke up and got dressed for work. It was on her mind when she was stuck in traffic, leaving school and headed to the music store listening to Musiq sing about "love."

It was on her mind as she listened to the messages Craig left on her voice mail at home and on her cell phone.

"Hi, Kayla. I know you're at school, but I woke up with you on my mind and I wanted to hear your voice. So, your voice mail will just have to do until I talk to you, if you decide to grace me with a phone call. Have a great day, beautiful."

Kayla could not help but smile as she hung up the phone late that Thursday evening. She still had not decided what she would do for Valentine's Day. Yvonne wanted everyone to go out, but Roni of course had plans and so did Tia. Kayla figured she would play it by ear. She had a long week and didn't really feel like going out and seeing other couples all hugged up, knowing that this time last year she was happily involved herself. *Geno. Wonder what he'll be doing tomorrow? Probably with his new trick*, she thought. At that moment, the phone rang and she was surprised to see Geno's cell number on the caller ID.

Taking a deep breath, she answered with a low, "Hello."

"Hey, Kay. How's it going?" He sounded great, as usual. The sound of his voice caused waves of memories to come flooding back.

"Great, G. And you?" she asked, monitoring her breathing.

"I've been good. I just called to check on you. I mean, it's been a while since we talked and I just wanted to make sure you were okay."

"I'm fine, G." She didn't know what he wanted to hear at this point.

"You weren't busy, were you? I mean, you sound kinda distant. Am I disturbing you or something?"

"No. I just got in from work. But I do have some papers I am about to grade. And I gotta get these gift bags together for my kids." She sighed, still wondering what brought this phone call on. She and Geno had not parted on the best of terms, but they had gotten to the point where they were at least friends. It still hurt her to know what he had done, but it hurt even more that they were no longer together.

"Well, I'm not gonna keep you long, Kay. I just wanted to wish you a happy Valentine's Day and make sure you're doing all right," Geno said quietly. She could hear him fumbling in the background.

"Where are you, Geno? You sound muffled," Kayla asked him, straining to decipher the background noise.

"The door is locked!" She heard a female voice yelling.

"I'm picking my friend up from work. Hey, it was nice talking to you. I'll call you back later," he quickly said and the phone went dead.

That nigga had the nerve to call me while he was picking up some other chick from work. She shook her head and threw the phone on the bed. She had to remind herself that they were no longer together so she had no right to be mad. Again, she told herself that he had moved on, so it was time for her to do the same thing. The kiss again was on her mind as she picked up the phone and dialed Craig's number.

3

"He's cooking you dinner?" Roni asked her as she put the hot curling iron in Kayla's hair. They were in Kayla's cluttered bedroom and Roni was helping her get ready for her big date.

"That's what he says. I mean, he *is* a cook. That's what he does for a living," Kayla answered as she tried not to flinch from the heat.

"Um, the way to a woman's heart is through her stomach." Roni smiled smugly.

"Ron, I thought that was the way to a man's heart."

"No, girl. The way to a man's heart is through his head, and I ain't talking about the one on his shoulder with two ears, either." Roni laughed and almost burned Kayla's forehead.

"Girl, you'd better chill. You know I ain't got enough hair to wear bangs." Kayla swatted at Roni.

"I can throw some tracks right in there. You know I can." Roni tilted Kayla's head and kept curling. It was a well-known fact that Veronica Jett was one of the best hairdressers this earth had ever seen; a talent inherited from her mother, Ms. Ernestine Jett, the owner of Jett Black Hair Salon on the south side of the city. But Roni decided that doing hair wasn't steady enough to be her thing, so she taught at the alternative school instead. She did her girlfriends' hair and occasionally went to work at the shop when she was strapped for cash, which was rarely, since she had enough male compadres to help her out whenever that occurred.

"Did I tell you Geno called me last night?" Kayla acted like it was no big deal.

"What the hell did he want?"

"I don't know. The girl he was picking up from work came to the car before he had the chance to tell me." Kayla shrugged.

"What girl?" Roni sucked her teeth as she reached for the spray bottle.

"I don't know." Kayla sighed. Roni reached for the makeup kit on Kayla's dresser and began making up Kayla's face.

"Close your eyes," she said and Kayla felt her applying the eye shadow. "Look, Kay. I want you to do me a favor. Go out tonight, have fun, don't even think about Geno. Let it go and move on. You are a beautiful, intelligent black woman with so much to offer. Forget that nigga. It's over. Okay? All done. You like?"

Kayla opened her eyes and was amazed at the transformation Roni had done. Her big brown eyes seemed brighter and her full lips were glossy and sensual. There was not a hair out of place on her perfectly curled head.

"Damn. I *am* a diva." Kayla smiled and hugged her girlfriend.

"Now hurry up. You don't wanna keep your chef waiting. And here." Roni reached in her purse and placed a small item in Kayla's hand.

"What's this?" Kayla asked and looked down at the small plastic wrapper. "Oh, hell, naw. I don't need this. You know I don't get down like that. I just met this man, Roni. He ain't getting nothing from me except maybe some tongue action— and that's only on his lips."

"Take it, Kayla. It's Valentine's and you might get lucky. You never know, girl. Better safe than sorry. I gotta run. Darren is picking me up at nine. Love you, Kay. Call me in the morning and let me know how it goes," Roni said as she left. Kayla looked at the condom and put it in the top drawer of her dresser.

"That girl is a fool," she said out loud and proceeded to get dressed. She decided to dress down, but cute. Craig told her he would cook dinner and they would get to know each other better. She liked him more and more every time she spoke with him.

Pulling on her black silk shirt and fitted Parasuco jeans, Kayla took one last look in the mirror. She turned and noticed the photo of Geno and her. *Time to move on,* she thought as she picked it up. She placed it in the top of her hall closet when she grabbed her leather coat.

The drive to Craig's house only took twenty minutes, but to Kayla it felt like hours. The neighborhood was fairly new and she took notice of the perfectly manicured yards even though it was dark. She found his townhouse nestled at the back of the cul-de-sac, his blue Honda parked right out front. As she parked behind it, she saw the lights go dim and the porch light come on. Checking herself in the rearview mirror, she touched up her lipstick and opened her car door.

"My, my, my. You look too good to stay in, Kayla. Maybe we should go to State Street's so I can show you off." He grinned and gave Kayla a hug.

"You are so silly." Kayla could smell his Calvin Klein cologne as he pulled her close to him. She took notice of how sexy he looked dressed in the simple wife beater and blue sweat pants, white socks on his large feet.

"Come on in. Dinner's almost ready." He led her into the sunken living room and she was immediately impressed. Sounds of jazz filled the room. There was a brown leather sectional surrounded by African artwork and statues. They were all beautiful. On the wall was a huge print of a warrior, standing with staff in hand in the African jungle. The coffee and end tables were adorned with carvings and hand blown glass. Kayla had never seen anything like it.

"Make yourself at home."

"This is gorgeous. I mean, absolutely gorgeous," she told him.

"Thanks. I try," he answered. "Have a seat. I gotta check on something in the kitchen."

Kayla took a seat and continued to admire her surroundings. *This brother has taste*. The mahogany entertainment center held a thirty-two-inch television and a stereo system. There were what looked like hundreds of CDs and DVDs on mahogany shelves.

"Did you find my place okay?" he called from the kitchen.

"Yeah. Your directions were easy to follow. This is a nice neighborhood," she answered. "How long have you lived here?"

"Almost a year," he said. She turned around and saw he was walking toward her with a glass of wine.

"Thank you," she said, taking the glass from him. "Something smells delicious."

"Chicken. It's finishing up. Would you like a tour while we wait?"

"Sure." She shrugged.

"Let's start upstairs and work our way down." He took her by the arm and led her up the Berber-carpeted steps. At the top there was a loft with a small office, outfitted with a desk, computer, file cabinet, and a bookshelf full of books. The wall held framed photos of Miles Davis, Dizzy Gillespie, and Etta James. There were also jazz statues on the shelves.

"You read?" she asked him, impressed by the titles, including historical greats such as Zora Neale Hurston, James Baldwin, and Richard Wright.

"Jazz and reading, my two favorite hobbies." He smiled. They continued further and he showed her a bedroom, which was modestly decorated in taupe. There was a full bed and a dresser, but not a lot of artwork, as the rest of the house had. "This is the guestroom."

"Nice."

"It's a'ight. I haven't got it finished yet." They returned to the hallway and he opened a second door across the hall. "Now this is the master bedroom." He grinned as he opened the door.

Kayla's mouth dropped as they entered the huge room. It looked like something off *MTV Cribs*. The grand lair was an ivory dream. The king-sized bed was raised in the center of the room. There was a separate sitting area with a cream leather love seat and matching ottoman. As she inhaled, Kayla smelled vanilla and noticed candles burning in each corner of the room. On the far wall, she was stunned by a flat screen television.

"Wow," was all she could say. As she walked closer to the bed, she had to blink several times to make sure she was seeing clearly.

"It's mink," Craig informed her as she touched the bedspread.

"Cooking must really be paying well," Kayla commented. She could feel Craig's hand on the small of her back and she turned to face him. As he reached and touched her face, there was a beeping noise coming from downstairs.

"Saved by the bell. Sounds like dinner is ready. Shall we eat?"

Kayla took one last look around the room, still amazed at its beauty. "May I use your restroom?" Kayla asked.

"Yeah. You can use the one downstairs," Craig answered. She followed him down the steps and he showed her to the bathroom. Like the rest of the house, it was an impeccable array of browns and beige with gold detailing. She stood in the bathroom a few moments, just looking at herself in the mirror. *Maybe he is worth more than a little harmless fun,* she thought.

"You okay?" Craig tapped on the door, startling her.

"Yeah. I'm coming out right now," she called. She washed her hands and opened the door where he was waiting for her.

"Right this way, Madame." He looped his arm through hers and guided her into a beautiful dining room. He had dressed the elaborate table with flowers and candles. He pulled a chair out for her to be seated and out of nowhere, presented her with a long-stemmed white rose. "For you."

"Why thank you, kind sir." She laid the rose in front of her.

"Dinner is served." He imitated a formal waiter and bowed as he went into the kitchen. She could not help giggling to herself as she drank the remainder of the wine in her glass.

Craig returned carrying two plates. He placed one in front of Kayla and the other at the empty seat near hers. She looked at the salad, which she could tell was freshly prepared.

"I didn't know what type of salad dressing you like, so I have a variety to choose from. I like this one myself. It's raspberry vinaigrette. Sweet, yet tasty." He licked his lips sexily at Kayla.

"I'll bet," she said, blushing.

They feasted on a fabulous dinner which Craig had prepared, consisting of salad, shrimp cocktail, Chicken Alfredo, garlic bread, and cheesecake. He amazed her not only with his culinary skills and witty conversation, but he even went so far as to grind fresh Parmesan over her pasta and butter her bread. By the time he placed the strawberry-topped dessert in front of her, she was too full to eat it.

"I'm stuffed," she whined as she looked at the thick slice of cake he gave her.

"At least take a bite and save the rest for later," he pleaded.

"Okay. Just a taste." Kayla took a small bite and closed her eyes. "Oh my God. This is the best."

"Naw, I got some better recipes if you wanna try 'em." He winked and continued to clear the table. "Excuse me for a moment. I need to run upstairs."

Kayla looked at him inquisitively, but Craig just kissed the top of her head and left her sitting at the table, the sound of Boney James serenading her. *I wonder what he's up there doing?* She didn't even want to think about it. She poured herself another glass of wine and gulped it down. She heard him coming down the steps and regained her composure.

"Wanna come upstairs for a little while?" he asked.

"Uh, I don't think that's a good idea." She could feel her heart beating faster as he walked closer to her.

"I have something for you." He looked deep into Kayla's eyes. She wanted to look away but couldn't. "Please, it's not what you think."

A million thoughts seemed to go through Kayla's mind, including Roni telling her to live it up and have fun. Curiosity won over apprehension and Kayla smiled at him.

He reached for Kayla's hand and she followed him up the steps and into his bedroom. She was surprised when he continued past the bed and opened another door. He motioned for her to come inside. Kayla slowly walked in and gasped. It was the biggest bathroom she had ever seen. There were candles everywhere and she could hear Brian McKnight coming from a wall mounted CD player, asking her if he ever crossed her mind anytime. Craig pulled her closer, pointing to the jetted tub.

"I took the liberty of drawing you a milk bath, with rose petals, of course. Your towel and washcloth are right here. It's a pair of shorts and a T-shirt on the counter for you to put on when you get out. I can bring you another glass of wine if you'd like. This is a time for you. A brother ain't trying to be all up in here or nothing like that, unless you want me to be." He laughed.

"I . . . uh . . . " Kayla was at a loss for words.

"Water's getting cold. Enjoy. I'll check on you in about forty-five minutes. Tub jet button is right here." He pointed to the switch on the wall. "I'm going back downstairs to finish cleaning up the kitchen. Holla if you need anything." He closed the door before Kayla had a chance to respond.

Alone, Kayla put the top down on the commode and sat down to think. She looked at the steaming tub of white liquid with the flowers floating on top. *What have I gotten myself into?* She wanted to call Roni, but remembered her phone was in her purse, downstairs. S*tuff like this happens to Roni and Tia, not me. What, what, what?* As if prompted by Kayla's thoughts, Phyllis Hyman began singing through the speakers that she was "moving on." *Why not? Me too!*

Kayla removed her clothes and stepped into the Jacuzzi. *What if this nigga is some kind of freak with a camera hidden somewhere?* She quickly looked around for a red light hidden somewhere and then smiled at being so paranoid. The soft, hot water felt like heaven on her skin as she submerged her body. She reached and flipped the jet switch and the tub began to massage her body. She relaxed like she never had before. The candles reflected in the bathroom mirror and caused an ambiance that whispered, "Let go and enjoy." She closed her eyes and obeyed.

"You need anything?" Craig quietly tapped, causing her to wake. She looked at her watch and saw that forty-five minutes had passed.

"I'm fine. I'm getting out right now," Kayla replied. She stood up and got out of the tub. Drying off, she realized that her skin was soft and supple. She looked at her reflection and smiled. Maybe it was the wine, but she looked and felt damn good. She decided to scrub all of her makeup off and get a little more comfortable. She bent over to pick up the shirt and shorts Craig had laid out for her. Usually conscious of what her grandma called an "onion butt," Kayla turned around in the mirror and admired herself. She ran her hands along her full breasts and down her flat stomach, resting them on her hips. Bottle shape; blessed with it and worked hard to keep it. She pulled the T-shirt over her head and the shorts over her hips. She slowly opened the door expecting to see Craig, but his room was empty. She looked at the magnificent bed and decided to see how it felt. She sat on the side and rubbed her fingers across the bedspread. *Mink. Go figure.* Kayla laid back and closed her eyes.

"I think you got a little too relaxed."

She sat up when she heard the deep voice. "Oh, my. Sorry. I just wanted to sit down for a few moments. I'm sorry," Kayla said, embarrassed.

"Ready to go back down?" Craig looked amused.

"I don't think I can make it." Kayla smiled.

"I'll help you." Craig reached and gently pulled Kayla up. When they got to the top of the steps, he got in front of her and put her on his back.

"What are you doing?" She giggled.

"Told you I'd help. Jump on." He laughed. Kayla hesitated then climbed on Craig's back. She could feel and see his muscles through the thin T-shirt he wore and noticed part of a tattoo on his left shoulder. She looked closer and saw that it was a cross with a rose wrapped around it.

Somehow, they made it back into the living room. Craig had lit the fireplace and had a huge blanket lying in front of it. Kayla got off his back and stood in the middle of it.

"You're amazing," she told him.

"It's Valentine's. I wanted it to be special." He pulled her to him and kissed her like he had before. Kayla responded, for it was what she had been waiting for all night long. She could feel him leading her to the floor and she obliged. They kissed for what seemed like hours. Exploring each other's mouths, tasting each other, neither one wanting to be the first to pull away.

"Turn over," he whispered.

"Huh?" Kayla stopped and realized what he said.

"Turn over. On your stomach."

"Hold on, Craig. Maybe I need to let you know up front," she began.

"I wanna rub your back. Come on." He began rubbing her neck in a circular motion. Kayla's eyes began to close and her head fell forward. "I told you I'm good with my hands." He reached under one of the end tables and pulled out a bottle of oil.

Kayla lay on the blanket and Craig massaged her back and shoulders. His hands worked their way along her body, picking up where the tub jets left off. His touch was firm yet gentle, and there was something about the way his fingers lingered along certain spots that sent a chill down Kayla's spine. She began to feel heat in places she hadn't felt in a while. She heard herself moan as Craig's hands kneaded her lower back.

"Feel good?" he asked her. She could feel him shifting and suddenly she felt his breath in the small of her back as he began nuzzling. Kayla's body tensed, shocked by what he was doing. "Relax," he told her.

He pulled her shirt up, began nibbling his way back up her torso, and licked her shoulders.

"Craig," she whispered. She did not want it to feel this good. It was too hard to say stop. *Tell him you want him to stop,* her mind told her. "What are you doing?" were the words that came out of her mouth.

This was too much for Kayla. Somehow she managed to roll over, but once again got lost in his alluring eyes. Craig continued to sing as he removed her T-shirt and kissed her neck.

Don't do this, her mind said. Her back arched, reaching for his kisses as his mouth found her hard nipples. He kissed each one gently and continued down her stomach, stopping only to pour more oil.

"You are so fine," he paused long enough to say. Before she could thank him, she felt him kiss the inside of each thigh, bending her legs, nibbling her calves.

This is wrong. You don't even know this man, her brain warned her. It was as if her body and mind were at war, but the physical was determined to beat out the mental. When Craig poured oil on each of her feet and began sucking her toes, Kayla knew that her mind had lost all control of her body. She could not remember taking the shorts off, but she knew they were not there when she felt Craig's fingers opening her dripping canal. She gasped as she felt his tongue going where only Geno's had gone before. Craig licked and sucked her like she was one of his sweet recipes that he had perfected. She could hear him moaning and it turned her on to the point where she thought she was gonna lose her mind totally. Her legs began to shake as he buried himself between her legs. And at the moment when she had reached the pinnacle of the voyage he was taking her on, he stopped.

"Not yet. I want to cum with you and feel it," he said. He removed his sweats and her eyes widened at his long, thick penis. His hand never left her clitoris, continuing to stroke it, and before she knew it, he had entered her, taking her even further.

"Oh God, please don't stop," Kayla groaned from the back of her throat.

"I won't, baby. I wanna cum with you. How long you want me to ride, baby?" He looked deep into Kayla's eyes.

"Forever," Kayla answered. He pleasured her and stroked her with a rhythm like no other and as she felt herself gushing while he pumped into her, they came with a fierceness that shocked the hell out of both of them.

"Dang, Kayla. You certainly had a better night than mine," Roni commented. It was a little after nine in the morning and Kayla had to be at the music store by ten. She had been home since seven, having fallen asleep in Craig's arms as he entertained her with stories about growing up in Mississippi. He had to be at work by six thirty and told Kayla she could stay as long as she liked, but she chose to leave when he did.

"So you see my little package I gave you came in handy, huh?"

"What package?" Kayla asked as she lay across her bed, not wanting to go to work.

"Uh, the condom." Roni said it like Kayla was slow.

"Oh, yeah, it did. Thanks," Kayla said, not wanting to tell her friend her night of sexual pleasure had been an unprotected one. "Look, Ron. Don't tell anyone about this. I just want this one to stay between me and you, okay?"

"Sure." Roni was surprised. Kayla usually shared everything with Yvonne. "They don't know about the date?"

"They don't even know we went out last weekend. I just wanted to keep it on the DL. You know how Yvonne is, and Tia has been wrapped up in some guy named Theo. Hold on, I got a beep." Kayla hit the flash button and answered the other line. "Hello."

"Good morning, beautiful. You up yet?" Craig asked her.

"I never went back to sleep. I have to be at work at ten, remember?" she responded.

"Oh, yeah. I forgot you were a teacher by day and a CD bootlegger by night," he said, trying to be funny.

"Ha-ha. I get off at five, though. What time do you get off today?" Kayla questioned, trying to feel out whether he was trying to hook up later.

"Uh, I gotta work a double so it'll be pretty late," he said quickly.

"Okay. Well, I gotta get ready and get out of here." She sat up and noticed how late it was.

"I'll call you later. And Kayla, thank you for a great Valentine," he said sexily.

"No, I should be thanking you. Talk to you later." Kayla smiled as she hung up the phone and threw it on the bed. It quickly rang again and she answered it. "Hello."

"Why was I on hold forever? It must have been a man. What did he say?"

"He has to work a double and he'll call me later, nosy," Kayla replied. "But I gotta get out of here."

"At least he's sending you to work with a smile on your face," Roni yelled before Kayla had a chance to hang up.

That was the one and only time Kayla ever slept with Craig. After that night, she only talked to him a few times, nothing serious, and she would see him occasionally when she and the girls went to State Street's. She learned early on that he was full of crap. He would say he was coming over and wouldn't show, but it was all good with Kayla because although the sex was off the hook, it made her realize she still wasn't over Geno, and a relationship wasn't what she needed right now.

4

I need a drink, Kayla thought as she looked down at her vibrating cell phone. Unfortunately, Craig was calling her for the third time in the past fifteen minutes. Kayla hit the END button and sent the call to her voice mail. She had experienced the day from hell and was in no mood for lying, no-good niggas. She had a fight break out in her classroom and her boss actually insinuated that it was her fault, her car was acting like it had an attitude, and most importantly, she was stressed as hell working two jobs and still being broke. This is not how her life was supposed to be working out.

"TGIF, girl," her girlfriend Yvonne said as Kayla walked to the school's parking lot.

"You can say that again, girlfriend," Kayla sighed.

"You ready to go? You look worn out," Yvonne said as she unlocked her car.

"Yeah, just frustrated."

"Girl, you need a drink. You wanna go by State Street's for happy hour tonight?" Yvonne asked.

"I don't know. I'm tired, Von."

"Come on. Roni has been calling my cell and I know that's what she wants. Let's go for a little while. At least get our eat on for free." Yvonne smiled and Kayla couldn't help but laugh. "Besides, you may even meet Mister Right."

"More like Mister Right Now." Kayla giggled. "I am not staying all night, Von."

"Cool. You know I'm not gonna be in there for long either, Kay." Yvonne told her friend. "You're taking your car?" she asked as Kayla unlocked her car door.

"I might be ready to leave before you are. I told you I'm tired," Kayla answered and got into her car.

She pulled out of the parking lot behind Yvonne and opened her sunroof. The air felt good on her face and she immediately felt rejuvenated. She turned on the CD player and let the mellowness of Jill Scott relax her as she drove. Her cell rang and recognizing Tia's number, she answered it.

"Hey, ho!" Tia sang into her ear.

"Hey, girl. Where you at?" Kayla asked. Tia was a fitness trainer and she worked varied hours, depending on her clients.

"On my way to da club to meet y'all." She laughed.

"I know you are all diva-fied, so let me warn you that I am not. I have on my jeans, a black shirt, and some casual shoes."

"But I know you got your spare pair in your trunk, trick, and you'll probably mousse that good hair and make that face up before you step up in there, so I ain't even worried," she answered. She knew Kayla too well. Kayla did have a spare pair of shoes in her trunk, as well as a full makeup kit, complete with extra hair products.

"I'll see you in a minute. We're almost there. Ms. Yvonne is leading the way."

"All right, I'm pulling into the parking lot right now, so I'll get us a table," she said and hung the phone up. Kayla's cell immediately rang again and this time it was Roni.

"What up, Ron?" she answered.

"What's wrong with you? Von said you don't feel good."

"Just tired, I guess. Dealing with them bad-ass kids is wearing me down."

"You need a vacation. I don't know why you don't call out sometimes."

"Unlike you, I don't teach public school. We don't have a million subs to come in when we call out. We are short staffed. And even if I call out at one job, I have another one to go to," Kayla replied.

"What you need to do is find a guy that's paid to help you out for a minute. Geno is over and done with. You need to find another to step in and take over," Roni continued. Just the mention of Geno's name made Kayla's heart beat faster. Despite everything, she still missed him.

She pulled into the club parking lot, parked beside Yvonne and noticed Roni walking toward them. She shook her head at her and put the cell into her purse. "That's why you got a two hundred dollar cell phone bill. Why didn't you tell me you were already here?"

"I was caught up in the conversation." Roni shrugged. They gave each other a quick hug and Kayla opened her trunk to change shoes. She set up her big mirror and touched up her hair and makeup. Times like this she was glad she opted to cut her shoulder length hair to the short, funky style. She had surprised everyone when she did it, but she was going through a lot and decided it was time for a change. Roni and Yvonne watched as she handled her beauty business.

"You ready, Diva?" Yvonne asked.

"Yep. Let's go." Kayla turned and smiled a weak smile as she closed her trunk.

"'Bout time," Roni joked as they joined the line that began to form outside of State Street's Sports Bar. Each time the Lonely Hearts Club visited, the crowd seemed to get bigger and bigger. After a few moments waiting in line and getting their ID's checked, they made their way inside.

"You see Tia?" Yvonne said loudly above the sound of Craig Mack's "Flava in Your Ear."

"No, let's look over by the wall." Kayla pointed to the round tables lined along the side of the club. "You know she's not far from the dance floor."

"I'll call her." Roni reached for her cell but Kayla snatched it before she could dial. Yvonne laughed at her two friends who always provided her with comic relief.

"Put that phone down! She's right over there." Kayla pointed to Tia who was waving her arms to get their attention. She was decked out in a black linen pantsuit and heels. She had her braids pulled to the top of her head and looked like she had just stepped off the cover of a magazine with her beautiful face.

"Hey, Ms. Thang," Roni said as the ladies made their way to the table.

"Hey yourself. Everybody ready to get their groove on?" She raised her glass toward the bar where a nice looking gentleman was smiling at them.

"Cute. Friend of yours?" Yvonne asked Tia.

"Too early to tell, girl. But he did buy me a drink and he hasn't been all up in my face. That's a good sign," she told them. They all took their seats and a waitress came over to take their drink orders.

"Blue Malibu," Roni said.

"Apple Martini," Yvonne added.

"White Zinfandel," Kayla murmured. She felt drained and really didn't feel like hanging out. The thought of having to be at the music store the next day from nine in the morning until four, was not helping her mood.

"What's wrong with you?" Tia frowned at her.

"I'm okay, just tired," Kayla said to her friend.

"I told her she needs a couple days off," Roni said. "That's why they give you vacation and sick days."

"Not at our school. We are so short staffed that it is not even funny," Yvonne told them. "Mrs. Warren guilt trips employees into not calling out."

"Well, maybe you'll feel better after you've eaten. Let's hit the buffet," Tia said as she led the way to the soul food buffet the club offered every Friday night. Usually, Kayla could not get enough of the chicken wings, but she didn't even have an appetite. She watched her girlfriends pile their plates up as she put a dab of 'this and that' on her own plate and maneuvered her way through the crowd, returning to her seat. Suddenly, she felt someone put his arms around her and whisper in her ear.

"I knew you'd be here. Why didn't you call me back?" the husky voice said.

She tried not to smile, but could not help herself. "Because I knew you would give me some lie about not being here, so I figured why bother?" She turned and faced him.

"Come on, Kayla. Why you wanna treat a brother like that?" Craig asked her.

"Geno, I'm tired. I've had a long day and I don't feel well," she said.

"Yeah, you must really be sick, because my name is Craig, not Geno. Call me when you feel better." He turned and walked away. Kayla could not believe she had called him Geno. She knew it was time for her to leave.

"What's wrong with him?" Yvonne asked. She knew Kayla talked to Craig every once in a while, but from what she saw across the room, it looked like Kayla had hurt his feelings.

"I accidentally called him Geno," Kayla said as she sat at the table and took a big gulp of her wine.

"You what?" Tia laughed out loud, causing Kayla to smile.

"I called him Geno."

"Oh, no you didn't. What did he say?" Roni was tickled to death.

"He told me to call him when I could get his name right, basically," Kayla said. She picked over her food, watched her girls dance and flirt, had a second glass of wine and decided to call it a night. As she stood up, she nearly lost her balance.

"Are you all right, Kayla?" Yvonne reached out to grab her before she could fall. Roni took notice and rushed over to the table.

"How much did she have to drink?" Yvonne glared at Roni.

"Two glasses, and why are you rolling your eyes at me? It was your idea to meet here, if you recall. Kayla never gets lit," Roni threw back at her.

"I'm okay. Dang. I just got a little light headed. I'm fine." Kayla regained her composure and gathered her purse.

"I'm gonna drive you home," Yvonne said and looked for her keys.

"Von, I am fine. I told you I'm tired. I'll call you and let you know when I get home." Kayla hugged Yvonne and Roni and waved at Tia as she left. Her eyes met Craig's as she watched him dance with another female on the dance floor. *Good, let him find someone else to lie to for a change.*

5

As broke as she was, Kayla called in and didn't go to work the next day. After a full week of teaching, she was too tired to even move. When Roni called, Kayla told her that she had the flu and assured her that she would be fine. She got up to get some water and a wave of nausea came over her. Grabbing the side of the toilet, she threw what felt like her entire insides up. Then she remembered she had missed her period. Hell, she had missed two periods. Beads of sweat began to form around her brow and she crawled back into bed. *Please God, let me just have the flu.*

She slept until Sunday afternoon and somehow found the strength to make it to the drugstore and get a pregnancy test. She sat on the side of her bed and looked at the pink line, thinking that it must be wrong. There was no way that she could be pregnant. She had been on the pill for years, ever since her mother took her to the doctor when she turned fifteen and told her to take them "just in case." Her mother. She was going to be so pissed. She and her father had worked so hard for her and Anjelica, giving them a good home. Her dad worked as a city bus driver for the past thirty years and her mother was a secretary. Both still worked hard. She had never even told them the truth about Anjelica and Geno. She didn't want to cause conflict within the family, even though it wasn't her fault. Kayla hated to disappoint her parents. Their respect was too important to her. But she knew that her having a baby would be a letdown for them, because she had let herself down.

Kayla needed to talk to someone, but she was too embarrassed to tell her girlfriends. She hadn't told anyone that she had slept with Geno a few months ago. It wasn't anything that was planned. She was working at the music store when he walked up to the counter.

"Do you all have any Go-Go?" he asked, so focused on the sales paper that he didn't look up.

"G?" she asked, looking at him and smiling.

"Kayla. What in the world are you doing here?"

"What does it look like? I work here," she said.

"For real? You get a discount?"

"Only for my family and friends. You don't fit either category." She smirked at him.

"That is real cold, Kay. You act like you ain't got no love for a brother."

"When I did have love for you, you did my sister. What are you doing on this side of town anyway?" she asked.

"Funny. I came to visit my moms."

"You here alone? Where's your new woman I heard so much about?" She couldn't resist asking. Rumor had it that he was living with some older chick.

"Jealous?"

"Please. I just hope she doesn't have any sisters. The Go-Go section is this way," she said and led him to the right aisle.

"You are a real comedian, you know that?"

"Whatever. You'd better hurry up because we close in ten minutes." She turned and went back to her register. He returned with three CDs and she rang them up.

She handed him his bag, adding sarcastically, "Thanks for shopping. Have a great night."

"I really want to talk to you, Kayla. Can we go somewhere after you get outta here?" he asked.

"I don't think that would be a good idea, G," she answered and watched as he reluctantly walked out of the store. She tried not to admit it, but she missed him terribly.

Her manager locked the store up and Kayla quickly braved the cold wind and ran to the parking lot. When she got there, Geno was standing next to her car.

"What do you want?" Kayla inquired. It was cold and she wanted to go home.

"Kayla, can we just go somewhere and talk?" Geno asked her.

"About what, G?" She unlocked her door and hopped in her car. Geno remained standing in the cold. She cranked the engine and rolled down the window enough to hear what he was saying.

"Shit, Kayla, I don't care. I just want to talk to you. I miss you. I miss hanging out with you. We used to have fun, Kayla. I ain't saying we gotta talk about what happened, but let's just go out and chill for old time's sake. Please?" She could see the mist coming out of his mouth as he talked.

"Are you begging?" she asked.

"What?"

"I said, are you begging?" She knew Geno hated to be played like a sucker, but she wanted to see how far he would go to talk to her.

"Don't play with me, Kayla. It's cold as hell out here." He blew into his hands and rubbed them together. "Yeah, Kay, I'm begging."

"Where you trying to go?" She couldn't help but smile.

"Follow me. And you need to get this raggedy car of yours checked out. It sounds like a moped." He laughed.

"Don't push your luck, Geno. I ain't followed you yet," she warned.

She followed him to an old hangout spot they used to shoot pool at back in the day. They laughed and talked like old times, taking shots of tequila and drinking beer. She got caught up in the moment, enjoying just being with Geno. She didn't resist when he suggested they get a hotel room. The good feeling ended when she awoke, curled by his side with his arms around her, to the sound of his cell phone ringing. He nuzzled against her and kissed the top of her forehead while she pretended to be asleep.

Geno slipped out of bed and quietly retrieved the ringing phone out of his pocket. He looked over at Kayla again and went into the bathroom. She could hear him mumbling through the door, lying about where he was and who he was with. Knowing this had been a mistake because she still had feelings for him, she quickly got dressed and left him without saying a word.

Now here she was facing a situation she never thought she'd have to face. They were no longer together and the night they shared had just been one of physical pleasure, not emotional.

She threw the white plastic entity in the trash and went back to bed, too depressed to think about her next move.

Somehow, Kayla made it to work by seven o'clock Monday morning. She knew she looked a horrid mess with her hair barely wrapped the night before and not a drop of makeup on other than a little foundation, but she had to get to school early and talk with the principal, Mrs. Warren. Kayla dreaded telling the woman that she needed the day off, because it was a well-known fact throughout the staff that unless you were dead, Mrs. Warren expected you to be at work—no exceptions. It was one of the few things Kayla hated about her job.

"Mrs. Warren. I need the day off," Kayla told her.

"What seems to be the problem, Ms. Hopkins?" she asked.

"I think I have the flu. As a matter of fact, I was sick all weekend. I really need to go to the doctor and maybe take a few days off," Kayla pleaded.

"Ms. Hopkins, you know we are extremely short staffed and subs are hard to come by these days. Why don't you at least get started this morning and then we'll see how you feel. Get your class settled and I will work on finding someone to cover your class this afternoon," she told Kayla. Kayla dragged herself to her classroom and Yvonne stopped in to see how she was doing.

"You look like death warmed over. You still don't feel well, huh?" She placed a cup of hot tea on Kayla's desk.

"Thanks, Von. No. I'm trying to go to the doctor this afternoon, but Mrs. Warren swears she can't find a sub for me. Go figure, but she can go and get her hair done every Friday morning with no problem." Kayla stirred the hot liquid.

"I can cover for you today. No one has anything scheduled in the library, so I don't think that would be a big deal," Yvonne suggested.

"Thanks, Von. Can you go and tell her?" Kayla greeted her students half-heartedly as they entered the classroom. Once Yvonne had cleared with Mrs. Warren that she would cover for Kayla and her students were settled, Kayla went home.

I need to make an appointment with Dr. Bray as soon as possible," Kayla told the receptionist at her doctor's office.

"I'll be happy to see what we have available. Name?"

"Kayla Hopkins."

"Okay, Ms. Hopkins, let's see. She has a cancellation at ten fifteen. Can you make it then?" she asked.

"Yeah. That's fine," Kayla mumbled.

"Ten fifteen it is. And what is the nature of your visit?"

"I think I failed a pregnancy test," Kayla told her.

Sitting in the examination room, she waited for the doctor, trying not to throw up. *I have finally done it. I have ruined my life. My dad is gonna have a heart attack. How am I gonna have a baby and work two jobs? What am I gonna do? What is Geno gonna say when he finds out he's gonna be a father? Me and Geno are having a baby. This can not be happening to me.*

"Kayla, Kayla, Kayla. How you doing, girl?" Karen was her usual chipper self. She had been Kayla's doctor since her junior year of college and she always made her feel comfortable.

"Hey, Karen. I'm not doing all that great. I failed a home pregnancy test." Kayla sighed.

"You failed an office pregnancy test, too, sweetie. But let's not look at it as failing. I know many women who would love to have these positive results." She washed her hands and read Kayla's chart.

"I wish it was them rather than me. I can't believe this."

"Believe it. Well, let's check you out. Lie back." Kayla lay back on the table and Karen began her examination. Kayla closed her eyes and tried not to think about why she was there. For a moment, it felt like a regular exam until Karen pulled out an odd looking probe and said, "Now, how about we take a look and see what we're working with?"

"What's that?" Kayla almost began to panic.

"I'm gonna do a vaginal ultrasound and see exactly how far along you are. It may be a little uncomfortable, but no pain." She could see Kayla was worried.

"I been on the pill for years. How did this happen?"

"Well, even the pill isn't one hundred percent foolproof. Women get pregnant on the pill too, Kayla."

Karen wasn't making Kayla feel any better. She didn't know what she wanted to hear, but she knew that it wasn't what Karen was saying.

"How far along am I?" Kayla asked. She figured that she had been with Geno about three months ago.

"Well, the ultrasound puts you at around ten weeks. That would give you a due date of about November twenty-first. Thanksgiving Day. I guess that would give you a conception date of, uh, February Fourteenth, Valentine's Day," Karen said matter-of-factly as she calculated.

"Dear God, no." Kayla sat stunned and could not move.

Kayla went home, called both her jobs and took the rest of the week off. She turned the ringer off on her phone and climbed into bed. She thought about the baby she was carrying and what she should do. Here she was single, not even able to make ends meet while working two jobs, and now she may have another mouth to feed. And she didn't even want to think about the father. That bastard couldn't even commit to a movie date, let alone a baby. She had barely even talked to him in a few weeks, now she was gonna call him and tell him she was knocked up? Be for real. Kayla didn't even want to think about her parents' reaction. Everything she had worked so hard for could now be ruined by a fucking one-night stand. There was no way she was gonna keep this baby. It made no sense.

I can't have this baby, she thought as she drifted off to sleep. She woke to the sound of her doorbell ringing. "Hey, girl," she said and opened the door for Yvonne.

"I see you're not feeling better." Yvonne followed Kayla into her bedroom and watched her climb back into bed. "I tried to call you, but you didn't answer. Mrs. Warren just left a message that I would be subbing for you the remainder of the week, so I decided to come by. Did you go to the doctor?"

"Yeah."

"And?" Yvonne sat at the foot of the bed.

"She said I have a virus and it has to run its course." Kayla slid deeper under the covers. She wasn't ready to share the truth with anyone, especially after she decided to have an abortion. She knew that would be one decision she'd take to her grave.

"I figured you did. You know it's been going around the school. I'm surprised I haven't gotten it yet," Yvonne told her.

"This is one virus you don't want to catch," Kayla murmured.

"Let me get you something to drink." She took Kayla's empty glass off the nightstand and went into the kitchen. Whcn she came back, she gave Kayla a cup of tea and a bottle of water, then filled her in on her students. "Do you need me to do anything else while I'm here?"

"No. I just wanna sleep." Kayla managed a weak smile. "But can you let Tia and Roni know that I am okay? I turned my ringer off and I don't want them to worry."

"Done."

"Thanks, Von." She sat up and took the saucer holding the steaming liquid.

"Okay. Call me if you need anything." Yvonne gave her tired looking girlfriend a hug and made sure the door was locked behind her as she left.

She was lying back in her bed trying to watch *Law & Order* when there was another knock. She grabbed her robe and hobbled to the door. She looked through the peephole and saw Roni standing outside.

"Didn't Yvonne call you?" Kayla shook her head at her.

"Yeah, but I wanted to check on you myself. And since you're not answering your phone, here I am. What's wrong with you?" She followed Kayla back to the bedroom.

"I got the flu, that's all. Damn." She could not look at her as she answered. Roni knew her too well. The two shared a sisterly bond that she and Anjelica never had.

"The flu, Kay?"

"Yeah, Roni. The flu. Let it go, okay?"

"You're the one on the defense, Kayla. I just asked what the hell was wrong with you. Now it would be something else if you were lying, wouldn't it?"

Kayla tried to brush her friend off, but it wasn't working. She was scared and had to tell someone. Roni was her best friend, but she was embarrassed. Shit, it was Roni who gave her the condom that she didn't use. How could she tell her that she was that irresponsible? All of the questions and feelings that Kayla felt overwhelmed her and she began to cry.

"Kayla, talk to me. What is going on?" Roni hugged her girlfriend and tried to comfort her. Kayla told Roni about her unplanned pregnancy. She even told her about the night she spent with Geno, and how it made her feel even worse knowing that he had moved on, but she was still harboring feelings for him.

"Kayla, it's okay. Geno is gonna be a good father. He still loves you and he will love this baby too."

"But, Ron. You don't understand. I can't have this baby. You don't get it. Geno isn't the father. Craig is," she admitted to her best friend. She had finally said it. She even felt somewhat relieved.

"Damn."

"Exactly. I *cannot* keep it. It makes no sense."

"Kayla, it doesn't have to make sense in order for you to keep it. You don't know what you're saying. You have never believed in abortion, Kay. But now because the man you wanted to be your baby daddy *ain't*, you want to get rid of it? That's not even you, Kay. You don't even think like that." Roni sat up and looked at her.

"But Ron, I don't have no money to take care of a baby. And what about Mama and Daddy? They are gonna be pissed too. And Craig, don't even get me started on him," Kayla cried.

"You know that if you want to have this baby for real, Kay, it's gonna be taken care of. Your mama and daddy are still gonna love you no matter what. And we can let the child support judge take care of that nigga if he don't wanna act right. I just want you to see all the sides of this before you decide to do something I know you don't want to, Kayla. Take it from someone who's been there. It's not an easy thing to do. But I am here for you no matter what you decide to do."

"Ron, I—" Kayla began, but Roni cut her off.

"Senior year, sweetie. Remember? But I did what was best for *me* at the time. Why do you think I stay on y'all about condoms? A lot of good it did *you*, I see."

Kayla could not help but laugh. She was glad she had decided to confide in Roni. They talked a little while longer and then Roni stood up to leave.

"Know that I love you and support you, and so do a lot of other people, Kay. Unconditionally, no matter who your baby daddy is." She hugged Kayla and said good-bye.

6

For three days Kayla's routine consisted of sleeping, taking showers, drinking tea and water, eating crackers and throwing up. On Thursday morning, she rolled over and looked at the alarm clock. The numbers read eleven twenty-one. *November twenty-first, my due date.* Kayla did the only thing she knew how; she began to pray.

Okay, God, I am finished having my pity party. It's just you and me now. What I did was wrong, and I am asking you to forgive me. But I know that what has come out of it is a blessing, not a curse. Please, God, guide me and tell me what to do. Give me the strength to make it through this, because I can't do it without You. She closed her eyes and did not realize that she had gone back to sleep until she checked the time, and this time it read two fourteen. Kayla knew what her next move had to be. *Okay, God, here goes*, she thought as she reached for the cordless phone and dialed the numbers.

"Hey, beautiful. I was hoping you would call me," Craig said when he answered.

"Hi. Are you at work?" she asked him. She could not remember his schedule.

"I get off at three. Why? What's up?"

"I need to talk to you. Do you think you can stop by on your way home? Or maybe I can meet you at your house?" Kayla felt that this was something she should tell him in person rather than over the phone.

"No! I mean, I'm not going straight home."

"Then can I meet you somewhere?"

"What's the deal? I guess I can swing by your place. Is this gonna lake long, because I have somewhere to be."

"No. I just need to talk to you." Kayla tried not to be irritated by his covertness. She gave him directions to her apartment and got up to prepare for what she was about to do.

***

"Nice place." Craig gave her a quick hug and kissed her lightly.

"It's not quite as lavish as yours. Have a seat. Would you like something to drink?" She remembered to be cordial. *He is a guest*, she reminded herself.

"No, no thanks." He looked down at his watch, "So is this just a ploy to get me into your bed?" He smiled his sexy smile; always the flirt. He sat on the soft, hunter green sofa that Kayla had inherited from her parents' den.

"Definitely not. That's the reason I'm in the shape I am in now." Kayla tried to say what she needed to say without coming straight out and telling him.

"Um, you look like you're in great shape to me, Beautiful."

"Not for long." She chose to sit in the chair across from him so she could look him right in his face.

"All right, Kayla. What is this all about? Come on. I told you I gotta be somewhere."

"Okay. You know I've been sick, right?" she began.

"Yeah. I know you called me some other nigga's name at the club last week. You said you were tired. What's wrong?" He began to look worried.

"I'm pregnant," she told him quietly. She looked in his face for some type of reaction. He just nodded his head.

"Okay." He shrugged his shoulders.

"By you," she whispered.

"What? Me? Are you sure? We were together only one time." He responded like she had made a bad menu choice, rather than told him she was carrying his child. She thought it would go a lot worse than it was. Kayla had heard horror stories from other women when they told guys they were pregnant and it was unplanned.

"It only takes one time, Craig."

"All right. So, how much you need?"

"What do you mean?" She was confused.

"For the procedure. I mean, you want me to pay half. Isn't that why I'm over here?"

"What procedure?" the realism of what he was talking about sunk in. "The only procedure I'm having is a full-term delivery," she said angrily.

Craig looked down at his watch. "Look, Kayla. Obviously you haven't thought this all the way through. I ain't in no position to have a baby. I mean, you said so yourself you gotta work two jobs to make ends meet. How you gonna take care of a baby?"

Now, this is the reaction Kayla was expecting. She felt the anger rise in her body. "I plan on doing what I need to *and* do a hell of a job taking care of *my* baby! I mean, it is *my* body!"

"This baby might not even be mine. I ain't even gonna get into this with you, Kayla. But if it is, I'm telling you that I *can't* take care of a baby. Not right now. I just can't. Now you can be a superwoman and do what *you* want to do because it's *your* body or whatever. But I'm just trying to tell you up front. I ain't trying to have a kid right now!"

"Then your ass shoulda considered that when you went raw dog on me. And furthermore, you ain't my prime choice to be the father of my child. Nigga, ain't nobody trying to trap your ass if that's what you're thinking!" Kayla got up and stood in his face, taking him by surprise.

"The only thing I'm thinking is that you done lost your damn mind!" He took a step back for fear that she would swing on him.

"I ain't lost my mind yet! Look, I did not call you over here to argue. I'm just trying to talk to you about the situation at hand." She took a deep breath and rubbed her temples, trying to calm down.

"The situation at hand is this, you are not trying to hear nothing I have to say right about now and I gotta go. I'll call you later once you've calmed the fuck down and are rational." He stood up and walked out, leaving her stunned, wondering what she was supposed to do next.

7

It was May and Kayla was now three months pregnant. She still hadn't told anyone, with the exception of Roni and Craig, because she didn't feel ready yet. She was still trying to convince herself that she was making the right decision by keeping this baby. She hadn't talked to Craig since the night she'd told him about the baby. She didn't call him and he didn't call her; not that she expected him to. She figured that she wouldn't really start to show until after school was out, so she wouldn't have to do a whole lot of explaining to her parents or her students until the start of the new school year, if they let her return.

Kayla was sitting at her desk, grading papers as her students worked on their Mother's Day cards. *Next year, I will be celebrating Mother's Day,* she thought. Suddenly, David, one of her students was on the ground.

"Stop!" She heard him yell out. She stood just in time to see another student, Nate, snatch something out of his hands as he tried to get up.

"Gimme my glue stick, punk!" he responded.

"It's not yours!" David began. The remainder of the class began to crowd around to get a front row view.

"Nate! David! What is going on?" Kayla rushed over to stop whatever was about to start.

"This punk took my glue stick! I just took it back!"

"It's mine, Ms. Hopkins. Look at the bottom. My mom put my initials on it. He picked it up when it rolled on the floor," David explained.

"Give me the glue." Nate stood, looking at her like he wanted to kill her, but Kayla was determined not to bend. She looked at him just as hard and yelled, "Now!"

"I hate you!" Nate yelled as he picked up the desk and hurled it at her. The students began to duck and scream as Kayla watched it fall in front of her.

"Pick it up," she told him calmly. He looked confused, so she told him again, "Pick it up. You missed the first time. Now this time I need you to hit me so I can sue your parents for your house *and* their cars, *and* I can sue the school, too. Now let's try it again. Pick it up."

"No!" He spat at her.

"I'm giving you another chance. Pick it up. If you're gonna get suspended for it, at least get the satisfaction of knowing that you hit me, Nate. Now pick it up."

"I ain't getting suspended," he laughed. "Don't you know how much money my parents donate to this school? Mrs. Warren ain't suspending me, 'cause if she do, my parents are gonna pull me out. Can't you see? I rule this school."

"We'll see. Well, I gave you a chance and you didn't take it. Don't even bother taking your books. I'll bring them down when I bring your referral." She walked back to her desk and went back to grading her papers.

Her students were still stunned by the incident and were not moving. "Finish your gifts so you can take them home," she announced. Nate stormed out of the room, slamming the door behind him.

Kayla waited about fifteen minutes before she went down to the office, giving Nate and herself some time to cool off. She was so mad she wanted to smack him. She was going to demand expulsion for him. Nate was more of a problem than the school deserved to deal with, and she was no longer going to tolerate his behavior. She walked into the office and found him sitting in the waiting area.

"Where is Mrs. Warren?" she asked the secretary.

"Giving a tour. She should be right back. Did he really throw a desk at you?" She looked shocked.

"Yep," Kayla answered and looked at the crude little boy, sitting like he owned the joint. "I've gotta go back to the class. Tell Mrs. Warren she can buzz me if she needs me." Kayla proceeded down the hallway.

"Ms. Hopkins?" She heard Mrs. Warren's voice and looked up. "We just left your classroom."

"You did?" Kayla commented, not realizing who "we" were. She hated the dimly lit hallways of the school.

"Yes, this is Mr. and Mrs. Coleman. They are enrolling their son, Nigel, in the fall." Mrs. Warren introduced the couple. As Kayla extended her hand, she looked at the gentleman's face and nearly passed out.

"Ms. Hopkins is one of our best teachers." Mrs. Warren beamed.

"Avis Coleman." The dark skinned woman with the bad weave job shook Kayla's hand. "This is my husband, Craig."

"Nice to meet you." Kayla did not look at them. She kept her focus on Mrs. Warren. "I hope my students were on their best behavior?"

"Of course. They have made some beautiful gifts for their mothers. They will be so pleased on Sunday," Mrs. Warren said to her.

"Your classroom is so nice," bad-weave wife commented.

"Yes, it was beautiful," Craig had the audacity to say. Kayla wanted to punch him in the forehead. The motherfucker was actually smiling at her.

"Thank you. Well, I have to be getting back to help them finish up. Enjoy the rest of your tour." She quickly returned to her classroom and sat down. Her head was going in fifty million directions and she felt like she wanted to throw up. Somehow, Kayla made it to the restroom in the teachers' lounge and stood over the sink to splash cold water on her face.

Married. How can he be married? I have been to his home, in his bed. He cannot be married. Kayla tried to think of every detail of the house and could not come up with anything that might have indicated that a woman lived there, let alone a wife and a family. *All the times he couldn't make it when we were supposed to go out, the supposed 'double shifts' he had to work—all lies.* Kayla was furious. She didn't know who she was angrier with, Craig for being so damn deceitful or herself for being so damn naïve. *And this nigga smiled at me in front of his goddamn wife.*

Kayla thought about marching into the principal's office and telling the ghetto woman about her husband who tried to come off as so fucking polite. But then, there was no way she could look into his face without smacking the shit outta him, so she decided to chill, *for now*. The sound of the bell startled her and she caught a glimpse of her reflection in the mirror. She quickly got herself together and returned to the classroom. Sitting at her desk, she remained motionless, unable to think.

"Ms. Hopkins?" She looked up to see Mrs. Warren standing in the doorway. "Can I speak to you in the hall?"

"Yes, ma'am." Kayla tried to think of a way to explain to Mrs. Warren that she had no idea Craig was married.

"I wanted to talk to you before Nate's parents got here," Mrs. Warren said when Kayla reached the hall.

Nate. The desk. Kayla had almost forgotten about the incident.

"Okay." Kayla shrugged.

"What brought this on, Ms. Hopkins?" Mrs. Warren walked closer to Kayla.

"Nate took David's glue and when David took it back, Nate pushed him. When I told him to go to the office, he picked up the desk and threw it at me," Kayla told her.

"Did David aggravate Nate in any way?"

"No." Kayla was confused at this point.

"Did you say anything out of the way to Nate?"

Kayla could feel heat rising to her neck and she had to tell herself to remain calm. "Are you asking me did I somehow provoke this incident, Mrs. Warren?"

"I know that you have had some conflicts in your classroom a few times these past couple of weeks involving Nathaniel. I just want to hear your version before I speak with his parents." Mrs. Warren began to read the bulletin board. Kayla could not believe what her boss was trying to say. *She don't have my back,* she thought. *She is trying to make this my fault and keep that bad-ass boy in school. Nate was right.*

"Mrs. Warren, Nate bullies others, he doesn't get bullied. He harasses his classmates and he is disrespectful to the staff. We give him chance after chance and he does not improve.

And now, you're still not kicking him out, are you?" Kayla said incredulously.

"Ms. Hopkins, Nathaniel Morgan has been at this school since he was four years old. His parents are some of our biggest contributors and support this school in all of its endeavors. Now, I know that Nate has been going through a rough time of it, but his parents and I feel that it would not be in his best interest to remove Nathaniel from school at this time."

"You mean he is not even being suspended?" Kayla was appalled at what Mrs. Warren was saying. "He could've hurt me or another child with that desk. You've gotta be kidding me, right?"

"It's near the end of the school year and he will need to prepare to take his final examinations, Ms. Hopkins. This school is in the habit of solving problems, not expelling them. That is one of the goals of Academy."

"Okay, Mrs. Warren. But it's in my best interest to educate my students without having a menace in my classroom trying to prevent that from happening. And since the *Academy* and I don't have the same goals or interests, I quit!"

Kayla went into her room, gathered the remainder of her things and strutted out of the classroom, pausing before she left. "You may have the pleasure of letting Nate's parents know that I won't be provoking him anymore, because I am no longer their son's teacher. I will let my other parents know personally. Good-bye, Mrs. Warren. Good luck finding a sub!"

8

It can't get any worse than this. Kayla looked on the caller ID as her phone rang later that night and then realized it could.

"Hello."

"Kayla Denise Hopkins, why haven't you called me?"

"Hi, Mama. I'm sorry. I've been busy. You know I work two jobs," Kayla answered. She knew her mother was mad because she used Kayla's full name. She wanted to call her mother, she really did, but she just couldn't bring herself to do it.

"I don't care how many jobs you work. Your Daddy and I been worried sick. I know you know I been calling because you got caller ID. Did you get the message I left for you last week? And don't lie to me, either."

"Yes, Mama. I told you, I've been working." Kayla sighed.

"Are you coming home this weekend?" her mother asked.

"No, Mama. You know my car has been acting up." That was the truth. Her car had been acting crazy over the past couple of weeks.

"I can send Anjelica to pick you up Friday night," her mother offered.

"No! Do not do that. You know I don't want her doing nothing for me, Mama," Kayla told her mother.

"Kayla, that is your sister. Now I don't know what has happened to cause you two to become so distant, but that fact will never change and don't you forget it. You understand?"

"Yes, ma'am." Kayla felt as if she was a little girl again the way her mother scolded her. She could not stop the tears from falling down her cheek.

"Kayla, what is wrong with you? Why are you crying, Baby? I know your feelings don't get hurt that easily."

"I quit my job, Mama." Kayla told her mother about the desk incident that had happened in her classroom.

"You'll find something else, baby. What the Devil means for bad, God always means for good. That is with every one of your *situations*. There's no point in crying about it. You know what you have to do. Get yourself together and get another job," her mother told her. "Just know that you have our love and support."

When her mother said that, Kayla began to cry even harder.

"Kayla. Something else is going on. Tell me." She could hear the worry in her mother's voice and decided that telling her would be the right thing to do.

"Mama, I'm pregnant," she said in barely a whisper.

"Oh, Kayla." Her mother sighed.

"Mama, I am so sorry. I didn't mean for it to happen, I mean, I swear, I . . ." Kayla could not go on. She was sobbing. She knew that her mother was devastated by this news. She had raised Kayla to be a respectable young woman and now look what had happened.

"How far along are you?" her mother asked her.

"Three months. I'm due Thanksgiving Day." Kayla sniffed.

"So, you *are* having it?"

"Yes."

"Good, and the father? What does he have to say about this?" Her mother questioned. What little relief Kayla had begun to feel now left her. She began to whimper again.

"That's what makes it even worse, Mama. I had a one-night stand and we really don't even have a relationship. I am so sorry."

"Stop apologizing, Kayla. You are a grown woman, not some fifteen-year-old high school student. Granted, I *am* sorry that this happened under the circumstances, but you'll be okay."

"I just wanted you to be proud of me."

"Your father and I are proud of you, Kayla. Let me let you talk to him."

"Mama, no. Please, not now. I can't tell him now."

"Kayla, he's gonna find out sooner or later."

"I know. But I just need a little more time."

"Suit yourself. But please don't dwell on us being mad or thinking that you are a failure because of this. We love you Kayla, no matter what. Do you need anything? You have enough money?"

"Yes, Mama." Kayla laughed a little.

"How're you feeling?"

"Better. I was really sick, but now I'm over it, I guess."

"I got a beautiful Mother's Day bouquet from Geno. Have you talked to him lately?"

Kayla could not believe he sent her mother flowers. "I saw him a few weeks ago," Kayla told her. "I still love him, Mama."

"You always will, baby. I wish I could tell you that your feelings for him will stop, but I can't lie to you. I just don't understand what happened."

"Things just happen, Mama. Look at what has happened to me. I am now knocked up and unemployed on top of that."

"But you're gonna be fine. I know that. But, you need to tell your daddy. You owe him that much."

"I will, Mama. I promise." Kayla felt as if a ton of bricks had been lifted from her shoulders. "I'll call you on Sunday and wish you a Happy Mother's Day."

"No, this year I can call you." Her mother laughed. "I love you, Kayla."

"Love you too, Mama." She lay back on the bed. The sound of the doorbell caused her to jump. She looked over at the clock and saw that it was after eight.

"Hey, Kay. Am I intruding?" Kayla was stunned as she opened the door and saw Geno standing there. He looked good. He had let his facial hair grow out to a full beard and it was trimmed perfectly, reminding her of a built Craig David. His thick arms protruded from his Sean John T-shirt and in his perfect hands he held a plastic bag.

"Geno. No. Come on in." She opened the door and followed him into the living room. When they reached it, he turned around and faced her.

"Can't a brother get a hug?" He reached and pulled her to him, laughing. It was a sound she hadn't heard in a while and until then, she didn't realize she missed it. "You cut your hair again. And you filling out. Damn, Kay. You look good."

"You grew a beard. And you working out. You look good, G."
She quickly pulled away from him for fear that he may figure
out why she was filling out.

"Still crazy. How you been?" He looked at Kayla and sat on
the sofa.

"Okay. How is everything with you, Geno?" Kayla sat on
the other end of the couch and they faced each other. "Wait a
minute, how did you find out where I live?"

"I have my resources." He smiled at her.

"Okay, *resources*. They do have laws for that now. I believe
it's called stalking."

"Damn, that's cold. I figured after our last encounter you'd
be glad I found you." He took her hand and looked at her
curiously. "Ma sent me over here to invite you over Sunday.
You know whether we are together or not, you are still a part
of my family. She says she hasn't talked to you in a minute.
That's not like you, Kay. What's going on?"

"Nothing, G." Kayla tried to lie but she could not keep the
tears from falling. She missed Geno and hoped they would
somehow get back together. Now the reality of carrying
another man's child, a married man on top of that, had
wrecked that possibility. Geno had always said he would never
date a woman with children because it was too much drama.

"Kayla, come here." He reached for her and she cried into
his arms, imagining for a moment that she was his again.
"What's wrong, baby?"

She mentally began to panic. For a second, she started to be
honest and tell him the truth in its entirety, but she thought
better of it and blurted out, "I quit my job."

"You quit?" He wiped her tears and stood up. She watched
him go into the kitchen with the bag and when he returned, he
had two glasses of wine and a wet paper towel. She took a sip
of the drink so he wouldn't question why she wasn't drinking,
then wiped her face.

"Yeah, I quit," Kayla continued and told him about Nate,
the desk and Mrs. Warren's reasons for not suspending him.

"That's crazy. So she would rather endanger the other
students and staff members because his parents give the
school money?"

"That's what it seems like," Kayla answered.

"Where's the remote to the stereo? I made you some CDs."
He reached into his pocket and pulled two CDs out. She
pointed to the bookshelf and he opened the player. He put
a CD in and smiled as Brian McKnight began to sing about
what's going on tonight.

"So, now what am I gonna do?" Kayla shrugged.

"Find another job, Kay. That's what. One with some decent
pay and some real benefits." He grinned at her. "It ain't that
deep."

"I missed you, Geno." She smiled back at him. "So what's
going on with you? How is your job?"

"It's cool. You know I like what I do."

"And the older woman?" Kayla dared to ask him.

"She's just a friend, despite what everyone thinks. Rent is
expensive, Kay, and she had a room for rent." He looked down
at her hands in his.

"It's okay, Geno. Even though we aren't together, we will
always be friends. We can still talk. Are you happy?" Kayla
asked him.

"Her name is Janice and she's cool," he said nonchalantly.
Kayla knew that he was lying. If she was just a friend, they
wouldn't be living together. Rent wasn't that damn expensive
and Geno made decent money. She decided to ask the inevitable.

"You love her?" Kayla had to know. *You got a lot of nerve,
knocked up with a married man's baby and you asking him
if he's in love,* Kayla scolded herself.

"I don't know, Kay. I mean, she is so good to me. She's
smart, intelligent, funny. She has her shit together. Know
what I mean?" he said

"Yeah, she's perfect." Kayla smirked.

"No, Kay. Not perfect. I don't feel the same way about her
as I feel about you. That's what scares me. There was never
any doubt that I loved you, Kay. That's how I know it was real.
Hell, Kay, I still love you. You're still my best friend," he said.

Kayla couldn't respond to what he had just said so she just
sat. The doorbell broke the silence.

"Were you expecting company?" he asked.

"No, I wasn't even expecting you." Kayla went to the door
and looked through the peephole. She closed her eyes and
wished the tall figure on the other side away. She looked
again, but obviously the wish did not come true.

"Kayla, open the door. I need to talk to you," Craig yelled out.

"Go away! I have nothing to say to you!" Kayla hissed.

"Open the door! At least let me explain. Please," he moaned.

"I don't need an explanation and furthermore, I don't want one. The only thing I want from you is for you to get the hell away from my door," Kayla answered. Suddenly, Geno nudged by her and opened the door before she could stop him.

"Is there a problem?" Geno asked Craig. They both had strange looks on their faces as they looked at one another.

"Naw, bruh. I just needed to talk to Kayla for a minute. You mind?" Craig took a step back.

"*Naw, bruh.* I don't mind at all, but evidently she does. So I think you need to leave." Geno flexed and crossed his arms, standing protectively in front of Kayla.

"Who the fuck are you?" Craig looked suspicious. He and Geno stood about the same height and were the same size, so neither one seemed intimidated.

"None of your fucking business!" Geno answered with a growl.

"You here with my girl, nigga, so obviously it is my business." Craig feigned a callous smile and stepped toward Geno.

"Your girl? I think you got that all wrong." Geno didn't back down.

"Look, both of you need to back the fuck up! Now!" Kayla stepped between the two men.

"She carrying my mothafuckin' seed. According to her, it's mine!" He looked accusingly at Kayla.

"What?" Geno looked at Craig like he was crazy.

At that moment, Yvonne, Roni, and Tia walked up to the door.

"Oh, snap!" Roni jeered as she realized both Craig and Geno were in front of Kayla's door.

"Geno!" Tia shrieked.

"So you're that punk nigga Geno?" Craig leered.

"Craig, you need to leave." Kayla faced him.

"Naw, this nigga is the one that needs to be leaving," he continued.

"I ain't going nowhere!" Geno retorted to him. The two men were squared off and she knew they were about to rumble. Kayla knew she had to do something.

"Craig, I asked you to leave. Now, if you don't get your married, thug ass off my property, I will call the police and have you removed and then call your wife and tell her where to find your ass."

"Oh, shit!" Kayla heard Roni say.

Kayla's comment must have hit home with Craig because he stepped back.

"Fuck both of you!" he said as he left. Kayla closed her eyes and took a deep breath.

"What the hell?" Yvonne asked as she pulled Kayla into the house. Geno, Roni, and Tia followed.

"I'd like to know the answer to that myself," Geno murmured.

"Geno and I were sitting here talking and Craig just showed up. The same way you guys did, I might add." Kayla flopped onto the couch and shook her head.

"She's right. We were just sitting here chilling and this nigga came banging on the door. He looks familiar. I just can't figure out where I know him from," he said. The girls looked at each other knowingly. *He looks like your twin,* is what they were all thinking, but no one said it.

"I think we need to be leaving, too," Roni said to Tia and Yvonne. "Call us tomorrow, Kay."

They left Geno and Kayla in the living room.

"Who the fuck was that, Kayla?" Geno asked. "And what the fuck was he talking about when he said you carrying his seed? You fucking that nigga?"

"G." Kayla looked down.

"Don't tell me you're pregnant by that wannabe, hard mothafucka for real, Kayla." He looked at Kayla like he was disgusted. "I can't believe you."

"Hold up! You *living* with a broad and you going off on what I'm doing?" Kayla could not believe the nerve of him. It was she who looked at him like he was a fool this time.

"I know you're smarter than that. You don't even know this nigga."

"And how long have you known the woman you're living with, G? You know what? We really don't even need to be discussing this. You can leave, too. Go home to your woman." Kayla opened the door for him and he left without saying another word.

9

"So that was it?" Roni asked. "Yep. That was it," Kayla answered. She had gotten up early and gone over to Roni's and told her what happened after they had left the night before. They were sitting at her small kitchen table.

"Girl, when we walked up and saw Craig and Geno, I almost died. I thought they were gonna throw down."

"Me too. I can't believe Geno had the nerve to be mad, can you?"

"You were mad when you found out about him and that other woman. It's a natural reaction. You two are still in love with each other. Face it," Roni told her.

"I am not in love with Geno. I still care about him, yeah. But I ain't in love with him." Kayla reached into Roni's refrigerator and grabbed a piece of fruit.

"So, you decide what you're gonna do yet?" Roni asked her.

"About what?"

"Don't play, you know what I'm talking about."

"Honestly, Ron, I don't know. I have so many messed up situations right now to decide on. A job, Geno, Craig, my car." Kayla leaned back in her chair.

"About the baby, Kayla," Roni interrupted her.

"Oh, I was gonna get to that situation eventually, but you jumped in. I'm gonna have it, I guess."

"Really? I think that's a good decision." Roni hugged Kayla.

"I told Mama."

"Ooh, what did she say?"

"Nothing, really. She wasn't even upset as I thought she was gonna be."

"And your father?"

"He doesn't know. I told Mama I would tell him later. I'm not ready to tell him yet, Ron."

"Tell who what?" Tia asked as she and Yvonne came in. Roni looked at Kayla and she looked back.

"What are y'all talking about?" Yvonne sat in the chair across from Kayla.

"Nothing. Have either of you heard of knocking?" Roni asked quickly.

"For what? I got a key." Tia shook her head. She looked too cute in a white cotton short set. "You got any juice, Ron?"

"In the fridge. I think it's some in there. Use one of the glasses on the top shelf."

"What aren't you ready to tell, Kayla? Geno and Craig obviously already know about each other."

Yvonne giggled. Kayla decided she would just go ahead and tell them about the baby. There was no point in keeping it from them. They were, after all, her best friends.

"I'm pregnant," she announced. The sound of breaking glass startled all of them.

"Tia!" Roni yelled, looking at the broken pieces on the floor.

"Sorry." Tia continued to stare at Kayla as Roni picked up the mess.

"What did you say?" Yvonne wanted to make sure she heard correctly.

"I'm having a baby," Kayla confirmed.

"Wow. Is that why Geno was at your house?" Tia questioned.

"No, it's not his baby." Kayla knew what the next question would be, so she answered before it was asked. "It's Craig's."

"Kayla," was all Yvonne said.

"Okay, I'm confused. When did you sleep with Craig?" Tia reached for another glass.

"Valentine's night," Kayla told her.

"Where was I?" she continued.

"Obviously not having as much fun as *she* was," Roni laughed. Tia gave her a high five.

"What are you gonna do?" Yvonne had been quiet the entire time. Kayla expected this reaction from her.

"I am gonna be a mother," Kayla told her. She fought the urge to look away from her girlfriend; she knew she had to keep her pride.

"So, you're gonna have a baby by *him*? You don't even know him like that, Kayla." Yvonne continued, "You mean you slept with him without using protection, Kayla? That's so irresponsible."

"I know it is and I'm not trying to make any excuses, Yvonne. I'm accepting responsibility now, though." Kayla felt the tears swell in her eyes.

"It's too late to be responsible. You're about to have a baby by practically a stranger you met in the *club*, of all places."

"Hold up, Yvonne. You're outta line, girl." Roni stopped her.

"She's right, Von. You can't judge her like that." Tia added, "You're out there living it up too."

"The only difference between you and her is that *she* got caught. Shit happens. But that doesn't mean I love her any less or think I'm better than her. I thought I knew you better than that, Von," Roni frowned.

"I'm so sorry, Von. My life is so screwed up right now that sometimes I feel backed into a corner with nowhere to turn." Kayla cried.

"That's your choice, Kayla, because you can always turn to us. We have always been there for you." Tia reached out to Kayla.

"And I need *you* to be there for me, Von. Be here for me right now. Please." Kayla put her head in her hands.

"I am here for you, Kayla." She felt her friend reach and rub her back. The women embraced each other and Kayla knew she would be okay.

"Happy Mother's Day, Mama."

"Hi, baby. I told you I'd call you. How you feeling?"

"I'm fine, Ma. I wanted to call because I'm about to go to the store and I didn't want to miss you. You know how you think I'm dodging your calls." Kayla laughed.

"That's because most of the time you are." Her mother laughed. "Your father just asked had I talked to you. Hold on, I'll get him."

"Mama, no. I told you I'm about to leave out. I will talk to him later," Kayla said quickly. "I just wanted to tell you Happy Mother's Day and I love you."

"Love you too, Kayla. But you better talk to your father soon. No use putting it off."

"I will, Mama. Bye." Kayla hung up the phone and headed to the door. She wanted to get a paper and go through the classifieds.

"What do you want?" Kayla asked as she flung open the door.

"I been trying to call you, Kayla. I called your house, your cell. You gotta talk to me. Where you going?" Craig asked her as she closed the door behind her.

"No you didn't! What business of it is yours? I certainly ain't going to see your wife and your son, though maybe I should." She walked toward her car, Craig right on her heels.

"Kayla, I am so sorry. I was gonna tell you, but—"

"Save it, Craig. I don't even wanna know what you were *gonna* do. I can't believe you got a wife and a kid! Where the hell were they on Valentine's, huh? What? Did you take down all their pictures and hide all the toys?"

"No, I mean, that wasn't my house, Kay. It was my brother Darryl's crib. He's a sport's agent and he was working. Avis and Nigel were gone out of town for the weekend." He looked down as he confessed. "But we are having problems. We are actually filing for a separation. It's over between her and me. I promise."

"You don't have to promise me anything, Craig. What we had wasn't even that deep. Believe me, there is no love lost here." Kayla looked at him like he was crazy.

"I need for you not to say anything about this, though, Kayla. Now do you see why I don't need the stress of a baby? You are gonna be teaching at the academy and . . ."

"You can stop right there. Not that it's any of your business, but I no longer teach at the academy, so me running into your wife at the school is the least of your worries." Kayla folded her arms and glared at him. She could not believe she liked him at one point. He was pathetic.

"But I don't need for you to tell anybody, either. If she finds out, she's gonna haul my ass to court for real. I'll do anything, Kayla. Please rethink this shit. Don't do this to me. Don't have this baby." He began to shake his head at her. "I can't take this stress."

"Get the hell away from me, Craig. What you should be worried about is how you're gonna pay child support to two different baby mamas. If you gonna be stressed, be stressed about that. Because you are really gonna have to pay me to keep our 'little' secret." Kayla got into the car and pulled off, leaving Craig standing in the middle of the driveway with his mouth hanging open.

10

Kayla was determined to get a job and get one quick. She knew that it would have to be one with benefits because she would have to be out on maternity leave, preferably with pay. Theo, who was Tia's new boyfriend, worked for an insurance agency and told her they were hiring. He passed her resume on, but Kayla had not heard anything and it had been a week. She found out the Human Resources person's name and decided to go see her in person.

"Good morning. Hunter Davis, please," Kayla told the elderly security guard. "Okay. And you are?" He smiled and reached for the telephone on the cluttered desk.

"Kayla, Kayla Hopkins," she answered.

He mumbled into the receiver and then hung the phone up. "She's in a meeting. Leave your number and she'll call you back." Kayla looked at her watch and saw that it was quarter to ten. She didn't feel like leaving her resume anywhere else or filling out any more applications. She took a deep breath and walked back over to the desk. "If you don't mind, I'll wait until she has a moment to speak with me."

"No, I don't mind. You can sit right over there." He pointed to a leather sofa in front of a table full of well-worn magazines. Kayla went and picked up a subscription of *Better Homes and Gardens*. The lobby was pretty much empty and remained that way with the exception of an occasional courier dropping off or picking up a package.

"You want me to try her again?" the security guard asked her for the third time since she had been waiting.

"No, you've already left two messages. I'm sure she will be out soon," Kayla told him.

"Well, it's twelve o'clock and I'm about to go to lunch. I'll be back in a half-hour. You need anything?"

"No, thanks. I'll wait."

"Suit yourself, ma'am." He came from behind the desk and went through the glass doors separating the lobby from the remainder of the building. At one point, Kayla thought about calling Tia and having her call Theo to let him know she was in the lobby. *No, he did what he said he'd do. Now it's up to me.* She sat back and reached for another magazine. Soon, the guard returned and found her still waiting. Several employees began entering and exiting the building. Checking her watch again, Kayla's stomach began to growl. *Maybe I should go and get something to eat and come back.*

"Ms. Davis, this is the young lady that has been waiting for you all day," the security guard quickly said to a tall, attractive brunette as she came through the doors.

"Ms. Hopkins, you're still here? But it's after two." She looked surprisingly at Kayla.

"I decided to wait until you got a moment. You can go to lunch. I'll wait."

"Nonsense. By all means, you've waited long enough. Come on back." She used a keycard and she and Kayla stepped through the glass doors and onto the elevator. They rode to the third floor, walked down the corridor, entered a door labeled Human Resources and then went into Hunter's office. "Have a seat. Can I get you anything? Coffee, soda, water?"

"Water, if that's okay." Kayla took a seat and hoped her stomach was not growling loudly.

Hunter reached into the small refrigerator located beside a file cabinet and took out two bottles of water, passing one to Kayla. "Believe it or not, calling you is on my to-do list for this week. But our district manager came into town and announced that we will be developing a new division and that has the entire place going crazy."

"I can imagine." Kayla nodded.

"I have reviewed your resume and I see you are a teacher. I am a former teacher myself, but I got burnt out." Hunter sat down and opened a file folder on her desk.

"That is the point where I am now," Kayla explained. "I definitely need a change. " Kayla looked deep within herself and told Hunter everything she thought the woman wanted to hear. She had prepared herself mentally for this interview and she was determined to get a position. She had to. She had to get herself together. Getting a job was just the first step in that direction.

"Well, Ms. Hopkins, you certainly are what we are looking for here at Atkins and I will definitely be calling you in the next month or so," Hunter said.

"In a month? I need a job now, Ms. Davis. I can't wait a month." Kayla felt her heart beating faster and her breath quickened. Tears began to well into her eyes.

"I'm sorry, Ms. Hopkins. The hiring for the new division won't be until then. As a matter of fact, our last training class starts on Monday afternoon and it is full."

God, please help me. I have a child to provide for. Open a door for me. I need this, Kayla prayed in her heart.

"I can start Monday, Ms. Davis. Please, just give me a chance," Kayla pleaded.

"But today is Thursday. You would need to have a drug screening and security clearance. That takes about a week to complete and today is Thursday. The head of security works half days on Friday and he does not take kindly to being rushed." She looked at Kayla sadly.

"Please. I will take care of everything I need to by Monday." Kayla was beginning to cry at this point.

Hunter looked at her and Kayla could see the wheels turning in the woman's head. She stood and reached into the file cabinet, passing Kayla a pack of papers. "Call this clinic and see if they can take you this afternoon or first thing in the morning. You need to be back here by noon tomorrow for your security paperwork."

"Huh? You mean . . ." Kayla began.

"I respect your resilience. You have the courage to go after what you want. We need that here at this office. Welcome to Atkins." Hunter stood and extended her hand to Kayla. Kayla threw her head back and laughed. *Thank you, God.*

"Thank you, Ms. Davis. I won't disappoint you," she said as she shook her hand.

"I'm sure you won't," Hunter told her.

***

The next day Kayla looked around the small security office as she completed her paperwork. There were several TV monitors transmitting different entrances to the building and the parking lots as well. She watched employees pass by the screens and was grateful that she would be among them. She had rushed over to the clinic, completed her drug screening and made it back to the Atkins Agency at precisely twelve o'clock.

She looked over onto a small table and noticed other pictures with names on them. There were several other women and a few men; one in particular was a big, cheesing, dark-skinned man wearing a sweater vest with a paisley bow tie. The name on his picture was Terrell. *He looks happy to have a job,* Kayla laughed to herself.

"In your haste to accept the job, I didn't get a chance to tell you exactly what department you would be in, the hours, your salary or your benefits. I guess we should take care of that, huh?" Hunter said as she collected Kayla's paperwork.

"I think we should." Kayla smiled.

Hunter told her about the customer service position that she was hired for and went over the thick benefit packet. "Now here's what the starting salary is, but there is a ten percent night differential because the hours are from noon until nine. After a year, you will be reviewed for an additional salary increase based on merit."

"I need to tell you something," Kayla said quietly.

"What's wrong?" Hunter looked concerned.

"I'm pregnant."

"Congratulations. When is your due date?" She smiled.

"November twenty-first."

"Well, that works out perfect for you. Your ninety-day probation will be up and you will be entitled to two months paid maternity leave. Now you can take up to a year, but only the first two months are paid. We love giving baby showers around here. Gives us a reason to eat cake."

"Wow." Kayla thanked Hunter for all she had done and walked out of the building happy that she was once again fully employed.

11

"I can't believe you quit one job last Friday and you got a new one on this Friday," Yvonne said as she looked through the sale rack. It was Saturday afternoon and she had taken Kayla to brunch to celebrate her new job, and then they had made their way to the mall.

"Believe it, girl. I just got it like that." Kayla faked a vogue pose.

"So, what about the music store?"

"I had to quit. The hours were conflicting. But with the new job, I make more money than the two jobs I was working anyway. Do you like this?" Kayla held up a cute, green sundress.

"I sure am gonna miss that discount. Yeah, that's cute."

"I'm gonna miss it too. I think I'm gonna try it on." Kayla took the dress and went into the dressing room.

"Let me see it?" Yvonne called out to her as she was trying on her fashion disappointment.

"No. It's too small," Kayla pouted.

"Too small? But isn't that a twelve? I thought it would be too big."

As Kayla was coming out, she bumped into a woman coming in. "Oh, excuse me."

"You need to watch where you going," the familiar woman said as she brushed past Kayla without looking. *Oh, no she didn't. And I know that trick from somewhere, too.* Kayla tried to remember where she knew her. *Avis, Craig's wife.*

"Do you have this in a bigger size?" she heard her call out to the salesperson.

"I'm sorry, ma'am, a twenty-two is the largest that comes in."

"This must be mislabeled or somethin'. It ain't fittin' right."

She came out of the dressing room and Kayla saw that they were holding the same dress. She could not resist walking up to the counter next to the woman. *I wonder why she didn't recognize me? It doesn't matter, but it's a good thing she doesn't.* Kayla decided to have some fun.

"I think she's right, ma'am. I know I'm a size ten and this eight is too big for me. I think they are cut big. Come on, Yvonne, let's go over to the petite section."

"You are crazy. She looked mad as hell."

"She ain't mad as she gonna be. I can't believe her fat tail. Try to disrespect me 'cause she weigh nearly three hundred pounds and can't fit in the dressing room. I see why Craig leaving her big behind. Let's get out of here and go get some ice cream." Kayla grabbed Yvonne's arm. She looked around to make sure Avis was gone.

"That's why that dress was too little." Yvonne laughed and followed her girlfriend out of the store.

The following Monday, Kayla entered the training room and sat at the round table. There were a few people already seated and she smiled as she spoke to them. There were snacks, soda, and water in the center of the table and the guy whose name she remembered was Terrell, was sitting across from her. The training class was scheduled to begin at twelve thirty and it was quarter after. As other people came in, she recognized them from their pictures. The trainer entered and introduced herself and they began. Finally, after about two hours, the trainer called for the first break. Kayla gathered her bag and went into the break room along with some of her classmates. She found a quiet spot outside and sat down. She looked up and saw Terrell looking at her.

"You can come and sit with me, Terrell. I promise I won't bite." Kayla smiled.

"I know how you women are. I ain't trying to get caught up in a harassment charge. You know I'm a prime target, being the only brotha in the class." She laughed as he sat down, and they talked until he looked at his watch and announced, "We gotta get back."

The first week of training went by fairly quickly. Kayla and Terrell hung out together during breaks and lunch. He kept her laughing and amused her with his tales of being a mack, or so he said. Every time she talked to one of her girlfriends, she had to tell them what Terrell had said or done. He was intelligent, funny, street-smart and respectable. He knew when to speak up and when to shut up. A lot of guys hadn't mastered that skill nowadays. And to be as thick as he was, he could dress his tail off. The boy had style and class.

"Okay, is there something going on between you and this Terrell dude that I should know about?" Yvonne asked her one night on the phone.

"No, Von. It's nothing like that. We are just real cool, that's all. Come on, now. I'm pregnant. What do I look like trying to holla at another nigga? That's like adding fuel to the fire. I got enough problems with Geno and Craig."

"I was just asking. You seem awfully excited when you talking about him. And as sneaky as your ass is, I have to ask or I'm the last to find out." Yvonne smirked.

"Terrell and I are just friends, Von. He's like the male version of me. I mean, we think alike, and he always has a story to make me laugh," Kayla explained. It was like everyone assumed that she had something going on with Terrell. The truth was, he was just what she needed right now: a friend.

12

"What's up for tonight, Ms. Kayla? You know it's Friday and the club will just be jumping when we get off. You down?" Terrell asked.

"I'm going home and fall out. It has been a long week and I am tired to death," Kayla said.

"Let's hit Dominic's. The deejay that's gonna be there tonight is off the hook!" He started singing, "Can I get a what, what?"

Kayla could not help joining him and started dancing. "It sounds like fun, but I am too tired."

"Come on, Kayla. Let's go. You can sleep all day tomorrow."

"Okay, for a little while." Kayla shook her head. "I'll call my girls and see if they wanna come too."

"Bet. Hold up, are they fine?" Terrell asked.

"Of course they are." Kayla grabbed her cell and left a message for Roni, Tia, and Yvonne, inviting them to Dominic's. Everyone agreed to meet at the door at ten thirty. By the time they got off from work, the adrenaline was flowing and Kayla was just as hyped as Terrell to go out.

"Hey, you! Look at you. You look good!" Roni ran up to Kayla and hugged her.

"You are so silly, Roni. You act like you haven't seen me in months." She laughed and hugged her girlfriend.

"It seems like it. The job must be agreeing with you. You are glowing," she said and they went to join Tia, Theo, and Yvonne in the line. Dominic's was a new club but it was packed. The line was wrapped around the building and seemed to go on forever. They had waited about twenty minutes when Terrell walked up and beckoned for them.

"Where are we going?" Kayla asked.

"Come on, let's go." He motioned for her to follow him.

"But what about the line? And I have my friends . . ."

"Come on and follow me. Bring 'em with you," he said. Kayla shrugged and she and her crew followed Terrell right up to the door. Other people waiting in the line did not seem too thrilled that they passed them. The bouncer saw them coming and immediately opened the door for them.

"What up, Terry," he said and gave Terrell a pound. "How are you all doing?" He greeted everyone else and let them in.

"How much is the cover charge?" Kayla asked, reaching for her small Coach bag.

"I'm a baller, girl. And you are my guests." He grabbed Kayla and ushered her into the huge club. She was taken aback when they made it all the way in.

"This place is incredible!" Theo said over the loud music.

"Come on, we can get a table up here," Terrell called out.

"But that's the VIP section," Yvonne said.

"I *am* a VIP." He smiled, and greeted the security guy who held a red velvet rope. The guy opened the walkway and they made their way to an empty table.

"Okay, you a player." Kayla laughed and sat down. She was suddenly exhausted. Although she was no longer nauseous, she tired very easily these days. But she was determined to have a good time and not let her friends see any changes in her behavior.

"This is so fly," Roni said. "Now *this* is how a sister is supposed to go out."

The waitress came and took their drink orders and Yvonne and Roni didn't waste any time hitting the dance floor. A couple of females came to the table to speak to Terrell and he seemed to be in his element. After finishing their drinks, Theo and Tia headed to get their dance on, too.

"You wanna dance, yo?" Terrell asked Kayla.

"No thanks. You go ahead." Kayla shook her head.

"Well, I was asking to be polite. I didn't want to show you up on the dance floor anyway. You know a big brother got some moves." He nudged Kayla.

"Whatever, Terrell. Why don't you ask one of your adoring fans that have been flocking to you?"

"Do I detect a hint of jealousy?" He grinned.

"Hell, no."

"Dag, I was just playing. But you know how it is. You never dance with anyone you meet when you first arrive. Then they expect you to be with them for the rest of the night. You understand?"

"Oh, but you can dance with *me*, huh?" Kayla was beginning to enjoy this quick lesson in club etiquette. She looked around and all of a sudden she spotted Geno. She could not believe it. She stood, but quickly turned when she realized he was not alone. She couldn't resist turning around to get another look.

"I've already introduced you as one of my home girls, so the chicks know that we are just cool. Friend of yours?" He stood to see who Kayla was looking at.

"Huh? Oh, nobody special." She tried not to seem disappointed, although she knew Terrell could read her face. He looked and saw her watching a guy at the bar, hugged up with an attractive woman, whispering in her ear.

"Come on, yo. Let me make you look good on the floor." He grabbed her and they made their way in front of the deejay booth, jamming to TLC singing "Scrubs." Terrell was right about one thing: he had some moves. That boy could dance and she fell right into rhythm with him. Before she knew it, there was a circle formed around them and the deejay was pumping them up even more by screaming, "Go Terry!" into the mic. She decided she couldn't take anymore and signaled for Roni to take over. She eased her way back to the side of the floor and watched. She forced herself not to look for Geno.

"Whew, girl. Y'all were tearing that floor up!" Theo said as he and Tia joined her. "Big boy can go."

"I know. He told me he could dance, but I didn't know he was like that," she responded.

They joined the rest of the crew at the table and Terrell whispered in her ear, "What's up with your friend? She is fine as hell. You think I can holla?"

"No offense, Terrell, but she is a little out of your league. She's just as much a pimp as you are," Kayla whispered and laughed. She looked at Roni, who was focused on the dance floor. She slid next to her friend to see what she was finding so engrossing. "Who are you looking at?"

"Girl, the deejay is the bomb. Did you see him?" Roni leaned further over the balcony, pointing him out to her girlfriend. Kayla saw the sexy, chocolate brother as he was whispering into a scantily clad female's ear, giving her what Kayla assumed was a business card.

"He is fine, Ron. But he's been all up in females' faces all night. You know he's a ho." Kayla scanned the small tables on the opposite wall of the bar.

"You're probably right, Kay. And you know I don't sweat no nigga. But it's something about him." Roni continued to look at the fine brother as he did his thing.

"Kay, I gotta tell you something. While we were coming upstairs I saw . . ." Tia began and put her hand on her girlfriend's shoulder.

"I already saw them." Kayla didn't let her finish. She didn't even want his name to come out of anyone's mouth.

"You wanna leave, Kay?" she asked, looking at Theo for assurance.

"It's still early. We can hit State Street's or another spot," he suggested.

"No. I'm cool. Seriously, everyone is having a good time, including me. Come on. Let's go back to the table." Kayla turned to go back down the steps when she heard the sound of Teddy Riley coming from the speakers. She turned around and looked into the eyes of Geno. His date was pulling for him to dance with her but he could not move. For a moment, both he and Kayla were frozen, remembering the first time they had made love. From that moment, Blackstreet's "Stay" had been their song. She looked at him, daring him to break the stare, but he was just as determined as she was.

"Geno, come on. I love this song." The woman was grabbing his shirt by now. "What is wrong with you?" She turned and saw him looking at Kayla.

Geno did not move.

"Is that her, Geno? Geno?" She grabbed Geno's face and he pushed her hands away. The woman looked at Kayla with fire in her eyes.

"Let's go," he said to the woman and turned to walk away, pulling the woman by the arm.

"I want to know if that's her. Are you Kayla?" She stepped toward Kayla, snatching away from Geno.

"Yes, I am," Kayla answered daringly. "And you are?"

"Janice. Geno's girlfriend."

"Let's go, Janice. I need a drink." He reached for her arm again but she pulled away.

"You can go to the bar, Geno. I'll be right here when you get back, chatting with your ex." The girl continued to look Kayla up and down.

"I don't think we have anything to chat about, *Janet*. Is that your name?" Kayla asked her sarcastically.

"Janice, bitch. Get it right."

"Geno, you better check your girl. And do it quick." Kayla glanced past the crazy woman and straight at Geno. She gave him a look that let him know she meant what she was saying. He took heed and stepped between the women.

"Come on, Janice. You're making a fool of yourself," he told her quietly in her ear.

"What? Geno, I will whoop her ass in here. I know you don't call yourself shutting me up, do you?" The woman was yelling at this point. Without warning, she tried to swing around Geno at Kayla, but he grabbed her arm. Kayla prepared to defend herself. She wasn't no punk.

"What the hell are you doing?" Roni yelled and jumped in front of Kayla.

"Who the hell are you?" Janice tried to swing at Roni this time. Geno pulled Janice and forced her out, kicking and screaming. By this time, a crowd had formed and everyone came to see what the commotion was.

"You okay, yo?" Terrell asked Kayla.

"I'm fine. She's the crazy one." Kayla smiled at him.

"Everything okay over here, Terry?" one of the security guards asked.

"Yeah. It's cool," he informed him.

"I'ma get that ho. Messing wit me, she'd better watch out!" they heard Janice scream.

"Yo, Kayla. Why was she tripping?" Roni asked as she and Terrell stood by her.

"I don't know. She just flipped out." Kayla began to ascend the steps.

"If your nigga was looking at another female like she was his wife, you'd be pissed too," Terrell told her and smiled.

13

"Can I get my hair like that?" Kayla asked Roni, pointing to a girl in the nail salon. It was the Friday before Father's Day and Kayla had to be at work in an hour. She decided to get her nails and feet done because she knew the salon would be packed tomorrow.

"Those are tracks, Kay," Roni said.

"I know. But you can do tracks, Ron." Kayla picked out a pretty lavender polish for her hands and feet.

"I know I can do tracks. I'm just surprised you want some. I thought that was the whole point of you cutting your hair."

"I just feel like something different. Will you do it for me?" Kayla sat down in the princess chair in front of the nail technician.

"You gotta come to the shop tomorrow if you want that done. And you know it's gonna take a minute to put in. I don't wanna hear your mouth, Kayla," Roni warned her.

"I know, Ron. I'll come and I won't complain." Kayla smiled.

"I'll pick your hair up tonight. Be at the shop by noon. On time."

"Thanks, Ron. I know you love me."

"I'll love you even more if you come with me to Dominic's," Roni pleaded.

"Ron, I can't. I am so worn out that I can barely drive home. I can't be hanging out at the club in this condition. Besides, I am getting too fat to fit into any of my clothes."

"You're barely showing, Kayla. It's just for a little while. I just want to check out the deejay. Please, Kay."

Kayla could not believe her girlfriend was sweating the deejay from Dominic's. This was a total change for Roni. She had the guys looking for her. And what made it worse, Roni still had yet to meet the man. Every time they went to the club, he had a flock of chickenheads lined up at the booth.

"Ron, he is a straight dog. You of all people know the type. I am not going to Dominic's so you can fantasize about a man who has just as many women as you have men."

"Fine, Kayla. But you have got to admit that is the sexiest brother you have seen in a while. I think he is my type. I am so attracted to him," Roni said as she blew her wet nails.

"No, you're attracted to him because he is a challenge. Unlike every other nigga you meet, he is not all up in your face."

"Not yet, anyway." Roni winked at her girlfriend who shook her head.

Kayla made it to the shop at twelve fifteen the next day. She tried her best to be on time, but she had been having these funny feelings in her stomach. She prayed that nothing was wrong as she looked at her tummy getting bigger. She took her time getting dressed and stopped to pick up a doughnut. She craved sweets to no end. The shop was pretty full when she got there.

"Hey there, stranger. Roni didn't tell me you were coming in here today." Ms. Ernestine greeted her as she came in the door.

"Hi, Ms. Ernestine," Kayla greeted. She put her bag of goodies down on the table in the waiting area and walked over to Ms. Ernestine's station. "Where's Roni?"

"Back here. Mama got me washing hair," Roni called from the shampoo bowl.

"Kayla, is that you?" a voice called from under the dryer. Kayla turned to see who it was. It was Geno's mom, Ms. Gert.

"Come here, girl, and give me a hug." Ms. Ernestine reached and gave Kayla a big hug. All of a sudden she stood back and looked at Kayla strangely. "Girl, Roni ain't tell me you were having a baby! When are you due?"

Kayla felt her heart beating and looked into Ms. Ernestine's eyes. She looked from Ms. Ernestine to Ms. Gert, but knew there was no point in lying to either one of them.

"Baby? Kayla's not having a baby," Ms. Gert said as she lifted the dryer all the way up. "She would have told me."

"Thanksgiving Day," Kayla said and took a deep breath. She could not turn around and face Ms. Gert, so she walked back to the waiting area and sat down. It was so quiet in the shop that even the dryers seemed to have stopped humming.

"Kayla, you're having a baby and didn't tell me?" Ms. Gert came and took a seat next to her.

"I'm sorry, Ms. Gert. I just didn't know how. I mean, it's not Geno's, and . . ."

"That doesn't matter to me, Kayla. You do. I love you like you are one of my own children. Does Geno know?"

"Yes."

"He still cares about you, Kayla. You do know that, right?"

"We were engaged, Ms. Gert. Geno and I will always care about each other."

"So you still love him?"

"Ms. Gert, I'm pregnant by another man and Geno is living with another woman. I don't think how we feel about each other is relevant. It's over. We have both moved on." Kayla looked at the woman she had grown to love over the years. They were as close as she and her own mother at one point, and like everyone else, she could not understand why Kayla and Geno broke up.

"I understand, Kayla. And if that's how you feel, I respect that. But you will always be a part of my family and nothing will ever change that." She reached over and hugged Kayla as a chorus of "awww" was heard in the shop. The women looked up and saw that everyone had stopped and all eyes were on them.

"Are you two finished with your Hallmark moment so Roni can get some work done?" Ms. Ernestine smiled at them.

"Mama, I know you ain't trying to rush nobody when they working for free!" Roni put her hands on her hip.

"Free? Child, you still owe me for that college education I paid for. You just lucky I don't garnish your wages like the student loan people do."

"What is you doing, dawg?" Terrell asked her Monday afternoon when she got to work.

"What are you talking about, Terrell?" Kayla knew she looked fly. Her white rayon outfit was perfect from her manicured hands to her perfect feet, which wore Kenneth Cole heeled sandals. Roni had hooked her hair up and it was flowing down her back. Her eyebrows were arched and she had put on her M•A•C makeup like a professional artist.

"You are trippin' for real." He sighed as he sat at his desk.

"Terrell, what are you talking about?" Kayla knew he would have a smart comment. She was prepared for it.

"You can not, I repeat *can not* leave on Friday night with a short bob and return on Monday with hair down to your behind." He touched Kayla's tracks and acted like he was gonna pull them.

"You can if you're a diva." Kayla batted her eyes at him and stuck out her tongue. The rest of the class laughed as he took his seat, smiling.

During lunch break, Kayla bought a honey bun and a bottle of Pepsi. She sat at their regular table and pulled out the *What to Expect When You're Expecting* book that Roni had dropped off to her that morning. She was determined to find out why she kept having those strange feelings in her stomach. The book confirmed that the butterflies in her stomach were called flutters. Kayla smiled as she realized she was feeling her baby move for the first time.

"Who's having a baby?" Terrell asked as he sat down and looked at her book.

"I am." Kayla smiled.

"Yeah, right. When?"

"In November." Kayla opened the honey bun and decided to put it in the microwave for a few seconds to get it soft. She returned to the table and saw Terrell flipping through her book.

"You having a baby for real, Kayla?" he asked.

"For real," Kayla said and prepared herself for the sweet, gooey food she had sitting before her. She picked up the warm honey bun and was about to bite into it when Terrell snatched it from her and tossed it into the trash.

"What is your problem?" Kayla stood up and asked him angrily.

"You can't be eating that stuff. It's not good for you," he answered and went back into the cafeteria. Kayla wanted to cry. She had been thinking about that honey bun all day and now his big behind had thrown it away. She sat back down, too furious to move.

"Here," Terrell said, placing a tray in front of her. On it were a grilled chicken sandwich, some baked chips, an apple and a glass of milk. As bad as Kayla wanted to stay mad at him, she couldn't.

"You know I wanted to stab you, right?" Kayla told him.

"Whatever, diva. You wouldn't dare if you want that hair to stay pretending like it's yours," he joked.

"You're just mad because I won't let you touch it."

"My uncle has a stable down South. I know what it feels like."

Kayla stuck her tongue out at him and began to eat her food.

"Man, you don't even look pregnant," he said.

"Coming from anyone else I would take that as a compliment, but from you, I don't know." She looked up from her plate.

"Was that your baby daddy the other night at the club?" he asked as he reached on her plate and grabbed some chips. Kayla raised the fork over his hand and pretended to stab him.

"If you must know, no, that was not my *child's father*. That was my ex-fiancé and his new girlfriend," she told him.

"He's still feeling you. Does he know you're pregnant?"

"How do you know he's still feeling me?"

"Because I saw the way he looked at you. That's the reason ol' girl was mad at him, because he was more interested in you."

"Well, we're over."

"Where is your baby daddy?"

"That's a whole 'nother story and he's out of the picture too." She finished her sandwich and gave him the remainder of the chips. He didn't hesitate to take them and she laughed.

"What happened to him?"

"I didn't appreciate the fact that he was married," she informed him. He gave her a surprised look.

"You, somebody's mistress? I underestimate you and your *playerability*." His shoulders shook as he laughed at her. Kayla was not amused.

"I am *not* anybody's mistress. I didn't know he was married and, like I said, he's out of the picture. I'm all alone," she said sadly. Kayla realized that indeed she was alone. She thought about having to go to birthing class and doctors' appointments by herself. There wouldn't be a proud father with her in the delivery room waiting with a camcorder in one hand and a digital camera in the other. She looked down at the empty tray, reminding her of her empty heart.

"Hey, you're not alone. You got your girls. I know they got your back. And you got me. You're my dawg." He gave her an encouraging look and Kayla shook her head at him. Over the past few weeks, she had learned that Terrell was a great listener. They would share stories and thoughts with each other and he always seemed to understand what she was going through.

"Your *dawg*?"

"My ace, my buddy, my girl, you know . . . my dawg! Now come on, before we're late," he told her and pulled her up from the table.

14

The June heat was bearing down on Kayla as she sat on the hood of her car. She was traveling along the interstate when it went dead. She got out and popped the hood as if she knew what she was looking for. She called Roni, but got no answer on her cell or Yvonne's. She knew Tia was at work and she wouldn't be able to reach her. Luckily, her father had her on his AAA account and they came and towed the car to her house. The tow truck driver told her that her transmission was gone and it would take about two thousand dollars to repair. *Where the hell am I supposed to get two thousand dollars?* She wondered as she rode home in the tow truck. *I don't even have two hundred dollars in my savings account.* Her situation was going from bad to worse. *How am I gonna raise a baby with no man, no car, and no money?*

She slammed the door as she went into her house and sat on the sofa. The phone rang and she picked it up on instinct.

"Hello."

"Hey, Beautiful. I was calling to see how you were doing." The sound of Craig's voice pissed her off even worse.

"Why the hell do you care? All you wanted was for me to have an abortion, right? I didn't and I haven't told your wife, *yet.*"

"I know you didn't. That's why I'm calling. I appreciate that, for real. How are you feeling?"

"Not good. My car broke down and I don't have the money to get it fixed. Are you gonna help me out?"

"How much you need?"

"Two thousand."

"Dollars? Hell, you can buy another car for that much."

"Are you gonna give me money to buy another car then?"

"I don't have no money like that. I mean, I can get you some loot, but it ain't gonna be no two thousand dollars," he told Kayla. She was totally surprised. She didn't think he was gonna offer her any help.

"How much can you get me?" she sat up and asked him.

"Let me check some stuff out and I'll get back with you," he told her. She had heard this from him before and she wasn't even falling for it this time.

"Whatever, Craig. Don't lie to me. I know you ain't gonna call me back," she told him.

"I am, Kayla. I just gotta check on something and then I'll call you back." Craig sounded as if he meant what he said.

"I need for you to call me tonight so I'll know what I need to do," Kayla told him.

"Okay. I'll talk to you then," he said and hung up the phone. That was at quarter after seven. At twelve fifteen, Kayla went to bed. *I knew he was lying.*

She woke up early the next morning. She had to figure out how she was gonna get to and from work. She went on line and found a bus schedule and mapped out her route. She made it to work twenty minutes early. *At least I know I can make it here on time everyday*, she thought, relieved. The only bad part was catching the bus home at ten o'clock at night. But Kayla knew she had to do what she had to do. Walking to the bus stop after work, she tried not to panic when she saw a car pull beside her.

"What are you doing, dawg?" she heard Terrell call as the window rolled down.

"Going home. The same thing you're doing," she answered.

"Where's your car?" he asked.

"My electrical system went out. Costs almost two grand to fix."

"I'll give you a ride. Come on. Get in." He reached and opened the door. Kayla looked at him, hesitating.

"Where do you live, Terrell?"

"Do it matter? I'm the one taking *you* home. Get in, girl." He smiled.

Kayla got in his Altima and they pulled off.

"So, where am I taking you?" He fumbled with his radio.

"Terrace Gardens, the townhouses." She sat back.

"That's not far from where I live. As a matter of fact, it's on the way. Why didn't you say anything about your car being broke, yo?"

"Because that's my problem. I don't want to be airing my issues to everyone," she said.

"So you were just gonna catch the bus to and from work, not expecting me to offer you a ride? Come on, we peoples. You know that by now. This is my joint right here." He turned up the volume on the radio and began to nod to the music. "You don't know nothing about that, girl."

Kayla laughed and directed Terrell to her house. "Thanks, Terrell."

"No problem, Kayla. I'll see you tomorrow. Be ready at eleven thirty. I'll blow the horn. And have me some lunch ready." He smirked.

"Imagine that." She got out and closed the door, shaking her head.

"Well, at least be ready on time. I'll let you slide with the lunch part. Tell your girl Roni I said what's up, though."

"She's out of your league, Terrell. Besides, she's caught up with another guy right now. I will give her the message, though." She started to go in the house.

"Peace, Kay. And eat something healthy before you go to bed," he called out as he pulled off. Kayla shook her head and was grateful that they had become friends.

15

"So what are we gonna do to celebrate the Fourth of July, prego?" Tia asked Kayla as she flipped through the CDs.

"I don't know," Kayla answered. They were having a Lonely Hearts Club night at Kayla's and while they drank wine, Kayla sipped on a Pepsi and they listened to music.

"What did your dad say when you told him you were pregnant, Kay?" Yvonne passed her a bowl of tortillas and she dipped one in the guacamole.

"I haven't told him," Kayla said between bites.

"He doesn't know?" Roni sat up on the sofa.

"He knows. If your mother knows, then he knows," Roni and Tia looked at each other and said, giggling. There was a knock and Kayla went to answer the door.

"Hey, Terrell. What's up?" Kayla opened the door and he followed her into the living room where the other ladies were.

"Now this is my type of party. Four beautiful women, all shapes, sizes, and flavors." He grabbed a handful of chips and sat beside Roni. Kayla looked at her and laughed. She had told Roni of Terrell's crush, but as she suspected, Roni was not even trying to go there.

"What? You don't have one of your hot dates tonight?" Yvonne asked him.

"Yeah, I did. But she began to bore me so I decided to check on Kay while I was in the neighborhood. If I would have known y'all were over here chillin', I would've cancelled it and came here from the jump." He laughed.

"What are you doing tomorrow for the Fourth, Terrell?" Tia asked.

"I am making my rounds. I got some dates lined up, but my brother is having a nice little cookout at his spot. You guys wanna come?" he asked. "You got something to drink?"

"Yeah, look in the fridge. It's wine, juice, and soda," Kayla replied. Terrell got up and headed for the kitchen.

"Anybody else need something while I'm in here?" he asked and picked up Kayla's almost empty glass.

"I'm good."

"No thanks."

"I'm cool."

He returned with a glass of wine for himself and a glass of juice for Kayla. She looked at him and frowned as he took her can of Pepsi away.

"I'm not having my godchild come out all hyper. I told you about that," he informed her.

"Your godchild? That's my godchild." Yvonne threw a pillow at him.

"Correction. Theo and I have already claimed that child as our first joint venture." Tia laughed.

"Well, I'm glad it's my niece or nephew. Kayla is my sister, even if it's no blood between us," Roni aimed at all of the other claimants.

"Well, if anyone deserves to be the godfather of this child, it's me. If it wasn't for me, the poor kid would be trying to survive on Kool-Aid and Now n' Laters. You'd better want me to be the godfather, because then the kid is straight. Because I am a *pimp*," Terrell joked.

Roni punched him in the arm and told him, "My niece or nephew will not have a *pimp* for a godfather."

"If Kayla's baby is your niece or nephew, yes it will. Now are y'all coming to my brother's crib tomorrow or what? It's gonna be plenty of food, plenty of drinks, and plenty of fun." He looked around at the beautiful women.

"Are there gonna be plenty of men?" Roni asked.

"I'm gonna be there. I'm more than enough. It's plenty of me to go around." He moved closer to her.

"You can say that again." Roni laughed and moved further away.

"I'm down. What time?" Tia asked.

"It's supposed to start at three. But you know how black folks are. I'd say get there around four, four thirty. It's gonna be off the hook, for real. My brother *can* throw a parry. He learned from the best."

"I'm afraid to ask who that might be," Yvonne said.

"Me, of course." His cell phone began to ring and he looked at it. "Well, ladies, duty calls and I must leave you now. I'll meet y'all here at four and you can follow me to his crib. That cool?"

"That's cool," Tia said.

Kayla got up to walk him to the door. "Thanks, Terrell."

"Be on time. You know how you can get." He smiled as he closed the door and left.

"You look so cute," Tia said as Kayla opened the door. Kayla had on her first maternity outfit. She wanted to wear some cute shorts and a midriff top like she usually wore on the Fourth of July, but her condition this year did not allow it. Kayla had on some red maternity shorts and a red and white striped sleeveless top along with some white socks with a red ball on the back and a fresh pair of white Classics.

"I look like a strawberry." Kayla frowned. "Hey, Theo."

"You look cute, Kay," he said as he came inside.

"I can't believe your stomach. It's so cute," Tia continued and touched Kayla's somewhat noticeable belly.

"Shut up, Tia." Kayla laughed and slapped her hands away.

"Roni and Yvonne just pulled up," Kayla said as she looked out the front window. "And there's Terrell. Go tell them I'm ready. But I need Roni to come put my hair in a ponytail. *Don't* tell Terrell. Just tell Roni I need her."

"Okay. But you know Terrell is gonna be fussing," Tia said. "Come on, Theo. Talk him to death to distract him."

"What are you trying to say,?" she heard Theo ask as they departed.

"What's up, Kay?" Roni asked as she came in the door.

"I need you to pull my hair up, Ron."

"I thought something was wrong. Come here, girl." Roni twisted and twirled Kayla's hair until it was perfect.

"I don't see how you do this." Kayla smiled at herself in the mirror.

"Come on, let's go!" They heard Terrell's voice booming from the front. Kayla grabbed her purse and sunglasses and they left.

"Wow. It's a lot of cars here," Kayla told Terrell as they parked in front of the pretty condo. "These are big."

"Yeah, they got three floors," Terrell commented and got out of the car. He took the time to fix his shirt and made sure his pants fit perfectly over his Timberlands.

"Anybody ever tell you you're vain?" Roni said as she joined them. She was touching up her lip-gloss.

"I know you not talking, yo." Terrell smirked.

"Both of you take vanity to a whole other level," Kayla said and they followed Terrell to the house. He opened the door and there was a crowd of people. They were sitting in the well-decorated living area and there was what sounded like a live deejay coming from the backyard.

"Terry! What's up, man?" They greeted Terrell like he was a superstar.

"What's up? Yo, where's Toby?" he asked.

"He's out back working the grill," a tall red-bone told him.

"Come on, y'all. Let me introduce you to your host." Terrell led them through the living area, down a hall past the dining room and kitchen to the huge backyard where a live deejay was set up. A huge grill was filling the air with the smell of barbecue. Theo nodded toward the fully stocked bar and beer keg. There were long picnic tables full of food—salads, fruit, breads, and vegetables, anything you could ever imagine at a cookout. Kayla looked to her left and saw one guy holding a beer, frying fish in a deep fryer. Yvonne nudged her and pointed to another table with a big container in the middle. Kayla looked at her and they knew what the other was thinking—Crabs!

"Now this is a cookout!" Roni nodded. "What does your brother do again?"

"Here he is now. Yo, Toby!"

"Terry. I knew you was gonna be late." The voice came from behind the grill. The cover closed and Kayla saw Roni's jaw drop.

"Hey y'all, this is my brother Toby, otherwise known as Deejay Terror. You know, at Dominic's."

"Nice to meet you. Terry has told me a lot about you all." Toby came and shook all of their hands, stopping at Roni. "I'm glad you could make it."

"Thank you. I'm glad we were invited," Roni said, her eyes never leaving Toby's.

"Toby, I think the meat is ready," a big girl with long hair called from the grill. She did not seem too pleased that he was in Roni's face.

"Well, eat, drink, and be merry. Please have a good time. Let me know if you need anything. We'll talk more later," Toby said.

"Toby!" the girl called again.

"A'ight, Darla. Gimme a break. If it's ready, take it out!" he growled at her as he returned to the grill.

"Do you think that was directed at all of us or just Roni?" Tia laughed.

"I think the last part was for Ron," Theo replied.

"Why didn't you tell me that was your brother?" Roni fumed and asked Terrell.

"You never asked. I mean, I don't go around saying my brother is Deejay Terror. That's some gay type stuff."

"I can't believe this." She shook her head and tried not to look at Toby.

Kayla decided to look for her. The brother was beyond fine. He was dark chocolate in color and at six three, two hundred forty pounds, he was cut just right. His chiseled face had deep set, amber eyes and he had deep dimples when he smiled. *I see why she's digging him.*

"Well, let's eat," Terrell announced. They set out to fix their plates.

"Hi, I don't think we've met. I'm Darla, Toby's girlfriend," the heavy-set girl who had interrupted them earlier walked up and said to Roni.

"I'm Roni," she said mildly, staring the girl in her face. She was never one to be intimidated by anyone.

"And you are?" she directed at Kayla.

"Kayla."

"You here with Terrell?" she asked, looking at Kayla's stomach.

"He invited us." Kayla looked Darla up and down.

"That's cool," she said.

"Darla! Go to the store and get some more ice," Toby yelled from behind the bar.

"Okay." She scurried away, leaving Roni and Kayla standing.

"If she's Toby's girlfriend, why is she worried about if I'm here with Terrell?" Kayla laughed to Roni.

"She better chill, because she messing with the wrong one. Let me get her *boyfriend* to fix me a drink." Roni smiled and headed to join Toby at the bar.

Kayla and her crew feasted and more than enjoyed the food. The deejay, although not as tight as Toby, did an excellent job mixing old school and current favorites. They ate and ate and laughed and joked and ate some more. Soon the sun began to set and Toby joined them at their table, sitting next to Roni.

"I don't think your girlfriend would appreciate you sitting over here with me." Roni smiled at him as he brought her another margarita.

"What girlfriend?" He looked at Terrell, confused. Terrell just put his head down and shrugged.

"What's her name, Kay?" Roni turned to Kayla.

"Darla," Kayla answered.

"Darla? I don't have a girlfriend, and if I did, it definitely wouldn't be *Darla*. That's just my STD." He and Terrell looked at each other and laughed.

"What's a STD?" Tia asked.

"Something To Do. You know. If I get bored and want someone to come over and cook, I'll call her. I need my dry cleaning picked up or someone to wait for the cable man, I know she'll do it. She hangs around me at the club, helps me load my equipment in the car."

"Gives you some," Roni interrupted.

"I didn't say that." He smiled.

"You didn't have to," Roni replied and sipped the frozen beverage seductively through a straw. Toby tried not to stare. He glanced down at his watch and checked the time.

"Hey, you know y'all can see the fireworks from back here. They're about to start in a little while." Everyone was kicked back, having a good time when Kayla caught a familiar face from the corner of her eye.

"G! What's up, baby?" Toby called out.

"Deejay Terror!" Geno started for their table and stopped before he made it, noticing who was sitting there.

"Kayla," Geno said.

"You two know each other? Cool!" Toby got up and offered Geno a seat. "Let me get you a beer, man."

"Hey, Geno," Roni offered.

"What's up, everyone? I didn't think I'd run into you all here," he said. Kayla spotted Janice talking to Darla at the opposite end of the yard. Obviously, she didn't see Geno talking to her. Although he didn't seem too worried about being caught.

"Where's the bathroom?" she asked Terrell.

"Come on, I'll let you use the one upstairs," Terrell told her. They went inside and walked up to the second floor. He showed Kayla the bathroom and told her he'd wait for her. She went inside and looked at herself in the mirror. *What the hell is Geno doing here? I'm not even in the mood to deal wit' no ignorance tonight.*

"You a'ight, Kay?" She heard Terrell tapping on the door.

"Yeah. Give me a few minutes, okay?" she called out.

"Okay. Take your time. I'll wait for you downstairs," he said. She could hear him talking to someone down the hall. She washed her face and hands and opened the door. She found Geno waiting outside the bathroom.

"I told Terrell I needed to talk to you. He said we could use the room at the end of the hall." He grabbed her hand and led her into the bedroom. She sat on the bed in the middle of the massive room.

"What do you want, Geno? Ain't your psychotic girlfriend gonna be looking for you?" she asked him.

"I need to know something, Kayla," he asked, ignoring her question.

"What?"

"When is the baby due?"

"November."

"We were together that night, Kayla. That would be nine months."

"You can't go by months, Geno. It takes forty weeks from conception to birth. I got pregnant on Valentine's." She looked at him.

"But it still might be . . ."

"It's not, Geno." She stopped him. As bad as she wanted him to be, she knew she couldn't make Geno the father of her child.

"Look, I know you are mad about me and Janice."

"You and Janice? I don't give a damn about you and her," Kayla fired at him.

"Chill out, Kay! Don't act like the thought of me being the father never crossed your mind!" he yelled back at her.

Kayla sat on the side of the bed and tried not to cry. The door opened and Terrell stuck his head in.

"You a'ight, yo? Everything cool, man?" he asked, looking at Kayla and then Geno.

"Yeah, man, we just talking," Geno answered him.

"Try to keep it down. Y'all don't want everybody up in your business. Know what I'm saying?" He nodded as he left out and closed the door behind him.

"You wouldn't lie about this, Kayla. Would you? Please, tell me."

"I wouldn't lie to you period, Geno. You know that. Your being with Janice has nothing to do with it. I've never lied to you," she told him.

"Then I guess I owe you an apology, Kay. I mean, I remember that night, and . . ." He smiled weakly, but she knew he was hurt. They sat silently for what seemed like an eternity, just looking at each other. "You look . . ."

"Big as hell." She finished the sentence for him.

He smiled weakly. "No, you look beautiful."

"Come on, we'd better get back downstairs. The fireworks are about to start." She struggled to get up. He reached his hand out and helped pull her to her feet. They giggled as they went into the hallway.

"What the hell are you two doing?" an icy voice said. Kayla and Geno turned around and Janice was standing at the bottom of the steps looking at them like she could spit daggers. Kayla could tell that she was drunk.

"We were talking, Janice. That's all. Come on, let's go back down," he said and tried to get past her, but she blocked him.

"Oh, hell naw!" she yelled. "You come out the bedroom wit' your ex-bitch, who by the way is knocked up, and you wanna act like it's all good? You gotta come better than that, Geno!"

"You know what? I ain't even gonna entertain this bulIshit." Kayla laughed as she went to walk by them. "Excuse me."

"Don't run. What the hell were you doing wit' my man?" she slurred. Kayla looked over the rail and saw a crowd had begun to gather.

"Janice, you're drunk. Come on, let's go." He pulled her arm and she spun around and looked him in the face.

"You still love her, Geno? Is that it?" She waited for him to answer.

"Come on, Janice. Let's go home." He reached for her arm again and she stumbled as she stepped back.

"Tell me. Tell me in front of her, while she standing here, big belly and all. Do you still love her?" This time, she pointed to Kayla.

Kayla looked down at the floor so he wouldn't have to look at her face. As bad as she wanted to know the answer to that question, she dreaded hearing the answer. Either way, it wouldn't matter.

They were over.

"Answer me, dammit!"

Suddenly, Geno bent over and picked up a screaming Janice, carrying her down the steps past the audience that was observing the moment. He looked back at Kayla but didn't say a word. She watched as the door closed behind them.

"Man, that was better than the fireworks," Terrell said. "That was the highlight of the party."

"Shut up, Terrell! You okay, Kayla?" Yvonne ran next to her girlfriend to make sure she was all right.

"Yeah, girl. That bitch is crazy," Kayla said as they went outside.

"No doubt. What were you and Geno doing up there anyway?" Tia asked.

"We were just talking, that's it," Kayla answered.

Everyone had made their way back outside and the party had picked up where it left off. Soon, the sky was lit up with bright, colorful fireworks. Kayla looked up and felt her baby kicking; she couldn't help but smile. *Next year, I'll be watching the fireworks with you.* She put her hand on her belly.

"I got a date this weekend," Roni whispered in her ear.

"I'm not surprised." She smiled at her friend. She looked around and saw Tia and Theo hugged up and Yvonne laughing with a guy by the beer keg. Everyone seemed so happy and content, their lives predictable and settled. Kayla felt the movement in her stomach again and told herself that one day, she and her baby would be happy too.

Despite all the drama earlier, the evening's festivities continued well into the night. Everyone was having such a good time that no one wanted to leave. Kayla tolerated the merriment for as long as she could and then decided she couldn't take it anymore. At ten after eleven, she looked for Terrell. She went inside to check the kitchen where she found him kissing Darla.

"Oops, my bad," Kayla said, embarrassed as she quickly turned around.

"That's okay. You ready to go?" He pushed the plump girl away and she excused herself, walking by Kayla with a smile.

"I'm tired. I can see you're not, though. I'll just get Tia and Theo to drop me off. You go handle your business, Terrell." She smirked at him. They went back into the backyard.

"It ain't even like that. But naw, we can go. I think I might hit a few spots tonight and get my dance on. Is she rolling with us?" He motioned toward Roni who was dancing with Toby.

"I'll go and ask." She shrugged. She waved at Roni and pointed to her wristwatch. Roni nodded and whispered something into Toby's ear. They walked over to her.

"I'm sorry, Kay. I didn't even know it was that late," Roni told her.

"No, I'm sorry, Ron. You can stay if you want. I'm sure Theo will give you a ride. I think Yvonne left, though. I can't find her," Kayla replied.

"I can take you home. That is if you don't want to spend the night." Toby rubbed Roni's arm, smiling.

"You must think I am one of your STDs, huh? Don't think so." Roni pushed his hand away.

"I heard that. Well, let's roll, then," Terrell announced.

"Terry, you not gonna help me clean up?" Toby asked his brother.

"Sorry, bro. I'm quite sure Darla got it under control for you. You know I chauffeured these ladies tonight. I gotta get 'em home, too." He laughed and motioned toward Geno who was walking back into the yard, alone. "I think your boy wanna talk to you."

"I'ma go tell Theo and Tia we're out," Roni said. "You gonna be okay?"

"Yeah." Kayla nodded. She sat back down and watched as Geno walked toward her.

"I'll meet you all out front," Terrell said and waved toward Geno. "We outta here, G!"

"I wanted to come back and apologize for earlier, Kay." He sat beside her.

She wanted to ask him where Janice was, but kept quiet.

"She gets kinda crazy when she drinks. I'm sorry."

"You didn't do anything, Geno." Kayla shrugged. "You might wanna tell her to get some help, though. Any other time you know I wouldn't have been so nice. But I *am* pregnant."

"No, your being pregnant ain't got nothing to do with it. You are *you*. Listen, I just want to let you know that we're still cool. No matter what, okay? You call me if you need anything, you understand?"

"Yeah, G" She turned and faced him. Roni came from around the side of the house and Terrell pulled up all at the same time. "Well, take care of yourself, Geno."

He gave her a quick hug and kissed her cheek, then hugged Roni. "Look out for her, Ron."

"I always do, Geno. Hey, see where Toby's head is at for me, okay?"

"I already know where it is. You got him open." Geno laughed.

"I know that. I got 'em all open. But I gotta figure him out. Let him know I'm not your average chick," Roni said.

"He been in your face all night and he had around forty female guests that came to be in his face. It ain't that hard to figure." Geno waved as they got in the car.

Terrell dropped Roni off and then proceeded to Kayla's. As they pulled up, he noticed something sitting outside her door.

"What's that?" he asked her.

"I don't know." She opened the car door and hesitated going up the sidewalk, turning to look back at Terrell.

"Now I gotta be security too. Jeez." He commented as he opened his door and got out. He picked up the package and read the note. "It's a cake. From your baby daddy."

"Quit playing." Kayla went and grabbed the note from him.

Hey, Beautiful.
I came by to check on you and bring you something sweet. But you weren't here—I guess it's my loss. Call me later so I can see how it tastes.
Love,
Craig

"I can't believe his lying ass. What did he want? And where was his wife and kid?" Kayla snatched her door open and threw the cake on the counter.

"Call him and find out," Terrell told her. "I thought you said he wasn't around."

"He's not. I haven't seen or heard from him since that day I cussed him out in my driveway." She flopped down on the sofa. Terrell wasted no time getting a knife and cutting a slice of the cake.

"Damn, this is the bomb," he said. "That nigga can cook."

Kayla tried to resist but she couldn't. "What kind is it?"

"Chocolate something," he said between bites.

"Bring me a piece," she called out sweetly. He brought her a big slice of the chocolate frosted inferno. It was chocolate with chocolate chips, nuts and caramel. "Who's pimping who, now?" She laughed.

"That's not even funny, yo." He tried not to smile. He knew she had caught him off guard.

"Oh God, this is sinful," she said as she took a bite.

"Well, you good? 'Cause I gotta be out," he said and wiped his mouth.

"Oh, that's right. You're going out," she murmured. "What was up with you and homegirl?"

"Who?"

"The one you were slobbing over." She looked at him knowingly.

"What? Darla? Please. She was trying to get back at Toby for being all in Roni's face. But what she doesn't realize is that Toby ain't her man, and will never be her man because she is too weak. Toby likes strong women. They are a challenge for him. Darla is a chickenhead, a freak chickenhead at that. That was nothing."

"Okay, *nothing*." Kayla wrapped the remainder of the cake up.

"Yo, tell that nigga that cake is the bomb when you call him. I'll holla at you tomorrow."

"Be safe." Kayla hugged him as he left. She made sure her door was locked and picked up the cordless phone. She dialed the numbers and waited for Craig to answer.

"Hey, sweetheart. Did you get your cake?" he asked as if it was the most natural question in the world.

"Don't even try it, Craig. What the hell was that all about? You popping over my house again? I thought you got enough of that the last time you showed up over here unannounced."

"There you go. Why you always gotta trip, huh, Kayla? I made that because I thought you'd like it." She could hear a lot of laughter in the background.

"I thought you were gonna call me back the other week, huh, Craig? Don't tell me, you had to work and didn't get a chance, right?"

"No, I—" he began but Kayla didn't give him a chance to finish.

"I don't care what happened. It doesn't even matter anymore. Nothing you tell me is the truth. The sad part is that you lie for no reason. I can take anything but a liar and a cheat, Craig, and you are *both* of those."

"Kayla, I'm sorry. I know I've fucked up and you have no faith in me. Hell, I don't blame you. But I'm telling you I'm gonna do right by you. This is a messed up situation for both of us, and I was taking all of my frustrations out on you. I'm sorry."

Craig was breathing hard into the phone and Kayla could tell that he must've changed rooms or went outside or something, because the background noise that was there earlier was gone. "Hello, Kayla?"

"I'm here," was Kayla's only response. She didn't know what to say. She wanted to believe Craig, but she knew that he was lying. She had been set up one too many times by him and her guard was up.

"I'm gonna bring you some money, Kayla. And I'm gonna take care of my baby. You understand?"

"If you say so, Craig," she answered.

"Can you call me tomorrow after you get off? I can come through whenever you tell me to. Is that a'ight?"

"I'll call you after ten. I'm 'bout to go to bed. I've had a long day." She sighed into the phone. Kayla was beyond exhausted and she couldn't think straight.

"I guess you don't feel like company then?" Kayla could hear his flirtatious grin through the phone.

"No, I don't. I'll talk to you tomorrow, Craig."

"Good night, Beautiful. I'm gonna do right by you, just watch," he told her and she hung the phone up.

16

"I'm so excited. My first ultrasound," Roni whispered as they waited for the radiologist to come into the exam room.

"You are so silly, Ron. You'd think you were having the baby." Kayla tried to find a comfortable position on the table. There was a light knock and the door opened.

"Ms. Hopkins? Hi, I'm Kelly and I'm gonna be doing your sonogram today. You feeling okay?"

"Fine. This is my friend Roni."

"Nice to meet you. Well, let's get started." Kelly lifted the gown and measured Kayla's stomach with her hands. "You feeling the baby move?"

"A lot." Kayla smiled.

"Now, this is gonna be a little cold," she said as she put the blue gel across Kayla's stomach. She reached for the scope and moved it around Kayla's belly. "There's the heart, liver, kidneys, all looking good. There's the head. Look at the arms, the legs."

Kayla watched in amazement as she saw her baby on the small monitor. Tears began to form in her eyes and she did not bother to stop them. This was her baby. At that moment, she knew without a doubt that she had made the right decision. She saw the form on the small screen and the love that she felt was overwhelming.

"Can you tell what it is?" Roni whispered.

"You want to know the sex?" the woman asked Kayla.

"Yeah." Kayla nodded and continued to focus on the screen.

"Well, let's see. Now I'm not one hundred percent certain because of the position, but I'd say you're having a healthy boy," Kelly said.

A boy, a son, my son.

"Yes, yes, yes. I am gonna have a nephew. He is gonna be spoiled rotten!" Roni gushed.

"I can tell. Let me print some of these out for you and then you can get dressed. Karen will see you in her office in a few minutes." Kelly passed Kayla some paper towel to wipe her stomach and helped her sit up. "Congratulations, both of you."

"A son. Wow, I'm having a baby boy," Kayla said as she got dressed.

"I gotta call Tia and Yvonne and Mama. Girl, we got some shopping to do. We are cleaning that junk room of yours out this weekend, Kayla. It's time to design a nursery."

"You are crazy, Roni." Kayla shook her head.

"What did your dad say, Kayla?" Yvonne asked as she put Kayla's college books into a box.

"About what?" Kayla reached into the closet and pulled some bags out.

"Having a grandson. I know he's excited." Yvonne had closed the box up and began to go through the bags Kayla pulled out.

Her cell phone rang as they were cleaning out what used to be Kayla's guestroom and she excused herself. They knew it was Kayla's father by the way she was talking.

"So, what did he say?" Yvonne asked Kayla.

"I still haven't told him. I'm going to, though." Kayla sat on the floor and crossed her legs.

"When? At his kindergarten graduation? What are you waiting on, Kayla?"

"You know my father. This is gonna break his heart. I just don't know how," Kayla told her friends. She had tried and tried to think of the right way to tell her dad. But no matter how she tried to play the scenario out in her head, it always ended with him being hurt and disappointed.

"You'd better tell him, Kay. I'd hate for him to hear it from someone else, which would be even worse. He'll be even more upset because *you* didn't tell him."

"He's gonna be upset, period. I am just trying to keep the peace for a little while longer. Trust me, I know what I am doing." Kayla hoped she did, anyway.

The girls finally finished clearing the room out and then went out to grab a bite to eat. They were studying their menus at IHOP when a sexy gentleman approached their table. He was short, but cut like LL Cool J. He had perfect skin and the cutest smile.

"Excuse me, but don't I know you from somewhere?" he asked, looking at Yvonne.

"Oh, how original," Roni groaned and shook her head at him. Kayla looked at him, but she didn't recognize him from anywhere.

"I think so, but I'm trying to figure out where," Yvonne told him.

"The school. You work at my nephew's school. I pick him up sometimes," the guy said, realizing who Yvonne was.

"That's right. I've spoken to you in the hallways sometimes. See Roni, he does know me from somewhere."

"I see," Roni replied.

"I'm Darrell, Darrell Coleman." He extended his hand to Yvonne. Kayla frowned at him as she began to comprehend who he was. *It was my brother Darrell's house. The sports agent.* Craig's voice echoed in her head.

"Yvonne Majors. And these are my friends, Kayla and Roni." She pointed to her friends.

"Nice to meet you," he said and noticed that Kayla didn't seem too friendly. "Well, I won't interrupt you ladies any further. Enjoy your meal. I'll see you next time I pick up my nephew."

"I look forward to it." Yvonne smiled and he walked away.

"Cute, Von. You should have given him your number." Roni grinned at Yvonne.

"No she shouldn't have. Don't you know who he is? That's Craig's brother," Kayla hissed across the table.

"Shut up. His brother is that fine?" Roni turned to get a better look.

"Don't turn around! He's looking over here," Yvonne whispered. "Kayla, he seems nice."

"So did Craig, remember?" she muttered, trying not to look across the room at Darrell. "Oh God, he's coming back over here."

"Excuse me, Yvonne. I wanted to leave my number with you. Call me some time if you want to hang out."

"Uh, thanks." Yvonne smiled at him. Kayla was not impressed.

"When's your baby due?" he turned and asked Kayla. *Why don't you ask your brother,* was what she started to say, but thought better of it.

"Thanksgiving Day," she answered with a fake smile.

"That's nice. Well, I look forward to hearing from you. Nice talking to you ladies again." Darrell turned and walked away, leaving the ladies smirking at each other.

"Shut up and eat," Kayla warned before anyone could say anything.

They enjoyed the rest of their meals and went to the register to pay.

"It's already taken care of, ladies," the cashier said.

"What?" they asked in unison.

"Someone already paid for your meal," she said to them like they were slow.

"Who?" Roni demanded.

"The gentleman already left a few moments ago." She gave them their receipt.

"Compliments of DC," Yvonne read aloud. "Darrell Coleman."

"Now that brother has taste," Roni told her.

"You should see his crib," Kayla mumbled.

"What?" Yvonne turned to Kayla.

"Can't believe he paid the bill," Kayla lied.

"If I would have known he was paying, I would have gotten dessert."

17

"A godson. My first godson," Terrell said to Kayla. They were sitting at their desks and Kayla finally told him the results of the ultrasound. She tried to lie and say she didn't know, but Terrell in his eternal nosiness had seen her writing down boys' names on a piece of paper, so she had come clean. "Now we have to come up with a tight name."

"We?" Kayla looked across at him.

"I'm not letting you screw up his life with some cornball name."

"I am not picking cornball names, you jerk." Kayla threw a rubber band at him.

"What do you have so far?" Kenosha asked.

"Okay. How about Xachary Denzel Hopkins," Kayla said proudly. "But spell Xachary with an X, not a Z."

"Annnn!" Terrell made the sound of a game show buzzer.

"I like it," she said.

"Hell, no. First of all, Zachary with a Z isn't even player. It's a nerd name. And then you're gonna really confuse him, his teachers and everyone else by spelling it with an X? And when he plays football, he's gonna be big Xach. That is ugly. And Denzel? Come on."

"Well, what do you suggest, Terrell?" Kayla waited for him to think.

"Tyranny. Now that's player." He smiled.

"Annnn!" It was Kayla's turn to make the buzzer noise. "What the heck? Tyranny? Doesn't that mean oppression? What about Montel Jordan Hopkins?" Kayla asked.

"His first words are gonna be 'this is how we do it'," Terrell joked. They tossed names around every day for weeks until Kayla decided on the perfect one, telling no one. She did, however, let everyone know that she appreciated their input, but they would just have to wait.

***

"Why won't you tell me, Kay?" Roni asked as they were painting the nursery walls a pretty shade of sky blue. It was the end of August and Kayla was getting bigger by the day. She decided they had better get this done before she couldn't get out of the bed.

"Because it's a surprise, Ron. I'm not telling anyone until he's here."

"Not even Craig?"

"No, not even Craig," Kayla told her. Kayla and Craig had come to terms on their relationship. He would come by once a week to check on her and see if she was okay, bringing her banging desserts that she began to thrive on. They would talk for a little while and he would see the progress she was making on the nursery. The entire theme was denim, and everything was OshKosh thanks to her childless girlfriends who got a kick out of outfitting the room. He agreed to purchase the two-hundred-dollar stroller she wanted and surprised the hell out of her when he showed up at her door one night with it. At this point, Kayla had no complaints about him. He tried to push up on her every now and then, but she stopped that real quick. They were just cool and Kayla made sure that he and every one else knew that.

"Is he excited?" Roni began painting the opposite wall.

"I don't think so. I mean, this isn't his first child and he already has a son. It's really no big deal. Calm down, boy." Kayla rubbed her belly.

"Oh, let me feel." Roni walked over and Kayla put her hand where the baby was kicking. "Kay, it's a baby in there."

"Naw, for real? Let's take a break." They went into the living room and Roni looked out the window.

"You expecting company?" she asked.

"No, Yvonne is out with Darrell, and Tia and Theo went to the movies."

"It's a burgundy Explorer pulling up in your driveway. Oh my God!"

"Please don't tell me, Ron." Kayla closed her eyes as she thought of the only person in the world she knew with a burgundy Explorer.

"I'll open the door." Roni went up the hallway and waited for them to knock. Kayla went into her private bathroom so she could think for a minute.

"Ron, hey there girl. How you been doing?" Kayla heard the deep voice say. She tried to calm herself and took a deep breath.

"Fine. You look good."

"Thanks, where's my baby?"

"She's in her room. I'll get her." Roni went to close the door when she realized the rest of the family was getting out of the truck. "Be right back. Make yourself at home."

"Kayla, come out." She tapped on the bathroom door. She knew this was the moment Kayla had been dreading and she wanted to be there for her friend.

"I can't," she whined.

"Yes, you can. Come on, Kayla. They're out there waiting for you." She tried the door but it was locked. She turned around and was startled when she realized she was not alone in the room.

"Move!" the woman commanded. Roni wasted no time doing what she was told. She sat on the side of Kayla's bed and waited for this scene to play itself out.

"Open the door and come out right now."

Kayla opened the door slowly. "Hi, Mama."

"Your hair is growing back. It looks good," her mother said as she hugged her. "Look at you."

"Kayla! I did not drive almost three hours for you to be in the bedroom all day. Come on out here and see me." She jumped at the sound of her father's voice.

"Go on, baby. Time to face the music." Kayla's mother rubbed her back. "She's coming right out, John. Give the girl a few moments. We did show up unexpected."

"Well, if she would call home every now and then she would have been expecting us." He laughed heartily.

"Does he know?" Kayla quickly asked her mother.

"Did you tell him? He'll know in a few minutes." She pulled Kayla out the door and down the hall. "Come on, Roni."

"Hi, Daddy," Kayla said as she walked toward her father. Her dad reached out and hugged her, then quickly let go.

"Kayla? Are you . . . ?" He frowned as he looked at his youngest daughter. The one he taught to ride her bike and scramble eggs. He couldn't believe that she was having a baby, and worse, that she had kept this from him.

"Yes, Daddy." Kayla looked down, ashamed.

"Looks like we're gonna be grandparents, John." Kayla's mother put her hand under Kayla's chin and raised her head. "Don't you hold your head down. You know better than that."

"Is that why you haven't called or come home? But Jennifer, you talked to her. Did you know?" He looked at Kayla's mom.

"I smell paint. Are you painting something?" Kayla's mother quickly asked.

"We're painting the nur—I mean guest room," Roni answered.

"Well, Roni, why don't you show me and we can give Kayla and her dad a chance to talk." They disappeared down the hall, leaving Kayla alone with her father. He sat down on the sofa, still shocked.

"I'm sorry, Daddy. I wanted to tell you, but I was too ashamed. I knew you'd be mad and I wasn't ready to deal with that. Not yet, anyway."

"Mad? Kayla, you are a grown woman. Why would I be mad? I am disappointed, but that doesn't mean I don't love you. What is Geno saying?"

Kayla really wasn't ready to tell him that the baby wasn't Geno's, but she knew that the time had come to be honest about everything. "It's not Geno's, Daddy."

"What? Then whose is it?" Her Dad was truly baffled by what she was saying.

"Craig's," she answered.

"Who the hell is Craig?" He looked up at her.

"A friend."

"So let me get this straight. You get pregnant, don't call or visit for months and the father is your friend, not your ex-fiancé?"

"That's about right, Daddy. But I'm going to be all right. I have a great job and a support system from my friends. This isn't anything I've planned, and believe me, I have gone back and forth with myself about this decision. My child may not have been conceived under the greatest of circumstances, but I *am* gonna be a great mother. You and Mama raised me to do the right thing and I am."

"Baby, baby, baby. You are doing the right thing. But you could have come to me. I could have—" Tears filled his eyes.

"I'm sorry for not coming to you, Daddy. But there was nothing more you could have done for me except what you're doing now, loving me," she said and gave her father a big hug.

All of a sudden there was another knock at the door and it opened before Kayla could answer it.

"Yo, Kay. Let's roll to the mall," Terrell's voice yelled as he came in the door. He realized she wasn't alone and began to apologize. "Oh, my bad."

"Dad, this is . . ." Kayla started.

"You don't have to tell me who this is. My daughter tells me you're the father of this child she is carrying," her dad stood up and said coldly.

"She told you what?" Terrell looked at Kayla, appalled.

"Hey Terrell!" Roni greeted as she and Kayla's mom entered the living room.

"Terrell?" John looked totally baffled. "I thought you said his name was Craig."

"No, *you* said his name was Craig. This is my coworker and friend, Terrell." Kayla introduced Terrell to her father.

"You thought Terrell was Craig?" Roni giggled.

"Who's Craig?" Jennifer inquired.

"The baby's father," John told her.

"Oh, yeah."

"Craig is the father. Terrell is the godfather. And Geno and I are just friends." Kayla sighed. "Everyone understand now?"

"I got it," Roni said.

"Me too," Terrell replied.

"Now, I see the walls are being painted blue. Does that mean I am having a grandson?" Jennifer put her arm around Kayla.

"Indeed you are." Kayla smiled at her mother.

"A grandson. I like that." Her dad smiled at her.

"Well, Kayla, you don't need to be in there painting. Why don't we leave and let your father and Terrell finish the room and we go shopping? Maybe even register you at some stores for your shower," Jennifer said. Kayla looked at Terrell and knew he wanted to object but didn't out of respect for her parents. "You don't mind, do you, Terrell?"

"Uh, no ma'am," he answered and Kayla and Roni suppressed their laughter.

"Go get changed, Kayla. We gotta go shopping for my grandson." She pushed Kayla toward the bedroom.

"I didn't know I drove all this way to paint. And by the looks of what you're wearing, you didn't either, huh?" John asked Terrell. "I appreciate it, though. And I'm sorry about assuming you were the father."

"Happens all the time," Terrell told him. John excused himself and went out to his SUV.

"Thanks, Terrell," Roni told him.

"For what?" He looked confused.

"Making an uncomfortable situation better."

"Why didn't she tell him, anyway?"

"I don't know. She knows her parents have and always will support her. She didn't want to upset him."

"Your girl and her emotional confrontations. That's why I call her DQ."

"What's DQ?"

"Drama Queen. The funny thing is, she doesn't go looking for the drama. It just always seems to find her." He laughed. "Her parents are cool, though. But I did get pimped into painting the room."

"Hey, that's what godpimps are for," Roni told him.

"I like that. Godpimp." He nodded.

"That was supposed to be a joke."

"Now it's my new title." His cell began to vibrate on his hip and he answered it. "What up? Over here at Kayla's. Yeah. She's right here. You wanna speak to her?" He passed the phone to Roni.

"Hello. Oh, it's in my purse. Okay, that's cool. I'll check my schedule and let you know. I'll call you later. Bye." She passed Terrell his phone back, glowing.

"You know he's really feeling you, right?"

"Yeah. Me and how many others?"

"Naw, you are good for him. You don't jump when he wants you to, like all the others. He likes that. I bet he wanted you to go out tonight, right?"

"How do you know?"

"That's how it works for him. He's known since y'all went out the other night that he wanted to see you again, but he'd never tell you that then. He'll wait until the day of and call to ask you. Now, most chicks would've said yes. But you held it down and said you'd let him know. That's player."

"So he already planned to take me out? Why did he wait?"

"Because you are supposed to sweat him, not him sweat you. That's his MO. How long have y'all been going out?"

"Since July, so two months."

"He's never sweated anyone that long before. Whatever you're doing, keep doing it. That is if you really like him." He nodded at her.

"I do. He's a male version of me, kinda what I been looking for."

"Then it'll work because you're a female version of him. I can see why you are so compatible. He talks about you all the time and believe it or not, the games are about to stop. You just need to make sure you're ready for that."

Roni thought about what Terrell was telling her and thanked him. She really liked Terrell because he was the realest guy she had ever met. He was a good friend and just what Romi needed right now. She respected him because he spoke his mind, even though he was so full of himself that he made her want to throw up sometimes.

Kayla, Jennifer, and Roni shopped well into the evening. By the time they returned to Kayla's townhouse, they found John knocked out on the sofa and Terrell long gone. Kayla and Roni took the bags into the nursery. They cut on the light and smiled when they saw that the room was completely done. Not only had they done the walls and trim, there was a neon moon in the corner and glow in the dark stars had been applied to the ceiling.

"Grandpa and godpimp did a good job," Roni whispered to Kayla.

"They always do," she replied and almost cried.

18

The first few weeks of September went by so fast that the days began to run together. Kayla was standing in front of her closet one afternoon when she heard Terrell blowing his horn. She looked at the clock on her nightstand, making sure she had the correct time. The clock read ten forty. She went to let him in.

"You up yet?" he asked her.

"Naw, I'm still in the bed opening the door," she retorted. "I don't feel like going to work today. Let's call in."

"What?"

"Let's call in. I gotta start looking for a car anyway. I'm gonna need one by the time the baby gets here and I got my money saved, plus my trade-in. So, you can help me find a car."

"You're serious?"

"Yeah, I'm serious. Then we can go to lunch, my treat. We need a mental health day." She picked up the phone and called their manager, letting him know she would be absent. Then she passed the phone to Terrell who followed suit.

"I think they're gonna put two and two together and see that we're both calling out."

"Why give us vacation days if you don't want us to take them?" she said. She got dressed and they departed for their day of mental relaxation. They enjoyed test-driving all the latest vehicles, although Kayla knew she couldn't afford them. But by the end of the day, thanks to fast talking Terrell and her nice savings, Kayla was driving a black Maxima.

"Now you gotta get a system and some tint. You already got rims on it. Whoever had it before you took care of that."

"No, now I gotta get a car seat." She laughed. "Thanks, Terrell. I appreciate this."

"No, thank you, Kayla. It was almost enough to make me forget my own drama for a change." His cell began to ring and he checked it. "Hello. Hey, yeah, I took the day off. Um, sounds good. I'll be there in twenty." He clicked the phone and put it back on his hip.

"I don't even wanna know. You are so pitiful."

"Don't hate me 'cause I'm a player. I'll call you later," he told Kayla as he got in his car. She opened the door of her new ride and he rolled down his window. "That car almost looks good enough for me to push."

"It doesn't have any tint, jerk."

"You're right. But you look a'ight in it." He pumped up his music and drove off.

19

"You still working every day?" Karen asked her as she completed her exam.

"Every day." Kayla tried to sit up. Karen had to reach out and help her. "You okay with that? I mean, you only have a few weeks left. Are you tired?"

"Tired, hungry, exhausted, fat, can't breathe. But if I stay home, I'll be bored. And I wouldn't be able to stand that." Kayla put her hand on her stomach. "Is being home gonna stop him from doing pull-ups on my ribs?"

"Unfortunately, no. But look at the bright side. It's almost Veteran's Day and by Thanksgiving, he'll be out of there."

"Promise?"

"Promise. I'll see you next Wednesday." Karen smiled as Kayla left. When she got home, Craig was waiting in her driveway.

"What did the doctor say?" he asked when she got out of the car.

"She said by Thanksgiving I'll be able to breathe. What are you doing here?"

"Came to check on you, beautiful. I swear, Kayla, pregnancy agrees with you."

"Shut up. Where is your wife? And why aren't you at work?"

"I go in at four and she's my soon-to-be-ex-wife."

"Whatever. You still live there."

"Not for long. I'm gonna move in with Darrell." He followed her into the house and she turned to face him.

"Not a good idea," she said.

"Why not? He has an extra bedroom and I definitely ain't staying there with her much longer."

"Look, I need to let you know. We bumped into your brother a couple of months ago at IHOP. He's been trying to holla at

Yvonne ever since. Before you freak out, he has no idea who I am or that this baby is yours. I know you haven't told anyone about the baby."

"Really? I guess I need to let him know then, huh?"

"You're gonna tell him?"

"Yeah. That's my brother. Don't worry, Kayla. You just worry about getting my baby outta there." He put his hand on her big tummy. "I'll take care of announcing his arrival."

"You'd better make it quick. He ain't gonna be in there for long. Believe that," she warned him.

"So what are we gonna do with this head?" Roni asked the Saturday before Veteran's Day.

"I don't know. I don't care. I can be bald at this point and it wouldn't matter," Kayla whined.

"What about some braids, Kay?" Tia suggested.

"I can't sit on the floor that long. My back is already aching."

"I'll do it at the shop," Roni told her. She looked knowingly at Tia.

"That'll take all day."

"Who's doing it, me or you?"

"You."

"Then quit complaining. Come on, let's go."

"You're gonna do it now?"

"Yes, and you'd better hurry up because I have a date with Toby tonight."

"You coming, Tia?" Kayla looked at her girlfriend, who seemed preoccupied.

"Uh, no. Theo's on his way to pick me up. You two go ahead. I'll call you later, Kay."

Roni insisted on driving and they stopped at the beauty supply store to get some bags of hair for Kayla, then proceeded to Jett Black.

"Well, look who wobbled in. Hi, Kayla and company."

"Hi, Ms. Ernestine." Kayla dragged herself to the nearest empty chair and plopped down.

"Miserable, huh?" her friend's mom asked.

"Beyond miserable. And now Roni wants to braid my hair," she moaned.

"Well, at least your hair will look good in your delivery room pictures." Roni began to comb through Kayla's hair.

"What delivery room pictures? I'm not having any pictures taken in the delivery room."

"You think that I'm gonna be your birth coach and not take pictures? This is the birth of my nephew."

"She already bought a new camera, Kayla." Ms. Ernestine shrugged.

"And she can take all the pictures she wants in the hospital nursery," Kayla told them. They laughed and joked until the sun set and Roni finished the last braid.

"That looks good, Roni. Well, it was nice having you, Ms. Kayla. I guess the next time you visit us you won't be by yourself."

"I guess not."

"Do you need anything?" Ms. Ernestine asked her, helping her out of the chair.

"No, I pretty much got everything. Between my mama and the Lonely Hearts Club, I am pretty well set."

"Well, call me and let me know. No matter what time it happens."

"You know we will, Mama. I'll see you later." Roni kissed her mother's cheek and they headed for Kayla's house.

"I would invite you in, Ron, but I know you have a date. I wish you could keep me company for a little while at least." Kayla reached in her purse and pulled out her keys.

"Fine, Kayla. I'll call Toby and tell him I'll meet him later." Roni pouted as she followed Kayla inside.

"Thanks, Ron. You know I love you." Kayla went in.

"Surprise!" People yelled when Kayla turned on the light. There were blue, yellow, and white balloons everywhere and what looked like a hundred people in her house.

"I'm gonna kill you, Roni." Kayla hugged her friend.

"It was Tia, Yvonne, and Terrell, too," Roni told her. Kayla greeted all of her guests and looked at the big banner hanging in the living room, welcoming baby boy Hopkins. There was a long table spread with food on top of food and a huge, blue and white cake in the shape of a rocking horse.

"Thank you so much," Kayla said as she wobbled to her lounge chair and sat down.

"Surprise, baby," she heard her mother call out. She turned to find her.

"Mama! Where's Daddy?"

"You know he was not trying to come to no baby shower, although Terrell told him other males would be here." She pointed to Terrell who was talking to Theo and Toby in the corner of the room. "But your sister did come."

"What?" Kayla looked at her mother and she felt her heart pounding. Her mother walked off before Kayla could speak.

"Hello, Kayla," Anjelica said. Kayla looked at her pretty sister. She looked nice in a red, sleeveless sweater and some jeans. Her hair was pulled back off her face and fell past her shoulders. "Congratulations."

"What the hell are you doing here?" Kayla asked as her sister bent down to hug her.

"Look, I don't wanna be here any more than you want me here, but mama made me come. So calm the hell down before you embarrass you and her in front of all your friends."

"I don't give a damn. I want you outta my face. Now!" Kayla yelled. Roni quickly came over to her friend's side. She was glad the music was loud enough to drown out the two sisters' arguing.

"Anjelica, I think you might wanna go in the other room for a while, please," Roni told her.

"Fine." Anjelica rolled her eyes at Kayla as she walked by.

"I want her out, Ron. Please get her outta my house." Kayla grabbed Roni's arm.

"Your mother made me invite her, Kayla. I couldn't say no. I'll keep her out of your way, I promise," Roni assured her. She had no idea what had gone down between Kayla and Anjelica, but she knew it was deep.

Kayla calmed down and began talking to her other guests. Some of her coworkers were there, even though they had given her a huge shower at work. Ms. Ernestine arrived shortly after she and Roni did. And the most surprising guest of all presented Kayla with a huge box.

"Congratulations, my Kayla," Ms. Gert said as she gave her a kiss.

"Ms. Gert. I . . . Thank you." Kayla was lost for words.

"For what? Child, I keep telling you we are family no matter what. You are still my daughter-in-law. I love you, okay? Where's your mama? I haven't seen Jennifer in ages. Let me go find her." Ms. Gert set off to find Kayla's mother.

It was a shower like no other. Kayla got everything on her gift registry and more. She got enough diapers to last a year and even Toby surprised her with a blue stereo system for the nursery along with some classical and jazz mix CDs.

"Start him out early as a music pro." He laughed.

Terrell had purchased his first leather coat with fur trim.

"Where did you find that?" someone called out. "What size is it?"

"A small." Kayla read the tag.

"'Cause my godchild has to look player." Terrell smiled at Kayla.

Tia, Yvonne, and Roni took the job of writing down what was from whom, and Theo and Toby carried armloads of gifts to the nursery.

"Thank you all for coming." Kayla stood and said as the shower ended.

"Let us know when he makes his arrival," everyone told her as they left. Her girls were busy cleaning up and putting away the food. Kayla wanted to change into something more comfortable. She passed the nursery and noticed the door was cracked. She pushed it open and startled Theo, who was pushing Anjelica away from him.

"What the hell are you doing?" Kayla demanded. Her sister stared at her and Theo wasted no time evacuating the room. Anjelica looked at her with no remorse.

"Nothing happened, Kayla. Chill," she said, running her fingers through her hair.

"What the hell is wrong with you? You try to push up on my best friend's boyfriend in my house?"

"You need to calm the hell down. I already told you nothing happened. And the key word here is boyfriend. I don't recall seeing a ring on his finger or hers. To me, he's free game."

"You really are a skank! You know Tia and him are together and you still pushed up on him? You are a trifling wench!" Kayla yelled, getting angrier and angrier by the minute.

"True words from a pregnant woman knocked up from a one-night stand. And I am the trifling one?"

Those words hurt Kayla and she swiftly moved and raised her hand to slap her sister back to reality, but a strong hand caught her before she could make contact. She turned to see everyone crowded in the doorway watching the entire incident unfold.

"I think you need to leave," Terrell told Anjelica, turning Kayla away.

"Who the hell are you supposed to be? Her bodyguard?"

"No, I'm her friend and the brotha that's keeping her from whooping your ass, whether she's pregnant or not. Now, if you can't respect your sister or her friends, then you need to leave her house."

"Whatever! I didn't want to come here anyway." Anjelica stormed out of the room and they heard the door slam behind her. Kayla went into her room and sat on her bed. Beads of sweat began to form on her forehead and she could feel her heart beating a mile a minute.

"You okay, Kayla?" Roni asked and sat next to her friend.

"I hate her. Always have, always will." The tears fell from her cheek and onto the bed.

"Don't say that, Kay. That's just her. Always has been, always will be. She's just her."

"Ain't that the truth." Tia came and joined them on the bed. "We all know how she is."

"Can I have a moment, please?" Kayla's mom tapped on the door.

"Sure. We gotta go finish cleaning up anyway," Roni said. She and Tia left Kayla and her mother alone to talk.

"Your sister was wrong. Terrell was right. She disrespected you, your friends, and your home." Her mother rubbed her back.

"Why did you even invite her? You know we hate each other. She only came to do something like this." Kayla wiped her face.

"Because like it or not, she's your sister. And she was right to come. I don't know why she does what she does. And I am not gonna make any excuses for her obnoxious behavior. Maybe she's jealous."

"Of what?"

"You."

"Why would she be jealous of me? I am single, pregnant, broke, and I don't know what life holds for me from one day to the next."

"But you accept every challenge that is presented to you, Kayla. No matter what it is. When Anjelica caught her boyfriend with that white girl, she didn't get out of bed for a week. When she found out she was pregnant, she got rid of it and then got so depressed she nearly lost her mind. She's never really had any close friends and here you have Tia, Roni, Yvonne, *and* Terrell. She would never move twenty miles from home, let alone two hundred. You are a conqueror, Kayla, and she resents that."

"Mama, I know she is your child and you think you know her, but you don't. Anjelica is evil. She's done some wicked, hurtful things to me and I couldn't care less whether I ever see her again. Sister or not." Kayla went into the bathroom and closed the door behind her.

After a few minutes she came out, expecting to find her mother still sitting there. To her surprise, her room was empty. She went into the living room and found her three best friends sitting next to a pile of gifts, still wrapped.

"I thought I opened all the gifts," she said as she sat down. "Where's Mama?"

"She went to get something out of the car. She'll be right back," Yvonne answered.

"I just want to thank all of you. This really meant a lot to me. I thank you and love you, as my son will too." She told all of them. Her mom came in carrying another wrapped gift and Roni lit some candles on the mantle.

"Now, we have some things for you," Tia told her.

"I got enough things. Where did these gifts come from?" Kayla was still wondering what they were about to do.

"The shower gifts you got earlier were for the baby. Now this shower is for you," Yvonne said and handed her a box. Kayla opened it and smiled at the foot massager and pedicure set. "Thanks, Von."

"For those tired feet, girl. Walking that baby to sleep at night." She hugged Kayla and sat back down on the sofa.

"This is from me and Theo," Tia said and handed her the pretty, wrapped box. Inside Kayla found a giftset from Bath and Body Works and an envelope. She opened it and found a gift certificate to a day spa. Kayla squealed in delight.

"Do you get to bring a guest?" Von asked.

"Sorry, only good for one." Tia laughed.

"And this is from me." Roni could hardly push the big box in front of Kayla.

"What in the world?" Kayla asked. She opened the top of the box and looked down into it. "A suitcase."

"Help her take it out," Tia said. They slid the rolling bag out of the box and laid it on its side.

"Open it," Roni encouraged. Kayla unzipped the bag and her eyes filled with tears.

"Oh, my," she heard her mother say. Tia and Yvonne came closer to get a better look. The bag was fully packed with nightgowns, slippers, underwear, socks, soap, comb, brush, toothpaste, toothbrush; everything Kayla would need at the hospital, down to an outfit to wear home. Kayla could tell that Roni put a lot of thought and effort into packing it.

"Roni, I don't know what to say." Kayla did not try to stop the tears from falling. By now, every eye in the room was watery.

"Well. I guess it's my turn now." Jennifer stood and handed Kayla the gift she had gotten her. When Kayla opened it and saw what it was, she really began to cry.

"Oh, Mama, it's beautiful." She held up the gold locket for her friends to see. She opened it and found her baby picture.

"Read it, baby," her mom said.

"From one mother to another." Kayla barely got the words out because she was crying so hard.

"The other side is for you to put your baby's picture. We all love you, Kayla. We know this hasn't been easy for you, but we are here for you and we just wanted to show you." Her mother sniffed.

They all gathered around Kayla and hugged her, big belly and all.

20

Kayla was two days from her due date and she was beyond miserable. She came back from lunch and laid her head on her desk. All of a sudden, she felt a pain go down her back and spread across her abdomen. It caused her to suck her breath in and sit straight up.

"You okay, Kayla?" her manager asked.

"I got a pain in my back," she told her.

"Just one?"

"Yeah, so far." She looked at her watch and mentally noted the time as six forty-two. She began work and after a while, another pain shot through her body. This time it was six fifty-one, less than ten minutes apart. She waited until she had a set of six pains.

"What's wrong, yo?" Terrell asked.

"I think I'm in labor," Kayla told him.

"For real? You want me to call Roni?"

"I wanna go now. Can you take me, Terrell?"

Terrell looked at his friend and then his watch.

"Okay, Kayla. It's after seven now. That means I'm gonna miss two hours on my paycheck. You gonna pay me back?"

"Shut up, Terrell, and let's go." She grabbed her purse and cut her terminal off. Her coworkers wished her good luck and Terrell wasted no time in getting her to the hospital.

"Which floor?" he asked as they got on the elevator.

"Fourth, labor and delivery." She groaned. He reached out and rubbed her shoulders. She looked at him and noticed the worry on his face. They got off the elevator and Kayla wobbled to the nurse's station.

"Hi, I'm having a baby," Kayla told the pretty nurse.

"Well, we're here to help you do that." She smiled at Kayla. "I'm Nicole and your name?"

"Kayla Hopkins. Karen Bray is my doctor." She felt another pain and grabbed the counter.

"Okay, Ms. Hopkins, follow me. You're already pre-registered so you don't have anything to fill out. Just sign. We can get that done after you're settled in the labor room. You need a wheelchair?"

"I think I can make it," Kayla told her.

"Okay. Mister Hopkins, you can wait in here while I examine your wife."

"I'm not Mister Hopkins. That's her father. I'm Mister Sims," he corrected her.

"I'm sorry, Mister Sims. Excuse me for making that assumption. You can follow Ms. Hopkins to the labor room. I know you're excited. Is this your first child?" she asked.

"Yes, my first baby," Kayla answered as they left Terrell and went into one of the birthing rooms.

Nicole helped her settle in and Kayla quickly felt comfortable with her. Kayla changed into a hospital gown and Nicole wrapped the monitor around her belly. Sounds of her baby's heartbeat filled the room. Kayla couldn't help but smile. *It won't be long now,* she thought. Nicole continued to examine her and told her to relax for a little while as she went to get Terrell.

"She's nice," Kayla said to Terrell when he came into the room.

"And she's fine. I like her."

"You okay, Mister Sims? Can I get you anything?"

"Um, your number. That is, if you'd like to maybe have dinner with me."

"I don't think now is the appropriate time or place for you to be flirting." Nicole laughed as she checked Kayla's vitals. "How are you gonna disrespect your child's mother like that?"

"God, Kayla, I swear. People call me your baby daddy so much that I'm beginning to believe it. No, Nicole, I am not the father of this baby. I am the lucky godfather."

"I thought you changed it to godpimp," Kayla told him. He looked at her like he wanted to hit her.

"Quit playing, girl. What kind of name is that? Godpimp?" He laughed lightly and Kayla opened her mouth in amazement.

"Well, you're a good godfather, bringing her to the hospital and waiting this long. Especially since she's not in active labor." Nicole wrote something down on Kayla's chart.

"What do you mean? I'm having contractions, aren't I?" Kayla wailed.

"Yes, but they aren't strong enough to make you fully dilate. When I checked you, you were only three centimeters dilated. Now, you can stay for a couple hours and walk, maybe making you further along, but I don't think you'll have that baby tonight."

"Aw man, so you mean we've been here for nothing?" Terrell whined.

"Not for nothing," Nicole said and wrote her number down, giving it to him. "Let's just say I have a thing for godfathers."

"Told you I was a pimp." He winked at Kayla when the nurse left the room.

"Whatever. I can't believe I'm not having this baby tonight." She covered her face with the back of her hand.

"Kayla, Kayla. I got here as fast as I could. I brought your suitcase and Toby is bringing the camera. Thank you, Terrell. You okay? You need any ice chips?" Roni came rushing in.

"You could've took your time. She's not having the baby tonight. She's not in active labor," Terrell informed her.

"False alarm?" Roni asked.

"False alarm. Call Toby and tell him he may as well turn around." Kayla sighed.

"That's okay, Kayla. He'll come out when he's ready." Roni rubbed her friend's stomach and laughed. "Still comfy in there, li'l man?"

"Who wouldn't be? He's got it good. He got three squares and a warm bed," Terrell said.

"You make it sound like I'm a jail," Kayla told him as she sat up.

"You are. He can't get out, can he?" Terrell laughed. Kayla didn't find it funny.

Kayla decided not to return to work until after the baby was born. She spent the next day walking as Nicole had advised her to do. She walked around the neighborhood, she walked the mall, and she walked around the grocery store and Wal-Mart.

"Mama, what am I doing wrong?"

"Nothing, baby. You just gotta wait. He'll come when he gets ready," her mother told her.

"But Karen promised that he'd be here by tomorrow. And now you and Daddy are getting ready to go out of town. I wanted you all to be here." Kayla's parents were going to her aunt's house for Thanksgiving.

"You'll be fine, Kayla. I promise you we will be there to spoil our grandbaby enough. Look, I have got to get out of here. Your father has a list of things for me to do before we hit the road. I love you, Kay. And keep walking. Or you can always call Craig and have sex; that causes labor."

"Mama!" Kayla yelled into the phone.

"What? It's not like you haven't slept with him before. Now you need to. I'm just playing. Love you and call us if it happens before I call and check on you."

Kayla was even more depressed when she hung up the phone. All of her friends called or came by to make sure she was okay, but she knew they had plans for the holiday weekend. Yvonne was gone with her family, Tia was taking Theo to her grandmother's, and Roni was invited to the Sims' for dinner.

"Come on, Kayla, you should come," Roni told her Thanksgiving eve on the phone.

"No, I am too tired to move. I'm gonna stay in bed all day and be the warden for my son."

"You're crazy. I'll be over there after dinner," Roni told her.

"That's okay. I'll be fine. Enjoy meeting your future in-laws," Kayla mumbled. She climbed into bed and somehow found a spot comfortable enough to sleep in. The phone rang as she began to doze off.

"Hey, beautiful. What are you doing?" Craig asked her.

"Trying to sleep," she murmured.

"Well, I'll let you go then. Call me if anything happens."

"Like what?" Kayla knew she was being mean, but she couldn't help it.

"Go to sleep, Kayla. I hate when you get like this. Call me if you need me." She heard the dial tone and put the phone on the receiver. She woke to the sound of the Macys Thanksgiving Parade and dialed Terrell's number.

"Hello," he groaned into the phone.

"Happy Thanksgiving, Terrell. Are you watching the parade?" she asked him innocently.

"No. What time is it?"

"Nine seventeen."

"Bye, Kayla. Call me after twelve. I can't believe you called me this early." Again, Kayla's ear was filled with the sound of the dial tone. She got up, took a shower and got dressed. As she was sitting at her kitchen table eating a bowl of cereal, her mom called to wish her a Happy Thanksgiving and make sure she was okay. That call was followed by Roni, Tia, and Yvonne. By the time Kayla told everyone she was fine, she was tired all over again. The burst of energy she had when she woke up was gone and she was again having the pains in her back. She grabbed a blanket and relaxed on the lounge chair in the living room, watching television. She tossed and turned from the discomfort until she fell asleep. She thought she was dreaming when the doorbell rang. She sat up and looked at her watch. It was after seven and her back was killing her. She stood up and doubled over in pain.

The bell rang again and she called out, "Give me a minute. I'm trying!"

Taking careful steps, she slowly made her way to the front door. She didn't even look to see who it was. She just opened it.

"Happy Thanksgiving! I knew it was your due date so I decided to stop by and check on you! Kayla, what's the matter?"

She lifted her head and saw Geno standing there, carrying plastic bags, "My back is killing me, G."

"Come on. I'm taking you to the hospital!" He put his arm around her and helped her to his SUV.

"My bag, Geno. I need my bag," Kayla told him and he ran back in to get it.

While he was in the house, Kayla felt water run down her legs. She could not believe this was happening. She was standing in the middle of the sidewalk, legs straddled, when he came running out of the house. She looked at him, dazed and told him, "My water broke!"

"Don't move. I'll get some towels." He ran back to the door, realizing he'd locked it and raced to get her keys out of her purse. He flew in and got some towels then ran back to Kayla. He covered the passenger seat and helped her in. Kayla flinched as he pulled out of the driveway.

"It's gonna be okay, Kayla. Hold on, baby." He sped to the hospital and rushed her to Labor and Delivery. Kayla was in agony the whole time.

"Hi, Kayla," Nicole greeted her. "You back for good?"

"I hope so." Kayla let out a long moan and Nicole grabbed a wheelchair. They got her into a room and when Nicole checked her this time, she frowned at Kayla.

"What? What's wrong?" Kayla asked her.

"Why did you wait so long to get here?" she asked Kayla and reached for the phone on the wall.

"I don't know. I didn't want it to be a false alarm again so I waited, and when I got up to answer the door, I couldn't walk."

"Page Doctor Bray and get her here. Her patient is fully effaced," Nicole said into the phone.

"What does that mean?" Geno asked.

"That means in about fifteen minutes she'll have a baby."

"What about my epidural and my breathing techniques?" Kayla asked.

"Too late, Kayla. Your baby's almost here. Are you gonna stay with her?" she asked Geno. He looked at Kayla and she reached for his hand.

"You don't have to do this, Geno." He looked at the fear in her eyes and knew he had to do this. There was no way he was leaving her side. She began to wail and writhe in pain.

"I'll be here. What do I need to do?"

"I gotta go to the bathroom. I need to get up!"

"That's your baby you feel, not your bowels." Nicole looked at Geno. "Grab her leg when I tell you to. Okay now, Kayla, on the next contraction I need for you to bear down and push.

Ready? One, two, three, push." Nicole counted and Kayla screamed. It felt as if her bowels were being ripped from her body.

"God, I can't do this!" she yelled and sweat began to mix with tears on her face.

"Yes, you can, Kayla. Look at me. You can do this," Geno told her. She shook her head fiercely at him, but he stopped her and moved her head up and down. "Yes, you can."

"Okay, here comes another one. You ready?" Nicole said. "Push, Kayla, push! That's it!"

"I gotta stop! It's splitting me wide open!" Kayla screamed and panted.

"It's the head, Kay. I see the head. Come on! It's almost over. You're doing it, baby!"

"Looks like I made it just in time. Good thing I was with another patient upstairs." Karen burst through the door with a smile.

"Hey, Karen. Look. The head is right there."

"I see. Now let's get him out. Come on now, Kayla. I need you to push for me. And go!"

Kayla bore down, chin on her chest, and pushed as hard as she could.

"That's it, the head is out! It's almost over, Kayla," Karen told her and she felt Geno's chin on her head. She closed her eyes as she heard his voice encouraging her to keep pushing, and then it was over. She heard the cry of her baby and she knew she had done it.

"Uh-oh!" Karen said. "We made a boo boo!"

"What? Is he okay?" Kayla began to panic.

"She's beautiful," Karen said and put the wriggling, wet baby on Kayla's chest.

"She?"

"Yes, you have a beautiful baby girl. Geno, would you like to do the honors?" She held the scissors clamped on the umbilical cord.

"I don't think . . ."

"Do it, G. I want you to," Kayla told him. He reached and snipped the cord connecting Kayla and her daughter.

"Let's clean you up, Little Miss. Geno, you want to help while Karen finishes up with Kayla?" Nicole said as she took the baby. She put an ID bracelet on her little foot and on Geno's arm.

Just when Kayla thought the worst was over, Karen told her she had to deliver the birth sack.

"It's not another one in there, is it?"

"No, but it's gonna be some pressure." She felt Karen pulling on what felt like her insides and began to moan again. "All done."

"Seven pounds, three ounces. Nineteen inches," Nicole called out. "Vitals are great."

"I told you it'd be today," Karen said.

"You also told me it was a boy," Kayla said wearily. "I don't even have a name for her."

Geno walked over with the baby and handed her to Kayla. "What a day. What a day."

"It sure is. Congratulations, Kayla. You did good. Geno, you did good too!" Karen said as she was leaving. "I'll check on you later. Happy Thanksgiving."

Kayla was exhausted. They moved her to a regular room and she fell asleep immediately. When she woke up, Geno was still there, holding the baby.

"Hi, Mommy. You feel okay?" he asked.

"Yes, a little tired. What time is it?" she asked.

"A little after ten. I called Roni and she's on her way. She's mad because she missed the whole thing. You hungry?"

"Not really."

"Well, someone is. Nicole said you're going to breastfeed. I'm supposed to get her when you wake up. Here, hold her while I get Nicole." He passed the tiny little girl to Kayla and she could not help but smile.

"Hi, Sweetie. I'm your mommy. You ready to eat?" She kissed the top of her forehead and looked at her. She tried to see who the baby looked like. She was light in complexion, but Kayla knew that would change by the caramel color of her ears. Her eyes were closed, but Nicole said that they were brown. And she was bald, with the exception of a patch of hair on the very top of her head.

"Ready to do this, Kayla?" Nicole asked as she came in the room.

"I guess so. She's gotta eat." Kayla laughed. Nicole showed her how to hold the baby properly as she fed her, and Kayla felt like a pro as her daughter greedily sucked on her breast.

"Let me see him, let me see him!" Roni cried as she entered the room. "He's gorgeous. I can't believe I missed it, Kayla. How are you feeling? Did it hurt? How did Geno wind up here?" She didn't give Kayla a chance to answer. Geno came in with a big bouquet of balloons announcing, *It's a Girl.*

"You must have the wrong room," said Roni.

"You're crazy. How is she, Kayla?"

"It's a girl? How in the world? It's a girl!" Roni looked from Kayla to the baby to Geno.

"Say hello to your niece, Aunt Roni." Kayla passed the baby to Roni.

"Hi, Sweetie. You are so beautiful. You are gonna be a diva, just like your mommy."

"Don't curse her, Roni," Geno said as he tied the balloons to Kayla's bed.

"I can't believe I had a girl. She doesn't even have anything to wear home from the hospital." Kayla looked at Roni holding her daughter.

"That's the least of your worries. Aunt Roni will have her hooked up. Now what you do need to worry about is a name."

"Yeah, you need to pick one, Kayla, or she will be Baby Girl Hopkins," Geno said. "What was the boy's name gonna be?"

"Joshua Maxwell," Kayla told them.

"That was nice, but it definitely won't work for a girl," he said.

"You got that right. What about Destiny?" Roni asked.

"How about no. That's corny and everyone is using that because of Destiny's Child."

"She's right," Geno said. "You had to think of some girls' names before you knew it was a boy. What were they?"

"Knock knock! Everyone decent?" Terrell stuck his head in the door, followed by Toby. He looked at the balloons and shook his head. "How'd you manage that?"

"Ultrasound reading was wrong, I guess," Kayla told him and he gave her a hug.

"She's beautiful," Toby said as he looked over Roni's shoulders at the baby. "I guess you don't need the camera, huh?"

"Sure we do. This is a video worthy moment. Start filming. I'll be the host, of course." Roni handed the baby to Kayla as Toby took out his video camera. "Today is Thanksgiving Day, and we have so much to be thankful for. We are here with Kayla Hopkins, who has just given birth to a beautiful baby girl. Kayla, what are you thinking about naming your precious daughter?"

"Her name is Jenesis Sade Hopkins. But her nickname is Day," Kayla said proudly.

"Day," Toby said. "I like it."

"It's not as tight as London," Terrell said recalling one of the girl's names he had suggested to Kayla early in her pregnancy, "But Jenesis Sade is pretty. And Day is player for a nickname."

"Beautiful Day." Geno took the baby from Kayla. He was amazed at her tiny body and thought the name suited her. Kayla had always talked about naming her daughter Jenesis with a J, after her mother.

"Now how did you wind up taking my place in the delivery room, Geno?" Roni asked.

Kayla and Geno recounted the events of the night for everyone until Nicole came in and announced that Kayla and the baby needed to rest. She took Day back to the nursery and everyone said their good-byes.

"Thank you again, Geno," Kayla whispered as he kissed her cheek before he left.

"I told you I would always be there for you, Kay. She's beautiful and so are you. I'll come back and visit both of you tomorrow."

"Okay. We'd both like that." Kayla closed her eyes.

"Kay and Day. What a pair." He chuckled as he walked into the hallway.

21

The hospital registrar came by the next morning to get the info for Day's birth certificate. Roni told Kayla she had called Craig and left a message on his cell phone that she had given birth and was in the hospital, but he still had not called or come by.

"Father's name?" the crabby white woman asked.

"Craig Coleman," Kayla answered.

"Is he here?"

"Not right now."

"We need him to sign the certificate if he is to be registered as the father. If not, a name won't be listed."

"He'll sign," she told her. She wanted Day to know her father's name, even if he opted not to be an active part of her life. She called his cell and again got no answer. When she hung the phone up, it rang instantly. Kayla thought it was him returning her call, but it was her parents calling to congratulate and let her know they were on their way.

"Hi, Kayla. You feeling okay?" Yvonne knocked as she came in the door. "Let me see my goddaughter. She's gorgeous! Hi, Day. Auntie Von bought this for you to take your pictures in and wear home."

"Thanks, Von. I told Roni last night that she had nothing to wear." Kayla looked at the soft pink and white outfit with the matching hat that Yvonne had given her.

"We got that all taken care of. Don't worry about a thing. You just rest up. When are they releasing you?"

"Tomorrow morning." Kayla sighed.

"What's wrong, Kayla?"

"I left messages for Craig but he hasn't called or come up here. I need him to sign her birth certificate."

"He'll show up. You told me he's changed, right? He's been coming around and he promised to be there for his baby. Just relax."

"Okay, Von." Kayla sighed. They dressed Day and got her ready for the photographers. The nursery had just brought her when Craig arrived along with Darrell.

"I hear I have a princess in here." He winked at Kayla. She was not amused.

"About time you decided to make an appearance." She scowled.

"Is this my new niece?" Darrell asked, "Hi, Kayla. It's nice to see you again."

"Can I at least hold her, Kayla?" Craig reached for the small bundle Kayla was clinging to as if her life depended on it.

"We've been calling and leaving messages for your trifling behind since last night and now you want to waltz in here and hold her like the proud papa?"

"I didn't get any messages, Kayla. I lost my cell the other night at the restaurant. We had mad dinner parties for Thanksgiving and I don't know what happened to it. I swear. The only way I knew was when Darrell called me a little while ago. We came straight here." He pleaded with her. She looked at him doubtingly and he looked at Darrell for support.

"He did lose his phone. So if that's what you were calling, he wouldn't have got the messages," Darrell added.

"Lying for your brother?" Kayla asked.

"No. The only way he knew was because Yvonne left a message on my voice mail a little while ago." Kayla looked over at her friend who shrugged at her.

"She looks just like you, Kayla. Hi, Princess. What are we gonna name you?" He rubbed noses with his tiny daughter.

"She already has a name," Kayla told him.

"How you gonna name her without my input?" He looked at Kayla.

"Don't go there," she warned him and he knew it wouldn't be worth the fight.

"Well, what is your name?" he asked the baby.

"Day," Kayla and Yvonne answered simultaneously.

"Day? What kind of name is that?" Craig frowned.

"It's her nickname. Her full name is Jenesis Sade Hopkins," Kayla informed him.

"Genesis, like the Bible?" Darrell asked as he took the baby from his brother.

"More like Geno," Craig said accusingly.

"First of all, it's Jenesis with a J, as in Jennifer, which is my mother's first name. And Sadie was my grandmother's name. That's how I came up with it. Secondly, Geno's real name is Antonio Giovanni. His nickname is Geno. So you can kill that thought before it even enters your mind."

"Jenesis Sade. Day. I think that is very elegant, Kayla. You picked a beautiful name." Darrell looked at her, seeing why Craig liked her.

"Okay. Since you've explained how you got it, I like it too." Craig rubbed her arm.

"I need for you to sign her birth certificate," Kayla told him.

"I know. What do I need to do?" He took a deep breath. He knew that news of Day's birth was gonna come out sooner or later, and now it was time to pay the piper. He had a plan, though. Looking at his brother holding his daughter, his heart filled with love, he knew this was the right thing to do.

"Sorry, I didn't know you had visitors," Geno said as he peeked in the door.

"It's okay. Come on in, Geno." Kayla motioned for him to enter. And he did with a big vase of pink roses and the biggest teddy bear Kayla had ever seen.

"Aww, Geno! That is so cute!" Yvonne stood to help him with his gifts. "Where did you find a bear that big?"

"If I tell you, I'd have to kill you." He smiled at her and passed her the flowers. She put them on the nightstand next to Kayla's bed.

"What's up?" he said to Craig and Darrell.

"Geno, this is Darrell. And uh, I think you met Craig," Yvonne said.

"Wussup?" Craig mumbled.

"Nice to meet you." Darrell smiled.

"Hi there, Miss Day. You're all dressed up." Geno walked over and looked at the baby.

"She had her first photo shoot." Yvonne laughed.

"The first of many. You just watch," Geno told them. "How you feeling, Kay?"

"Good. Our first night was okay," she answered.

"You ready to go back to Mommy?" Darrell asked Day as she began to squirm.

"Let me take her for a sec." Geno held out his arms and Darrell passed the baby to him. He paced the floor and rocked her, rubbing his face against hers affectionately. He turned and looked at Kayla whose eyes met his and they smiled at each other. Craig knew the look well. It was the look he gave Avis the first time he held his son. A look that said, "Look what our love for each other created."

Kayla looked over at Craig who was sitting, looking at Day's birth certificate. "You sign it?"

"No." He looked up at her.

"What are you waiting for, her eighteenth birthday?" Kayla chuckled.

Craig glared at Geno then looked her in the eyes and replied. "I want a blood test before I sign anything."

You could hear a pin drop in the room as all eyes landed on Craig. Even Day seemed stunned by what her alleged father had just said.

"What are you saying, Craig?" Kayla felt her blood go ice cold as she sat up in the bed.

"I think we need to give them some privacy," Yvonne said as she pulled Darrell's sleeve.

"Yeah, no doubt," Darrell told her as he stood up.

"You okay, bro?" he asked Craig as they headed out the door.

"I'm fine." Craig nodded.

"We're going to the gift shop for a while. Kay, you need anything?" Yvonne touched Kayla's hand. She knew that Kayla was offended by what Craig had said and she had good reason to be.

"No, you go ahead. Can you send the nurse in to take Day to the nursery, though? As soon as possible," Kayla told her, still staring at Craig. She did not want to expose her child to what she was about to say, whether she thought she could comprehend it or not.

"I'll get her right now." Yvonne hurried out of the room and gave the nurse Kayla's request.

"I'm here to pick up a package?" the cheerful nurse said as she entered the tension filled room.

"Yes, can you take her for a while?" Kayla asked.

"Sure thing." She smiled as Geno passed Day to her and she placed her in the bassinet. "We'll change her out of these fancy clothes and bring her back for her next feeding."

"Thank you," Kayla said. She watched the nurse wheel the baby out and then closed the door behind her. "Now, I'll repeat my question. What are you trying to say?"

"I'm saying I want there to be no question whether this child is really mine."

"*This child* has a name. It's Day. And I have no reason to tell you that you're her father if I had any doubt that you weren't," Kayla told him.

"Naw, Kayla. Here this brother comes waltzing in like he's fucking Father of the Year, you're looking at him like he's Romeo and you're Juliet. I'm not gonna be played out like some sucker taking care of a kid that might, just might not be mine."

"Have you lost your damn mind? I think you forgot something. I am not your girlfriend, lover, significant other or wife. Hell, I'm not even your mistress. I don't care if I look at Sam Sausagehead like he's the greatest thing that ever walked into my life. That's my business!" she yelled.

"Hold up, Kayla. You don't even have to justify that with a response," Geno said. "Look, man, if you want a blood test, that's your business. But believe me, if I was lucky enough to be Day's father, you'd better believe I am more than willing to step up to the plate and take care of my responsibilities. Quiet as it's kept, I was begging Kayla to tell me I was the father. I wanted to be. So don't come up in here trying to hate because Kayla and I are friends. And hell yeah, I'm acting like Father of the Year, because I was there when she was born, unlike you!" Geno sat down in the chair.

"Whether I was there when she was born or not . . ." Craig yelled.

"Hey, hey, hey! Y'all need to chill. I can hear you all the way down the hall." A voice stopped Craig before he could finish. "Whatever the problem is, y'all need to squash it. This ain't the time or the place."

"Who are you?" Craig gritted on the big guy who walked through the door.

"What's up, Terry? You're right, man. I didn't realize it had gotten out of hand." Geno stood and greeted his friend's brother.

"What's up? I'm Terrell, a friend of Kayla's." Terrell introduced himself.

"Another friend, Kayla?" Craig looked Terrell up and down and stood to leave. "Yeah, I'm definitely gonna need that test before I put my name on anything. You call me so we can have that taken care of. I'll holla."

"What was he talking about?" Terrell asked Kayla. Her head began to pound and she closed her eyes and sat back. She tried to make the room stop spinning, but she couldn't.

"Kayla? Kayla?" She heard Geno and Terrell calling her name as she passed out.

22

Kayla could hear a faint beeping in the distance. She frowned as she tried to figure out what it was. Her eyelids fluttered as she opened her eyes. She looked around the room and remembered that she was in the hospital. *Day! Where is my baby?* were her first thoughts. She tried to recall what had happened. Her room was dark and as she looked out the window, she saw that it was pitch black outside. The beeping sound got louder and she turned to see that it was a heart monitor. There were several IV bags hanging by the head of the bed and running into her arm, and there was an oxygen tube in her nose. Her throat was dry and she pushed the nurse button.

"Hi, sleepy head," Nicole whispered to Kayla. "It's nice to see you finally awake."

"Can I get something to drink?" Kayla closed and opened her eyes, trying to focus.

"I'll be right back with some juice for you."

Nicole continued to whisper. She came in and gave Kayla a small can of apple juice and a straw. Kayla opened it and began to drink; she emptied it immediately.

"I feel funny. Like everything is foggy," she told Nicole.

"Probably the medicine they have you on. It's pretty strong. You gave us a scare, girl." Nicole talked low, confusing Kayla even more.

"Where's Day?" Kayla asked her.

"She's in the nursery. I'll get her for you in a little while. The staff has gotten quite attached to her over the past couple of days." She took Kayla's vitals.

"She was just born yesterday, Nicole. They can't be that attached." Kayla smiled.

"Kayla, you've been asleep for two days." Nicole looked at her.

"Quit playing. And why is it so dark in here? You are funny, Nicole. I see why Terrell likes you. Pass me the phone, I need to call my parents." Kayla looked on the nightstand and saw that there was no phone, "Where is my phone? And where is the TV? I know I have the bomb insurance. Isn't all of that covered?"

"Kayla, Karen had the phone, television and radio taken out of here. You can't have any visitors either, except for your mother." Nicole pulled a chair and sat beside Kayla's bed.

"Why?" Kayla was beginning to get frustrated because she didn't know what was going on.

"Kayla, your blood pressure shot up to one ninety-eight over one twenty-seven. You were a heartbeat away from a stroke. Your body shut down in order to prevent that from happening. That's why you passed out. You basically went into shock."

Kayla couldn't believe what Nicole was saying. She felt the tears fall from her eyes and she wiped them away. Nicole went and got her some Kleenex.

"But what about my baby? Who's been taking care of Day? I'm breastfeeding." Kayla sniffed.

"Because of the meds that they have you on, you can't breastfeed, Kayla. Not right now, anyway. But Day has been well taken care of."

"But, but, she's not gonna know me. Strangers have been taking care of her. We won't have a bond."

"Yes you will, girl. You're her mother, she knows that. And she hasn't been taken care of by strangers. Your mother comes and sits with you and her, and Geno does her feedings, too."

"Geno?"

"He's the only other one with a wristband for the nursery security. Your mother had to go through hell and high water to get permission to sit here with you knocked out in the same room." Nicole laughed. Kayla remembered the armband being placed on Geno's arm after he cut Day's umbilical cord. "Let me go call Karen and tell her you are doing better, and then I'll bring Day."

"Thank you, Nicole." Kayla looked at the beautiful nurse and was grateful for her.

"Sweetie, you're up." Jennifer rushed to her daughter's side and hugged her.

"Hi, Mommy."

"I am so glad you're okay. Your father is worried sick. He is going to be relieved." She rubbed her hand across Kayla's cheek.

"I'm fine, Mama. Did you see the baby?"

"She's beautiful. Just like her mother."

"Did they tell you her full name?"

"Her name is just as beautiful as she is. Thank you so much, Kayla. I am so flattered, and Gramma would be proud, too." Jennifer cried when Roni told her the baby's full name. She was hoping to have a grandson, but when she heard Kayla had a girl she couldn't have been happier.

"I guess I overdid it, huh, Ma?"

"Kayla, why in the world did you have all of those people visiting and all of that nonsense going on in the first place? You had just given birth, not signed a record deal. From the way I hear it, if Terrell hadn't arrived when he did, Geno and Craig were about to start fighting. You are lucky they didn't call security." Jennifer knew she was wrong to be laying her daughter out, but she was angry. Kayla could have died.

"Mom, Craig had the nerve to ask for a blood test," Kayla responded.

"Is it his baby?"

"Ma! Yes, it's his. I am not some loose floozy who sleeps with everyone. I know it's his baby."

"Then let him take the test. You didn't even have to go there with him. You know what the results would say, do you not?"

"Yes."

"Then take it. And when you take him to court for child support, you'll have all the proof you need!" Jennifer told her. "Who do he think he is, gonna question my baby's integrity?"

"You are crazy, Ma." Kayla laughed. Nicole wheeled the bassinet into the room and Kayla happily took her baby. "She's gotten bigger!"

"No, you are the crazy one." Jennifer shook her head and silently said a prayer of thanksgiving for the recovery of her daughter and the birth of her grandbaby.

23

Kayla had just gotten out of the shower and was packing to go home. She was beyond ready to leave. She had been in the hospital five days, including the night that Day was born. She wanted to take her baby home and get on with her life. They had already brought Day from the nursery. Kayla made a mental note to send the nursery staff a thank you note and a basket of cookies from herself and the baby. They had been so attentive.

"Looks like you're ready to go," Karen said. Kayla was sitting on the side of the bed, waiting for her parents to pick her up.

"I've been ready," Kayla told her. "Day needs to go and see her new room."

"Well, I am gonna discharge you, but we need to get a few things straight before I sign these papers."

"Okay, what?"

"There are two young men outside who say they need to see you. Now, I have listened to both of them begging me to see you for the last two days. I have agreed to give them five minutes each. I am going to connect you back up to this blood pressure monitor and if it shows a high reading at any time while they are here, it's back in the bed and you will stay there. I cannot risk having you leave here and having a stroke. Understand, Kayla? You have a little one to care for."

"I understand. Who's outside to see me?" Kayla asked. She figured it was Geno and Terrell. They had probably been worried to death, and Kayla already knew that Geno came to see Day regularly.

"I'll send the first gentleman in," Karen said as she affixed the blood pressure cuff on Kayla's arm. "Remember what I told you."

"I will." Kayla took a deep breath and reminded herself to stay calm. She leaned over and checked on Day to make sure she was still asleep.

The door opened slowly and Kayla smiled at Geno as he entered.

"Hi, G. I knew you were here."

"You feeling okay, Kay?" He kissed her cheek and walked over to see Day. "Hey, Princess."

"I would probably be doing better if I was at home," Kayla admitted.

"Kayla, I'm so sorry for what happened the other afternoon. I was out of line and I was wrong. I know you think it wasn't my place to get into it with Craig, but when he made it seem like we were scheming on his punk ass, I got mad."

"Don't worry about it, G. It wasn't your fault. But I'm glad you're here. I want to thank you for looking after Day while I was sick. They told me that you gave her 'round the clock feedings and everything." Kayla wondered how he was able to get away from that crazy Janice to do it, but she didn't ask.

"That's my princess. I didn't do anything you wouldn't do for me, Kayla. Hell, if it wasn't for you, I never would have finished school. I keep telling you that I will *always* be there for you. I'm not playing. No matter the circumstances." He sat next to her and put his arm around her. Kayla did not know what to think. She still loved Geno, there was no doubting that, but she did not know what he was trying to say and didn't want to make a fool of herself by asking.

"Time's up." Karen interrupted her thoughts before she had a chance to respond. She checked the monitor and looked at Kayla and Geno. "Very good, Kayla. No high readings. Now, Geno, I really need for you to make sure Kayla gets some rest while she is at home. Don't be calling her all times of the night and no surprise visits."

"I know. Karen, I know this sounds crazy, but are you sure there is no possible way that I could be the father? I am not saying that Kayla's not sure, but is there any possibility?" He looked at Karen, pleading.

"If the last time you were together was when you said it was, Geno, then there's no way. Now if you want to take a blood test then I'd be more than happy to have it done."

"No, it's just like I love her as if she's mine. She's only a few days old, but I know I couldn't love my own child any more.

We have a bond," he said. It took everything in her power for Kayla not to breakdown and cry. She wished more than anything that Day could have been hers and Geno's child. It would have made a hell of a lot more sense than Day being the result of a one-night stand with Craig.

"Childbirth is a very bonding experience, Geno. And you already had a bond with Kayla. That's a lot of emotions, when you think about it. And Day will also have a bond with you, if you choose to continue. But know that bond comes with a lot of responsibility. You are talking about being a part of a child's life. That's nothing to take lightly."

"I know," he said.

"Kayla, you have another visitor waiting. And your parents are waiting to take you home as well." Karen opened the door.

"Good-bye, Kayla. I'll call before I stop by later." He looked at Karen for approval. "To see Day, of course."

"How about tomorrow? Give Kayla and Day a chance to get settled their first night."

"Okay. But I'm gonna call." He kissed Kayla, Day, *and* Karen as he left.

"Ready for your next gentleman caller?" Karen asked.

"Send Terrell with his retarded self in." Kayla prepared herself for the smart comment she knew he would have when he came in. Karen shook her head and walked into the hallway.

Kayla could not help but frown when instead of Terrell, Craig walked in. She was about to curse him out when she caught a glimpse of the blood pressure cuff on her arm and began to breathe deeply.

"Hi, beautiful." Craig spoke smoothly. He walked over and gave Kayla a hug, then touched Day's back. "And little beautiful."

"You are the last person I expected to be here," she told him dryly.

"Okay, I can't risk you falling the hell out again, so I'm asking you just to chill while I say my peace." He looked at her intensely. Kayla didn't want to hear anything he had to say, but she decided to let him talk so he could hurry and leave.

"Go ahead." She took another deep breath.

"Okay. I am sorry for saying what I did. It's just that I was looking at you and Geno and it was like it was *your* baby—*yours and his*. I know you wouldn't lie to me, Kay. And Karen confirmed what you said about the date of conception. I already made my peace with Geno, now I'm making amends with you *and* Day." He reached inside his jacket pocket and passed Kayla a folded piece of paper. She took it from his hand and slowly opened it. It was the registration for Day's birth certificate and he had printed and signed his name under the space for father's information.

"Thank you," Kayla whispered. She looked up at him and saw him standing next to Day.

"Can I?"

"She's your daughter. Of course you can." Kayla reached in and passed the baby to him. He gently rocked her in his arms.

"I want to be a part of her life, Kayla. I know you and I will be nothing more than friends, but I still want to be there for her and you. Please, give me a chance." He looked at her with that intense stare and Kayla could not help but smile.

"I don't have a problem with that, Craig. But I will not have you walking in and out of her life like some distant relative that she gets to see on birthdays and holidays. If you're gonna be a father, I have no problem with that. But I don't have time for your games, either," Kayla warned him.

"All right, I understand. Well, I guess I need to let you finish up and get out of here. Do you need anything? Or does she?"

"No, we're fine for now. Thank you for stepping up, Craig." She took Day and placed her back into the bassinet.

"Well, call me if you need me." He gave her a hug.

"But are you gonna answer when I call? You know how you conveniently lose your phone sometimes." Kayla smirked.

"You're a trip." He opened the door and she could see her parents talking with Karen.

"Mister and Mrs. Hopkins, she's ready," he told them as he turned and waved to Kayla. "I'll call you later."

"Good-bye, Craig." Kayla waved. "Hi, Daddy. You ready to take all of us women home?"

"You'd better believe it. Where's my newest baby luv?" Her dad kissed her as her mother followed him into Kayla's room.

"I thought we took all of this kind of stuff home?" her mother said as she picked up a pink and white vase full of flowers that had been delivered earlier. She read the card then turned to Kayla and asked, "Who's Uncle Darrell?"

"Craig's brother," Kayla answered as she bundled Day up into the bunting Roni had sent.

"Well, that was nice of him," her dad said as he picked up Kayla's suitcase.

"He's a nice guy," Kayla told them.

"Mom, can you please grab Day's pictures out of the drawer?"

"You'd better not forget them pictures," her father warned. "I gotta have plenty to take when I go back to work. My grandbaby," he said proudly as the nurse and Karen came in and Kayla sat in the wheelchair, holding her precious daughter.

"Thank you for everything, Karen," she said. "I couldn't have done this without you."

"Yes, you could have. It just wouldn't have been as easy." Karen grinned. "Now, I have given your parents specific instructions, so I know you're in good hands. I'll see you next week in my office."

"Well, Day. We're finally going home." Kayla smiled and kissed Day's forehead.

24

Kayla's transition into motherhood came naturally. Her mother stayed with her for two weeks to make sure she and Day got settled. By the time she left, they had exchanged all of Day's blue clothes for pink ones and the nursery was still blue, but it now had pink accents.

"Mama, I can't thank you enough for being here for me and Day. You know you didn't have to do all of this," Kayla told her as she watched her pack her suitcase. Day was asleep in the porta-crib that Kayla had in her room.

"Please, Kayla. Wait until Day has a baby and then you'll know why I did it," her mother stopped packing long enough to say.

"Whew, that is over thirty years from now, Mama." Kayla raised her eyebrows. "Yeah, that's what I thought when I had you. But somehow it didn't work out that way, did it?"

"I guess not." Kayla put her head down.

"Sometimes things work out better. Kayla, no matter what the circumstances that got Day here, she is still our grandbaby and you are still our daughter. And we love you both very much."

"I know, Mama. I still feel that I somehow disappointed you and Daddy, though. I know you wanted me to be married first."

"Kayla, your father and I are very proud of you. You could be doing a lot worse, you know. We raised you and Anjelica to be productive, successful young women, and you are."

At the sound of her sister's name, Kayla felt her pressure rise. She had not spoken to her since the baby shower and she wanted to keep it that way. "At least *I* am," she said before she could stop herself.

"Kayla. Your sister is successful too, in her own right. Your guidelines for success are different from hers because you are two different people. But I am going to say this one last and final time. You are sisters and that fact will never change."

"Okay, Mama," Kayla said. She didn't want to argue with her mother so she just let it go. She knew that her mother would never believe what Anjelica had done if she told her the truth. The doorbell rang and Kayla went to open the door. Her father had arrived to pick up her mother.

"Hey, Daddy." She greeted her father with a kiss.

"Hey, honey. You doing okay?"

"Yes, I'm fine, Daddy."

"Where's my sweetie?" He walked into the nursery.

"Are you referring to me or the baby, John?" Kayla's mother asked her husband. He walked over and took her into his arms.

"Of course I was referring to you, Sweetie." As he kissed her, he peered into the crib looking for Day.

"She's not even in there, you big, fat liar." Kayla's mother pushed him away.

"Where is she?" he asked.

"In my room. She's asleep." Kayla led him into her bedroom. He went to pick her up but Kayla's mother protested.

"Leave her alone, John. We finally got her on a schedule. You can't wake her up. It'll throw her off."

"But I'm her grandpa. I get special, unscheduled visitation rights." He winked at Kayla and gently picked the baby up. He kissed her cheek and laid her back down, never waking her.

"Well, I guess we'd better head on home, Jen. Kayla, you take care of my baby luv and call us if you need anything." He put his arm around Kayla and they walked into the hallway.

"My bag is in the nursery, John. Grab it for me."

"Yes, ma'am," he answered.

"Thank you again, Mama." Kayla fought back the tears. She loved her parents so much and was grateful for them.

"I will call you when we get home. And don't you have a bunch of people running in and out of here fawning over that baby," she warned Kayla. Her daughter was all grown up with a baby of her own, but that would never stop Jennifer from being her mother.

"Okay, Mama." Kayla smiled.

"Let's go, sweetheart. Love you, Kay. We'll talk to you later on tonight," her father called as they departed. As soon as Kayla locked the door, the bell rang again. Kayla laughed at her father standing outside her doorway.

"What'd you forget?"

"This is for you, Kay. Don't open it now, but put it to good use for you and Day." He put an envelope in her palm and rubbed the tops of her hands as he left for the second time. After she saw them pull out of the driveway, Kayla sat on the sofa and opened the card. It was simple, with a pink flower on the cover and a handwritten message on the inside.

To my daughter, Kayla, with love,

As you embark on this new journey, may the lessons of love, life, and laughter that we have shared over the years be the compass that directs your life, as you are now a leader for your little one.

I love you and I am so proud of you,
Dad

This time, the tears did not surprise Kayla as she removed ten hundred-dollar bills out of the card.

25

"What are you doing?" Geno asked Kayla.

"Watching cartoons." Kayla balanced the cordless phone on her shoulder as she bounced Day on her lap. She was sitting in the middle of her bed and was deciding what they should do on this fine December Saturday.

"Well, get dressed. I'm on my way to pick you and Day up," he said.

"What do you mean you're on your way? What are you doing home anyway, and where's your girlfriend?" she said in one breath.

"Just get ready. I'll be there in fifteen minutes." He chose not to answer any of her questions.

"I can't get myself and an infant ready in fifteen minutes. Are you crazy?"

"Jeez, Kay. Look, can you be ready in an hour?"

"Where are we going and what is the rush?" Kayla looked over at the clock and saw that it was only ten thirty in the morning.

"Just be ready." He hung up before she had a chance to ask anymore questions.

"Well, Day. I guess we're going out for the afternoon." She looked into her eyes and kissed her chubby cheeks. At almost a month old, people said she looked just like Kayla, but Kayla didn't see it. "What shall we wear?"

Kayla put Day into her bouncer and went rummaging through her closet. She was almost back down to her pre-pregnancy weight, but because of her new, well-rounded hips and thick butt, her jeans still didn't fit right.

"I need to go shopping, Day," Kayla called out. The phone rang and she picked it up.

"Hey, girl. Theo and I are going to the mall. You want to go?" Tia asked.

"I can't. I'm going somewhere with Geno," Kayla mumbled.

"Geno? Where is his girlfriend?"

"I asked him the exact same thing." Kayla pulled out a pair of black stretch jeans and a red sweater. *Well, it is Christmas. May as well look festive.*

"Where are you going?"

"He wouldn't say. Just told me to be ready," she said as she went into Day's room and began to scavenge her closet for the perfect ensemble for her as well. She found what she was looking for and laid it on the bed next to her own outfit.

"Well, go and have fun. He must have had it out with his girl again. Every time she pisses him off he calls you. I don't see why he's with her crazy ass anyway."

"I don't know, girl." Kayla ran a tub of water and grabbed a towel for her and Day, and then got all of their toiletries, making sure she would have everything in arm's reach. She flicked the small radio she had on the shelf to the jazz station and it began to play softly.

"So, have you talked about getting back together?"

"Uh, hello. I just had another man's baby and he is living with another woman." Kayla could not believe Tia asked her that. She got undressed and then undressed Day.

"What? It's no secret that you and Geno still love each other. Hell, that's the reason Craig nearly flipped out at the hospital. I'll be the first to admit that neither of you are in the best circumstances, but you can't help who you love."

"That's not what Roni says," Kayla laughed.

"Humph, she's so in love these days that even her mama is shocked. I never thought I'd see the day. But ain't it funny how the two biggest players in the entire town hooked up?"

"I think it's cute. I am glad she finally found someone. You have Theo, she has Toby." Kayla took a moment to look at her naked body in the mirror. *I gotta work out harder,* she thought as she pinched her sides. "Yvonne and I are the only members left in the Lonely Hearts Club. Maybe we need to recruit new members?"

"Girl, please. Ain't nobody got a ring on their finger. Heck, I don't even think any of us are really ready for marriage."

"I am. And you are, too. Don't even try it. If Theo were to ask you to go and get married today, you'd be calling me to borrow my white wool suit," Kayla joked.

"Girl, please. Although you should let me have it anyway, because you can't get into it anymore." Tia laughed.

"You know what? On that note, I am hanging up."

"Bye, girl. Tell Geno I said hello."

Kayla picked Day up and went into the bathroom. She stuck her foot into the tub and made sure the temperature was okay. She carefully got in and lay Day on her chest as she cascaded warm water over her tiny body. Although she flinched at first, Kayla knew Day loved the tub. They were both treasuring the moment, when Kayla swore she heard someone calling her name. She sat up and before she could reach for the towel, the bathroom door opened.

"Kay!"

"What are you doing?" Kayla covered herself and Day as best she could, using her hands and Day's tiny body.

"My bad! I thought you had left the radio on in here." Geno smiled as he looked at her and the baby in the tub. "I was about to be mad because I thought you had left with someone else, and you knew I was on my way. Hey, Day, come here."

"Get out, Geno!" Kayla screamed.

"Why are you screaming? Give me the baby."

"No, get out." She was beyond embarrassed.

"Kayla. It's not as if I've never seen you naked before. Hell, I saw all that long before you gave birth. I saw all up *in* there while you were giving birth. Now pass me the baby. She's shivering." He laughed and grabbed the small pink towel off the rack near the tub.

"Get out of here. How did you get in here, anyway?" She reluctantly passed Day to him and he wrapped her warmly in the towel. He stood looking at Kayla as he rocked the baby.

"The door was unlocked. Need help getting out?" He grinned. Damn, he missed her.

"No, can you just get out?" She tried in vain to cover herself.

"Come on, Day. Let's give Mommy some privacy." He giggled as he turned and left the steamy bathroom. "Are these her clothes?"

"Naw, they belong to the other baby in there. What you think?" Kayla answered as she wrapped a fluffy towel around herself and stepped out of the tub. She let the water out and cut the radio off. Geno was sprinkling powder on Day's bottom when she entered the room.

"I thought I told you to be ready in an hour," he said without even looking up. Kayla grabbed her clothes off the bed and returned to the bathroom, closing and locking the door behind her.

"You're early," she said.

"It's twelve fifteen," he informed her.

I must've talked to Tia longer than I thought.

"Well, you know I have to get me *and* Day ready. I can't do that in an hour. You *did* call at the last minute. I still have to pack her diaper bag."

"Well, I already got her dressed. You just hurry up."

"I am. Did you brush her hair? And did you put lotion on her face?"

"Get dressed, Kayla. We're going to pack the bag," she heard him call out.

Kayla made sure he was out of the room and completed getting dressed. She was finishing up her makeup when she heard him talking to someone. She looked at the 'In Use' indicator on her phone and it wasn't lit. *Must be his cell phone,* she thought.

"I don't want to discuss it right now. Forget it. Look, Janice, I have to go," he said as Day began to whimper. "None of your business. I will call you later tonight. No, because I got stuff to do. Bye. You ready, Kayla? Day, your Mama is s-l-o-w, you know that?"

"I heard you, Geno. I'm dressed, if that's what you mean. I still have to pack the diaper bag," Kayla told him. She went into Day's room and grabbed the big diaper bag. Looking at the smaller, more compact one she asked, "Where are we going, anyway?"

"Just pack the bag and come on. You got a stroller?"

"We need a stroller? It's in the hall closet." She heard him fumbling and then the closet door closed.

"This is more like a baby limo. Day, you're gonna be riding in style, huh, boo? I bet you picked this big thing out, huh, Kayla?" He unfolded the monstrosity and then realized he didn't know how to fold it back up. Kayla came in carrying a huge, pink diaper bag. "We are just gonna be gone until tonight, Kayla, not the entire weekend."

"Shut up. I don't know what I'm gonna need and I want to be prepared." She went into the kitchen and grabbed bottles of prepared formula and extra cans, just in case. She picked up Day's extra pacifier off the table and then remembered to get the ice pack out of the freezer and put it in the bag. She looked at her watch and saw that it was now after one o'clock.

"How do you fold this thing back down?" Geno asked, still struggling with the stroller.

Kayla flicked a button with her foot and it collapsed instantly. "Ooh, that was so hard."

"Bring your smart mouth on before Day and I leave you here," he said as he grabbed the handle of the stroller with one hand and the diaper bag with the other one.

Kayla, Day, and Geno spent the entire afternoon shopping. They walked the mall, buying Christmas gifts and enjoying the hustle and bustle of the season. Kayla and Geno had always loved Christmas shopping together. Actually, they loved all shopping together—Christmas, birthday, grocery, whatever the occasion. The mall was where they had their best times. It felt like old times, only now Geno was pushing Day in the stroller in front of them. A few people stopped and told them they had a beautiful baby and how precious their family was. Geno didn't correct anyone; he just smiled and thanked them.

"I am starving. What do you feel like eating?"

"I don't know. How about Chinese?"

"Red Dragon?"

"You really are trying to make this a tradition aren't you?" Kayla laughed as they arrived at their favorite post-shopping restaurant.

"No doubt," he said. He picked the baby up out of the stroller and put her on his shoulder as they waited to be seated. The doors opened and both Geno and Kayla were shocked when Avis, Craig, and a small boy stepped out, arms full of bags. Craig was so busy talking on his cell phone that he didn't notice them.

"Oh, Craig, look at that pretty baby," Avis squealed as she paused in front of Geno. "How old is she?"

When Craig looked up and realized whom she was talking to, the look on his face became sheer panic. He quickly closed his phone as Kayla stared at him, not saying a word.

"Three weeks," Geno answered, shaking his head at Craig.

"Oh, she is so cute. What's her name?" the woman directed at Kayla.

"Ask her father," Kayla smirked. Craig's eyes widened in shock and he could not believe what Kayla was doing. She turned and looked at Geno, wrapping her arm in his and rubbing Day's head.

"Jenesis, but we call her Day," Geno replied.

"Day, that is nice, ain't it, Craig?" She smiled at her dazed husband. He stood, not moving, too shocked to do anything.

"Are you gonna have me a baby sister, Mommy?"

"One day, Nigel. He been asking for a little sister for years," she informed them.

The waiter called Geno's last name and he placed Day back into the stroller.

"That's us," he said.

"Bye, Day," Avis gushed as they maneuvered past her. Kayla's eyes never left Craig's. It took all of her mental restraint to keep from saying what she was feeling. He was still with her. All this time he was telling Kayla that they were no longer together and they were. She was beyond furious.

"Man, that was weird," Geno said as they sat down.

"I can't believe his lying ass." Kayla shook her head. She looked at her sleeping daughter and took a deep breath. "I am gonna kick his ass."

"For what, Kay? I don't understand why you're so mad. You knew he was married." Geno shrugged. "I mean, I can understand you being uncomfortable, but mad?"

"He told me he was leaving her. He said they were no longer together," she responded. She couldn't believe Geno's nonchalance at the situation.

"So what if they're still together? As long as he takes care of Day, it shouldn't matter," he said.

"It does matter. He lied to me." She sat back and frowned. She was no longer hungry.

"Are you feeling this nigga, Kayla? Is that why you mad?" He looked over at her and lay the menu down.

"No."

His cell phone began buzzing and he looked at the caller ID. Ignoring the call, he put it back in his pocket. Kayla could tell he was getting frustrated. "Then you shouldn't care who he's wit' then. You don't need that nigga and neither does Day."

"Why not, G? Because we got you?"

"Yep."

"Really, did you forget you have a girlfriend? What? You think every time you get mad at her you can run to me? I don't think so. Neither my house nor my heart has a revolving door. I'm ready to leave," she told him.

"Fine. Let's go." They left the restaurant without eating.

The ride home was quiet, neither one saying anything. He carried the stroller and bags into the house, kissed Day goodnight and left, locking the door behind him.

It was after eleven when Kayla heard a knock at the door.

"Can I come in?"

"Hell, no! I know you have got to be out of your mind!" Kayla yelled back.

"It wasn't what it looked like, Kayla. We were just taking Nigel out Christmas shopping, that's all. I still have to be a part of my son's life," he told her.

"I didn't say you didn't, Craig. I can't believe you lied to me!"

"Lied about what? I am not with her anymore."

"I can't tell the way she was hugging up on you. And you trying to have another baby? I don't think she'd be feeling that way if she knew the baby she was cooing all over was *yours*, would she?"

"She didn't say we were trying to have another baby. She said Nigel wanted a little sister. Shit, he does! You're jumping to conclusions, dammit!"

Kayla thought about what he was saying and cracked the door open. She tried to remember what Avis said, verbatim, but couldn't.

"Let me in, Kayla. Please." He looked at her with that intense stare and she obliged. He followed her into the living room. "Where's Day?"

"Don't start with the small talk. It's after eleven. Where you think she is?" She sat on the sofa and he sat next to her. He began rubbing her back. She tried to shrug his hands off, but he kept on running his fingers across her shoulders. She had to admit it felt good.

"I'm sorry. But seriously, Kayla, I had to come over here and talk to you. I knew you wouldn't answer the phone if I called. I wanted to squash this shit before you blew it out of proportion."

"You know I was pissed when I saw you with her ass." She turned to look him in the face.

"You know I was pissed when I saw you wit' his ass." He raised his eyebrow at her. "And he was carrying my daughter. That's why I couldn't even say nothing."

"I thought you were scared I was gonna call you out."

"Shit, you almost did!" He laughed. "But I ain't mad at you, Kayla. I need for you to understand that I ain't tryin' to disrespect you. I care about you and Day. I just wish you would cut a brotha some slack. I told you, I'ma do right by you. Have I not been doing that?"

"You have," Kayla admitted. He would drop off diapers, wipes, and formula twice a week and he bought more shoes and outfits than Day could even wear. He *had* been doing right by them.

"So, truce?"

"Truce. But if I find out otherwise, you'd better believe it's on," she told him.

"I like when you talk like that. You know I love a woman wit' spunk. I know she 'sleep, but can I at least see my daughter?"

"She's in her crib."

Craig went into the nursery for a few moments.

"I gotta go, but I'll holla at you later, okay, beautiful?" he said when he came out.

"A'ight." Kayla smiled at him. As mad as Craig made her, he still had a way of making her change her attitude toward him. He was definitely a smooth talker.

26

Day's first Christmas was an eventful one. Kayla bought more dolls, clothes, and stuffed animals than she had planned, but Day was worth it. Her parents drove up to spend Christmas morning with her and then everyone was having dinner at Ms. Ernestine's with Roni and her family.

"Merry Christmas!" Roni, Toby, and Terrell hugged and kissed as they came in, carrying arm loads of gifts. Kayla did the introductions and put the packages under the tree.

"How is my goddaughter enjoying her first Christmas?" Terrell asked, looking at Day swinging peacefully in her swing by the Christmas tree.

"I think she's enjoying it. She's been 'sleep most of the day," Kayla told him. They laughed and exchanged gifts as Christmas carols played on Kayla's stereo. Kayla was headed for the kitchen when the doorbell rang again.

"Merry Christmas, Kayla."

Kayla's mouth fell open when she saw Geno outside. They hadn't talked since their falling out at Red Dragon two weeks prior.

"Merry Christmas," she told him.

"I hope you don't mind. I wanted to see Day and give her a gift." He smiled sheepishly.

"No, I don't mind at all. Come on in, Geno." Although they had fought, Kayla really missed him.

"Merry Christmas, everyone," he greeted as he followed Kayla into the living room.

"Geno. Merry Christmas." Her mother stood and embraced him and her father shook his hand. They were happy to see him. Kayla knew that deep down they wanted her and Geno to resolve their issues and get back together.

"This is for Day," he said, giving Kayla a large box.

"Thanks, G. But where's mine?" she asked him jokingly.

"When you become a mother, you lose all gift privileges."
He grinned.

"I'm learning that the hard way," she told him. She opened
the box, which contained several DVDs. *"Cinderella, Snow
White, Sleeping Beauty, The Little Mermaid,* and *Beauty and
the Beast."* Kayla announced the titles as she opened the gift.

"She is a princess after all," he told her. Day began whining
in the swing and Kayla lifted her out.

"She needs to be changed," Kayla said, nuzzling her beautiful daughter.

"I'll do it," her mother offered.

"No, you stay. I'll take care of her." Kayla took her into the
nursery and began to change her.

"Long day for her?" Geno walked up behind her.

"Long day for me." Kayla rubbed her whining baby's head.
Once again, the doorbell rang and Kayla shook her head.
"Now who in the world could that be? Everybody's been here
to visit already."

"Her father hasn't," Geno whispered.

"He's not coming. He said he had to work."

"Maybe he got off early," Geno suggested. Kayla felt the
hairs stand up on the back of her neck when she realized the
voice that was coming from the front of the house.

"God is punishing me. I know He is." She folded her arms
and began to shake her head. Geno stood frozen, not wanting
to move.

"Kayla, come out here. And bring Day!" her father called.

"She fell back to sleep," she told him.

"Just bring her for a few minutes, Kayla. She has a guest."

"I'll stay here," Geno said quietly.

"No! I don't want to take her out there," Kayla hissed.

"Kayla, did you hear what we said?" her mother said as she
came into the room and reached for the baby.

"Mama, no. She just went to sleep. Leave her alone!" Kayla
startled herself at the tone of her voice.

"Now, you listen here. I will not have you yelling at me like
I am a child. It's Christmas and this is a time for family. Now,
pick Day up and bring her out right now." Kayla knew her

mother was not joking. She had never blatantly disobeyed her before and she wasn't about to start. She carefully picked Day up and held her in her arms, making sure not to wake her. She could hear laughter as she made her way down the hallway.

"Kayla! Merry Christmas." Anjelica held a fake smile on her face. Kayla just looked at her. "Geno! I didn't expect to see you here. Merry Christmas."

"Anjelica," he said and quickly excused himself, politely.

"Is this my new niece? Can I hold her?"

"She's asleep," Kayla said as she cradled Day's head and held her close.

"Well, I can see she looks just like her daddy. I can imagine your baby pictures looking just like her, huh, Geno? Oh, what was I thinking? You're not her father, are you?"

"Anjelica, that is enough," her father said.

"I'm sorry. It's just that seeing Kayla and Geno together with the baby, they look so natural. I haven't the slightest idea why they ever split up. They make such a nice couple," she said maliciously. Geno couldn't stay a minute longer. He quickly got up and got his coat.

"You're leaving so soon, Geno?"

"Yes, I think that's best," he said, making sure not to look at the hateful woman.

"I'm quite sure you have a lot to celebrate today. I hear congratulations are in order. Have you set a date?"

"What are you talking about, Anjelica?" Roni asked. She had been watching Anjelica since she arrived and she knew she was up to no good.

"He's engaged to my friend's sister. Janice, Janice Miles." She smiled knowingly. The entire room got quiet and waited for Geno's response.

"What is she talking about, Geno?" Kayla rolled her eyes at Geno. "What the hell was that all about, G?"

"She was just tripping, Kay. That's all. You know how Anjelica is." He shrugged.

"You're engaged to Janice, Geno? And you didn't even tell me?"

"I'm not engaged, Kayla."

"Is she wearing a ring?"

"Yeah."

"Then you're engaged, Geno." Kayla was so hurt that she wanted everyone to clear out of her house so she could be by herself.

"Kayla, let me explain. It's not what you think," Geno began.

"There's nothing to explain." Kayla smiled. "Congratulations. Well, I know you must be going and I don't want to keep you from your fiancée. Thank you so much for your gifts and I hope you have a Merry Christmas."

"I guess I should leave now, huh?" Geno frowned.

"I think that would be best."

"Kay, I'll call you later."

"Don't bother," she said dryly. She couldn't even look at him.

"Merry Christmas, everyone," he said as he departed.

"Mama, do you want to open your gifts now?" Anjelica turned and asked her mother.

"I don't think so. I would like to see you in Kayla's room though." She motioned for Anjelica. Kayla's sister rose and tossed her hair as she exited down the hallway.

She could hear her mother's voice getting louder from the bedroom and she looked over at her father, who was sitting on the sofa. "Did you invite her here?"

"That's your sister, Kayla. She don't need an invitation to your house." Her Dad looked at her like she was foolish. "It's Christmas Day and the family is to be together. What is wrong with you?"

"I don't care what day of the year it is, Daddy. Anjelica is still a conniving, mean, hateful dog, and I don't want her in my house."

"Kayla! Now I know you and her don't get along, but she is still your sister." Her Daddy frowned.

Kayla could not believe her father. Once again Anjelica had come into her house and disrespected her and yet her parents were still defending her. Kayla wouldn't have cared if they were Siamese twins. She wanted Anjelica out of her house. She walked into the kitchen and leaned against the refrigerator.

"You a'ight, dawg?" Terrell asked her after a few moments. Kayla forgot he was still there.

"Anjelica does this shit all the time and they still act like she's God's gift." She was too mad to cry, even though she wanted to.

"Stop tripping, Kay. I'm talking about Geno. I know you're pissed."

"Uh, that's where you're wrong. I'm happy for Geno. I am glad he has finally found someone to spend the rest of his life with," Kayla lied. She could not believe he was engaged to someone else. Her heart felt as if it had been ripped out of her chest; it took everything she had to not curl into a ball and cry. But she was determined to be stronger than that.

The phone rang before she could go on. She snatched it up without checking the caller ID.

"Hello," she snapped.

"Dang, Merry Christmas to you too, beautiful." Craig laughed into her ear.

"Yeah, whatever," she replied.

"I guess Santa damn sure wasn't good to you. How is my gorgeous Day? She enjoying her first Christmas?"

"Yeah, she is."

"Well, can I come through and bring Day her gifts? And you too?"

"You bought me a gift?"

"Of course. You are the mother of my child. And a good mom too, I might add."

"Well, I have company right now, but I'll call you when they leave."

"Bet. I will check you later."

"Bye." Kayla found herself smiling as she hung up the phone. Craig bought her a gift. She had no doubt that he was getting Day gifts. But he had gone so far as to get her a gift, too. She was digging that.

"Who was that?" Terrell asked.

"Craig." She shrugged.

"Why are you smiling?" He looked at her funny.

"He got me a gift."

"So did I, but you ain't smile like that. Don't do nothing dumb," he warned.

"What are you talking about, Terrell?"

"I mean, I know you're pissed at Geno and here this nigga is buying you a gift."

"I am the mother of his child. Besides, it is Christmas."

"Whatever. Just be mindful of the games niggas play."

"Okay, Terrell. Ain't nobody playing no games. Damn, it's just a Christmas gift." She laughed because he was always suspicious. They went back into the living room where her mother and sister had rejoined her dad.

"Kayla, I want to apologize," Anjelica began.

"Save it. Mama, Daddy, we need to get ready to head over to Aunt Ernestine's. I have to get back here so Day can spend time with her father." Kayla ignored her sister completely, hoping she'd get the picture.

"Well, your father and I have decided to head to Aunt Margie's for dinner. You go ahead to Ernestine's and tell her we send our best," her mother said.

"Well, I'll talk to you all later." Kayla kissed her parents as they left behind her sister, who made no comment. She closed the door behind them and breathed a sigh of relief.

"Your life makes the soap operas look boring." Terrell shook his head. "I wouldn't have missed this for the world."

27

Kayla made it home by nine o'clock Christmas night. She called Craig as soon as she got in.

"Dang, you just now getting home?" he whined.

"Yeah."

"Is Day still up?" She could hear a lot of people in the background. "I still haven't given her the last feeding. If you come now, you can do it. Where are you anyway?"

"Uh, I'm not that far. I got one stop to make and then I'll be there. Just keep her up until I get there."

"You'd better hurry. When she gets hungry she gets demanding."

"Like her Daddy. I'll be right there." He laughed.

"Yo, Craig, you got something good for me?" She could hear a woman laughing in the background.

"Who is that?" Kayla demanded. He had been swearing to her that he was no longer with Avis and she never questioned him about other women. Maybe she should.

"Nobody. Give me fifteen minutes, Kay, and I'll be there." He hung up.

Kayla changed Day into her pajamas and set her in the swing, hoping she would be content until Craig got there. She had just begun to get feisty when the doorbell rang.

"You're right on time," Kayla said as she opened the door. Craig's arms were full of wrapped boxes and gift bags. "What did you do, rob the mall?"

"It's my baby's first Christmas. What do you expect?" He followed Kayla into the living room and placed the gifts under the tree. He walked over to the swing and picked Day up. "Hi, Day. Merry Christmas."

"I have no room for all of this stuff. I can't believe this." Kayla looked at the mass of gifts under the tree.

"Open them for her while I feed her and put her to bed, Kay," Craig said, reaching for the bottle sitting on the table. He sat down and began to feed Day, looking like a natural. Kayla knelt down beside the tree and began opening gifts. Craig bought Day any and everything for an infant age six months and up. He had musical activity sets and games, toys that attached to her stroller and car seat, he even bought her a piano that she could kick and play with her feet. Kayla laughed every time she opened a gift. She was delighted when she opened a small box that contained Day's first pair of earrings.

"Diamonds, of course," Craig informed her.

"Just like her father," Kayla commented, noticing the studs he wore in his ears. He stood and took the sleeping baby into her room and placed her in the crib.

"I'll be right back," he said and opened the door.

"Where are you going?" She jumped up to go behind him.

"Chill. I gotta get your gifts out of the trunk," he told her. She sat back down and waited for him to return. He came back with another armload of packages.

"I know all this isn't for me." She raised her eyebrows at him.

"Merry Christmas, Kayla. These are from Day." He passed her three large boxes. She was too shocked to even thank him. She just began to open them one by one. The first one contained a beautiful, ivory cashmere sweater and matching leather pants.

"Oh my God. Craig."

"Keep opening." He laughed. She opened the second box and found an ivory Coach bag and wallet. Kayla could not believe it. She had never bought herself a Coach bag because her mother had told her that there was no point in spending more money on a purse than you had in your wallet.

"One more from Day," he said, sliding a longer box toward her. She opened it to find a pair of ivory leather boots. She sat back on the sofa, stunned by what he had just given her. No man, not even Geno, had ever given her such elaborate gifts. Stuff like that only happened to Roni. "What's wrong? I got the right sizes, right? You don't like it?"

"I love it. I'm just surprised. I never expected this," she said.

"Well, you still have your gift from me to open." He pushed a long box into her hand. She carefully opened it and lifted a thick, gold chain out, holding a heart-shaped charm with a diamond. "Open the heart."

Inside there was a small picture of Kayla holding Day in the hospital. She had given him a copy of it after he started being a good father. She felt the tears swell in her eyes and tried to brush them before they fell.

"Look at the back," he whispered in her ear as he stroked her hair. There were three small words engraved on the back of the charm: *Kay & Day*. She fell into Craig's arms and cried. All of the emotions she had gone through that day came pouring out at that very moment. Craig just held her and let her cry.

"Thank you, Craig," she finally said after she had gotten herself together.

"Kayla, you are my daughter's mother and more importantly, you are my friend. I give you mad props because you deserve and earn your respect. You don't hassle me, you let me know in a proper way if I ain't handling my business and you are a damn good person. Hell, I been feeling you from the moment I met you and you know this. But I have my issues; you know that. I just want you to know that I care about you and appreciate you, even though I ain't that nigga Geno," he added.

"You don't have to be Geno. I appreciate you too, Craig. You have really surprised me. I thought you were gonna be one of these dads. Missing in action, but you proved me wrong." Kayla wiped the remainder of her tears and smiled at him. Craig's cell began to vibrate and he took it out and looked at it.

"Look, Kay. I gotta dip. But check this out, I would like to take you out tomorrow night if it's cool. If I get my moms to watch Day, you wanna go grab a bite at Dolce's?"

Kayla did not have to think twice. Dolce's was the premiere spot for dinner.

"That would be nice. I would love to go." She stood and walked him to the door. He bent down and caressed her neck as he hugged her. She tilted her head so that her lips met his. She closed her eyes and felt her mouth open as he began to suck on her bottom lip. She didn't want to stop and knew he didn't either, but the vibration from the phone stopped him.

"Mmmmm, see you tomorrow night, beautiful. I'll pick you up at seven," he whispered and kissed Kayla once more on her forehead. *Too bad he don't act right, or else he just might be the one for me,* Kayla thought as she went to try on her new outfit and boots.

28

"I need to talk to you," Geno said when Kayla answered the phone. She had been avoiding him for weeks now and he still hadn't let up.

"For what, Geno? I ain't your fiancée, you don't need to talk to me about shit." Kayla grabbed her purse and the diaper bag. She and Craig had an appointment with a childcare provider and she knew she couldn't be late.

"Kayla, I swear. I thought we were much cooler than this. You don't return my calls, and on the off chance that you do answer the phone, you still won't talk to me. I'm getting real pissed." Kayla could hear that Geno was frustrated, but she did not care. He wasn't her man; let Janice deal with him.

"Look, Geno. I am on my way out the door, I have an appointment and I can't be late." She picked up the carrier, where she had already placed Day, and opened the door.

"Look, Kayla. I gotta go outta town for a few weeks, but I need to see you when I get back. Face to face. This is an entire month's notice, so you have plenty of time to clear your schedule. You owe me that much, Kayla. And I wanna see Day, too."

Kayla sighed. Geno was right. She did owe him the opportunity to apologize to her face to face. "Fine, Geno. Just let me know when."

"The last Saturday in March."

"Fine. I gotta go." She hung the phone up and rushed out to meet Craig. Kayla was scheduled to return to work the first week of February. As much as she hated to leave her baby, she knew she had to go back to work in order to survive. She had diminished her savings down to almost nothing and although Craig was a good provider for Day, she still needed her own income to live comfortably. Tia had told them about a woman named Ms. Cookie who had an awesome childcare center, but she was always full. Craig had told Kayla to let him worry about getting Day in. She had no idea what he did, but he had called Kayla that morning and told her to meet him at Ms. Cookie's for their tour and interview. The neatness and cleanliness of the center impressed Kayla. There were four different rooms; three of them set up with cribs and tables. The other was a multi-purpose room, holding a large screen television and shelves of toys and books. The unique thing about Ms. Cookie's center was she exclusively kept infants up to age two.

"Well, we will see you all next week then." Ms. Cookie smiled as she walked them out.

"You mean she's in? I thought you had a waiting list." Kayla was stunned.

"She has a very persistent father." Ms. Cookie nodded. "I can respect that."

"Thanks, Ms. Cookie. We'll see you next week." Craig carried the carrier to the car and strapped Day in.

"What did you do?" Kayla asked him, incredulously.

"I got my daughter in school. I handled my business."

"How?"

"Don't worry about all that. You said you wanted her in, now I got her in. She's in and I paid her first month's tuition up front, so you don't have to sweat that either. Now I got some other business to handle. I'll be by there later, and tonight I'll do the three a.m. feeding." He winked and kissed Kayla as he jumped into his new Jeep. He told her he had gotten a major raise because they sold the restaurant to a new man, and rather than see him quit, he offered Craig double what he was making. Kayla waved as he drove off. The sight of a red car caught her eye and she turned, but it was gone. She had been seeing a red Benz following her for a couple of days now. The tag read LIBRAGAL. She knew Avis drove a red Benz. She scolded herself for being paranoid and got into her own car.

She knew she had a surprise planned for Craig. Karen had already given her the okay to have sex, but she wanted tonight to be special. She raced home to prepare. She covered her bed with the navy blue satin sheet set that Tia had given her for Christmas and placed candles all over the bedroom and bathroom. She thought about cooking but decided against it when she remembered she had no culinary skills. So she ordered some Chinese delivery. Once the food had arrived, she called Craig to see what time he would be coming and reminded him to pick up some wine and strawberries. She already had whipped cream in the fridge. She put a slow jams CD in the stereo, double checked Day and waited for her soon-to-be re-lover's arrival.

"Damn, I shoulda got Day in school earlier." He laughed as Kayla opened the door. She was wearing a blue, silk kimono and matching slippers. Her hair had grown out to its original length and she had it pulled on top of her head. She had sprayed herself with Escada, knowing it was his favorite scent for her to wear.

"Come on, dinner's ready." She turned to go into the kitchen.

"Oh, no. I hope you ain't cook." He groaned.

"You'll have to come and see." She rolled her eyes and he followed behind her. The table was laid out beautifully and she had the variety of oriental dishes in her glass serving plates and bowls.

"This is beautiful," he commented as he sat down.

"You get the wine and strawberries?"

"Yeah, right here. Give me a corkscrew so I can open the bottle."

She passed him the opener and reached into the cabinet to get two glasses. She could feel him walk behind her and reach around her waist. Her body got hot and she had to catch her breath.

"Here," she said as she turned around, holding the two glasses. He took them from her hand and placed them on the counter with one hand, pulling her to him with the other. She put her arms around his neck and stood on her toes. His arms felt so good around her as he lifted her up off the floor. She wrapped her legs around his thick waist and they kissed each other hard. Kayla found herself biting at his mouth, matching his heat. She had never wanted anyone so bad in all her life. She could feel him through his pants as he carried her to the bedroom. Once there, he laid her on the bed and looked around at the sensual surroundings Kayla had created. He didn't waste any time removing his clothes and climbing next to her. She had already removed her robe and he was staring at her sexy body. She was now even thicker than the first time he saw her nude body. Her breasts were fuller and her nipples were inviting his touch. He took his time running his fingers all over her body and nibbling her every crevice. She moaned in delight as he blew erotic kisses over her body. He kissed and licked from the top of her head to the arch of her foot, which he teased with the tip of his tongue, causing her to squirm. He knew what he was going to do next and so did she. His tongue found his way into her now melted openness and the wetness invited him home. He enjoyed the invitation and let it be known. Kayla found herself lost in the ecstasy he was taking her to. She tried to be mindful that their child was now sleeping in the next room, but could not stop herself from calling his name and letting him know she was there. Just as she caught her breath, he mounted her and began riding her gently. She bucked at first, because it was painful, but soon began to enjoy the ride, her hips rising to meet his. It was Craig who began to moan this time as the heat and wetness from her body began to contract around his thick muscle each time he entered. He began to thrust faster and faster, the sound of their bodies connecting and the scent of their lovemaking making it even better. As they had the first and only time they had ever made love, they reached their climax together and with each other's names on their lips.

"I love you, Kayla," Craig whispered. Kayla didn't know what to say. She knew she cared for Craig, he was after all the father of her child, but deep down, she knew she still loved Geno. But he was with another woman. What was the use of holding on to those feelings? *Can I love two men at one time?*

"I love you too, Craig," she said as her mind told her heart to shut up. He kissed her once again and rose from the bed, walking into the bathroom. He returned with a warm cloth for her to clean herself up. "Thanks, but I think I need a shower after that one."

"We did get kinda funky. I think I'll join you. That is, if you don't mind."

"I don't mind at all." Kayla grinned as he pulled her up. "Start the water. I need to check on Day."

She peeked into the dim nursery and made sure Day was still sleeping. *I can't believe she slept through all of that,* she thought. She walked into the room just in time to hear Craig talking on his cell phone.

"Damn, man. I told you I couldn't meet up tonight. I got something to do. We just have to handle it in the morning. Man, naw. Because. Look, meet me in ten minutes and your ass better be there when I get there. Whatever."

"Who is that?" Kayla asked, causing Craig to damn near jump out of his skin.

"Don't be sneaking up on a brother like that, girl." He turned and smiled at her. "That was Darrell. I gotta go meet him at the crib right fast."

"But I thought we were gonna take a shower."

"Look, give me thirty minutes, baby. I promise you I will bathe you from your head to your feet," he said as he pulled on his jeans and Tims. He looked so sexy. Kayla sat on the side of the bed and rolled her eyes. "Thirty minutes. I promise, Kay."

He kissed her and nearly ran out the door, leaving her sitting on the side of the bed. He returned two hours later and climbed into bed, wrapping his arms around Kayla as she slept.

29

"Hello." The call was coming from Lynch Financial Group and Kayla knew it must either be a telemarketer or a wrong number.

"Can I speak to Kayla?"

"Yes, you may. Who's calling?" Kayla indirectly corrected the unknown female caller. She was waiting on Roni to arrive so they could go to lunch with the rest of their girlfriends.

"Avis. Avis Coleman." Kayla's heart began to thump in her chest. She knew this day was coming, but she still was not prepared. She took a deep breath and closed her eyes.

"This is she."

"I need to ask you a few questions." She could hear the ghetto attitude and New York accent in the woman's voice and knew that it was not gonna be pretty. Craig had assured her that he and Avis were finished, but she still had her doubts.

"Go ahead. I am listening."

"Are you and Craig fucking?" she asked. Kayla cringed at the crudeness of her question. She decided to attempt the intelligent way out.

"Craig and I are dating, if that's what you want to know. As far as us having a sexual relationship, well, I feel that that's none of your business, especially considering the fact that you two are no longer together."

"None of my business! Bitch, have you lost your mind? That's my husband. We may be taking a break right now, but we are still and always will be married. I just wanted to know for my own sake and my protection if you are fucking him, because I still am."

"Well, thank you for being concerned enough about me to let me know that. I will take it all under advisement." Kayla figured the dumb girl probably had no idea what the word "advisement" meant, and knew that her calmness was pissing her off even more.

"Let me give you a little more facts to take under ad . . . ad . . . *advisement*, since you wanna be so gotdamn funny. Craig is my husband!"

"You already told me that twice," Kayla said calmly.

"Listen to me, trick! I am his wife and I am the mother of his son. You will never be me. I have his seed. You may be his *piece* for right now, but I have his son. He will be taking care of me forever. You are nothing to him! I am everything!" she screamed. Kayla tried to remain calm and not let the worst of her come out, but this ghetto bitch had said the wrong thing.

"Guess what? He might have me be his '*piece*,' as you call it, for a little longer than you think, my dear. You see, I would never want to be your funky, uneducated ass for nothing in this world. Not only do I have my own, but I got his seed too, boo. I am the mother of his daughter." Kayla hung the phone up thinking, *Let her think about that*. When Roni came through the door Kayla was still *fuming*.

"You ready? What is wrong with you?" Roni looked at her friend who was so mad she was almost feverish.

"That stank ho Avis called me." The phone rang and Kayla read the caller ID. "This is her again. She's calling from her job. Hello."

"I know you are a liar, bitch. You know Craig is out in the streets blowing up and you trying to take him for what he worth. I know your so-called daughter ain't his. But you know what? You keep trying me and I am gonna really fuck you *and* your baby up."

"Listen, I don't take to threats too kindly, so let me warn you. Don't let your mouth write a check your ass can't cash. Don't call my house again." She hung the phone up and grabbed her purse. The phone began to ring again. "Let's go before I have to get ugly."

"You should let me talk to that bitch," Roni said as she grabbed the diaper bag and the car seat. "Aunt Roni knows how to handle hers, right, Day?"

"Mommy knows how to handle her own, too!" Kayla slammed the door as they left.

After a wonderful lunch with her friends, Kayla returned to find that she had thirty-eight new calls on her caller ID and twelve new messages. She looked at the small screen of the phone and there were different numbers, but they all came from Lynch Financial Group.

"I don't believe this. She called almost forty times and she left twelve messages."

"No she didn't. Play them on speakerphone so I can hear them," Roni told her. Kayla played each message. They were all full of profanity and threats to her and Day. She told Kayla she knew where she lived and was gonna kill her. She even offered to meet Kayla somewhere so they could fight like "real women".

"You really are crazy. Ain't no nigga worth fighting over," Kayla replied to Avis' voice. But there was something else about the messages that bothered Roni.

"Kay, what does she mean about Craig making big money in the streets now?"

"I don't know. She said something about that to me earlier. I thought she was talking about the raise he got at the restaurant."

"I don't think so. I betcha that nigga is hustling. You see, a woman like her ain't gonna be sweating him like that if he just a cook. And you said she drives a Benz. Unless she's a big time broker at Lynch, she wouldn't be driving a Benz. He's hustling."

The phone rang again as Kayla was thinking about what her friend had just told her.

"It's her again," she told Roni.

"Let her leave another message," Roni told her.

"I am, but in the meantime, I'm gonna get her ass." Kayla called the phone company and got her number changed immediately. She found the toll-free number for Lynch Financial Group and called them. "Yes, I need to speak with Corporate Security, please. Thank you."

"What are you doing?" Roni frowned.

"Outsmarting the dumb bitch. She is so stupid. Watch this. Hi, my name is Kayla Hopkins and I need to report harassment by one of your employees. Her name is Avis Coleman.

Yes, well Mrs. Coleman has called my residence several times today from your company and even left threatening messages on my voice mail. As a matter of fact, hold one moment and I will play them for you." Kayla clicked to the other line and dialed the voice mail number, playing the messages for the manager. "As you can see, these messages are time and date stamped, and if you compare that to Mrs. Coleman's schedule, you will see that they were made on company time. Now, I am sure you are paying Mrs. Coleman to do something other than bother persons such as myself. I have contacted the authorities as well as my attorney, and you will be hearing from them soon. I am calling you to ask Mrs. Coleman as a courtesy to refrain from contacting me. Yes, that's fine. Let me give you my new telephone number for them to call me. I had to go through the inconvenience of changing it due to this unfortunate circumstance. Yes." Kayla gave him the number and he assured her that the company's attorney would call her as soon as possible.

"Work it, girl. Be smarter than her!" Roni snapped her fingers at Kayla and she tried not to laugh.

"Thank you. And one more thing, can you let Mrs. Coleman know that it is a federal offense to use profanity over telephone lines in a threatening manner? The telephone company could prosecute her and have her home lines permanently disconnected. You have a wonderful day as well." Kayla tossed her head back with laughter as she hung the phone up.

"A woman after my own heart. I trained you well." Roni hugged her girlfriend. "One down, one to go."

"What do you mean?" Kayla asked.

"We're gonna find out if that brother is dealing. Come on. We'll drop Day off at Tia's." Roni jumped into the car. They dropped Day and explained to Tia that they had some emergency business to take care of. Tia just shook her head and took the baby and the diaper bag.

"Where are we going now?" Kayla asked.

"To Toby's. He'll know someone that could tell us if Craig is hustling."

30

Roni sped through the streets and pulled up behind Toby's Lexus truck. They hopped out and walked to the front door, ringing the doorbell. They waited a few minutes but there was still no answer. "I know he's here because he has to be at the club by eight. What time is it?"

"Six forty," Kayla answered. "I thought you had a key anyway."

"Not yet. 'Yet' being the operative word. He must be 'sleep." Roni laid on the doorbell, ringing it five or six times in a row. They finally heard footsteps coming toward them. "About time."

"Wha . . . Hey, what are y'all doing here?" Toby opened the door slightly, wearing some sweats and no shirt. Kayla tried not to stare at his muscular, chocolate body, but it was hard.

"Hey, sweetie. We came by because we need to talk to you. It's an emergency." She reached to open the door but Toby stopped her.

"I . . . I was uh, about to jump in the shower. Why don't y'all meet me at the club?" he quickly suggested.

"I told you it's an emergency. And why aren't you answering your home phone? I tried to call on my way over here."

"I was asleep. Look, I need to go get dressed. I'll check y'all at the club." He stood behind the slightly cracked door. A movement in the background caused Kayla to frown, but she didn't know what it was. She was gonna find out, though. She looked again and realized it was a foot, without a shoe, dangling off the sofa.

"That's cool. Come on, Ron. You know I gotta pick Day up in a little while. We'll check you later, Toby." She pulled at her girlfriend's jacket and gave her the look. Roni didn't know what was up and was about to go off on Toby, but she followed Kayla's lead.

"A'ight, Kay. I'll see you later, Ron. I love you." He watched them get into Roni's car and shut the door.

"What the hell was that? And why are you rushing me? You know Day is with Tia. She could stay there a month and she and Theo wouldn't care."

"Somebody's in there, Ron. Pull behind that car over there and we're gonna walk back and see who it is. Come on!"

Roni did as she was told and they crept back up to Toby's house. Sure enough, as they peered through the front bay window, they could see Toby hugging that fat nasty Darla on the sofa. Kayla could not believe Toby. He was just as bad as the rest of the trifling, lying men. She turned to see her friend's reaction and saw that Roni was not by her side. She quickly looked around and spotted her in the driveway next door, picking up a skateboard. Before she could react, Roni had tossed the board through the bay window, scaring Toby and Darla. They both screamed and ducked, not knowing what was happening. But Roni didn't stop there. She found a brick and headed for Toby's truck.

"Roni!" Kayla screamed. But the tears that were streaming down her face blinded Roni. She could see more hurt than anger in Roni's eyes and Kayla knew that made her more dangerous. Roni had vowed never to be hurt by any man.

"Veronica! Stop right now. I mean it. Don't make me stop you!" Toby ran after Roni but didn't make it to her in time. The brick seemed to be floating in slow motion as it crashed through his rear window. Kayla grabbed Roni's arm and dragged her to the car, rushing to get away from the now livid Toby. Kayla jumped behind the wheel and tried to think of where to go. They drove around in silence. Roni's eyes glazed over with sadness. Kayla knew the only place to hide. She pulled behind the back of Jett Black. They knocked on the back door and Ms. Ernestine opened it, letting them in.

"Y'all must have really gotten into trouble. Coming through the back door." She smiled at them, then policed Roni's forlorn face. "What happened, baby? What's wrong?"

Kayla followed mother and daughter into Ms. Ernestine's decked out office and explained what had just transpired between Roni and Toby. Kayla thought Ms. Ernestine would be mad enough to kill Toby, but she just laughed.

"My baby is finally in love. I never thought I'd see the day."

"I am not in love with him," Roni told her mother defiantly.

"Yes, you are. If you weren't, then you would've cussed him out rather than vandalize his property. It's nothing wrong with being in love, Roni. That's not a bad thing."

"I got played. I can't believe I got played." Roni began to cry again.

A knock at the door surprised them all.

"Ms. Ernestine, it's a man named Toby out here to see you and he is fine," the shampoo girl, Tameka, came and announced. Roni looked at her mother with a panicked look on her face. Ms. Ernestine touched her daughter's arm and let her know it would be okay.

"He doesn't know you're here. I am not gonna let anything happen to you, you understand?"

"Yes." Roni nodded at her mother. She sat behind the large desk and looked at Toby in the surveillance camera her mother had, displaying the center of the shop. Ernestine Jett kept watch over her shop even when she wasn't seen.

"How you doing, Toby?" Her mother walked up and gave the handsome young man a hug. "What brings you all the way over here? And on a Friday night, too? Aren't you supposed to be spinning records at Dominic's?"

"Yes, ma'am. I came to see if you've seen or heard from Roni," he asked her wearily.

"No, I'm sorry. I can't say that I have. Something wrong?" she asked.

Toby looked around at the crowd of women and then mumbled, "Is there somewhere else we can talk? Somewhere private?"

"We can go in my office. Just give me a minute to clear some stuff up," she said. "Be right back. And Meka, you can look but you'd better not touch."

"What are you doing, Mama?" Roni hissed as her mother re-entered the office.

"Go in the bathroom and wait, both of you. Don't make a sound," she told them. Kayla and Roni went into the small bathroom adjoining the office and held their breath.

"I hope your mama knows what she's doing," Kayla whispered.

"Lord, help her to calm him down so he won't call the cops," Roni prayed aloud.

They listened as Ms. Ernestine and Toby came back into the office.

"Now, what's going on, Toby? And why is my daughter missing all of a sudden?"

"She showed up at my house unexpectedly this evening and I was trying to help a friend of mine out. A female."

"A friend?"

"Yes, ma'am. This friend of mine has some heavy issues going on right now and I was helping her deal with them. I told Roni I was kind of busy and thought she had left, but the next thing I know she busts my window with a skateboard and bricks my truck." He dropped his head toward the floor.

"Are you sure it was just a friend? Roni has never been the jealous type. Did something else go on that you aren't telling me?"

"No, I mean I will admit that the female and I do have some history, but I swear to you, Ms. Ernestine, I would never do anything to hurt or disrespect Roni. I love her with all my heart, and believe it or not, I have never been faithful to anyone until I met her. I know that she is my soul mate and I am not gonna risk losing her for nothing and nobody. I want to marry her. That is, if I have your blessing. But I have to apologize to her for earlier and get her to forgive me."

"Let me get this straight. You were comforting a friend at your house and Roni got mad and broke your house window *and* your car window and you want to apologize and propose to *her*?"

"Yes, ma'am." He looked at her like he was confused.

"Toby, are you sure nothing else happened?"

"I swear. The girl was upset because she found out she was pregnant and the father wants nothing to do with her. I was just being a shoulder for her to cry on."

"And it's not your baby?"

"Absolutely not. I haven't been with anyone since I met Roni and we got together in July. I just need her to forgive me for not explaining and trying to be hush-hush about the whole situation."

"I think she'll understand. I will do what I can to find her for you. I believe that you love her, Toby, and as crazy as both of y'all are, I think you're made for each other. She tears up *your* stuff and *you* want to apologize. I have heard it all."

"Thanks, Ms. Ernestine. I appreciate it." Toby hugged her and left out.

"Girl, if you don't get your behind out here and call that man. Lord, I finally got a wedding to plan!" She hugged Roni and Kayla. Both were still in shock from what Toby had just said.

"And Terrell calls me Drama Queen." Kayla shook her head at her friend.

31

"Where have you been and where is my child?" Craig demanded as Kayla pulled up to her house.

"She's at Tia's. What is your problem?" Kayla flared at him.

"Goddamn Avis has been blowing up my pager and cell phone. She says you got her fired. What the hell is your problem? I told you to stay away from her."

"First of all, I didn't go looking for her, she came looking for me. She called *my* house harassing me and threatening me and Day."

"Day? How the hell did she find out about Day?"

"I told her."

"You did what? I know you didn't. Don't tell me that, Kayla. You told her? So basically what you did was give her a valid reason to take my ass to court for child support and alimony. I told you not to talk to her dumb ass."

"Look, you two need to take that into the house. You don't want your neighbors to call the cops," Roni encouraged.

Kayla had forgotten that they were standing in her driveway like common folk. She quickly unlocked the door and went inside with Craig on her heels.

"I didn't give her anything. I am not gonna walk around here like my child is some deep, dark secret to be denied. And her stupid behind would still have a job if she would've left me alone like I asked," she yelled at him. His pager went off and he pulled it out and looked at it.

"I got a errand to run. I will deal with this shit later," he mumbled.

"Before you go, let me ask you a question. What restaurant are you working at again?"

"What?"

"What is the name of the restaurant?" She looked him in his eye to see if he could lie to her face.

"I don't have time for this. I'll call you later." He stormed out of her house. She looked at Roni and told her to come on.

"Where are we going?" Roni asked as they raced to the car.

"Follow him. I don't care what you have to do. Run red lights, stop signs, just stay behind him."

Roni followed the SUV like a pro. She kept a safe distance and trailed Craig until he pulled in front of a row house on one of the side streets all the way across town.

"What up, Craig? You got that for me?" A tall, dark figure wearing a black jacket approached Craig as he got out.

"You paged me, Fred. If I ain't have it I wouldn't have come. Now, you got my money? And hurry up. I got other business to attend to," Craig grumbled as he reached under the back seat and got a small bag out. Kayla watched in disbelief as the transaction took place.

"Here, man. Now where's my money?" Craig walked toward the shadowy figure.

"Right here, player!" He reached into his jacket, but instead of pulling out money, he pulled out a nine millimeter and shots rang out. Kayla opened her mouth and thought the screams were coming from her mouth, but it was Roni's voice. The slim man looked around and ran off, stopping only to pick the package up from Craig's bleeding body.

32

Kayla rocked back and forth, cradling Craig's head in her arms. She began to pray and let him know he was going to be all right. She tried to look for a sign that he understood, but he never opened his eyes. She could hear the sirens in the distance coming closer, and the flashing lights were soon dancing across Craig's face, but she still rocked and prayed.

"Ma'am, we need to get to him. Are you okay?" the paramedic asked her. Kayla didn't answer. She continued to rock.

"Kayla, let them help him. Please." She heard Roni's voice in the background. She felt someone gently lift him from her arms and she watched them check for life. It was like she was in a movie.

"Are you okay, ma'am?" again someone asked. "Were you struck anywhere?" Kayla didn't realize what they were talking about until she looked down and saw that she was covered in blood. She shook her head at the police officer.

"It's not my blood. It's his. Is he going to be okay?" She watched as they began performing CPR.

"They're gonna do everything they can to save him. We need to ask you and your friend a few questions."

"Can we do it later? She needs to make sure he's taken care of first, as well as herself." Roni put her arms around Kayla. The attendants placed Craig on a gurney and lifted him into the back of the ambulance.

"I need to ride with him." Kayla pulled away from her girlfriend and ran toward the vehicle.

"It's okay. She can ride," the officer assured Roni.

"I'll follow you in my car," Roni yelled.

It seemed as if the ride to the hospital took an eternity. Kayla listened as they made comments in regards to Craig's condition. She tried to understand what everything meant, relying on her memory from watching episodes of ER. Most of it was still foreign, but one phrase was clear.

"He's crashing!"

They scrambled, poking Craig with needles and trying to stop the pouring blood from his chest. Kayla closed her eyes and prayed harder and harder. She could not believe that the father of her child was dying before her eyes. It was too much to take.

They rushed Craig into the operating room and told Kayla to wait. She didn't know what to do. The nurse came over and asked if she was Craig's wife. She thought for a moment and shook her head.

"I'll call his brother," she said quietly.

"Okay." The nurse smiled.

Kayla picked up the courtesy phone and dialed Darrell's house. She could hear the panic in his voice when she told him Craig had been shot and he needed to get there right away. He told her it would be okay and he was on his way. Kayla sat on the hard chair beside the phone and tried to think.

"How is he?" Roni asked her quietly.

"They haven't said yet. I don't know."

"He'll be okay, Kayla." Roni tried to comfort her friend and began to pray herself. This was why she didn't date thugs. She had been there when they told her mother that her father had been shot over a dime bag of weed. She was only seven years old. She decided right then that her mother deserved better and so did she.

A little while passed and Darrell came into the waiting room along with two people who he introduced as his parents.

"Where is he? What did they say?" Craig's mother asked.

"They haven't come out and said anything yet," Kayla told her. "He was shot three times, and one of those was in his chest."

"My God. Where did this happen? And who did it?" She cried, looking to Kayla for answers.

"We were on Brighton Street. We followed him. He didn't know we were there," Kayla tried to explain. "It was a guy . . ."

"Brighton Street. Why was he over there?" she interrupted.

"He was dropping something off to the guy and the guy pulled a gun."

"Jesus, I knew he had started selling again." Craig's father sat down and sighed.

"You don't know that, Eddie. He might have just been in the wrong place at the wrong time." She shook her head at her husband. She didn't want to think that Craig had gone back to dealing in the streets. He had stopped that a long time ago.

"Mister and Mrs. Coleman? I'm Doctor Win." The young Korean doctor came into the room, his scrubs covered in blood.

"Yes. How's my boy?" Craig's father jumped up and asked.

"He's stable. The bullet barely missed his heart. We've stopped the bleeding, but these next twenty-four hours are critical," he informed everyone.

"Can we see him?" Diane asked.

"You can, for a few moments. We are transporting him to intensive care. But you do need to know that he is in a coma."

"No! How long will that last?" Eddie looked solemn.

"We can't tell you. He may regain consciousness tomorrow, he may never wake up. As I stated earlier, the next twenty-four hours are critical. I'll tell the nurse to come and get you when he's moved." Dr. Win went back through the doors, leaving everyone to digest what he had just told them.

"He's gonna be fine," Kayla said. "I prayed and asked the Lord to heal him. Now we just gotta have faith."

"That's right."

"Oh God! Oh God! Where is he? Craig, Craig!" Kayla heard someone yelling from the corridor.

"Ma'am, ma'am. You are going to have to wait in there with the rest of the family. The doctor will inform you of his condition," the nurse said loudly over the wailing voice. The door opened and Avis nearly fell through the door, crying as if Craig were already dead.

"Oh God! Diane, did they say how he was? Oh, Craig, please be okay," she gushed and fell into Diane's arms.

"Avis! Get yourself together," Eddie grabbed her by the arm and told her. Avis turned to him and wept even louder.

"Ma'am, you are going to have to calm yourself. There are other families in nearby waiting rooms and you are causing a disturbance," the nurse warned.

"What the hell is she doing here? Did she shoot him?" Avis rolled her eyes at Kayla. "I thought this was a family waiting room. She ain't family! I am his wife! She is his whore!"

"Avis! That's enough. Now is not the time nor the place," Eddie warned. Kayla stood up and looked at Roni.

"I think it's time for me to go."

"You damn right. You shoulda been gone a long time ago, heifer! You know this bitch called and got me fired today, Diane? Now that I'm in her face, she wanna run off. Naw, be a real woman. Face me, you skank."

"Get out, Avis! My son is clinging to his life and you want to come in here and embarrass him and his family by acting a loudmouth fool. I don't need that, and neither does my son. I am telling you to leave right now or I will have you escorted out." Diane stood and looked Avis in the eye.

"So now you gon' defend her? I think you forgot who your daughter-in-law was. Better yet, the mother of your grandson," Avis said in a threatening manner. For some reason, Diane seemed slightly intimidated. Whatever was about to go down, Kayla wanted no part of it.

"We're leaving. I'll call later to check on Craig," She said to Eddie as she and Roni headed toward the door.

"I'll walk you all down," Darrell said.

"So now you wanna leave? Before you even get to see him? Typical." Avis spat the words at Kayla and it took all of her remaining restraint not to swing on the fat cow.

Kayla quickly walked out into the hallway and into the parking lot. Suddenly, she felt someone rushing toward her and she turned just in time to see Avis charging at her. She felt the punch Avis threw as it landed on her cheek. The pain jolted her but she recovered in time to dodge the next punch she threw. All of the anger that had been pent up came gushing out and she proceeded to whip her ass like she had been wanting to all day. Although the woman was bigger than Kayla by about eighty pounds, she was slower, too. After receiving a few blows of her own, Kayla sucker punched her and knocked her to the ground, then dove on top of her fat body, aiming strictly for her face. She showed no mercy.

"Kayla! Kayla!" She heard Roni screaming. The funny thing was that neither she nor Darrell tried to stop her initially. They let her get her hit on for a few minutes until someone yelled that security was on the way. At that point, Darrell lifted Kayla off Avis and carried her to Roni's car. They sped off before he could say a word.

33

"Kayla, Terrell's here to see you." Roni knocked and stuck her head in the door of Kayla's bedroom. "It's cool. He can come on back." Kayla sat up in the bed and clicked her television off.

"Hey. You okay?" Terrell looked at her sympathetically. She couldn't do anything but nod. It had been six days since Craig had been shot. He was still in a coma. Kayla hadn't had the strength mentally or physically to go and see him. She just lay in her bed, occasionally watching television. Her parents had come and taken Day back with them for a few days, and Roni had been staying at her house and looking after her. Although she had tried, Kayla still could not get herself together.

"How's he doing? I mean, have you heard anything?"

"He's still in ICU. He's stable, but he still hasn't woken up," she told him. "How are you doing? You look terrible."

"Man, I just been having issues of my own. You know what I mean?" He sat on the side of Kayla's bed.

"Terrell Sims with issues? I don't believe it. This I gotta hear. What's going on?" she asked him curiously.

"I was told I'm about to be a father."

"What? Nicole's pregnant! Congratulations. What's the problem?"

"She's not the only one." He looked down at the comforter and shook his head sadly.

"What do you mean? I don't understand." Kayla was confused.

"I have two children on the way by two different women, one of whom is *not* my girlfriend."

"And who is the other?" Kayla knew Terrell was serious about Nicole. He'd assured her of that when she asked him Christmas Day. He even admitted to being in love with her.

"Darla."

"STD Darla? I know you're playing." Kayla remembered seeing her hugged up with Toby the night Craig was shot, and what Toby had explained to Ms. Ernestine about the situation.

"I wish I was. And she ain't trying to get rid of it, either. I don't know what I'm gonna do. I love Nicole. I want her to have my baby. Hell, I love her and want to *marry* her." He looked at Kayla.

"No you don't. Don't even sit there and lie. If you loved her you wouldn't have been fucking Darla." Kayla was pissed at what Terrell was saying.

"It's not like that, Kayla. I do love Nicole."

"So you accidentally fell into Darla's twat? Is that what happened?"

"No. I mean, with her it was an ego thing. You see, before Christmas Nicole didn't have time for a brother like I needed. That 'me-time' that I gotta have. With Darla, I could go out to the club and then swing by her crib and she would have a sandwich and some chips ready on the table for me. She'd be waiting for a nigga to hit the door and she would slob me down from the jump. I had my own special Kool-Aid in her fridge, sweetened to my liking. She knew how to treat a brother like a man. Nicole never did stuff like that."

"What does Darla do again?"

"She does hair I think. Oh, and she work somewhere else, too. I forget where."

"So you went to her because Nicole was working full-time at the hospital, going to school part-time, and didn't allow you to disrespect her by staying out all night and coming to her crib to eat and sleep whenever you felt like it. Is that what you're saying?"

"No, not like that. I just—I don't—man, my life is so messed up right now."

"You damn right. You blew a perfectly good relationship with an educated, hard-working, respectable woman so you could have 'me-time' with a part-time hairdresser that your brother used to screw. Not only is that pathetic, Terrell, it's nasty. And now she's about to have your baby. And you think my life is drama-filled?" Kayla was disappointed in her friend.

He was supposed to be smarter than that. "And if you know you ain't care about that girl, why didn't you wrap it up?"

"I did. At least I thought I did. I don't know, Kayla."

"So you don't even know if it's your baby."

"She says it is."

She looked at Terrell and remembered how he had been there for her over the past few months with all she had been going through. She could not believe she was treating him the same way she didn't want to be treated when she found herself pregnant. She had no right to judge him.

"I don't know what to tell you. I do know that if Nicole forgives you, she's a good one and you better spend the rest of your life making it up to her."

"If she forgives me, you'd better believe I'm gonna marry her."

"You'll be okay, Terrell. I'm here for you. You're my dawg!" She took his hand.

"Thanks, Kayla." He smiled at her.

The phone rang and Roni answered it before Kayla could read the caller ID. She was still trying to help Terrell make heads or tails of his predicament when Roni came into the room.

"Kayla, it's Darrell. Craig has regained consciousness."

Kayla was quiet the entire ride to the hospital. After the last time she was there, she didn't know what to expect. Darrell did call her, so she hoped that was a key indicator that Avis would not be there. She held her breath as she entered Craig's room. His parents and Darrell were all standing over him as she walked in. He was still hooked up to tubes and machines, but his eyes were open.

"He . . . hey, b . . . be . . . beautiful," he stuttered. Kayla smiled at him.

"Hey yourself. You scared the hell out of me."

"I know. I scared the hell out of myself," he said and closed his eyes. Kayla wanted to confront him about the entire incident, but she knew this was not the time. The nurse came in and told them that he needed his rest.

"Kiss my beautiful Day for me," he managed to say.

"I will." Kayla squeezed his hand. They left him and met with Dr. Win in the hallway.

"Well, he's out of the woods. He has a lot of healing to do, but that will happen in time. There was no permanent damage done," the doctor assured them. "He will remain in here another ten days, but we'll move him to another room. He's a lucky young man."

"Thank you, Dr. Win. Thank you for all you've done," Diane said.

"We really do," Darrell added.

"You all take care and I'll check on him later." The doctor left them standing in the hall.

"How you holding up, Kayla?" Eddie asked her.

"I'm fine. I guess I can go back to work next week," she told them.

"I am sorry for all that has happened, including my ignorant daughter-in-law." He rubbed her shoulders.

"It's not your fault nor your place to apologize. I know how to handle trolls like her."

"I second *that*. Lord knows you handled her in the parking lot last week." Darrell laughed. "You tore her fat ass up!"

They all told Kayla about the damage she had done to Avis. She ripped her weave job out and broke her nose. Diane said she *still* had a black eye.

"I'm sorry. But you do know that she tried to jump me. I don't fight unless I am pushed."

"Don't worry about it. Darrell told us what happened. She just got what she been deserving for a while now. I just hope you watch your back. That Avis is a snake and this won't be the end."

"I will. I'll be back tomorrow to check on Craig." Kayla hugged all of them.

"Thank you, Kayla." Diane nodded. "I know this entire situation has not been a very good one, but you have handled it like a lady and that says a lot about you and your character. One more thing."

"Yes, ma'am?"

"When do we get to meet our granddaughter?" she asked Kayla. Kayla didn't know what to say. "We know."

"I, who . . ." Kayla began.

"It doesn't matter. When do we get to see her? We hear she's beautiful."

"Whenever you want," Kayla told them. She felt the weight she had been carrying around for days lifted off her shoulders. *Maybe things are gonna be okay after all,* she thought.

34

Kayla was getting dressed for her first day back at work when the phone rang. She checked the caller ID and it was an unavailable number. She knew that when Ms. Diane or Darrell called from the hospital that was how the number came up, so she answered it.

"Hello," she said, but there was no answer. She held the receiver a few moments longer but still heard nothing. She hung up the phone. The same thing happened three additional times and Kayla was getting pissed. When the phone rang once more, she snatched it up and yelled.

"Why the hell are you playing on my phone?"

"Whoa! Kayla, it's me. What is going on? Are you okay?" Geno asked. Kayla was relieved. She was almost in a panic.

"I'm okay, G. Somebody keeps calling here playing on my phone."

"I thought this was your new number. I had to beg Roni to give it to me."

"It is. I was gonna call you and give it to you myself, but everything has been so hectic around here."

"I know. I heard what happened. How are you holding up?"

"I'm okay."

"Thank God you and Roni weren't hurt. Your mom still has Day?"

"Yeah. She's gonna be there another week and then I'm going to get her. You still out of town?"

"Yeah, I'll be back next week. I still want to talk to you. I need to explain a few things."

"Look, Geno. I keep telling you that you don't owe me an explanation." Kayla saw that she only had half an hour to get to work. "I gotta get outta here. I have to be at work by twelve thirty. I'll call you later."

"Promise?"

"I promise." She hung up the phone and finished getting dressed.

"Well, look who finally decided to join the realms of the working class." Terrell grinned when she made it to her desk.

"Ha-ha." She stuck her tongue at him.

"Naw, dawg. I don't even wanna go there with you. I should've known that was your car in the parking lot. Who else would have 'Kay&Day' on their tag? You got personalized plates. Bad idea."

"Why? You got 'em." Kayla looked at him smugly.

"I ain't got the kinda drama you got, either," he answered.

"No, but you got drama of your own though." She winked at him.

"Don't go there."

"I didn't, you did." She smirked as he rolled his eyes at her. She sat at her desk and looked at him innocently and he could not help but laugh.

Kayla's first week back was a light one. Her supervisor told her to take it easy and she did. She would leave work every day and go visit Craig, although it was way past visiting hours. He seemed to enjoy her visits and they would laugh and talk like they were at her house instead of the hospital.

"Have they told you when you can leave yet?" she asked him Friday evening.

"No, not yet. I think the doctor is juicing me for my insurance money." He smiled.

"You'd better be glad you have insurance," Kayla told him. She wondered who he got it through, *The Dealers' Union?* She figured that now was as good a time as any to ask him what she wanted to know. She had waited long enough. "Craig, are you selling drugs?"

"What? How am I gonna be dealing from a hospital bed, huh? Yeah, after everybody leaves I go and stand on the corner and sell anesthesia." He tried to make her laugh.

"Before you got shot, were you dealing?" She was not gonna break. She needed to know the truth.

"I was dabbling. I wouldn't call the little bit of business I was doing dealing."

"Why, Craig?"

"I mean, after Day was born and I left Avis, things got real tight. I had not only one daycare bill. I had two. Avis was always crying about money for her and Nigel. And then you were so cool that I really wanted to do right by you. I wanted to make you and Day happy." He looked at her and reached for her hand.

"Don't put this on me, Craig. I did not tell you to start selling drugs. I would never tell you to do that. You could've gotten a second job at McDonald's if it was that bad, and I would have been fine with that. Please don't try to make me feel like you did this for me. You can't make no money for me and Day from a coffin or from jail, which is where you're gonna end up if you don't stop."

"Kayla, believe me. I just wanted us to be a family. I love you and Day, Kayla. I am so sorry that I messed up this bad. Please forgive me."

Kayla looked at his beautiful eyes and they were pleading along with his mouth. She did not know what to do or say.

"You gotta promise to stop, Craig. I don't do hustlers. I don't care how much money they have. I don't do jails and I don't do funerals. Now, the choice is yours."

"I'll quit, Kayla. I promise."

The word "promise" reminded her that she had promised to meet Geno at the Deck. He had finally convinced her that she needed to see him so they could talk.

"I'll be back tomorrow." She bent over him and kissed him gently.

"What time?" he asked.

"Around ten."

"I'll see you then, beautiful. I love you."

"I love you too, Craig," she said as she left. She thought about him as she drove to the restaurant. If he was willing to give up that lifestyle then she was willing to give him another chance. As she pulled into the crowded parking lot, her cell phone rang. She didn't recognize the number.

"Hello."

"Kayla, where are you?"

"Geno, I'm at the Deck. Where are you?" She looked at the clock to make sure she wasn't late. The numbers read ten forty. They were scheduled to meet at ten forty-five.

"I'm gonna have to meet you a little later. Uh, I left my phone and I gotta swing back and get it. Is that okay?" he asked her. She could hear someone laughing in the background.

"Look, Geno, I don't have time for your games, okay? You go and handle your business and I'll check you some other time."

"Kayla, wait. I gotta talk to you."

"Good-bye, Geno." She clicked her phone off and drove home. Pulling into her driveway, she realized that she had left her purse in Craig's hospital room. *I'll just leave it until in the morning,* she thought, but then decided to go and get it.

She quietly got off the elevator and sneaked past the nurses' station. Luckily, there was no one there. She proceeded down the hall and when she got to his door, she heard him talking to someone.

"I know, boo. I'm sorry that happened, really I am. I know she had no right and I'ma check her on it. Look, I'm just tryin' to do and say whatever so she won't take me for child support. You know we don't need that shit right now. Let me handle Kayla. I know what to do. As a matter of fact, baby, I already got her thinking I'm quitting the game. Hell no, you know I got too much invested in the streets to do that shit. But if she think I ain't hustling, she ain't gon' be having her hand out for no money. I'm gonna do everything outside of killing her ass to keep her from taking me to court. Trust me. Yeah, I told you I got this. Avis, baby, I know. I do love you. You're my wife and nobody can take that from you. You the mother of my firstborn son. You're my queen. I just want us to be a family again. I just want to make you and Nigel happy. I love you, too." She heard him hang up the phone and turned, accidentally bumping into a nurse.

"Can I help you?" she asked, startled.

"I, I left my purse in his room and I need it. Can you get it for me?" Kayla asked, still stunned.

"Sure. Be right back," she smiled and said.

"Don't tell him I'm out here. I don't want to go in."

"No problem," she said. The nurse returned with the purse in hand and gave it to Kayla.

"Thank you," she said and rushed out the hospital. She sat behind the wheel of her car and could not move. She didn't know what to do. She picked her cell phone up and dialed Geno's number.

"Hello." A female answered.

"I'm sorry. I must have dialed the wrong number. I was trying to reach Geno."

"You dialed the right number. He accidentally left his phone on my bed a little while ago. I'll let him know you called," she said and hung up in Kayla's face. Again, Kayla was dumbfounded. She felt as if her life were falling into pieces. She quickly dialed another set of numbers into the phone.

"Hey."

"I need to talk to you," she told Terrell.

"What's wrong, yo?" he asked. "You a'ight?"

"Can you please meet me at my house, Terrell?"

"I'm in the middle of something right now. Can I call you back?"

"Yeah, that's cool," she said.

"You sure you a'ight?" he asked her again.

"Yeah, I'm cool. I'll talk to you later." She quickly hung up the phone and her bottom lip began to quiver. She started to cry. She had no one to talk to. She knew that her girlfriends were probably tired of her and all of her problems, and she definitely could not call her mother. Kayla called the only other person she knew could help her. She closed her eyes and prayed to God.

"Lord, please help me. I am at my wits' end and don't know what to do. I am tired of putting my trust into these men and they are dogging me every time. I have no one else to turn to. Please help me."

She wiped her face and drove herself home. She took a quick shower and got into the bed.

As she began to dream, she felt a spirit of peace come over her as God told her, "That's your problem. You are trusting man when you should be trusting Me."

"Thank you, God," she said and entered into a deep slumber. She thought she was dreaming when she heard the sound of glass breaking from outside her house. She sat up in the bed and rubbed her eyes. There was another loud crash and she rushed to the front of her dark house, peeking out the front window. At first she could not find the source of the commotion and then her attention was drawn to her car. She knew she was dreaming when she saw it. She ran to the front door and flung it open.

"No!" she yelled as she looked at the vandalized mess. Her windshield and all of her windows had been broken. Her lights were smashed and the hood was dented in, her tires flattened. She scurried into the house to call the police, but when she picked up the phone there was no dial tone. She reached for the light switch but when she flicked it, it was still dark. She could make out a shadow going into the nursery. She crept into the kitchen and unexpectedly felt someone behind her.

"Avis!" She turned and screamed.

"Guess again, bitch!" the figure said, lunging at her. She grabbed the attacker's arms as they reached for her and flung them away. She tried to run toward the bedroom but felt hands around her neck. They were strong and forceful. Kayla knew that this was not the same person she had fought with a week ago. She struggled to get out of the grip, but couldn't. She reached for the knife set that she kept on the counter, but her assailant flung her the other way. "Trust me." God's words rang in her head. Thinking quickly, Kayla kneed her perpetrator in the groin. The attacker bent over in pain and Kayla grabbed the butcher knife. Her enemy grabbed another weapon and they charged at each other. Kayla felt the piercing heat of the blade as it penetrated her chest. But she was not to be outdone. She forced the knife into the attacker's body as hard as she could. They screamed simultaneously and Kayla began kicking and stabbing at the same time. As her knee connected with the body, she realized that it was a woman. She fought with everything she had until the shadow fell before her. As she realized who had attempted to take her life, Kayla passed out on the floor.

35

"Dawg, you gonna be all right. Hold on." Kayla could hear Terrell in the distance. He seemed so far away. Kayla could not breathe. She tried and tried, but she could not get any air into her body.

"Her lung has collapsed," she heard someone saying. "Get her to the hospital, now!"

Kayla decided not to struggle to breathe any more. *God, I am trusting You. I need You to breathe for me because I can't.* She closed her eyes and suddenly she could breathe. She thought about her beautiful daughter and her parents, she thought about her friends and coworkers. She thought about Craig and Avis and Geno. All the things in life she had accomplished and the goals she still had. She reflected on her drama-filled life and the lives of those around her. She was grateful. Grateful for the strength and tenacity to stand when others couldn't, and to try again when she failed. Come what may, Kayla loved her life and wasn't ready to give it up. *Okay God, I think I'm ready to breathe now.* She opened her eyes and focused on where she was. She knew she was in the hospital, that was a given. She looked over and saw her mother sleeping in the chair.

"Ma . . ." She tried to speak but there was a tube down her throat. She hit the side of the bed rail to wake her mother.

"Oh my God, Kayla. Wait a minute, I'll get the nurse." Her mother rushed out of the room and returned with the nurse. The nurse took her vitals and then told her to blow so the tube could come out. Kayla obeyed and blew as the nurse pulled the long, plastic tubing out of her mouth. She went into a coughing frenzy and they gave her some water.

"Are you okay?" the nurse asked after Kayla was calm.

"Yeah," she whispered. "What happened?"

"You were attacked, baby. But you're gonna be okay," her mother said with tears in her eyes.

"Day?"

"Day is fine. She's with your father. I need to call him."

"Tired." Kayla shook her head and closed her eyes again. This time when she woke up, Terrell was sitting where her mother last was.

"Yo, you finally up?" He smiled. She nodded at him. Her memory was much clearer now. She remembered hearing his voice in her kitchen and him picking her up off the floor. She could hear him calling 911 and giving her address.

"Thank you. How did you find me?"

"I rode by your house after I finished handling my business. I saw your car was all messed up and your door was open. Your neighbors were standing outside like they were scared to come in, so I did. I found you and old girl on the floor." He gave her the details from his viewpoint. "You got her pretty good, yo. I'm proud of you."

"Where is she?"

"Still in ICU. They're gonna transport her to county jail soon as she's well enough."

"I still don't understand why she did it." Kayla told him.

"Well, from what I understand, your boy told her he didn't love her and broke off the engagement. He admitted he was still in love and wanted to be with you and Day. She flipped."

Kayla tried to figure out what Terrell was telling her. "Janice? Janice did this?"

"Yep. But get this. Remember your prank calls?"

"Her?"

"Yep." He nodded.

"But how did she get my number or even my address?"

"Anjelica. She gave up everything to her. She set you up," he said. As much as Kayla disliked her sister, she was still hurt by Anjelica's vindictiveness. "I'm sorry, dawg."

"Not your fault," Kayla said with tears in her eyes. "Thank you. Have you seen Day?"

"Yeah, she's out there with her father. Let me get her." He winked at Kayla and left before she could stop him. She still had not told him about what she overheard on the phone and she didn't want to see Craig.

"Hey, beautiful," the deep voice said, and Kayla closed her eyes. As she opened them, she smiled. She saw Geno standing next to her bed, holding her beautiful daughter. "You ready to come home?"

"Geno. Terrell told me Craig was out there."

"Would you rather see him than me? 'Cause me and Day can leave." He smiled as he walked over to her bed. Kayla pushed the button and the bed raised to a sitting position.

"Quit playing. Bring my baby here. Hi, sweetheart." Kayla took Day into her arms and lay her across her chest, disregarding the pain she felt from her stitches. She kissed and nuzzled the infant against her cheeks.

"She missed you, Kay. How're you feeling?"

"All right. I still can't believe what happened. I hate Anjelica. I don't care if she is my sister. The sad part is that as much as I hate her, I would never do to her what she has done to me." Kayla felt the tears as they ran down her cheek.

"It's okay, Kayla. Please don't cry, baby. This is as much my fault as it is hers. I should have been up front with Janice from the jump. I knew I was still in love with you and couldn't marry her."

Kayla was still stunned by the fact that Janice tried to kill her.

"Then why did you buy her a ring, Geno?" Kayla looked at him, waiting for an explanation.

"I didn't buy her a ring, Kayla. She started talking about getting married after Thanksgiving and then began wearing her grandmother's wedding ring. I never even asked her to marry me. But I never told her I wasn't gonna marry her, either. I just let her think I would because I didn't want the confrontation."

"You never proposed?" Kayla was secretly pleased.

She wanted to be the only one Geno ever asked to marry.

"I've only proposed to one woman, Kayla. The one I'm in love with." He touched her forehead and she closed her eyes. She could smell his cologne and wanted to be in his arms again, but she knew this wasn't the time.

"Am I interrupting?"

Kayla opened her eyes and looked over in the doorway. Craig was sitting in a wheelchair.

"What do you want?" she asked him. After all she had been through, she still remembered overhearing his telephone conversation with Avis. He was the last person she wanted to see. Geno stood protectively by her side.

"They told me you were conscious. I had to make sure you were okay." He proceeded to roll into her room.

"I'm fine. Geno, can you excuse us for a moment?"

"Sure thing, Kay. You want me to take Day?" he asked her, rubbing the baby's back. Craig did not look thrilled.

"No, she's fine. This'll only take a few moments." Her eyes never left Craig. She was ready to set his lying ass straight. She was never one to be made a fool of.

"I'll be right outside." He nodded.

"Kayla, I'm so glad you're okay, baby. I can't believe that nigga. His girl stabbed you and he got the nerve to be up in here, wit' my baby? He better be glad I'm in this wheelchair." Craig rolled over to her bed and grabbed her hand. Kayla snatched it away quickly.

"Don't touch me!"

"What the hell is wrong wit' you, Kayla? Shit was all good between us, and now you trying to act brand new. What's wit' this change of attitude?" He frowned at her. This was not the way he thought this was gonna work out and she knew it.

"Where's your wife?"

"What? You know me and her ain't . . ."

"Don't lie to me. I am so sick and tired of your lying that I don't know what the hell to do. I heard you talking to her on the phone, Craig. I heard everything. Everything!" Kayla felt her voice getting louder as she talked. "You no good, dope dealing, cheating mothafucka. Well, you know what? You can go to hell and take your fat ass wife wit' you. I don't need you and neither does my daughter."

"Hold up, Kayla. I was trying to keep her calm. I would say anything so she would leave us alone. Don't you see that? It wasn't you I was lying to, it was her."

"I don't give a damn. Get the hell out! The next time I see you will be before a judge," Kayla told him. He had a look of defeat on his face. The door was pushed open and Geno stuck his head in.

"Everything okay, Kayla?"

"I'm leaving, man. Just know that this ain't the last of this bullshit, Kayla. All I wanted was for us to be a family and to do right. But you so stuck under this mothafucka that you can't see that. It's all good, though. You do what you gotta do and I'ma do the same. Believe that."

"You threatening me, Craig?" Kayla's nostrils flared in anger. Craig didn't answer her. He just touched Day's arm and wheeled himself out of the room. Kayla knew there was something to what he said, but she was determined to not let it bother her. Craig was so full of it, she didn't know when to take him seriously. She could only hope that this was one of those times he was just talking.

"So, now what?" Geno looked at her. Kayla really didn't have an answer for him. She knew she loved him, but could she really trust him? She looked down at her sleeping daughter and was grateful for her. She recalled what the spirit had told her the night she was stabbed. *Trust me.*

"Now we move forward," she told him.

"Together?" he asked her, hopefully. To make sure she knew what he meant, he got on one knee next to her bedside. "I love you, Kayla. I love Day. I want us to be together.

"You begging?"

"Kayla," he said threateningly.

"I'm just asking. Day and I want to know. Are you begging?"

"I'm begging," he answered and kissed her fully. She looked down at her squirming daughter and saw that she was smiling.

36

It was a week before the wedding and Kayla was too excited to breathe. She had checked and double-checked everything. Things were going perfect, too perfect. That was what worried her. She and her bridesmaids were meeting at the boutique for their final fitting. As she pulled into the parking lot, she had the feeling that she had forgotten something.

"My shoes," she said out loud. She quickly made a U-turn and headed out of the parking lot, stopping when she spotted Roni and Tia pulling into the lot. She pulled beside them, rolled down her window and told them, "I forgot my shoes."

"I'm not surprised," Roni said.

"I'll be right back. They're right by the door at home," she said. "Hurry up. I gotta meet Theo later," Tia warned. "I will." Kayla sped down the street and made it home in a record ten minutes. She quickly hopped out of the car and went inside. She could hear Geno talking to someone on the phone and walked into the bedroom where he was. His back was to the door and he hadn't heard her come in.

"No, I'll tell her. It's okay. I know. We'll be there as soon as we can. Okay, good-bye."

"Who was that?" she asked as she walked behind him and put her arms around his waist. He jumped because she had startled him.

"Damn, Kay. You scared me." He looked at her and took her into his arms. She could tell something was not right by the look on his face.

"What's wrong?"

"Sit down, Kayla. I gotta tell you something." He motioned for her to sit on the side of the bed, his eyes never leaving hers.

"What's wrong, Geno? Did you forget to take the check to the limo company? I told you to drop it off last week or they wouldn't be able to hold the limo. You know . . ."

"Kayla, that was your Aunt Lorrene."

"What did she want? I know she ain't tryin' to bring a whole bunch of people to the wedding." Kayla smiled, but Geno didn't smile back. She knew this was more serious than the limo or the guest list. "What's wrong, Geno?"

"Kayla, she called for your parents. Anjelica . . ."

"I don't want to hear about it. I don't give a damn who calls, she is not to come to my wedding. I never want to see or talk to her again. That's final." Kayla went to get up but Geno stopped her.

"Kayla, that's not what she was calling about. Baby, Anjelica's dead." His head fell and he looked down as he said the words. They sounded so final.

"What?" Kayla was confused. She began to gasp in small breaths as she tried to think. Maybe she didn't understand what Geno was saying. "What did you say?"

"Baby, Anjelica's dead. They found her body a few hours ago in her apartment." Geno looked at Kayla. She had the strangest look that he had ever seen.

"No, she's not. This is just another one of her stunts she's pulling to get some attention. This is her way of spoiling my wedding next weekend," she assured him. She tried to breathe, but could only gasp.

"Baby, she committed suicide. We need to get to your parents' house as soon as possible."

"She's really dead?" Kayla asked. Geno only nodded. She began to shake her head and he pulled her to him. She buried her face into his chest and cried, "No!"

On the day they were supposed to wed, Kayla buried her sister. The church was filled to capacity for what was scheduled to be a momentous occasion, but was now one of tragedy. As she sat on the front pew beside her parents and her fiancé, Kayla looked at the ivory casket that stood where she was supposed to be standing to say "I do." Her mind was filled with memories of growing up with Anjelica. Kayla tried to remember only the good times, but they were few and far between. After the choir sang and the minister gave *a moving eulogy, the casket was reopened for the family and friends to give their last good-byes. People hugged Kayla and her family after they had their last viewing. Anjelica looked beautiful in a gold, Oriental style dress, holding a red rose.*

Finally, it was time for Kayla to say good-bye. Slowly, she walked to her sister's casket, escorted by Geno. She leaned in and gave her a kiss on her cold cheek, whispering "I love you" as the tears streamed down her cheeks. As she took her seat, Craig came down the aisle, holding another rose. He walked up to the casket and placed the flower next to Anjelica's sleeplike body. After he paid his respects to Kayla's parents, he walked up to Geno and whispered loud enough so that Kayla could hear what he had to say.

"You ain't the only one that had both of them, player!"

37

Terrell rolled over and grabbed the ringing phone off the nightstand. He thought he was dreaming when it first rang, so he ignored it. Whoever was on the other end was persistent and determined to talk to him, so the ringing continued, letting him know that this was indeed reality.

"Yeah," he whispered into the receiver. He cleared his throat as he fought off the grogginess of sleep. "Terrell," the small voice came through the phone, "I'm sorry it's late."

"It's a'ight. You have that dream again?"

"Yeah, they're getting worse. This time she killed herself and Craig showed up at the funeral." Terrell rolled onto his back, listening as she talked. "In the dream, he told Geno he slept with her too. You think that happened for real?"

"I doubt that seriously," he laughed.

"It's not funny, Terrell. Look, I know you're 'sleep. I got a little freaked out, that's all." Kayla sighed.

"Have you talked to her?"

"Who?"

"Your sister. Isn't that who we're talking about?"

"Hell no! What am I gonna talk to her about? The drama she's caused? I ain't got no words for her."

"You need to talk to her, Kay. The dreams ain't gonna stop until y'all squash this and you find out what happened. Why or *if* she even caused all that stuff."

"I told you I have no words for her," Kayla restated. He knew that she wasn't changing her mind and he didn't feel like arguing, so he decided not to press the issue.

"You home by yourself?"

"Yeah, I mean Day is here with me," she said, referring to Terrell's six-month-old goddaughter. "Is Nicole there with you?"

"Naw, she's at her own crib."

"You decide what you're gonna do yet?"

"No, not yet. I got something else I got to take care of first."

"I hope that something is named Darla. I can't believe you slept with that shank. Are you at least gonna tell Nicole?"

"Look, I thought you called to talk about your nightmare."

"Well, now the convo has turned to your nightmare," she replied, voice dripping with condescension. Terrell knew it was time to end this conversation. He was not in the mood to discuss his multitude of problems, especially at 3:00 in the morning.

"A'ight, Kay. I'm hanging up now."

"I'll talk to you tomorrow, Terrell."

Hanging up the phone, he folded his arms over his face. He loved Kayla to death, but sometimes she seemed like a thorn in his side when she tried to be all up in his business. He didn't need her reminding him about his issues; they were ever present in his mind. *Darla.* He didn't even want to think about the fact that he had ever slept with her, but now it was evident because she was pregnant.

Then there was Nicole. There was no doubt that he loved her. She was beautiful, intelligent, funny, and ambitious—everything he desired in a woman. Possibly, wife material. Now, he had jeopardized all of that in a stupid moment of weakness. He could kill himself every time he thought about that night when he left the club. It wasn't even that memorable, but he was drunk and Nicole wasn't up for company. Darla, on the other hand, welcomed him with open arms, breakfast on the table, some bomb-ass Kool-Aid and a warm bed. What more could a man ask for? *How about a condom, stupid? But you didn't use one, and now she's pregnant, pregnant, pregnant.* The words had seemed to echo when they came from her mouth. He thought she had to be joking. There was no way she could be pregnant, especially since Nicole had just told him the exact same thing three hours earlier.

It was amazing how differently he felt when both women told him the same news. With Nicole, it was unexpected but still came with a sense of joy. With Darla, he felt as if he had just been handed a death sentence for a crime he didn't commit. Darla was threatening him with suicide because according to her, he broke her heart. Nicole was hell bent on him committing to her, which he planned to do, but he wanted to be sure. The stress of both women carrying his seed began to take a toll on him and he became frustrated with everyone around him.

Last night, he needed some chill time by himself. Avoiding both women, he drove around until he found himself at Floyd's, a small jazz bar he frequented when he wanted to disappear. A couple rounds of drinks, a few turns on the dance floor, a little small talk and he was ready to leave. He hadn't left alone.

"Was that her?"

Terrell turned to face the woman who was stirring next to him. "Who?"

"Your soon-to-be fiancée."

"No." He reached over and touched the naked shoulder. The glow from the streetlight came streaming in, casting shadows on the wall.

"Who was it?"

"None of your business." He pulled on the thick covers, revealing the contour of the naked body, and snuggled closer.

"Well, then it must have been Ms. Kayla."

"Whatever," he said, caressing the smooth skin with his fingers.

"Come on. Tell me what's going on now."

Terrell felt the hand moving higher up his thigh. "Nothing. She's just having these nightmares."

"Aw, poor baby."

"Let it go," he groaned.

"Oh, so you want me to let it go?" The hands teased between his legs.

"You know what I mean."

"No, tell me what you mean.

"I mean you and your sister need to squash the nonsense." Terrell pulled the firm body onto his and kissed Anjelica full on the mouth before she could say anything else. He felt her placing the condom on and as she mounted him, all thoughts of Nicole, Darla, and Kayla immediately vanished. Moments like this made him realize maybe he wasn't ready to settle down. *So many women, not enough time.*

38

Terrell sat in his Camry and watched as the rain fell on the windshield. As much as he loved the rain, he hated driving in it. He flipped the switch to turn on his wipers. For a moment, they swished back and forth to the same beat that Biggie was rapping to. He turned up the volume and nodded his head to the notorious one asking why she had to stick him for his paper. It was just the song he needed to put him in the right frame of mind for what he was about to do. He had told himself that no matter what, he would remain calm.

He pulled his cell phone out of his pocket and dialed the numbers as he pulled in front of the apartment building. She answered on the first ring.

"Yo, come out here for a minute. I need to talk to you." He knew he sounded cold, but he wanted to get this over with.

"Why can't you come in? It's raining."

"And what, you gon' melt? Come out here. And hurry up 'cause I gotta go to work." He hung up the phone and leaned back on the headrest. A few moments later, she came outside and walked to the car.

"Hey, baby." She smiled and tried to lean over to kiss him. He put his hand up to let her know that it wasn't happening. He noticed the look of disappointment on her face but disregarded it.

"Look, we gotta take care of this situation before it gets any further. You know what I'm saying?"

"I don't wanna handle it, Terry. I love you and I wanna have our baby."

"Darla, don't be crazy. There is no way that I can have a kid with you. I don't want a kid with you. It ain't happening."

"So, what do you want me to do, kill it? Kill our baby?"

"Be realistic. You already got two kids that you're barely taking care of now. You don't even have a steady job. Does it even make sense for you to have another kid? Come on. You and I aren't even all that tight." He looked over at the heavy woman with fair skin. Her long hair fell around her chubby face. "I mean, we cool and everything, but Darla, I don't love you."

"So, you do want me to kill our baby," she sighed.

He could tell that she was hurt, but Terrell didn't respond. They sat in silence with only the sound of the rubber blades whisking the raindrops off the heavy glass he was staring out of. He watched as the city bus stopped and an older woman with two small boys got off. They all held hands as they ran into the building next door. For some reason, it made him think of his own brother, Toby, and how their mom worked hard as a single parent.

"I'm telling you to be smart." He reached into his pocket and pulled out the card that he picked up earlier. "I made you an appointment for nine in the morning."

"Huh?" She looked up at him, confused.

"I'll pick you up at eight fifteen. I'm sorry that this all happened the way it did. You're a sweet girl, and—" The sound of his cell phone interrupted him. He looked at the caller ID and saw that it was Nicole. He sent the call to his voice mail.

"I'll be ready." Darla wiped the tears from her eyes as she opened the door and got out.

Terrell breathed a sigh of relief as he watched her slowly walk back to the building. It had gone better than he had expected. From the way Darla had been acting over the phone, he anticipated a teary-eyed, scream-filled temper tantrum.

He listened to the message Nicole left, telling him that she loved him and asking him to call her later. He reached into the back seat and grabbed his CD case. Finding the disc he was looking for, he pumped the volume as Jodeci sang "Forever My Lady." *Things may work out after all,* he thought.

39

"What are you trying to say, Roni?"

"I ain't trying to say nothing. What I'm saying is that your brother got set up. Darla couldn't get you, so she went after Terry. Now she's pregnant. That means she'll be tied to both of you," Veronica called out from the bedroom where she was getting dressed.

Toby checked the clock on the stove to make sure she wasn't running late for work. He knew she didn't intend on spending the night at his place last night, but as usual, he convinced her that it was too late for her to drive back to her apartment. He grabbed a dozen eggs out of the fridge and started preparing one of his famous omelets he knew she enjoyed. The sounds of his morning mix, which was aired on the local radio show, drifted from the other room.

"She ain't gonna be tied to me. It ain't my kid!"

"But it'll be your niece or nephew, Uncle Toby."

"If you think for one moment that Terry is gonna let her have his kid, then you're crazy. Hundred dollar bet it never happens. You want bacon or sausage?"

"Sausage. And it's not his decision; it's hers. Nasty, she's just nasty. I can't believe y'all slept with her. Both of y'all, at that."

He caught a glimpse of her as she walked past the kitchen and into the den. She had a way of being sexy without trying, and he loved that about her. He continued to spy on her through the breakfast bar which separated the two rooms. She casually sat on the edge of the sofa and placed her black high-heeled shoes on. He loved watching her dress. She stood and pulled her short, black skirt down, adjusting her white blouse. She caught him admiring her and licked her lips seductively then blew him a kiss. He remembered the food on the stove and focused on cooking.

"Hey, you wanna go to Jasper's tonight? They got a new band I wanna check out."

"You mean the infamous DJ Terror doesn't have to work?"

"Nope, not tonight, and I know you're not complaining about me working, Miss I-want-the-wedding-of-the-century."

"Baby, believe me. I ain't complaining about the work. I'm just surprised we can go out on a real date for a change," she said, hugging him from behind.

Toby understood that being engaged to a man who worked almost every night of the week might be a little difficult for Veronica Black. He knew that she was a diva in her own right and liked to be treated as such. Roni enjoyed being wined and dined and shown off by whoever was lucky enough to have her by his side, but between working at the club, radio station, and private parties, Toby really didn't have the quality time that he wanted to spend with his fiancée. He had decided that he better start making time and gotten one of his boys to work his Thursday nights, starting tonight.

"So, does that mean you wanna go?" He flipped the eggs and sausage onto a plate and she grabbed the orange juice out of the fridge.

"Of course. Why wouldn't I?"

"You know how you and your crew make plans. I thought you may have had to call Kayla, Tia, Yvonne, Susie, Cheryl, Margaret . . ." He began counting on his fingers.

"Shut up, Toby. You know that's not true," she giggled. They sat across from each other and bowed their heads as he prayed over the food. They quickly began eating.

"It is true. How many times have I heard 'Me and the girls' or 'Well, the Lonely Hearts Club . . .'"

"They kicked me out of the Lonely Hearts Club, thank you very much." She sighed, batting her eyes at him.

He faked a look of shock. "No. Whatever for?"

"I'm not lonely anymore, I guess."

"You don't sound like that's a good thing." His eyes fell on her empty ring finger and he thought about the black velvet box sitting on the shelf in his closet.

"Tobias Sims, you are the best thing that ever happened to me. Don't ever forget that. Now, I gotta go before I'm late. I love you and I'll call you during lunch." Roni jumped up and kissed him.

He walked her to the front door and helped her put on her blazer. She turned and he looked into her eyes. She was the most beautiful woman he had ever known, and she was perfect for him. He wanted nothing more than to make her happy.

"I love you, Roni Black."

"I love you too, DJ Terror."

She pulled him closer and kissed him full on the mouth. Her tongue teased his bottom lip and he opened wider and savored her taste. He ran his hands along the small of her back and he felt himself becoming aroused as a small moan escaped her throat.

"I gotta go," she said, pulling away.

"I know." He laid his chin on her forehead. "I'll pick you up at six thirty. Be ready."

Roni waved as she backed out of the driveway. His eyes fell on a skateboard lying in the neighbor's yard and he smiled at himself. *Yeah, no doubt I love the hell outta that girl.*

Toby had finished cleaning the kitchen and was about to jump in the shower when the phone rang.

"Yo."

"He wants me to kill our baby," a loud voice wailed in his ear. He knew that Terrell was going to tell her to have an abortion. He also knew that she wouldn't take it very well. Darla wasn't the most mentally stable girl in the club. That was why he always dealt with her in a special manner.

Toby had only slept with Darla twice. The first time, he was in a drunken stupor and she actually had to drive him from a party they both happened to be at. The second was when he had bronchitis and was so doped up on antibiotics and amphetamines he didn't even remember it happening. Funny thing was that both times, Darla swore she was in love with him, like there was a chance in hell he would consider being with her permanently. She was a nice enough girl; she would often come by with groceries for his crib and would clean up if she saw a need, but she definitely wasn't his type. She was his STD—something to do. If he needed something done, he would call her, and she always came through. There were times his utilities would have been turned off if she wouldn't have been on hand to drop off a payment. For that, he was grateful.

His brother, on the other hand, should have known better. Toby couldn't even understand how Terry got himself in this situation. Darla was not the kind of girl you sleep with unprotected. He didn't even want to think about the fact that Terry didn't even care that his own brother had already slept with this girl. He pushed that thought completely out of his mind for fear that it would show that Terry had a lack of loyalty to him. But she wasn't that important, so he wasn't that worried.

He didn't know what to say to her at this point, though. Not that he supported abortion, but this time, one would make sense.

"So, you talked to him?"

"He just left. He made the appointment and everything. He says he's taking me in the morning." She sniffed.

"Damn," was all he could say. He began making up the king-sized bed that he and Roni had just gotten out of.

"What am I gonna do? I don't want to kill our baby."

"But Darla, he doesn't want the baby."

"I want it, though. I love him, Toby. This baby is a gift from God. Are you telling me you don't believe that?"

That question made Toby uncomfortable and he decided that maybe he shouldn't be talking to her about this. "Look, this is a decision between you and my brother. I don't have anything to do with it."

"Talk to him, Toby. This is your blood he's about to get rid of, your niece or nephew."

"I'm sorry. I don't have anything to do with it, Darla."

"The night I told you I was pregnant, you swore you would support me and I was your friend. You lied!" she screamed at him.

"Hold up. I am supporting you. I'm listening to what you got to say. For real, yo, this really ain't even my business. This shit is for you and Terry to figure out. He's a grown man and whatever he wants to do is on him."

"So that's it? That's all you got to say, Toby?"

"That's all I got to say. I wish you the best."

"Thanks for nothing. You ain't shit and neither is your brother. I'm glad I'm getting rid of it. I wouldn't want to be bothered with anything with your blood running through it, you bastard."

Instead of responding, Toby hung the phone up. He knew she was hurt and was speaking out of anger. There really was nothing he could do; the decision wasn't his. One thing he did know was that Terry did have a cursing out coming to him. He called his brother's cell.

"What up, dawg?"

"Man, I don't even wanna know why the hell you slept with her, man. That don't matter. But you ain't use a rubber? I thought I taught you better than that."

"I know, I know. But I got it under control. It'll be taken care of tomorrow."

"Now she blowing up my spot, crying and yelling at me like I'm the one that knocked her up."

"She called you? What she say? She's still going tomorrow, right? Man, tell me you told her to do this."

"I can't tell her what to do, Terry. You think I'ma tell a woman to get rid of a baby I ain't have nothing to do with creating?" Toby thought his brother truly was crazy. He began looking in his closet for something to wear.

"Well, what did you tell her?"

"I told her it was between you and her and I ain't have nothing to do with it."

"And?"

"And what?" Toby was wondering where Terry was going with this line of questioning.

"Did she say she was gonna go tomorrow?"

I should play with his head and make him sweat. "She said she ain't going nowhere except her doctor to get some prenatal vitamins."

"What? Yo, you gotta call her. I can't have no kid with that chick. Man, I'm thinking about asking Nicole to marry me. Look, I gotta tell you something."

"What?"

"Nicole's pregnant."

"Man, do you ever wear a rubber?" He was shocked. He knew that Terry could be out there sometimes, but two girls knocked up at the same time was ridiculous. "You better pray that this Darla thing gets taken care of with the quickness. So, what are you gonna do about Nicole? Same thing?"

"Hell no. You know Nicole ain't trying to have no abortion. And I don't want her to, to be honest. I love her, man. I think I wanna marry her."

"You sure about that, Terry? I don't think you know what you want to do. Marriage ain't nothing to play wit'. You know that. Before you go doing something you know you ain't ready for, you better think and make sure."

"I know I want to take care of this thing with Darla and I wanna marry Nicole and get on with my life. Simple as that."

"Handle your business then. Just be sure. That's all I'm saying."

"I will, Toby. And believe me, this is the last time I'ma get caught up in some drama like this."

"I hope so, Ter. I hope so.

"Man, don't act like you ain't have no drama of your own a little while back."

"It wasn't like this, though." Toby snapped.

"A'ight, bro, I gotta take these calls. Unlike you, some of us have to work a regular gig. We all can't be living the glamorous life, DJ Terror." Terrell said.

"Whateva. Don't forget what I told you. Handle your business."

"See you tonight."

With that being said, Toby showered and dressed quickly. He had a lot to do and only a few hours to get it done.

40

Terrell called Nicole on his first break. She had left a message telling him she had to work a double shift at the hospital and wouldn't be getting off until late. He appreciated the fact that she was such a hard worker. Nicole was a nurse on the labor and delivery floor, and she was also studying to be a certified midwife. He loved an ambitious woman.

"Hi, baby. I got your message," he told her when she answered her phone.

"Hey, I tried to catch you before you got to work." He could hear the hustle and bustle of the nurses' station in the background. "You guys busy?"

"Not really. We got four patients in active labor and three already delivered. It's a regular day, I guess."

"How you feeling?"

"Okay, a little queasy, but that's to be expected. I'm just praying it doesn't get worse."

"I told Toby this morning," he told her.

"What did he say?" she asked after a pause.

"Nothing. He congratulated me," he lied. "So, what time you getting off?"

"I'm trying to leave by seven. Is that gonna be too late?"

"Naw, you should still be good. I'm not gonna be able to pick you up, though, because I gotta get there by eight. You good to drive?"

"Yes, Terry, I can drive." She laughed.

"I'm just making sure. I don't want you having to pull over on the side of the road, throwing up and stuff."

She laughed and told him she was being paged by a patient. "I'll see you later, Terry."

"I love you," he told her.

"Love you too."

He grabbed a drink for himself and Kayla on the way back to his desk.

"Aw, man, what's up with this tea stuff? Can't I get a Pepsi? I'm not pregnant anymore," she whined when he put the can in front of her.

"Did you pay for it?"

"What? You want your fifty-five cents? Now that I think about it, maybe I do need to pay you back. You might need to break off one of your baby mamas." She reached into her desk drawer and plopped three quarters on his desk. "Keep the change."

He rolled her eyes at her, picking up the quarters and putting them in his pocket. "I know you ain't joking, are you? Shall we start naming the issues you got going on right about now? Let's see, should we start with your married baby daddy or the psychotic ex-fiancée of your boyfriend?"

"Oh, so it's like that?" Kayla's eyes widened as she looked around to see if anyone overheard them. "I was just playing with your sensitive ass."

He had unintentionally hit a nerve and he regretted it. Kayla had been through a lot. She was always there for him as a friend. She was the sister he never had.

"I'm sorry, dawg. That was uncalled for. I just got a lot on my mind right now. I got this thing tonight and then Darla is still tripping."

"Does she know about Nicole?"

"Hell no," he shook his head.

His cell began vibrating and he didn't recognize the number. Making sure no supervisors were around, he flipped the phone open and whispered into the receiver. "Hello."

"Hey, big sexy, I just wanted to thank you for a wonderful night."

"Uh, that's cool, man. You good," he answered.

"So, what's up?" Anjelica whispered.

"Chilling at work." He swiveled his chair, turning his back to Kayla, who he knew was eavesdropping. "Yo, look, I'ma hit you back later. Is that cool?"

"Yeah, that's cool. It's no big deal, really. I know you really can't talk. My sister the drama queen is probably right there in your ear anyway. Call me when you get the chance."

"A'ight. Peace."

"Who was that?" Kayla asked, startling him. He turned back around to face her and it was like deja vu from this morning. It was amazing how much the two girls really did look alike. "I hope it wasn't one of your little tricks. You need to start telling them to stop calling. Cut them loose now, Terrell. I'm telling you."

"Can I help it if I'm a pimp?" he joked.

"I thought it was godpimp."

He laughed at Kayla. She was his confidante and he could tell her anything. He even considered telling her about last night, but knowing the hatred the two sisters held for each other, he decided that it definitely wasn't a story to be shared with Kayla. *Not right now, anyway*, he thought. *Soon, but not right now.*

"You and Geno coming tonight?"

"I wouldn't miss this for the world. Roni already called and told me that she was going on a 'real date' for a change, just her and Toby. She has no idea that we're all invited too? How is that gonna work?"

"Toby says he has some kind of master plan. All I know is that everyone is supposed to be there by seven thirty and wait in the lobby." Terrell had been working with his brother to concoct this event for a minute now. Everyone showing up in time seemed to be the only problem they could come up with. That was one of the reasons they told everyone 7:30. The moment wasn't scheduled to take place until after 8:00.

"Is he nervous?"

"About what? He loves that girl. Is she nervous?"

"Please, Roni's ready. You better hope Toby is. You know how his reputation precedes him." Kayla laughed.

"Don't front. Roni ain't nowhere near being Virgin Mary herself."

The two friends spent the remainder of the day going back and forth as they always did. Five thirty came sooner than either one expected, and they headed to the parking lot.

"I'll see you tonight, Kay. I'm praying that y'all be on time."

"We'll be on time, Terrell. You need to be praying that she says yes." Kayla jumped into her car and honked the horn as she pulled out of the parking lot.

41

Toby arrived at Roni's at 6:30 on the dot. He was surprised he hadn't thrown up because his stomach was a ball of knots and he thought he could pass out at any moment. Everything was going perfectly—a little too perfectly.

After leaving the house that morning, he dropped his car off to be detailed then walked two blocks up to get a haircut and a shave. He didn't have to wait to get into a chair and by the time he was finished, his truck was ready. He went to the radio station and mixed his tracks for the morning show, finishing in enough time to run his last minute errands. He accomplished all this without fainting. Now, hopefully the woman he was doing all of this for was ready and waiting like he told her to be.

"I'm almost ready, baby. I promise." She kissed him as she opened the door. "Damn, you look good. Maybe I should change."

"No!" he yelled. Toby knew that if Roni decided to change clothes, it would be a thirty minute wait, at least. "You look perfect."

"You just don't want me to look as GQ as you. That's okay. You look so nice. I love to see you dressed up." Roni ran her hands along the lapel of the dark suit he was wearing. Instead of a tie, he wore a wide-collar shirt with the top buttons undone. He put his hand in his pocket to make sure the ring was still secure.

"Oh, so I don't dress up?"

"You never wear a suit. I don't consider jeans, Timbs and a Sean John shirt dressed up, Toby. I gotta finish touching up my face and then I'll be ready." She disappeared down the hallway, leaving an anxious Toby standing in the living room.

"Are you sure you got permission from your girls to go out tonight?" he called, looking at a picture of Roni and her best friends sitting on the mantle. They were a tight bunch and he knew that tonight was just as important to them as it was her.

"Ha-ha, very funny. I don't need anyone's permission to go out. They were surprised that you didn't have to work tonight, though. Who's deejaying at the club tonight anyway?"

"Um, they're having Oldies but Goodies night on Thursdays now."

"Does that mean you're gonna be off *every* Thursday?"

He knew she would like that idea. He was going to wait and tell her later, but the present seemed as good a time as any. "For a little while, at least."

"And we can go on more dates, like regular people?" Before Toby could answer, her phone rang. "Hello. Hey. Good. Yeah, yeah, uh-huh. Um, sorry. I have plans. Yeah, nice talking to you too. Take care."

Toby fought the urge to ask who it was and what he wanted, although he was curious as hell. From the tone of her voice, he could tell it was a male. She used the throaty laugh that she would use when she was flirting. *Probably nobody. Somebody about work*, he told himself.

After a few moments, she emerged, looking perfect. "See, I told you I was almost ready."

Toby playfully looked at his watch and replied, "Yeah, but you're late and we missed our reservations. We may as well stay here and order pizza."

"Like hell. You'd better stop playing and come on," she said. She grabbed her purse and they were about to leave when the phone rang again.

"Don't answer it. Come on, Ron. We gotta go," he warned.

She checked the caller ID. "It's Ma."

Toby knew this was a call Roni was going to take. Ms. Ernestine could talk a hole in anyone's head and there was no doubt this was gonna take a while. He plopped down on the edge of the sofa. "Shit."

"What's your problem, Toby? It'll only be a minute. Don't get an attitude." She put the phone to her ear and began chatting. "Hey, Ma, what's up? For real? That's great. Well look, Toby and I are walking out the door. No, he got the night off and we're going to Jasper's. I don't know. Let me ask him. Toby, would you mind if Ma joined us?"

Toby looked at Roni without saying a word.

"Tell you what, Ma. How about I take you to Jasper's this weekend, just the two of us? I'll call you later. Love you too. Bye." She tossed the cordless phone on the sofa. "Happy? Now let's go, DJ Grumpy!"

Toby sat and stared at her for a few moments then stood. "You better watch it, girl. You never know when a DJ might change your life."

Jasper's was a premier supper club in the city. It was owned by JJ Sims, Terrell and Toby's uncle. Working there had been the first job that each of the boys had. Both started as busboys, then served as waiters at the restaurant. Toby had even tried his hand at bartending. They got their love of the nightlife from Uncle Jay. Jasper's was home. It was the perfect spot for Toby's plan.

"You're late," Uncle Jay said when they arrived. He greeted Toby and Roni with a hug.

"Hey, Uncle Jay. Take that up with Ms. Black here. I told her be ready by six thirty."

"I was ready, Uncle Jay. Don't listen to him. Besides, you think I haven't learned by now that Toby lies about what time I should be ready? It's ten after seven. I bet our reservations aren't until seven thirty."

"Uh, seven fifteen." The handsome older gentlemen looked at the hostess' book and corrected her.

"And since when do Toby and I need a reservation?" She tapped him on the shoulder.

"You must not've heard that Thursdays are our busiest night now. We got a new group called Liquid and they pack the place every week."

"I doubt if we need a reservation, though. I know if my mother doesn't need a reservation, then we don't." Roni winked.

Toby looked at his uncle, who was now insisting that they be seated. "What is she talking about, Uncle Jay?"

"Nothing, nothing. Come on. I got the best table waiting for you down front." He grabbed two menus and led them to the tables near the front of the stage.

Toby knew they made a stunning couple. As they walked, he placed his hand on the small of Roni's back. He saw people staring at them and he enjoyed the feel of being one of the beautiful people. The waiter had already been advised to take special care of them. They ordered drinks and Toby looked around nervously. The band hadn't started playing yet; a deejay in the corner was playing old school slow jams.

"What's wrong?" Roni frowned.

"Nothing. I'm just checking the place out. So, what's up with your mom and Uncle Jay?"

"I don't know. Every time I talk to Mom, she's always talking about eating here and what a good time she and *JJ* had. How long has he been single?"

"A little while. His wife died about five years ago." Toby sighed. "She was so nice and man, the most beautiful woman I had ever seen in my life. She looked like an angel."

"I thought I was the most beautiful woman you had ever seen. Or was that a lie?" Roni teased. "What happened?"

"She was killed by a drunk driver," Toby said sadly. "Jasper's was closed a long time after that. I was surprised he opened it back up, really. That's when I started deejaying at the club because Jasper's closed. I used to think I would own the place before she passed away. I was on a roll, too. Had worked my way from busboy to manager."

"That still may happen. You never know."

"Nah, Uncle Jay's having too much fun running the place right now, and I got my DJ Terror thing going on."

"That's right, you the man. I forgot." She noticed Toby checking his watch. "Why do you keep checking the time?"

"I thought the band was supposed to start their set at seven thirty and they haven't."

The waiter brought their drinks and appetizers and they talked until their food arrived. Soon, Uncle Jay came to the stage and introduced Liquid. The band consisted of a small brass quartet, a bass player, a drummer, and a talented guy who sang lead and played the keyboard. The evening was beginning to get even better as they enjoyed some of the best music they had heard in a while.

Toby loved being with Roni. She made him laugh and stimulated that part of his brain he had to utilize in order to participate in intelligent conversations. She was the best thing that had happened to him.

The band announced that they would be taking a break as the waiter cleared their dessert plates from the table. The curtains closed around the semi-circular stage and the deejay began playing again.

"They were off the chain," Roni commented as she applauded.

"I told you I heard they were good. I'ma go backstage and holler at Uncle Jay. I think I saw him go back there," he told her as he stood up.

"Go ahead. I need to use the restroom myself."

Toby's heart began racing as she reached for his hand. Her going to the restroom was not in his plans. If she went through the lobby, everything would be ruined. He tried to think quick. "You may want to wait until after the band begins; looks like every woman in here has made a beeline for the bathroom. You know you don't do lines."

Roni nodded as she took her seat. "You're right. I'll wait."

"Be right back," he said with relief. He kissed her on the cheek and hurried toward the back of the stage. Terry was waiting when he got there.

"Everybody here?" he asked his brother, who was looking dapper as ever in a two-piece black linen outfit.

"As far as I know. I came through the back door, though. I saw Tia, Yvonne, and Theo in the parking lot."

"What about Kayla and Geno?"

"I didn't see 'em. I saw a black Maxima, though, but I didn't look at the tag. That may've been her car."

"What time did you tell her to be here?"

"Everyone knew it was going down at eight thirty. Don't worry; she's here. You ready?"

"Yeah, let's just hurry and get it over wit' before I shit on myself."

"I know the cool, calm, collected DJ Terror ain't nervous. Come on, man. You love this girl. She already knows you're gonna marry her. You already told her."

"That's right. Calm your scared ass down and go propose." A deep voice came from behind the two men, causing them to turn around.

"Jermaine! Man, you made it!" Toby ran and hugged him.

"I had to see if you really gonna go do it." The tall, athletic man gripped Toby's hand and smiled. "What's up, Terry? How you been?"

"I've been a'ight, Jermaine," Terry said. "You all moved in?" He was pleased to see his brother's best friend, who was relocating to the area. It would give him someone new to hang out with now that Toby was about to be tied down. Jermaine had always been a suave brother who attracted women like honey to flies. Funny thing was, although they were all dark brothers, growing up, they always teased Jermaine about being blue-black. Toby was the cute, athletic one; Terry was the chubby, smart one; and Jermaine was the quiet, dark one. Needless to say, Toby was always first choice, Jermaine got the second cuts, and Terry got the leftovers. Sometimes, that was a good thing because they seemed to be the most flavorful.

"Well, both my best men are here, so let's go do this!" Toby put his arm around both men and they set off to take their places.

The second time Uncle Jay took the stage to introduce Liquid, Jasper's was standing room only. Toby took several deep breaths and said a small prayer for courage and strength to do what he was about to do. He could see Roni looking around for him as the curtain opened. The audience got quiet as the lights dimmed. Toby began playing the piano softly as he spoke into the microphone.

"Good evening, ladies and gentlemen. Welcome to Jasper's. We certainly hope you're enjoying your evening so far. My name is Tobias Sims, and tonight I will be accompanied by Liquid, along with the help of a few other special people. I have a very special dedication for a very special woman in my life."

"Go on, boy!" someone screamed from the audience.

Toby looked down at Roni, who was sitting with her mouth hanging open. He had never told her he could play the piano or sing, so he knew this was a total shock to her. He licked his lips and winked at her then began to sing the first lines of "Let's Get Married" by Jagged Edge. He saw the tears forming in her eyes and almost didn't make it to the chorus. He was glad to hear Jermaine's and Terry's voices combining with his. The remaining band members soon joined them. Terry stood up from the piano and jumped from the stage, landing in front of their table.

Females began screaming throughout the place as he got down on one knee and took Roni's hand into his. When he reached into his pocket and pulled out the black velvet box and opened it to reveal the three-carat platinum engagement ring, someone yelled, "He got a ring, too!"

"Roni, I love you with all my heart and soul. You are my soul mate, and I want to spend eternity with you. I thank God continually for putting you in my life. I am begging you to be my wife. Will you marry me?"

Tears were streaming down his cheeks as he touched her face, which was drenched with tears as well.

"You go boy!" a male called out.

"Yes! Yes! Yes!" She was finally able to answer between heaves. She pulled him to her and they embraced. The restaurant erupted with applause and Toby pulled her up as the house lights came on. He turned her so she could see all of her friends, as well as her mother, standing around them, crying and clapping. The band began playing "Spend My Life with You" and Uncle Jay ordered a round of champagne for everyone.

"Oh, baby," Ms. Ernestine gushed, wiping her eyes. "I'm so happy for you."

Kayla, Tia, and Yvonne raced to Roni's side, pushing Toby out of the way. He spotted Geno, Jermaine, and Terry at the bar and went over to join them. People came over to congratulate him and wish him luck, and it pleased him that everything worked out exactly as planned.

"That was tight, player!" Terry handed him a drink.

"Tight ain't the word. You know how many numbers I got when I made it offstage? You get much props for this one, T. Next time you wanna propose, I'm definitely down for it." Jermaine smiled. "Know what I mean, Terry?"

"There won't be a next time. And Terry, you better shut up. You need to hurry up and do the same thing so your life can be drama-free like mine."

They were interrupted by the sound of a woman on stage. "Ahem. Good evening. I'd like to send this one out to the happy couple. Congratulations."

She began singing a version of "Inseparable" that would have made Natalie Cole shut up. No one moved as she belted out the powerful notes. They didn't know what was more stunning; her amazing voice or her striking looks. She wasn't very tall, about five-foot-three, but it was enough to carry her curvaceous figure. She sported a sleeveless black top that criss-crossed at her ample cleavage. Her shapely legs extended from her short black skirt, and she wore black strappy heels on her small feet. Her amber skin was flawless, and the wavy texture of her long hair made it apparent that she was of mixed race. She swayed to the music as she sang, and she touched the microphone so seductively that the men were mesmerized as the notes escaped her full, pouty lips. By the time the song ended, everyone was once again on their feet, applauding.

"Bro, looks to me like your drama is just beginning," Terry said, leaning on the bar.

"No doubt about that," Jermaine said as he watched someone help the gorgeous woman from the stage. "That's a definite."

42

"Roni should definitely get that girl to sing at the wedding," Nicole said as she walked up to Terrell and put her arms around him. "Hey, baby. You made it. How long you been here?"

"Long enough to see my baby daddy sing. That was awesome. Toby, that was the best proposal I have ever seen in my life."

"Thanks, Nicole. You know I tried to come up with something to impress Veronica Black."

"Well, I think you impressed everyone here. Between your proposal and that girl singing, you all are making Jasper's the spot to be tonight."

"Jasper's is the spot to be any night," Uncle Jay said, joining them. "Toby, that was wonderful."

"Uncle Jay," Toby hugged his uncle, "I appreciate you helping me set this up."

"Tobias, I am so proud of you," his uncle told him. "You Sims boys are something else, I tell you."

"That they are."

Everyone turned to see Darla standing before them. Terrell and Toby looked at each other, neither one saying a word. She walked past them then turned and gave Terrell an evil look, adding, "I'm sure you'll make a great husband and *father,* too, Toby."

"Uh, thanks, uh. . . Darla," Toby stuttered. She turned and walked away, relieving the stressed men. Toby rolled his eyes at his brother, who just shrugged and shook his head.

"And that was so nice of Isis to come and sing, too. When did she get to town?" Jermaine picked up the conversation where it left off.

"You know her? She was awesome. Isis, that's the perfect name for her," Nicole said.

"Yeah, she's an old friend." Jermaine smiled.

Toby didn't find anything funny about the situation. A million questions filled his mind as his eyes scanned the crowded club.

"You looking for me?"

"You know I was. I need my fiancée by my side at all times," he answered Roni and kissed her. "You happy?"

"Um, let me think." She pretended to be deep in thought, then she looked deep into his eyes and told him, "I am beyond happy. I was happy from the day we met at your house last Fourth of July. Tonight, I think I'm more like ecstatic. I love you."

"I love you too, Toby," Ms. Ernestine interrupted. "You like the way I called as y'all were walking out the door? I added that for dramatic element."

"Gee, thanks, Ms. Ernestine. I appreciate your help in adding to my nervousness," he replied to his future mother-in-law.

"You were nervous, baby?" Roni tilted her head as she smiled at him. "I couldn't tell."

"That's 'cause I'm cool like that."

Surrounded by his family and friends, Toby tried to laugh and enjoy himself, suppressing the urge to walk around the club and find the cause of his distraction. After a while, Jermaine came over and whispered, "She's gone, man. She sang and she's out."

That being said, Toby reached in his pocket, passed his keys to his best friend, and told him, "Crash at my crib. I won't be using it tonight."

"Cool."

Kayla gave him the signal and he announced, "Well, I just want to thank all of you for making tonight a success. Roni and I love and appreciate you. And on that note, we are outta here."

He grabbed Roni's hand and led her through the crowd, followed by their small entourage. She squealed when they walked outside and saw the black limousine waiting for them. Everyone clapped and waved good-bye as the driver opened the door for them.

"Congratulations, DJ T," the driver said as Toby gave him a pound with his fist.

"Thanks, man." Toby laughed.

Roni took in the opulence of the leather interior, smiling as she sat back in the soft seats. "Toby, now you know you didn't have to do this," she said as he took his place beside her and pulled her close.

"This is nothing," he said and reached behind the seat, pulling out a long box and placing it on her lap. She opened it and smiled at the dozen long-stemmed white roses inside.

"Thank you," she said, kissing him full on the mouth. She loved the way he would caress her tongue with his, gently sucking it. Toby always felt that you could tell a lot from the way a woman kissed. He believed that if she had skills in kissing, she usually had skills in other sensual areas, too. And Roni definitely had skills.

He stroked her neck as she helped him out of his jacket and leaned back onto the seat. He cupped her full, double-D breasts in his hands and heard her moan as his fingers brushed across her nipples. Then, out of nowhere, music started playing. Her eyes flicked open.

"It's just the radio." Toby smiled and began sucking on her neck. Roni ran her hands across his smooth, bald head, savoring the moment. "You like that?" Toby asked.

"Mm-hmm," Roni managed to murmur. He loved making her sound like that.

Her hands found their way under his shirt and she let her fingers play with his nipples. He groaned as she licked along his earlobe. Just as things were getting to the point that he knew she could take no more, the car came to a stop and they heard the front door open.

"I think we've arrived at our destination," Toby whispered.

"And where is that?" she asked, readjusting her dress as she looked out the window.

"We are at the royal palace," he answered, helping her out of the limousine. She realized that they were in front of the Majestic, one of the largest, most lavish hotels in the city. The concierge held the door as they entered the massive archway leading to the lobby. She expected Toby to go to the desk, but there was no need. He waved to the front clerk as they passed by.

"Toby," she started as they got into the glass elevator and he pushed the number twenty-two. He kissed her again, distracting her from any other thoughts she could have had regarding what was going on. When the car stopped on the designated floor, he bowed as he stepped off the elevator and reached for her hand. She decided to play along and curtseyed. They embraced each other as they proceeded down the empty hallway. When they got to the room, he asked her to wait a minute. "I'll be right back." She frowned but nodded.

He slipped into the room knowing she wondered what he was doing. After everything else that had gone on that night, she wouldn't know what to expect. He looked around the room and made sure everything was set. Kayla hooked the room up for him. *I owe her big time*, he thought as he made the final preparations. Turning the knob slowly and opening the door, he welcomed Roni in. She was hesitant.

"Come on," he told her. "I promise I won't bite."

"Promises, promises," she grinned.

Roni was dumbfounded when she walked in. Toby had not only reserved a room, but a full suite with a Jacuzzi in the center. There were white candles and rose petals arranged around the jetted tub. She spotted a bowl of fruit and a chilling bottle of wine along with a set of glasses on a tray near the steaming water. Prince was drifting from a nearby CD player.

"I love you, Veronica Black," he whispered and hugged her from behind. He kissed the ring she was now wearing then put her entire finger in his mouth, sucking gently. He guided her to the mirror hanging on the wall and he stared at their reflection. They made a perfect couple.

She turned and kissed him with such passion that it scared him. Toby could not remember a time when he had put so much thought and effort into planning anything. Between the passion of the moment and the alcohol they had already consumed, he was now drunk with happiness. Before he knew it, she was naked in his arms and he was carrying her to the hot tub. He removed his clothes with a quickness and lowered his body into the steaming water.

"You are so beautiful, do you know that?" he asked as he fed her a ripe strawberry. She bit into it, juice dribbling from the side of her mouth. Toby leaned over and licked it off, nibbling from her lips down to her collarbone. With a quick movement, he sat her in his lap, and she threw her head back as he kissed across her chest. He buried his head into her shoulder, moaning as the bubbles enticed both of them.

Roni reached for a glass of wine, pouring it over his head, then used her tongue to catch the cascading liquid as it made its way from his head to his chest. His strong hands searched between her legs, and she tensed as his fingers found the spot they were looking for. She closed her eyes and became lost in the moment. It was as if he had found a rhythm and was playing a melody. She looked at him as her hands now found the treasure she was looking for. Her fingers massaged him in the same cadence that he played. She stared into his dark eyes, letting him know that she was not going to lose control; she was too much of a woman for that. He could tell that the intensity aroused her, and they played the duet together until neither one could take it anymore.

He didn't say anything as he stood and reached for her once again. She stood and he helped her out. Lifting her once again, he carried her into the enormous bedroom of the suite. He laid her in the middle of the bed, and for a moment, just looked at her. He pushed her legs open and began playing the tune again, this time using his tongue rather than his fingers. Roni bucked like she was losing her mind; Toby seemed determined to have her go crazy. She called his name over and over as her body shook with ecstasy. When he felt she was satisfied, he smiled.

"Having fun?" he asked. She nodded at him then began laughing uncontrollably. "What's so funny?"

She licked her lips seductively, smiling at him. "I'm just happy."

He joined in her laughter and she pulled him to her. He laid his head on her chest and began playing with her nipples. She knew what was next and she was more than ready.

"I know you came prepared," she whispered.

He nodded and reached for the condoms he had placed in the nightstand drawer. Roni was a stickler for safe sex, and he respected her for that. A lot of people, his brother included, didn't practice it very often. She took the plastic from his hand and tore it open with her mouth. Her eyes never left his as she rolled it on him. Then, like a graceful jockey, she straddled him and began to ride like he was a thoroughbred stallion. He buried his head into her ample breast as he thrust into her welcoming body. He gripped her strong thighs and his arms found their way to her firm behind. As if on cue, she leaned back and looked into his eyes, rocking faster and faster. She stared at him, his name escaping her mouth as she cried out.

"Toby. . . I . . . I . . . Yes, that's it!"

"Is that it?"

"God . . . yes . . ."

"Tell me."

"That's it," she moaned, rocking continually.

"And what is it?" He smiled at her, gripping her harder.

"It's . . . it's . . ." She could hardly talk.

"Huh?" He had her right where he wanted her. He was about to explode but was determined to make her talk.

"It's . . . yours. Toby . . . it's yours, baby!" she screamed, leaning forward and grabbing his shoulders.

"Show me, then." He reached up and pulled her so that her hair hung into his face. "Come for me, Roni! Now!"

He felt the tension that had built up in the moment release from deep within and explode from his body. Roni called his name over and over and he felt her legs begin shaking. Then, it was over. She collapsed on his sweat-covered chest and he kissed the top of her head.

"Damn, that was the best ever," she said as she panted.

"All that for putting a ring on your finger?" he teased, wrapping her hair around his finger.

"All that for being the love of my life." She kissed him.

Something about the way she said it bothered him. For a moment, it felt like deja vu, only it wasn't with Roni in the dream he had, it was with another beautiful woman who in the end had run away, taking his heart with her. That was two years ago, and he hadn't even thought of her in months, until she showed up again tonight, singing on stage.

43

"Where you going? I thought you were taking the day off," Nicole said sleepily.

Terrell leaned over and kissed her forehead. He had hoped she would still be asleep when he left, but that wasn't the case. "I got some stuff I gotta take care of this morning."

"What kind of stuff?"

"I'm taking my car to be serviced this morning."

"I can trail you and you can use my car if you want. That way you don't have to wait."

"That's okay. Stay in the bed."

"But you know we're supposed to—"

"I know. I'll be there at quarter to twelve. Promise."

He kissed her again and she reminded him to lock the door when he left. He hurried out to be sure he wasn't late picking up Darla. She was waiting when he got to her place and got into the car without saying a word.

"Hey," he told her.

"I'm moving and I need you to give me some money," she said, not looking at him.

He inhaled deeply, wondering where she was going with this. Her moving might be a good thing. That meant there was no way she could pull a stunt like she did last night or the several other times when she would just pop up at Toby's crib or the club.

"I feel you. When you trying to make this move?"

"Soon as possible. I already started packing. I need the loot, though."

He wanted to tell her that he was already paying for the abortion and didn't think he should have to pay her anything, but decided to chill for right now. "I don't have a problem helping you out."

It was a beautiful March morning and it seemed as if everyone was in a mellow mood. The weather was just about to break; not too cold, but not yet spring. Terrell noticed smiles on people's faces as he drove down the street, like they didn't have a care in the world. He, on the other hand, had the weight of the world on his shoulders, and was doing everything in his power to get rid of it, starting with Darla and this baby. *Which might not even be mine.* But he wasn't even taking the chance. The sooner he got rid of this baby, the better. *And now it looks like I'm gonna be getting rid of Darla, period. Hell, I betcha Toby will be glad to hear her whining ass will be long gone. She was always trying to pop up at his crib uninvited.*

Strangely enough, she didn't say anything the entire drive to the clinic. He was expecting an emotional temper tantrum, with her trying to convince him that this was a mistake, but she sat quietly looking out the window. He assumed she just didn't want to talk, so he turned the radio up and listened to Doug Banks. There was a radio advertisement promoting Dominic's nightclub featuring DJ Terror, and he smiled. He could remember a time when Toby would get in trouble for scratching up their parents' Kool and the Gang albums when they were little. After seeing *Beatstreet,* Toby was fascinated by deejays and determined to learn it like it was a science. Now, it seemed the beatings and practice had paid off because Toby's career was successful. Terrell was proud of his older brother; there was no doubt about that. He had the crib, the career and now, the girl. He looked over at Darla and decided, *I'm getting my life together too. I ain't going through this shit no more. She ain't even worth the gas I'm burning bringing her here.*

He pulled into the lot and parked on the side of the building rather than the front. It was then that Darla decided to speak.

"Good thinking. You wouldn't want anyone to spot your car outside the abortion clinic, right?"

He didn't respond verbally, but cut his eyes at her as he got out of his car. He walked ahead of her and went straight to the receptionist's desk, giving her Darla's name.

"Yes, sir, if you could just have her fill these forms out, someone will be with you in just a moment," the attractive woman told him in a sexy voice. She was a seductive blonde with an olive complexion, reminding him of one of the women from the TV show *Friends*. Terrell usually didn't go for women outside his race, but there was something charming about her that added to her appeal.

"Thanks. Do you know how long this is gonna take?" he asked.

"I'm not sure. It depends on a number of things." She shrugged.

"I understand. Look, can I go ahead and pay and then come back and get her?"

"We recommend you stay here with her, at least until after you speak with a counselor."

"Counselor? For what?" There was no way Terrell was going to talk to a counselor. This thing was getting more complicated than he anticipated. He had planned on dropping Darla off, paying, leaving, then picking her up and taking her ass home.

"So that you both understand your options."

"Is that really necessary? I mean, we've already discussed it and weighed our options. We've made our decision."

"Well, it's not a requirement or anything." She looked toward Darla sympathetically, then back to Terrell, who was pulling his wallet from his pocket. He had stopped at the ATM before he picked up Darla.

"Good. The lady I talked to yesterday said it was gonna be three-fifty. This should take care of it."

She took the money from him and gave him a receipt. "Come back around two."

"Cool," he said, thanking her. He turned and walked over to Darla, handing her the papers to complete. "Yo, you need to fill these out and they'll call your name. I'll be back to get you."

She took the papers without a word. He turned back and waved to the receptionist.

He began driving around, thinking of what he could do to waste time. He had taken the day off but didn't feel like going to his own home. Instead, he decided to go to Kayla's for a minute.

"What's up?" she asked, opening the door with one hand, holding Day in the other.

"Chilling. I came by to get some breakfast."

"You mean you came by to *cook* breakfast? Because you know I ain't cooking jack," she said matter-of-factly. He followed her into the living room where she was obviously packing Day's diaper bag and getting dressed for work at the same time. He took the baby from her arms.

"Hey there, princess. You been breaking any hearts lately?" he asked the vibrant infant. She cooed back at him, causing him to laugh. He sat on the sofa and bounced her on his knee.

"Well, I'm glad you stopped by. I can save my gas and ride with you," Kayla called out as she walked down the hall toward the bedroom.

"No can do. I got the day off."

"Huh? Then what are you doing out this early in the morning?"

"Your mama is nosy, you know that?" he whispered to the baby. "I had some stuff to do early this morning. Is that a'ight with you?"

"I don't care what you gotta do as long as it involves dropping Day off at the sitter."

"That definitely wasn't on my agenda this morning."

"Come on. You know I'm running late today, Terrell."

"You run late every day."

"Please. You're her godfather. You need to bond with her."

"We're bonding right now."

Kayla came back dressed in jeans and a sweater, carrying a pair of sneakers. Her long hair was held off her face with a headband. He shook his head at her.

"What? It's dress down Friday, Terrell. Don't even try it. Besides, I don't see where you look all that great either."

He looked down at his own jeans and Iverson jersey. "Whatever, yo, and I ain't talking about your clothes. I'm talking about that headband."

"I don't even have time to deal with you and your so-called fashion criticisms. Are you gonna take Day for me or what?"

"Don't even try to start making this a habit. You need to start getting up an hour earlier."

"Yeah, yeah, yeah. Thanks, Terrell. I appreciate it." She smiled as she kissed the baby. Grabbing her purse off the coffee table, she called out, "Her car seat is by the door. Don't forget the diaper bag. I'll call you later."

Terrell put Day into her swing and clicked on the television. After channel surfing for a few minutes, he settled on the news. He checked his watch and was disappointed that it was only

10:15. Time seemed to be creeping by. Day was beginning to drift to sleep so he decided he'd better put her into her seat and take her to the sitter. He gently took her into his arms and placed her into the carrier, buckling her in and covering her with the fuzzy pink blanket, which was lying in the chair. He noticed she was looking at him with her big, bright eyes like he was crazy.

"I know. Uncle Terry needs the practice, though, okay? Go back to sleep." He grinned. He made sure the door was locked and headed out to the driveway. Day must have understood what he told her because before he could even put her into the car, she was knocked out. He made sure the seat was fastened in and locked the door. His cell phone began vibrating in his pocket and he answered. "Yeah."

"What's up? You busy?"

"Naw, what's up with you?" he asked, walking to the driver's side and getting in the car.

"Nothing really. You drop your first baby mama off at the clinic?"

"Yep. Already took care of that. And quit calling her that."

"She is your first baby mama. And now you gotta go and meet your fiancée, right?"

"You know what Anjelica? You're getting to be as much up in my business as your sister. Must be something in the blood."

"Don't ever compare me to her. I told you about that. Keep on and our friendship will end right here and now. I'm surprised she's not in your face right now."

"She's gone to work already. I'm dropping Day off at the sitter for her."

"How is my gorgeous niece?" she asked. He could hear the hurt in her voice. Over the past few days, he had learned that although Anjelica tried her best to be a bitch, she still had a love for her sister and niece. "I bought her some cute outfits and a new diaper bag last weekend, but Kay thinks they're from my mother."

"Damn!" Terrell said loudly, slamming on the brakes.

"What's wrong?"

"I forgot the diaper bag, and I locked the door. Dammit!" He looked at the clock and saw that he only had thirty minutes to drop Day off and make it to meet Nicole. "I don't have time to deal with this."

"Calm down. Look under the flower pot on Kayla's porch and get the spare key," Anjelica told him. He wondered how she knew this and began to question whether or not the rumors that Anjelica was the mastermind behind the attack on Kayla a few months back were true. Janice, Geno's ex, broke into Kayla's home and assaulted her, nearly killing her. There was talk that since Janice and Anjelica knew each other, she had set her sister up to be attacked.

"I don't even wanna know how you know where her extra key is," he said as he turned around in the middle of the street and headed back toward Kayla's house. He left the car running as he quickly dashed to the porch and lifted the large flower pot sitting there. To his horror, there was no key. "Ain't no key here!"

"Look under the mat that it's sitting on, retarded! And stop yelling at me!"

He lifted the green mat under the plant and sure enough, a bronze key was there. He breathed a sigh of relief and proceeded to reenter the house. His phone began beeping and he saw that it was Kayla calling. He told Anjelica to hold then answered the other line. "Yo."

"Hey, everything okay when you dropped her off?"

"I ain't made it there yet. I forgot the diaper bag and now I gotta go back in and get it."

"And lock my door when you come out!"

"I know to lock the door behind me."

"Obviously you don't. It was open for you to go back in and get her bag."

"Look, I gotta go. I'm supposed to meet Nicole in a minute," he said, grabbing the bag and leaving once again.

"A'ight, I'll talk to you later."

He clicked back over and heard Anjelica singing along with Maxwell.

"Yo, chill with all that," he told her.

"Shut up. Did you get the bag?"

"Yeah, I got it. Thanks, I gotta go."

"A'ight, player. Call me when you get the chance. And don't forget to put that key back!"

"I already did," he lied and took the key out of his pocket, laying it back under the mat and replacing the plant on top. He got back into the car and checked on the baby. She was still sleeping. *Must be nice*, he thought as he sped off.

"Ms. Rogers, this young man is looking for you."

"Tell him he's late," he heard Nicole say. The women laughed and then he was told to come in.

"I'm sorry," he said as he entered the small room. She was giving him a fake evil eye.

"You're late," she repeated.

"I know. They took longer than expected with my car and then Kayla called and asked me to drop Day off so she wouldn't be late. I left the diaper bag and had to go back for it."

"Okay, okay. Kiss me and you're forgiven." She smiled. He leaned over and kissed her tenderly on the lips.

"Hey, that's how you two got like this in the first place," a deep voice interrupted them. "How you doing, young man? I'm Dr. Fisher."

Terrell looked up and shook the hand that was extended toward him. The man looked just like James Earl Jones. "Terrell Sims. I'm great."

"Well, it's nice to meet you, Terrell. I take it you've come to see your child's first picture?" The doctor walked over to the tiny sink and began washing his hands.

"Huh?" Terrell asked, looking at Nicole who had lay back on the examining table.

"He means the ultrasound, Terry." She shook her head at him.

"Oh, yeah." He laughed nervously. He wasn't really prepared for all this. He was under the impression that he would just be meeting with Nicole's doctor.

Dr. Fisher sat on the stool near the table and pulled over a cart holding what looked like a portable DVD player. He advised Nicole to lift her shirt then put some gel on her flat stomach. Terrell stood in silence as the doctor clicked on the machine and the dark screen lit up.

"There we go. Right there, Nicole. See?" the doctor said.

"Oh my God. That's my baby's heart beating," she whispered. "Look, Terrell."

Terrell leaned to see what they were talking about, but all he saw was a grey screen. Then, ever so faintly in the corner, he saw something moving fast. He put his finger on it. "Is that it?"

"That's it. That's your child. Tiny as a pea, but that's it." Dr. Fisher laughed.

"Wow, it's small all right."

"Terry, I'm only nine weeks pregnant."

Nine weeks. Darla was twelve weeks. A little further along than Nicole. It was strange that as he was watching the heartbeat of one child, across town the heartbeat of another was being stopped. He wondered how that baby would look on this monitor, but then told himself not to be stupid. *That probably ain't even your kid. Besides, that fetus is long gone, and after this weekend you won't ever have to deal with that trick again.*

He looked down at Nicole and took her hand into his. She looked up at him and he told her, "I love you."

"I love you too."

"Well, everything looks fine. I don't have to give you the specifics, Nicole. You know to eat right, take your vitamins, and get lots of exercise. No smoking or drinking, and I'll see you next month for your next appointment. Call my office if you need anything. Terrell, this young lady is one of the best nurses this hospital has. You get a gem and you need to treat her like one. You take care of her."

"I will, Dr. Fisher," he assured the doctor.

He helped Nicole get cleaned up with the doctor's words ringing in his ears. Nicole was a gem and he really cared about her. He had to get himself together if not for her, then for their baby that she was carrying. For the first time in his life, Terrell was ready to be a father.

After making an appointment for the following month, they walked to the parking lot. He saw that it was ten minutes before 1:00 and he had to go back and pick up Darla.

"You wanna go and get something to eat?" Nicole asked.

"I got a meeting at one, but we can meet up later." He pulled her to him.

"Well, I have some studying I really need to get done, especially since I didn't get anything done last night."

"Oh, you ain't get nothing done?" He looked at her provocatively.

"You know what I mean, silly." She blushed and put her arms around his neck. "We got more than enough done."

"I don't think we finished, either. We only went three rounds."

"We finished. Believe me, we finished."

He felt the vibration of the phone in his pocket and knew without looking at it that it was Darla. He walked Nicole to her car and hurriedly kissed her, promising to call after his meeting. He smiled as he thought about the image of his child on the monitor and the beautiful woman carrying it. He was definitely about to make some serious changes in his life. He would give Darla the money to get the hell outta dodge then make things work with Nicole.

By the time he made it to the clinic, he was damn near on cloud nine. The fact that Darla was already waiting outside the clinic made it even better. He figured he would have to push her in a wheelchair and help her to the car or something, and he just knew she would be putting on the performance of a lifetime, moaning and groaning as if she was dying. However, none of that took place. *Thank God,* he thought as he got out and opened the door for her.

"You a'ight, yo?" he asked her softly.

"I'm cool," was her response. He saw the folded up pieces of paper in her hand and asked if she needed to stop anywhere. "No. I just wanna go home."

He looked over at her and saw the tears streaming down her face. She rolled her eyes at him. He pretended not to notice and turned the radio up, nodding his head to the beat of Jay-Z. She turned and looked out the window, sniffling. As he turned his car into the parking lot in front of her building, he noticed a guy leaning against her black Neon. He was a grungy-looking older man wearing a baggy sweat suit and a pair of run-over Reeboks.

"Shit," Darla whispered as she saw the man, who was now scowling at Terrell.

"Who the hell is that?" He frowned, turning down the music.

"Turk," she said barely above a whisper, looking shocked.

"Who the hell is Turk? Man, I'm telling you I ain't for no shit, Darla. Who the hell is he?"

"Nobody."

"A'ight, *nobody*." He pulled into the empty spot on the other side of her car and the guy began walking toward them. "You better tell him something quick because I will knock him the hell out if he start acting crazy."

"I said it was nobody," she answered as she opened the door to get out.

"Where the hell you been?" Turk demanded as Darla stepped out of the car. "And who is *this* nigga?"

"Don't trip, Turk. He just gave me a ride from work, that's all."

"Don't lie, Darla. Your ass ain't even go to work. I went by there and they said you took the day off. And when I got here, Pooh told me you left wit' some dude. I'm guessing that would be this nigga here," he said, pointing toward Terrell, who was watching him, deciding whether to get out of the car. "Now, where the hell you been? Is this that nigga from the club?"

Ignoring him, Terrell rolled the window down and asked, "Yo, you gonna be a'ight?"

"What do you care? I'm sick of all y'all! Both of you need to leave me alone!" she screamed and rushed into the house. Neighbors began peeking out of windows, curious to see what was going on.

"I advise you to get the hell away from here, chump!" Turk growled at him.

Terrell was tempted to respond but thought better of it. *Forget it. She ain't my problem no more.* He kicked his car into gear and blazed out of the parking lot. For a quick second, he even tried to figure out who the loser was waiting for her at her house, but stopped himself. Relieved that the situation was now taken care of, he smiled to himself and decided to go to the mall and get his shop on. After all, he did have a new baby to buy for.

44

Toby flipped through the crates filled with albums, searching for some old school LL Cool J. It was only 9:00, but Dominic's was already crowded. It usually didn't get packed until after 11:00 on a Saturday night, but since spring finally seemed to be in the air, he figured people were ready to get their party on. Females were showing off flat abs and pedicured feet as they bounced to the bass pumping from the speakers. He loved this time of year; it gave him a new appreciation for the female physique.

"What's up, DJ T?" a voice yelled from the side of the booth. "A little bird told me you got married."

He peeked over to see who it was and a grin spread across his face. "Whatever, girl. What's been up with you, Meeko? You been hibernating or something?"

He opened the small door and let her into the booth, giving her a big hug. He inhaled the scent that he recognized as Miracle, one of his favorites.

"So, why didn't I get an invite to the big occasion?" she asked, folding her arms.

"Stop playing. You know I didn't get married."

"The rumors are coming from somewhere, and this one came from a reliable source. It all went down last month at Jasper's. You sang to Roni and then asked her to marry you, then you all jumped in a limo and headed to Vegas where you tied the knot. She must be pregnant . . . Is she?"

"No, she ain't pregnant!"

"Don't lie to me, Toby. Remember, I was almost your sister-in-law until your can't-keep-it-in-his-pants brother messed that up!" She laughed and Toby had to agree. A few years ago, Meeko was head over heels for Terry and everyone knew it, but he wasn't ready to settle down and she wasn't about to be strung along. Toby admired that about her.

She began flipping through his music and passing albums for him to mix.

"Something wrong with what I'm playing?" he asked.

"Whatever. Somebody gotta hype this crowd up!"

Sure enough, when he began to pump Mary J. Blige's "Real Love" mixed with Special Ed's "I Got it Made" the already crowded dance floor became flooded with people. She remained in the booth, helping him mix and shouting into the microphone until it was time to slow it down. He put on a slow jams mix CD he made and they exited the booth, heading for the bar.

"You look good, Meeko. I'm glad to see you," he said as they sat down. "You still drinking Long Island Ice Teas?"

"Naw, that was in my younger days. I can't take them anymore. Let me get some Stoli, straight."

"You can't handle Long Islands but you can handle Stoli? Go figure." He ordered their drinks then turned to look at her. It had been over a year since he had seen her and she hadn't changed a bit. She wore a fitted denim dress on her medium frame and her chin-length bob was tinted a color between burgundy and damn near pink. She wore red frames on her face the same color as her hair. Anyone could look at her and tell she was a firecracker.

"I ain't never been no punk, remember? So, how you been, Toby?"

"I been good, Meeko. What's been up with you?"

"You know how I do. I've just been working. That's pretty much it."

"You still writing?" Meeko could write songs like no one else Toby had ever met, and he had met some of the best.

"Not really. Guess I kinda been in a slump. Writing really hasn't been on my mind." She sighed. She looked over at him and took a deep breath. "I heard she sang for you that night after you proposed."

He swallowed the remainder of his Whiskey Sour and looked down into the empty glass. Meeko was the first one to bring up Isis since that night. He fought thoughts about her, but in the back of his mind he knew he wanted to see her, to talk to her, make sure she was all right.

"She sang for us." He nodded, not looking up.

"How did she look . . . I mean, did she seem okay?" Meeko asked, her voice full of concern.

"She seemed good. She sounded great—better than great. She was awesome. Blew everyone away, including Roni." He laughed. "I haven't seen or heard from her since that night. Have you heard from her?"

"I haven't seen or heard from her in two years. All I do is pray that she's okay and trust that God is taking care of her. She knows that if she needs me, I'm there. She's my best friend. Always has been, always will be," Meeko told him.

"Same here. It was just weird, though, Meeko. At first I thought I was dreaming. Everyone was clapping and congratulating us and then she was on stage. She looked and sounded perfect. Did you hear what song she sang?"

"Nope, but I bet you twenty dollars to a dozen doughnuts that it was 'Inseparable,' wasn't it?" She gave him a knowing look.

"How'd you guess?" he laughed. He could tell by the song that was playing that it was time for him to get back in the booth. Plus, the crowd was getting antsy and standing near the dance floor.

"Well, at least we know she's alive, so that's a good thing, right?" Meeko sounded like she was trying to convince herself as she said it. "She coulda called me, though. I wanted to see her. That's how *friends* do, though, huh?"

"True, but she'll call. She showed up, didn't she?" He stood up and stretched.

"Oh, yeah. I heard Jermaine was at Jasper's too. How is he doing?"

"Same old Jermaine. He's moved back here. You know he opened his own business and he's doing really well. I'm proud of him."

"You, Jermaine, and Terry. The Three Anegroes reunited." She smiled, referring to the nickname they gave themselves. "Hey, isn't that Terry over there?"

Toby looked over to where Meeko was pointing at a guy hugging and laughing with a familiar girl in the corner of the club. Although it looked like his brother, he didn't want to believe it was, not after all the bragging he had been doing about changing his ways and being in love with Nicole.

"I don't think so," he answered as they made their way back to the deejay booth.

"Well, it was nice hanging with you, Toby."

"You leaving?"

"Yeah, I told you I can't hang like I used to. I'm getting old."

"A'ight, Meeko. Call me some time, girl." He wrote his numbers down and passed them to her. She put them into her pocket.

"I will," she assured him. She hugged him and turned to walk away.

"Hey," he called after her. "When she calls, tell her I asked about her."

Giving him a knowing look, she nodded. "I will. Bye, Toby."

"Meeko!" Terell was headed toward her smiling like a kid on Christmas morning.

She looked back at Toby and shook her head. "I told you that was him."

Toby didn't respond. He watched them walk away then focused his attention on mixing music and refilling the near empty dance floor. He combined current hits and old school jams until it seemed like everyone in the club was grooving. He became engrossed in his work, filling requests and sending shout-outs so that time seemed to fly by. He was surprised when the bartender signaled him that it was last call. *One more hour then I can bounce*, he thought.

He scanned the crowd, hoping to see Roni or one of her friends. She told him she was coming tonight, but she hadn't shown up. They'd only been engaged a month, but she was already full swing into planning the wedding, which was probably the reason she didn't make it. Still, he thought she would have at least called and left a message.

"Man, Meeko looks good as hell, huh?" Toby didn't answer Terry, who was entering the booth. "I forgot how fine she was."

Toby began repacking his crates in preparation to leave. He was tempted to ask Terry about the girl he saw him hugged up with earlier, but didn't. Instead, he asked, "Hey, did you talk to Kayla tonight?"

"Nope. What, you were looking for Roni?" Terry waved at a group of women who were leaving the club.

"She said they were coming to hang out but I ain't see 'em. I was wondering if Kayla was with you."

"Sorry, bruh. I ain't talked to her." He shrugged as he helped his brother pack up. It was nearing 3:00 a.m. and the crowd was thinning. "You want me to take these out to your truck?"

"Yeah, grab those for me." Toby nodded toward the crates stacked in the corner of the booth.

"Where are your keys?"

Toby reached in his pocket and tossed him the keys. "Be sure to lock it when you come back in."

"Yeah, yeah, yeah. I know."

Finally, the last few stragglers had vacated the club and the wait staff began cleaning. He put on another CD for them to enjoy then went into the owner's office to get his check. He got his schedule for the next week and told everyone good-bye as he exited the back door. As he entered the parking lot, he could hear shouting.

"You are a trifling, no-good, nasty whore! That's what you are!"

"You're one to talk! How many men that come in this club haven't you slept with? So don't even come off at me like that, yo. I ain't even trying to hear that. Now, I'm warning you, you'd better get in your car and leave!"

"I ain't going nowhere. You ain't even call to check on me!"

"See, that's where you're confused. You're not my woman. I don't have to call and check on you. For what?"

"You just dropped me off like I was a hitchhiker or something! Like I hadn't just left the abortion clinic getting rid of *our* baby!"

"You had another one of your niggas waiting on you when you got home, remember? He shoulda checked on you. It was probably his kid you got rid of anyway!"

Toby noticed people stopping in the parking lot to see what was going on. He walked over to his brother, who was two feet away from Darla. She was yelling at the top of her lungs.

"Hey, what the hell is wrong with you two?" Toby asked.

"Your brother is a fool and he's trying to play me like I'm one! You think I don't know about Nicole being pregnant and you going around bragging about it?"

"I don't give a damn what you know. That's my business and I advise you to stay out of it!" Terrell turned to walk away when she reached out and grabbed his shoulder. Toby quickly intervened, jumping between them before Terry had a chance to react.

"Darla, you're out of line. Don't put your hands on him," he told her.

"Or what? What's he gonna do to me?" she growled.

"I ain't gonna do shit because you ain't worth it. What? You think that because you out here clowning that's supposed to make me scared of you? Yeah, right. You'd better get real." Terrell turned around and spat at her.

A white Acura Legend pulled up and the horn blew, causing all of them to turn around. The familiar girl who was with Terrell earlier was driving. He smiled and threw Toby his keys. "I'll holler at you later, T!"

"I want my money, you fat bastard!" Darla screamed. "You better get real and pay up. Believe that!"

"Imagine that! You gon' try and carry me in public and then think I'ma give you something. You played yourself, trick!" Terrell laughed in her face as he opened the car door.

Toby knew his brother hated to be embarrassed, especially in public, and Darla was making it harder on herself by clowning outside the club, even though he knew she was angry and hurt.

As Terrell got into the girl's car, it dawned on Toby who she was. He just could not believe that his brother was getting into the car with Kayla's sister, Anjelica Hopkins, of all people. "Terry. Terry! Man, hold up!"

"Face it, Toby. Your brother is nothing but a whore, a club hopping whore," Darla huffed. "But he's gonna pay. Believe that!"

"Leave it alone, Darla. Just go home," he told her and ran over to Anjelica's car.

"What's up?" Terry asked.

"Hey, Toby. How you been? Congratulations on your engagement." The pretty girl smiled at him. He looked at her like she was crazy because he had heard about how conniving and wicked this girl had been in the past, even from Terry. That was why he was confused as to why his brother would be caught dead with her.

"Uh, thanks," he told her. "Can I see you for a minute?"

"Hey, let me holler at him and then we can roll," Terrell told her. She shrugged as he got out of the car. He watched her pull into a nearby parking space to give them some privacy then walked over to his brother, making sure he was far enough out of range that she couldn't hear them.

"What the hell are you doing, Terry? I ain't even gonna talk about your acting a fool with Darla in the parking lot. But what the hell—"

"Man, I ain't thinking about her," Terry started.

"Naw, what the hell are you doing with that chick? Do you even think about what you're doing these days?"

"What? Toby, she's cool. I promise it ain't even like that."

"Like what? Kayla's supposed to be your best friend, man, and that's her worst enemy. That's just wrong."

"No, you're wrong, T. She's nothing like you think she is. I've talked to the girl and I know what's up with her. Kayla is my best friend, but her sister is not as bad as you think she is," Terrell told him. There was something in his voice that made Toby question his brother's sanity.

"And what about Nicole, man? You say you wanna marry her, but you're leaving with another female from the club. You think that ain't gonna get back to her? Come on now, Terry. You're not thinking."

"It's cool. I rode to the club wit' Jermaine. Anjelica's just gonna take me to get my car, that's it. I got it under control, bruh. I know what I'm doing."

"Man, it's your life. You do what you want. But you'd better start thinking about the repercussions of your actions."

"I will, T. I will."

The two men gave each other a brotherly hug that was interrupted by the sound of screeching tires. A low-rider truck came barreling into the parking lot, music blasting and headlights shaking. As it neared the two men, it slowed and the driver's side window rolled down. Panic filled Toby's body as he saw the hand holding the dull, metal pistol aimed at them. *God, help us,* he thought as he reached out and pulled his brother down. They fell to the ground just as the shots rang out. People began screaming and Toby watched Terrell lifting his head and cursing as the truck careened past them.

"Stay down, fool!" he yelled to his brother. *Thank you, Jesus*, he prayed silently as he remained low.

"Hell naw!" Terrell huffed as he maneuvered his large body off the ground. "I don't believe this! That bitch had him come after me!"

"Who? What are you talking about?" Sweat was pouring from both of them and Toby's heart was beating a mile a minute.

"Darla! The guy driving the truck was some dude Turk I seen at her house! I know it was him! I'ma fuck him up. Believe that!"

Sirens could be heard in the distance and Toby looked around to make sure everyone was all right. "Calm down, Terry."

"Are you two okay?" one of the security guards ran over and asked. They assured him that they were and Toby continued to try to calm his brother. Terry was walking back and forth like a panther ready to pounce. The police soon arrived and they each gave a statement. Terry continued accusing someone named Turk.

"Let's go, Terry. Get in the truck."

"I'm cool, T. Besides, I already got a ride," he replied, waving toward Anjelica, who sat across the parking lot, still looking stunned.

"Man, don't you have enough going on in your life right now? Come on. Get in and leave that girl alone. You're asking for trouble, you know that?"

"I told you I can handle mine," he said, walking toward the car.

Toby reached out and grabbed his brother by the shoulder. His brother was acting so stupid he couldn't believe it. There was no way he could stand by and let him ruin his life. It wasn't happening.

"Don't be damn stupid Terry! Leave that girl alone and go home to Nicole."

"Get off me! What's your problem, T?" Terrell snatched away from him, surprised that Toby put his hands on him like that. He looked at his brother, enraged that he would even go there.

Toby's eyes widened in anger and he squared off against his brother. Terrell was clearly bigger in size, but Toby's body was as cut as LL Cool J in the movie *SWAT*. Toby could feel his heart thumping in his chest and perspiration began to form on his brow. He hadn't fought his brother since they were in high school, and even then it wasn't serious. He was surprised at Terrell's actions.

"Hold the hell up, Terry. I'm just trying to get you to look at what you're doing!"

"I don't need you to get me to do nothing! That's your problem; you always trying to get me to do shit. I ain't you!" he snarled. Moments passed as they stared silently at each other. The few remaining people in the parking lot crowded around the two men, waiting for the fight to jump off.

Toby stared at his brother, confused by what was going on. There was so much animosity in Terry's voice and he didn't know where it was coming from. He frowned at him as he took a step back and told his brother, "You know what? You're right. It ain't my problem. You go and do what the hell you wanna do."

Terrell didn't say anything as he turned and got in the waiting car. Anjelica rolled down her window and began to say something. She must have thought better of it because she just shrugged at Toby instead and waved briefly as they pulled off.

All this over a piece of ass. I don't believe this, Toby thought as he got into his truck and headed home. *That brother was about to fight me over a piece of ass. Thank you, God, for looking out for him, because he almost got killed twice tonight.*

45

"What the hell was that all about?" Anjelica asked as they drove down the street.

"Man, I don't even know," Terrell answered. He leaned the seat all the way back and closed his eyes. He had a million thoughts running through his mind at one time, and didn't feel like thinking about anything. He couldn't believe that punk-ass scrub, Turk, had actually tried to take him out—over Darla's fat ass, at that. But he had a trick for her ho ass too. She wanted to play those kinds of games, he would play them and win. Then there was Toby. He could not believe his brother tried to buck up like he wanted to swing on him. Over the years, he had taken a lot from Toby, but at this point in his life, he was tired.

"When that fool started shooting, I was like 'What the hell?' I'm glad no one was hurt," Anjelica said, trying to make small talk.

"Yeah," he responded. He rolled down his window and enjoyed the air. Anjelica must've sensed his mood because she fumbled with the disc changer and Maxwell began playing. She leaned back into her seat and remained silent.

When they were in the club, Terrell told her his car was at Jermaine's crib, about a mile and a half from the club. Now he noticed she was getting on the Interstate instead. He didn't ask where she was going; he just decided to ride. He felt his phone vibrating in his pocket and didn't even look to see who it was. He figured it was Nicole calling to see where he was, and he didn't feel like talking to her right now. There was too much on his mind to even attempt to explain to her what had just happened. All he wanted to do was relax.

The sound of waves crashing caused Terrell to wake up. He hadn't even realized he had drifted off to sleep. He looked around, unsure of where he was, and then he saw the sand sprawled before him. They were at the beach. Maxwell was still singing, but there was no one in the car with him. He opened the door and got out, stretching his arms. He looked at his watch and saw that it was almost 4:00 in the morning. The sky was blanketed in darkness with the exception of a faint, twinkling star here or there, and the shape of a dull crescent moon. He inhaled, taking in the scent of the warm, salty air. He scanned the scenery until he spotted a shadow in the distance, sitting on the ground. He took his phone out of his pocket, turned it off without even checking the call log and tossed it into the back seat. Grabbing the keys from the ignition and locking the doors, he walked over.

"What's up?" he asked, sitting next to her.

"Nothing. Just chilling, enjoying the night . . . Or should I say morning?" She shrugged.

"Yeah, this is nice. I ain't been out here in a minute." He looked around.

"I come out here a lot. It's peaceful. I don't have a lot of peace in my life, but I'm sure you know all about that, huh?"

"What, not having peace in my life?"

"No, me not having peace in mine, Terrell," she told him. Her hands began playing in the sand, moving back and forth as she looked down. "You think I don't know what people say about me? How I'm the most hated person in my family?"

"I wouldn't say you were hated, yo. I'd say it was more like misunderstood."

"Misunderstood, huh? Let me ask you something. Why do you hang out with me? I mean, Kayla's your best friend. I'm her wicked sister, the one that has caused all this drama in her life. Why would you of all people want to be around me?" she asked without looking at him.

"Because I think you put up this front like you want to be this hardcore female that really doesn't care, but you do. Let me ask you this: why do you cause so much drama in your sister's life? Do you hate her that much?"

"See, that's where everyone has it all wrong. I don't hate her at all. She's not my favorite person in the world, but I don't hate her. I love her."

Terrell couldn't help laughing. "You what? Love her? Come on. You slept with her fiancé, in her house, in her bed! What? That was done out of love?"

"No, now *that* was a mistake. I went to a party and I was so drunk and high that it was unreal. I swear I've never been that blazed before in my life. The girl I rode with was drunk too, but she was gonna stay with her boyfriend. I told them to drop me off at Kayla's; I let myself in with the key. I knew it was Geno's bachelor party and Kayla was having her own li'l set at Roni's. I ain't think either one of them was coming home, I swear. I don't even remember much of what happened except that hot-ass water coming across my back."

"Damn." Terrell recalled how Kayla told him about tossing hot water on Anjelica and Geno when she caught them in her bed, but he thought she was exaggerating. His best friend was telling the truth after all.

"You know the saddest part about that whole situation? My friend's boyfriend found out later that this guy that had been try-ing to get with me all night had put something in my drink. They were gonna tell Kayla the whole thing, but what would've been the point? She called the wedding off. That was the last time I got high." She sighed as she reflected on the whole situation.

"Okay, then what about the whole Janice thing? Did you set that up?" Even he suspected her of having something to do with Kayla's attack, although he doubted that she meant for her sister to be hurt as badly as she was. He began asking questions that he wanted answered for the longest, and now Anjelica seemed to be in the mood to talk.

"Yeah, I had something to do with that too, right? I suppos-edly gave her Kayla's telephone number and address, right? I don't even *know* Kayla's telephone number. How about Janice followed Kayla from work and got her number from directory assistance?"

"But isn't Janice's sister your friend?"

"No, okay, I did lie about that. We work together, that's it. She ain't my friend."

"A'ight, a'ight, but what about when you pushed up on Theo at the baby shower?"

"I ain't push up on him. I was in his face, cussing him out because he had been blowing my friend, Yasmine's phone up trying to get with her. I was about to call him out when everyone came in the room hollering about me trying to push up on him.

So, since no one wanted to hear my side of the story, I left it alone. If Tia gets played, it's on her. It ain't my problem."

"You really think you're hard, huh?" He laughed.

"I'm not trying to be hard. Do you really think I care about what they say about me? No, that's what Kayla does. She has low self-esteem and needs to be accepted. She cares about what everyone is gonna think or what they're gonna say. I don't give a damn. She was a grown woman who hid her pregnancy from her father because she was scared of what he was gonna say. She went to school to be a teacher because that's what my mother wanted her to do. Kayla doesn't even like kids; she wanted to major in marketing, but she did what everyone wanted her to do. I wasn't about to go to school; I like working. I ain't about to move out until I can afford to build the house I wanna live in, but that makes me a bum. I'm not Kayla. She has to have everyone like her and be friends with everyone. I don't need a whole bunch of friends. That's where all the drama comes from," she said loudly.

"I feel you on that one. But you and your sister need to get this worked out."

"There's nothing to work out, Terrell. I'm cool with it like it is. I like being the villainess, the bad girl. Let me ask you this, since we're being all open and honest all of a sudden. Why did you sleep with me that night? I know you couldn't stand me just as much as the others, but you still had sex with me. Why?"

Terrell didn't have an answer. He tried and tried to think of one, but couldn't. She was right; he did have as much hatred for her as everyone else, but he was still deeply attracted to her for some reason.

"I know what it is, Terrell." She winked at him.

"You don't know nothing." He looked at her from the corner of his eye. She was so sexy. He tried not to stare at her full bust, which was very much inviting through the provocative, sleeveless fuchsia top she wore. Instead, his eyes fell on her thick hips wearing black fitted pants, and continued to her feet—even they were sexy. She had taken off her racy, stiletto heels, the same color as her shirt, and they were lying in the sand. He picked one up and examined it.

"What, your hooker shoes got too tight for you? How tall are these things anyway, four inches?"

"Four and a half, and don't change the subject. I know why you slept with me. Kayla is your best friend, right? You two been thick as thieves for what, at least a year now?"

"Yep, that's my dawg." He reached over, pulled her feet in his lap and began rubbing them. They were soft, just like he thought they'd be.

"You were there for her when she needed you the most. You shared a lot, and had each other's back."

"Yeah." He continued massaging the arch of her right foot as she talked.

"But nothing ever jumped off between you and her." She leaned back on her elbows and continued. He began to wonder where she was going with this. "Knowing you, it was probably because she was pregnant. Plus, she was all caught up in the Geno/Craig, Craig/Geno, who's-the-daddy, who-do-I-love drama. That right there, I guess, would have been a turn off, of course. But you stuck by her, no doubt. You were her friend. I've seen how you operate, Terrell. Had that not been the case, you probably would have tried to get with her."

He looked at her like she had just fallen from the sky. No female had ever tried to go there with him. She just lay there, smiling at him.

"Funny, I look just like my sister. People even say we could pass for twins."

"Obviously, you have lost your freaking mind, Anjelica." He pushed her feet out of his lap and frowned at her.

"What? It's cool, Terrell. Why are you mad?"

"I ain't mad, you're crazy! I don't believe what you just said. You're trying to make it seem like the only reason I got wit' you is 'cause you look like Kayla. That's sick. She's like my little sister! I don't even think of her that way!" Terrell shook his head, appalled at what Anjelica had even suggested. He had never thought about Kayla like that. The one reason that their friendship had gotten to the level that it had was because he had never thought about that. Granted, she was probably the *only* female that he had befriended that he had *never* thought of sleeping with, *and* it was due partly due to the fact that she was pregnant and her life was drama-filled, but it definitely wasn't the reason he had slept with Anjelica. He was offended by her even suggesting it. She, on the other hand, was amused at his reaction, unable to suppress her laughter.

"Well, if I'm wrong, I apologize, Terrell. I just thought you had a subliminal desire to sleep with my sister. Come on, she's a beautiful girl, smart and funny. A lot of guys try to get with her. There is nothing wrong with Kayla."

"I didn't say there was. I have no interest in getting with her."

"You don't have an interest in getting with me, but that doesn't stop you from sleeping with me," she pointed out. She put her feet back into his lap and he resumed his position as foot masseuse.

"How do you know I don't wanna get with you?"

"Terrell, you're not ready to get with anyone. Not even Nicole."

"That's not true. I love Nicole."

"I didn't say you didn't love her. You probably do, but you shouldn't settle down with her. Not yet, anyway."

"Okay, why shouldn't I settle down with her? She's got a great job, a future, she's wonderful." His hands began moving under her pants leg, along her strong calves, kneading into her muscles.

"That's why you shouldn't settle down with her until you're ready; because she's a good person. If you know you still want to be out there, then don't lie to her. In the end, she's gonna wind up hurt and she'll hate you. You don't want that. Being hated is not a good feeling. Trust me, I know."

"She's having my baby, remember?"

"According to—what was old girl at the club's name? Darlene?"

"Darla." He cringed at the thought of her.

"Whatever. She was having your baby, too, but you ain't make no rash decisions to settle down and be a family with her."

"She's a ho!" His hands crept further and further up her leg and he enjoyed the feel of her firm thighs. His manhood began to rise with thoughts of making love on the beach.

"So are you, Terrell. You slept with her knowing she was sleeping with Toby—unprotected on top of that. That's nasty."

"Since when did you become Ms. Morality all of a sudden? Don't go there with me, Anjelica."

"I ain't going nowhere, Terrell. See, you and I, we're cut from the same cloth. We have more in common than we'll ever know. I understand you and you understand me on a whole other level. That's why the sex between us was the bomb."

"Was?" He stopped caressing her leg.

"Was. I made the mistake of sleeping with one engaged man. I ain't making it again," she told him. He could see the seriousness in her face and knew she meant it. "You say you're with Nicole, then that's cool. I commend you for that. But don't think I'ma be Darla's replacement. Despite what you and everyone else thinks about me, I ain't a ho, and more importantly, I ain't stupid. You ready?"

She stood up and brushed the sand from her behind. He looked up at her, his arousal suddenly disappearing. This was definitely not how he thought this would be ending when he realized they were on the beach. She reached out her arm and helped him get to his feet.

"Thanks," he said and brushed himself off as well. Instead of heading back to the car, she bent down, rolled her pants legs up and began walking down the beach. He walked beside her and they continued talking until the dark sky brightened and they could see the amber golden hues of the rising sun.

46

"I guess you didn't have as much fun as you expected at the beach, huh?" she asked when she pulled up behind his car, still parked in the driveway behind Jermaine's Range Rover. It was just after 7:00 in the morning and he was contemplating asking her to breakfast.

"Naw, it was cool. You know I like chilling with you anyway."

"I guess that's something us Hopkins women have in common, right?" she teased.

"Shut up, girl. Oh, let me get my phone out the back seat. I wouldn't want you going through my numbers. Nosy as hell, that's another thing you Hopkins women have in common." He laughed, reaching into the back seat and retrieving his phone. He clicked the power on and the phone instantly vibrated. The screen alerted him that he had new messages. He decided to check them.

"You have eight new messages," the voice prompt announced.

"Damn, I got eight messages," he said aloud.

"Somebody been cussing you out repeatedly." Anjelica laughed.

"You're probably right." He sighed and listened to the first three, which were from Nicole, telling him to call her. By the third message, he could tell that she was pissed. The next three messages were from stupid-ass Darla, crying about how he ruined her life and she wanted her money so she could move. The next two messages were from Kayla, telling him to call her immediately. She sounded upset, as if she had been crying, and both messages were left after 4:00 in the morning, the same time he was at the beach. He wondered if maybe someone had told her about him being with Anjelica at the club or leaving with her. *Naw, she just had those nightmares again*, he told himself.

"Something wrong?" Anjelica asked.

"Naw, Kayla called me twice around four this morning," he said.

"Oh, no, not drama first thing in the morning." Anjelica faked a moan, but the sound of his phone interrupted them.

"It's her again. Something must be wrong," he said, answering it before it could ring again. "Yo."

"T-Terrell," Kayla said quietly.

"Yeah, what's wrong?" he asked. Anjelica was making faces at him as he talked into the phone.

"I . . . I . . . We're at the h-hos-hospital," she sniffed.

"Hospital? For what? What hospital, Kay? What happened?" Thoughts of the shootout at the club came flooding back and he wondered if Turk had come back and shot Toby. Anjelica's face now wore a look of concern.

"M-my father. . . he . . . he . . ."

"What? Tell me what happened."

"He had a heart attack. I'm here with Mama. We . . . we . . ."

He could hear the sound of the phone as it fell, then someone else picked up.

"Terrell, its Yvonne. We're here at Mercy Hospital. Mr. John had a heart attack around three thirty this morning."

"Damn." He sighed and looked over at Anjelica. "How is he?"

"What?" Anjelica whispered. "Who?"

"He's in critical condition. I'm here with Kayla and her mom. Geno is here too. I don't know where the hell Anjelica is. We've been trying to find her all morning."

"Who has Day?"

"Geno's mom has her. Where are you?"

The front door opened and Jermaine stepped out, looking at the car. Terrell opened the car door and got out, making sure he closed the door behind him. He waved at Jermaine, who took notice of Anjelica. He gave Terrell a nod of approval as he walked over to his truck. "What's up, Terry?"

"Chilling," Terrell told him then went back to talking to Yvonne. "Uh, I'm at my boy Jermaine's house. I stayed here last night. Tell Kay to give me a few minutes and I'll be right there." He sighed.

"Thanks, Terrell. I'll let her know," Yvonne said and hung up the phone.

Terrell leaned against the car and tried to think of what to do next. He knew he was going to have to tell Anjelica. She was already getting out of the car.

"What the hell is going on? Who's in the hospital?"

He walked around and stood in front of her, pausing before he let the words come from his mouth. "Anjelica, it's your dad."

"My dad? What about him?" Her face became clouded with confusion as she listened to what he was saying.

"He had a heart attack this morning, Anjelica."

For a moment, she just stared at him and he wondered if she heard what he told her. Her head leaned to the side and her stare was blank. Then, as if someone had slapped her, she straightened up. He saw her eyes quickly fill with tears and she began to shake, almost falling into his arms. Jermaine must have been looking because suddenly he was right there beside them.

"Yo, what's wrong with her? Is she sick?" he questioned. "Do I need to call 911?"

"Naw, man. She just found out her dad had a heart attack. I need to get her to the hospital," Terrell replied. He put his arm around Anjelica, who was now weeping quietly.

"Aw, man," Jermaine said. "I'm sorry."

"Is . . . is he—?" Anjelica started to ask, but she broke down before she could finish.

"He's in critical condition, Anjelica. That's all I know. Come on. We need to get going," he told her.

"I'll ride with you," Jermaine said suddenly.

"You don't have to do that, man. I got it," Terrell told him, leading a wobbling Anjelica back to the car. Just as he opened the door for her, she leaned over and began to heave. Vomit came from her mouth and he jumped back. "Shit."

"Sorry," she whined, still shaking. She looked down and noticed that she had soiled her shirt.

"It's okay. Come on. You can clean up inside before we leave," Jermaine told her, suddenly in charge.

Anjelica didn't resist when he reached out and put his arm around her. Terrell followed as his friend led her up the driveway. Jermaine was easily six-foot-five and practically had to lean to support her five-five frame. Her face was buried into his chest as they entered the house. For some reason, Terrell felt a slight twinge of jealousy, but brushed it off as he waited for them to return. He silently said a prayer for his friends' father as he leaned against the car.

A few minutes later, they emerged from the house. Anjelica was wearing a green-and-white T-shirt promoting Jermaine's security surveillance company, We Secure U. Terrell had about ten of the exact same shirts in multiple colors because every time he came over, Jermaine gave him one.

"You okay?" he walked over and asked. Anjelica barely nodded.

"Wait a minute," she said suddenly.

"What's wrong?" Terrell asked. He watched her as she looked down. He hoped she wasn't about to faint.

"I gotta get something out of my car."

"I'll get it for you. What is it?" Terrell asked, reaching for her keys.

"Grab my sneakers out the trunk."

"What?"

"Huh?"

He and Jermaine looked at her and shook their heads. Terrell walked to her car and opened the trunk. There were four different shoeboxes lying there. He grabbed the blue-and-white Reebok box and took out a pair of white classics.

"Are these good?" he asked.

She nodded her head and placed her arm on Jermaine's shoulder as she balanced herself, taking off her stilettos. She slipped her feet into the sneakers and handed him the pumps to put back into her car.

"You want me to drive, Terry?" Jermaine asked as he helped Anjelica steady herself.

"I can drive. Thanks for offering, though," Terrell answered, walking over to his car and hitting the alarm. He went to reach for Anjelica, but she clung to Jermaine's arm. Terrell realized that she was in shock. He looked at Jermaine and shrugged.

"We can just sit in the back." Jermaine opened the rear door and eased Anjelica inside the car. Terrell got behind the wheel and reached over to pull the passenger seat all the way forward so that Jermaine's legs wouldn't be in his chest. He couldn't help but smile as he watched Jermaine maneuver his long body into the back seat.

"You want me to try to call Kayla and check on your dad?"

Anjelica shook her head and the tears started flowing once again. "Just . . . just get to the hospital."

"We'll be there in no time," Jermaine assured her, looking in the rearview mirror at Terrell.

Terrell floored the car, maneuvering it with ease through the modish neighborhood, and merged onto the fairly empty highway. He knew the ride to Mercy Hospital would take at least thirty minutes. He turned the radio on and let the soothing sounds of Sunday morning gospel fill the car, praying that it would bring some comfort to Anjelica. He continually looked back to make sure she was okay. Jermaine still had his arm around her and her head was buried into her hands. Every now and then Terrell would see him whisper something to her and she would nod.

It was exactly twenty-one minutes later when he pulled into the parking lot of the hospital. He found an empty space and parked the car. Jermaine wasted no time hopping out and was opening Anjelica's door before Terrell even had a chance to get his seatbelt off.

"Do you know what floor he's on?" Jermaine asked as they entered the hospital lobby. "Is he in emergency or what?"

Terrell shook his head. "Yvonne didn't say. I'll ask the receptionist." The receptionist advised Terrell that Mr. Hopkins was in surgery on the seventh floor. She pointed them in the direction of the elevator, and they rode in silence. Anjelica hesitated when the doors slid open; Terrell and Jermaine stepped off.

"Come on, yo," he told her. She looked like she was about to throw up again and he couldn't blame her. The smell of the hospital almost caused him to be nauseous himself. He didn't understand how Nicole could stand working as a nurse. "It's gonna be a'ight, but you need to come on."

"I got her, Terry." Jermaine reached out and led her into the wide hallway. They proceeded under the sign pointing to the surgical waiting area.

Terrell could see Kayla sitting alongside her mother as he opened the heavy glass door encasing the waiting room. Her eyes were swollen and she looked as if she was barely holding it together. His heart went out to his friend and he knew there wasn't much more she could take. Her boyfriend, Geno, noticed him in the hallway and came out to meet him. Kayla didn't even look up.

"Hey, G. How is he?"

"He's still in surgery. They haven't told us anything yet." Geno sighed. His eyes went beyond Terrell and he realized Anjelica was there as well. "Anjelica, we've been looking all over for you. Your mom was worried."

"I'm okay," she said barely above a whisper. Geno took a step toward her, but she didn't move. Terrell saw her slip her hand into Jermaine's. The door opened again and Yvonne joined them in the hall. She spoke to Terrell then stood staring at Anjelica and Jermaine as Geno did.

"Oh," was the only thing she said. Terrell could tell she was lost for words.

"How're you doing?" Jermaine said to Yvonne. "Anjelica, your mom must be in here. Come on, so she'll know you're okay."

"Okay," Anjelica said. "Thanks for being here, Yvonne. You too, Geno."

Terrell opened the door and Kayla's mother rushed toward them. She reached past him and put her arms around her daughter. He eased past the two women and walked over to his friend. She stood and he took her into his arms, rubbing her back. For the second time that morning, a Hopkins woman cried on his shoulder. He searched his brain for the right words to say, but there were none. Kayla cried for a few moments longer then released herself from his grasp. Terrell moved his body so she could see her mother and sister.

"Your fam is here, Kay," he told her. The intensity in the room became apparent as the two sisters looked at each other. For what seemed like eternity, no one moved. The sound of the door opening once again caused everyone to turn as an older gentleman dressed in green hospital scrubs entered, a white surgical mask hanging between his chin and chest.

"Is he okay?" Mrs. Hopkins asked the doctor, her eyes wide with anticipation. Terrell felt Kayla reaching for his hand and he eased by her side, waiting for the doctor's response.

"Your husband suffered a massive heart attack, Mrs. Hopkins. We've stabilized him, but he's in critical condition," he told her.

Geno eased behind Kayla and put his hands on her shoulders. She closed her eyes and gripped Terrell's hands tighter. Terrell looked over at Anjelica, who was standing on the other side of her mother. Jermaine was still standing near, listening along with everyone else.

"What does that mean?" Anjelica asked. At the sound of her sister's voice, Kayla's eyes popped open. Terrell heard her inhale deeply as she glared at her sister. Her mother turned to the doctor for his reply.

"The damage to his heart was extensive, but we repaired it the best we could," the doctor said. Terrell could tell that there was forced optimism in his voice.

"And?" Anjelica stepped closer to the doctor and he seemed a bit disturbed.

"Anjelica, don't start," her mother said with a tone of caution. "I'm sorry."

"No, don't apologize for her. She's right."

They were all shocked to see Kayla step beside her sister. The two women stared at the man and waited for his response. Geno nudged Terrell, who just shrugged. Yvonne's mouth fell open.

"I know that you're upset, and we are doing all we can to take care of your father and make him as comfortable as possible."

"Look, don't try to blow smoke at us and sugar coat this situation, Dr. . . . . What's your name?" Anjelica asked.

"Stevens. Clifford Stevens," he answered, looking nervous. He wasn't much taller than either one of them and he began stroking his salt-and-pepper beard.

"Dr. Stevens, it's not his comfort that we're worried about. We want you to save his life!" Kayla told him.

The sisters made a powerful united front, which took everyone in the room by surprise.

"Now, again, how is my father's condition?" Anjelica repeated.

"If he makes it through the next twenty-four hours, he'll have a fifty percent chance of recovery." He looked over at their mother, who was trying to keep her composure, but was slowly breaking down. Yvonne walked over and put her arms around her, leading her to the small sofa in the corner of the room.

The sound of Kayla's sniffling could be heard, but just as Terrell headed toward her, the two sisters turned toward each other. He looked from one to the other as they stared into each other's faces. His heart began beating rapidly as he tried to think of something to do or say. *God, please don't let them start fighting in here. They've been through too much already.*

"Thank you, Dr. Stevens," Anjelica told him, her eyes remaining on her sister. "When can we see my father?"

"I can take you to him now. He's still in recovery," the doctor told her. He moved toward the door and held it open, looking around to see who was coming. Yvonne slowly helped Mrs. Hopkins up and she turned toward her children, who continued to look eye to eye.

"Anjelica, Kayla?" she said aloud, wiping her eyes and running her fingers through her hair nervously.

Neither one answered their mother, nor did they move. Then, to everyone's surprise, including her own, Anjelica extended her hand to her sister. At first, Kayla just stared at it, then slowly, she took it into her own and the three women exited together behind the doctor.

"Man, that was intense," Jermaine finally said. Terrell had forgotten that his friend was there with them.

"That was nothing," Geno sighed and took his seat next to Yvonne. "I've seen worse when those two were together."

"Ain't that the truth?" Yvonne added.

Terrell introduced Jermaine to them then asked, "Where's Roni? Toby was looking for her at the club last night."

"Roni left a little while before you got here. She had been trying to call Toby but couldn't get in contact with him," Yvonne told him. "We got here a little after four."

"Man, he probably went home and fell into bed. We had major drama after the club closed last night." He went on to tell them about the shootout that occurred in the parking lot. He left out the part about Darla being the cause.

"I know Nicole probably fell out when you told her about it," Geno replied.

"Nicole. Damn, I need to call her!" With all that had gone on, he had forgotten. Yvonne told him that he had to go outside the hospital in order to use his phone. He hurried to the elevator, dialing her number as he walked.

"Hello."

"Hey, baby. I'm sorry. I just got a chance to call you," he said before he even got off the elevator. He knew she was probably pissed and tried to think of how to explain why he hadn't come over or at least called the night before.

"I've been calling you all night, Terrell! I don't know what kind of game you're—"

"Kayla's dad had a heart attack last night," he interrupted her before she could finish. He felt bad about using his best friend's sick father as his alibi, but he had no other choice. He hoped Nicole would assume he had been at the hospital with Kayla the entire time.

"How is he? How's Kayla?" she asked, her tone quickly changing from irritated to concerned.

"He's still in surgery and we're waiting," he answered.

"Do you need anything? Is there anything I can do?"

"I'm good. Thanks for asking. You getting ready for church?" He knew she was. Nicole was a faithful member of Shepherd's Heart Memorial Chapel.

"Yeah, I have to usher this morning. I'll ride over to the hospital after service."

"Okay. Say a prayer for Mr. John, will you, baby? Hey, you feeling all right this morning? No morning sickness?"

"A little, but nothing I can't handle. I gotta get outta here. I love you."

"Love you too," he told her and ended the call. He thought about calling his brother but changed his mind. *I don't have the energy to deal with Toby's judgmental behind or his double standards this morning. I got my own problems.*

47

Toby tossed the keys on the coffee table and flopped down on the sofa. He took his cell from the pocket of his jeans, but it was dead. He picked up his cordless phone and dialed Roni's cell. Her voice mail picked up instantly, so he knew that either her battery was dead or she had it turned off. He had already driven by her house and found out that she wasn't at home, so he decided against calling there. He was tired both mentally and physically, and contemplated just staying on the sofa. He convinced himself that his bed would be much more comfortable and slowly got up.

As he climbed the stairs and entered his bedroom, he heard a noise. Someone was in the bathroom. He slowly pushed the cracked door open and heard the sound of the shower. He entered to the scent of jasmine and saw the silhouette of a woman's naked body through the frosted glass. Her back was to him, and she hadn't realized he was there. He watched her for a while, admiring her beauty and listening to her sing about finding love on a two-way street and losing it on a lonely highway. He meticulously removed his own clothes, making sure he didn't make any noise. His soldier was at full attention as he carefully opened the door and stepped behind her.

"About time you came home," she told him without turning around. His eyes took in her perfect body from head to toe. The drops of water clinging to her caramel shoulder were an open invitation for his tongue to lick, and he obliged. She arched her back and he pushed her long, black hair out of the way as he kissed her neck. His hand reached around her small waist and rested on her hips as he pulled her to him. His rock hard penis rested on her firm buttocks. "Mmm, seems like someone is happy to see me."

Slowly, she turned and put her arms around him, smiling. He felt his heart melt as his eyes met hers. He wasted no time *covering her mouth with his. He taunted her tongue and ran his hands through her thick hair, the steam of the shower surrounding them. She balanced herself on one leg as she wrapped the other one around him. His hands found their way to her center and he rubbed back and forth against her openness, causing her to gasp. Releasing the grip he had on her head, he lifted her into his arms and she wrapped her body around his. It amazed him that she was able to maneuver herself perfectly in one swift movement, and he smiled as he entered her.*

She rocked back and forth, never missing a beat as he nudged the shower doors open and stepped out. She felt so good, her breasts crushed against his chest as she continued to ride. His eyes took in the sexiness of her hard nipples. He could feel her muscles contracting against his hardness, arousing him even more.

He quickly made his way to the countertop and sat her down, making sure they weren't near the candles she had burning near the sink. He continued plunging into her as she clawed at his back and bit into his shoulder. Their lovemaking was ferocious and he loved it. The glow of the candles reflecting in the mirror seemed to cause her image to glow as she looked at him seductively. He was determined to control himself, but before he knew it, she had leaned all the way back and wrapped her legs around his neck. She tightened around him and he closed his eyes as he felt himself about to explode.

"Oh, God! Ice!"

"Toby! Toby!"

Suddenly, his eyes flew open. He quickly looked around and realized he was still on the sofa. He rubbed his eyes and saw that Roni was standing over him, looking at him like he was a stranger.

"Toby, are you all right?" she asked, frowning.

"Huh?" he asked.

"That must have been a hell of a dream."

She was right; the dream had been vivid. He hadn't had one like that in over a year. He sat up and stretched. "Yeah. It was crazy."

"You're all sweaty, baby." She ran her hand along his forehead and showed him the perspiration that was apparent on her palm. "And you were calling for ice."

His head snapped around and he stared at her. "What?"

"You were calling out for some ice. Let me get you a wet wash-cloth," she said and disappeared down the hallway.

As he sat on the edge of the sofa, he tried to get his thoughts together. He couldn't believe the dream he had just experienced. *Isis Adams.* When she had first disappeared, he had them all the time, almost every night. But as time went on, they had become more and more infrequent. He laughed at himself nervously and stood up. *Man, you are really tripping.*

"Here you go, baby." Roni gently wiped his face with the cool washcloth. Her touch was tender and he turned his head and kissed the inside of her wrist as she wiped.

"I looked for you last night. I called you too," he told her. "What happened?"

"I was at the hospital all night." She sighed and sat down.

"Hospital? For what?" he asked, sitting next to her.

"Mr. John had a heart attack. I was there with Kayla and her mom."

"How is he?"

"He was still in surgery when I left. Yvonne is there with them now and so is Geno. Anjelica is nowhere to be found."

He remembered Terrell leaving the club with Anjelica last night and reached for the phone to call him. He knew that the chances of them still being together were strong. He had begun dialing the number as Roni continued talking.

"Kayla was able to locate Terrell and he was on his way. Even he was M.I.A. last night. The club must've been off the chain."

Toby clicked the phone off, knowing that if his brother was en route to the hospital, then Anjelica was too. He took a deep breath and proceeded to tell Roni about the shootout afterwards, leaving out the fact that Terrell left with Anjelica, of course.

"Oh my God. Who would be shooting at you?" she shrieked.

"Some dude was beefing with Terry about Darla or somethi—"

"Darla! I should have known her fat yellow ass would have something to do with this. Her hood rat, sleep-with-anyone-with-a-car, always-in-somebody's-face, no-hair-doing self need to just go somewhere and stay!"

"Calm down, Ron. The important thing is that no one was hurt and everyone's fine. Let me take a quick shower and then we can head back over to the hospital."

"Are you sure? I know you're tired after everything that happened last night."

"I want to go. I wanna be there for Kayla and her family." He kissed her quickly and headed upstairs to his room. Pulling out a pair of sweats and a T-shirt from his drawer, he walked into the bathroom. Turning on the shower, he tried to push all thoughts out of his head, but they continued to flash in his mind like snapshots of a movie.

"Toby? You want me to make you some breakfast, sweetheart?" Roni called from downstairs.

"Naw, I'm good," he answered. *Man, get your head together,* he told himself. *You got a good woman downstairs that you need to be focusing on, and you're thinking about a damn memory of what could have been.* He stood in the shower and let his mind drift to thoughts of Kayla and her family, saying a quick prayer for them and Mr. John's recovery. He had just stepped out and was drying off when he heard the yelling.

"What the hell do you want?" Roni screamed.

"This ain't got nothing to do with you!"

"The hell it doesn't! You come knocking on my fiancé's door at eight in the morning demanding to see him and you telling me it doesn't have anything to do with me. You obviously don't even have as much sense as I thought you had."

"Look, I don't have to tell you shi—"

He heard the door slam and then someone began beating on it like a lunatic. The door opened again and this time he knew who Roni was talking to.

"Girl, I will beat your big ass into the middle of next week. You don't know who you're messing with."

"Toby!"

Toby quickly threw on his clothes and took off down the steps. His shirt clung to his still wet chest.

"What is going on?" he demanded. Roni was standing in the doorway about to bum rush Darla, who was standing outside the storm door, looking like a wild woman. Her clothes were rumpled and she kept folding and unfolding her arms as she demanded that Roni let her in. He knew from experience that Roni had no problem fighting, and he wondered if Darla remembered what happened the last time she popped up at his house and crossed Roni.

"I need to talk to you," Darla pleaded.

"I don't have nothing to say to you, Darla," he said calmly as he stepped in front of the door. Roni was right behind him, ready to pounce if necessary.

"Please, Toby. Just give me five minutes, that's all," she begged. Her face was swollen and he could tell she had been crying. He felt sorry for her, but was disgusted with her at the same time.

"Go away, Darla. There's nothing to talk to me about."

"I need to explain about last night. I need for you to understand what happened."

"What happened was that you almost got him and a whole lot of other people killed because of your ignorant ass!" Roni reached past him and tried to open the door.

"I didn't have anything to do with that! I swear. Toby, you gotta believe me. I would never have done anything as stupid as try to have somebody shoot at you or your trifling-ass brother. I need to talk to you, please."

"He already told you to get the hell away from here. What part of that don't you understand? Leave him alone!" Roni was using all her strength to get past him at this point and Toby had to actually struggle to restrain her.

"Darla, just go away. Now isn't the time or the place for this. Go," he said as he stepped back and reached to close the door.

"Toby, please wait," she pleaded. "That's it? After all the shit we been through? It's just that I told Terry—"

"Look, I didn't have anything to do with what you and my brother had going on. I got my own stuff to deal with and I'm not being in the middle of this. That stunt you and your friend pulled last night was crazy and uncalled for."

"Leave him alone. Leave Terry alone. Find somebody that wants you back for a change and quit being a doormat!" Roni yelled.

"Roni! Let me handle this," he turned and told her.

"Handle it then. I'm so sick of her," she huffed at him. It seemed that her attitude was now aimed at him and it took him by surprise.

"You're out of line," Toby told Roni.

"What? I'm out of line? You act like I should give a damn about her or her feelings, which I don't. Every time I turn my head she's over here crying on your shoulder about someone that's done her wrong. Maybe if her high yellow ass would stop screwing—"

"Just go inside," he cut her off.

She stared at him for a moment then rolled her eyes at Darla. "STD," she murmured as she walked away.

He made sure she was out of earshot then turned back to Darla, who was looking like she wanted to burn down his house with him and Roni in it. He went to say something, but she stopped him. "I thought I was your friend, if nothing else, but like your fiancée said, I'm nothing but a STD."

"I'm sorry, Darla, but right now the best thing you can do is let it go."

"Let what go? What are you saying?"

"I'm saying leave me and my brother alone." He closed the door, leaving her standing in the doorway with a defeated look on her face.

He stood there for a moment, staring at the back of the door, angry. Angry at himself for ever becoming involved with a girl whose self-esteem was so low that she would do anything to get anyone's approval. Angry for even bragging and joking that she was just an STD. Angry at Terrell for taking advantage of her too, then getting her pregnant on top of that. Angry at Darla for allowing them to treat her like she was nothing. Angry at Roni for talking to her like that, making an already bad situation worse. He looked out the window and double checked to make sure that Darla had left. He saw her black Neon still sitting in front of his house behind Roni's silver Celica. Their eyes met briefly, then she left. His anger turned to relief as something told him that she finally understood and wouldn't be bothering them again.

48

"Hey, baby. How's Mr. John?" Nicole greeted Terrell with a hug and a kiss as he walked through her front door. He was surprised she was still dressed for church because it was after 5:00 in the evening. He had remained at the hospital for the majority of the day, playing the waiting game with Kayla and her family. After making sure that there was no chance of any friction popping off between the sisters, he decided to leave for a while, promising to return later.

"Still in ICU. Everyone's pretty much still there. The doctor says the next few days are the most critical. I'm probably going back in a little while and take them some food. Did you cook?" He knew she did. Nicole cooked a full meal large enough for ten people every Sunday, although most days it was just the two of them.

"Yeah, I baked some chicken. You want me to fix you a plate?"

"Naw, I'll get it," he told her. "I wanna take a quick shower first, though. Is that cool?"

"Of course. You look exhausted. Why don't you lie down for a while before you go back to the hospital?"

He was tired, but he knew that if he lay down for a nap, he wouldn't wake up until the morning.

"Nickey, do you have any glossy paper?" A voice came from the room Nicole used for a home office.

Terrell cringed, knowing that it was her brother, Gary.

"Look at the top of the closet. It should be a pack up there," Nicole yelled to him.

"I looked and I don't see it."

"Never mind. I'll get it," she huffed and rushed down the hall.

Terrell shook his head in silence as he walked into the kitchen. Nicole had not only cooked baked chicken, but also cabbage, macaroni and cheese, rice and gravy, and cornbread. The growls coming from his stomach reminded him that he was hungry in addition to being tired. He grabbed a large plate and began piling it with food. Just as he sat down at the small kitchen table, Nicole entered with Gary right behind her. There was no denying that they were sister and brother. They were similar in looks, although she was older by two years, darker by two shades, and taller by three inches. Gary was barely five-five and she was easily five-eight.

Nicole had moved into the city to be near Gary after she finished nursing school. They never spoke of their father and their mother had passed away a few years earlier from cancer. Gary was protective, often overbearing of his older sister, and it wasn't a secret that he and Terrell didn't care for each other. He had served seven years in the penitentiary for drugs and acted like that fact alone made him hard-core. Terrell wasn't impressed with him, though, and didn't perpetrate like he was.

"Terrell," Gary said as he sat across the table from him. He was dressed in jeans and wife beater, which did nothing to complement his skinny frame.

"Gary." Terrell didn't look up from his plate.

Nicole offered Gary a plate, but he declined. "No thanks."

"I thought the reason you stopped by was to eat." She sucked her teeth at her brother.

"Changed my mind. I don't have much of an appetite now." He glared across the table. Terrell lifted his eyes and looked over at Nicole. He decided to let her respond, rather than giving Gary one of his own.

"Gary, don't start."

"Don't start what? You want me to sit here and act like everything is fine with this?" he snarled.

"Fine with what? You have a problem with me eating dinner at your sister's crib?" Terrell asked, placing his fork down and wiping his mouth. He had kept quiet long enough.

"Terrell, go ahead and eat," Nicole told him.

"No. What I have a problem with is you knocking my sister up!" Gary pulled out a piece of paper and threw it on the table. Nicole walked over and snatched it up.

"What? You're going through my stuff, Gary?" she shrieked.

"What is it?" Terrell asked, reaching for the paper.

"My ultrasound picture," Nicole answered. She shook her head at her brother in disbelief and began rubbing her temples. Terrell walked behind her and massaged her shoulders. He knew she was upset. The one thing she had been worried about for the past few weeks was how to break the news to Gary.

"I can't believe you, Nickey!"

"Calm down," she told him.

"You lied to me." Gary stood up.

"Gary . . ." Terrell's voice was calm. He knew this was going to be a difficult situation to diffuse.

"You shut up! I ain't talking to you!"

"Hold up, cuz." Terrell could feel his anger mounting although he was determined to maintain his composure.

"No, you hold up, and I ain't your cuz!" he spat.

Nicole shrugged Terrell's hands off her shoulders and took a step toward her brother. "Gary, you need to stop this right now."

"You lied. Straight-up lied to me to my face. I thought we were better than that, Nickey. I asked you if you were sleeping with him, if you two were serious. You said no."

Terrell felt his body tighten as he looked from Nicole then to Gary, who was still talking.

"'No, Gary, I'm not serious about him. It's not even that deep.' That's what you said, remember? Well, let's see how deep it is, huh, Nickey? Is he gonna marry you?"

Nicole stood there, obviously stunned by her brother's outburst. Her lips were pursed together in anger and her chest rose and fell with each breath she took.

"Maybe I should ask him since you don't seem to know the answer. Well, cuz, are you gonna marry her?"

"Don't answer that." Nicole turned and touched Terrell's shoulder. Her eyes told him she was pleading, and he remained silent. "Gary, don't be ignorant."

"How is that ignorant? What's wrong, *cuz*? You can't answer?" He paused momentarily. "I guess not."

"He doesn't have to answer you! Don't answer him, Terry."

"I'm outta here," Terrell told her. "I'll call you later."

"Terrell, wait." She walked behind him as he exited the kitchen and headed out the door. He felt drunk, like everything was moving too fast and he couldn't keep up. His day had been filled with emotional chaos and lack of sleep.

"Let that nigga go, Nickey. You don't need him anyway!"

"Terrell, please stop. Don't listen to him, please," Nicole said as he continued out into the hallway of her apartment.

"Look, I ain't gonna disrespect you or your house by disrespecting your short-ass brother, so I'm leaving. I'll call you later," he told her.

"Wait a minute, Terrell, I don't want you to leave like this. Talk to me," she demanded as she followed him all the way to his car.

"I ain't in the mood for talking right now, Nicole. Now's just not a good time for me. It's been a long night and I just need to go home, take a shower and lay down before I go back the hospital. We'll talk later."

"I wanna talk now."

"You wanna talk now? Whatcha wanna talk about Nicole?"

"I know you're mad, Terrell. I'm sorry my brother is a jerk."

"You told him you weren't serious about me, Nicole? This whole thing has been a joke to you?" he asked. He had told himself that he was going to let it go, but since she wanted to talk all of a sudden, he decided to just put it out there to discuss.

"I said. . . I mean . . ." She looked down as she talked.

"Don't lie to me! What did you tell him?"

"I told him I didn't know what was up with us. And I don't, Terrell. That's the God's honest truth."

"What do you mean you don't know? What the hell is that supposed to mean? I love you, Nicole. I tell you that all the time." He rested against his car and put his hands in his pockets.

"And? You know how many times I've heard that? Look, I love you too." She sighed and reached for his hand. He stared at her and frowned. He could not believe she was saying this.

"I can't tell. It's not even *that deep*, according to what you told your brother. And I don't give a damn about anyone else or what they told you. I'm talking about how I feel about you. Damn, quiet as it's kept, I do wanna marry you."

Nicole closed her eyes then let out a small huff. "No you don't, Terrell. I know you love me. I never questioned that. But you're not ready to marry me. I don't think you're ready to marry anyone."

"How can you tell me what I'm ready for? You know what? Forget it, Nicole. I don't believe we're even standing here having this conversation."

"Terrell, how are you gonna marry me when you're not even fully committed to me?"

"What? I am committed to you. You're having my baby, Nicole. I want us to be a family. You don't want that?" He was totally confused by her response. From the moment she told him she was pregnant, he thought she wanted to get married. Now, it seemed that marriage was the furthest thing from her mind. He didn't want to question whether the baby was his.

"So, you think that because I'm carrying your child that automatically means I want to be your *wife*? Sorry, it doesn't work that way. I'll agree to be your wife when you show me you're ready to be my *husband*."

"What do you want from me, Nicole? I love you, I'm there for you, there's nothing in this world I won't do for you. I've told you that from the moment we got together. And now I find out that we aren't that serious." Terrell's head was messed up and he was ready to leave. He leaned his head back and closed his eyes. He felt Nicole's gentle touch on his cheek and he looked into her beautiful face.

"I love you, Terrell, and I have no doubt that you love me, too, in your own way. But you still go to the clubs every time the doors open, and let's not talk about your phone blowing up. You stay out all night and then get mad when I don't condone that behavior and tell you how immature you are. You even accuse me of trying to control you. Terrell, until you show me you love me, the thought of marrying me shouldn't even enter your mind. True, I am carrying your child, so maybe instead of focusing on marriage you should start with fatherhood."

"So what, you don't wanna have anything to do with me, Nicole?"

"Baby, no, that's not what I'm saying at all. I'm saying that when I get married, it's gonna be forever, and right now, you are definitely not at the forever stage." She smiled.

He looked at this woman who was saying the opposite of what he thought she would. She never ceased to amaze him. She was smart, talented, and beautiful. He loved her and was going to marry her. He placed his hand on her stomach, which held their child. He knew that changing his ways was inevitable; he just assumed it was going to be after he was at least engaged. He now realized that he wanted to change.

Spending the rest of his life with Nicole and making her happy was that important to him. *She may think I'm not in love with her. I can show her better than I can tell her.* He kissed her, again told her he loved her, and got into his car.

Terrell could see her waving in his rearview mirror, slowly disappearing as he drove off. He thought about everything she had told him as he drove home, realizing that she was more intelligent than he had even given her credit for. He began respecting her more and more as he reflected. There was no way he was letting her down. *Little does she know, the forever stage is right around the corner.*

49

The sound of a baby crying on television caused Toby to stir in his sleep. He began feeling around in the bed, searching for the remote to turn the volume down when he realized that the sounds weren't coming from the TV, but the other side of the room. Roni got up and walked over to the port-a-crib where her goddaughter, Day, was whining. She picked up the baby and placed her in the bed between them. It had been seven days since Mr. John's heart attack and Roni had kept Day for the weekend to relieve Geno and Kayla.

"Aw, baby Day, what's wrong? You hungry?" Roni cooed.

Toby smiled at the beautiful little girl's arms and legs flailing in the air. Roni told him she was going to get Day a bottle from the kitchen. He picked Day up and placed her on his chest, snuggling her close to him. She began to quiet down and her wails turned into a simple humming. He placed his thumbs into her tiny fingers.

"You're just spoiled, that's all, Miss Day. You're not slick." He picked up the remote and clicked on *SportsCenter*. He checked out the scores of the NBA playoffs, glad to see that Miami had won. It was only 6:00 in the morning and he wasn't used to getting up this early. "You want anything while I'm down here?" Roni shouted.

"No, I'm good," he answered. The loudness of his voice startled Day, who raised her head in annoyance. "Sorry, sweetie."

He rubbed his hands across her back in a circular motion and her eyes began to close. Just as he thought she was asleep, a loud noise came from her bottom and a scent traveled to his nose. *Oh, no she didn't*. He grimaced. *That's so disgusting*. As if she knew what he was thinking, she raised her head once again, looked him in the face, and smiled as she grunted this time. He raised her off his chest and placed her back in the center of the bed.

"You smell terrible, pretty girl," he told her. She continued to look at him, still passing gas and grunting. He grabbed a diaper, the wipes and some powder out of the diaper bag and placed them on the bed. He stood there looking at the items, realizing he had never changed a diaper in his life. From the smell of it, he wasn't ready now, either.

"Okay, Day. I got your breakfast," Roni announced as she returned to the bedroom.

"Breakfast is the last thing she needs, Ron. She's already full enough!"

"What are you talking about?" She leaned over and picked up the baby. "Whoo whee! Girl, you stink!"

"I told you she don't need nothing else to eat. Then again, she may be hungry because everything she ate is filling that diaper up. I was about to change her." He stretched and lay back down on the bed.

"You were about to do what? You don't know anything about changing a diaper and you know it." She laughed.

"That's what you think." He watched her carefully unfasten Day's pajamas and lift her legs out.

"Wait a minute. Get a towel and put her on, man!" He hopped off the bed, hurrying to the linen closet for a towel. He nearly tripped over the diaper bag in the process.

"Lord have mercy, Toby. It's only poop. She ain't bleeding to death!" Roni laughed. She snatched the towel from him and placed it under the baby's bottom. As she opened the diaper, the stench increased and he tried not to gag.

"That is so disgusting," he commented. He went and grabbed the air freshener from the bathroom and began spraying. "I'ma have to have this place fumigated."

He was contemplating lighting some candles as well when Roni told him, "Here, boy. Take this to the outside trash can."

He stared at the small white bundle she was holding out toward him. *She can't be serious.* He looked over at her and realized that indeed she was and he had no choice but to take it. He grumbled as he took the foul package out the back door. *Maybe I'm not ready for fatherhood after all, taking crappy diapers outside at six in the morning, bedroom stinking.* When he returned to the bedroom and saw his beautiful fiancée sitting on the bed, rocking Day and humming as she fed her, his thoughts changed. It was a beautiful sight to see them there. Roni looked so natural, holding the bottle just right. He rarely saw her like this. So often she was dressed to the max, never a hair out of place, face made up perfectly, but here she sat, dressed in one of his old T-shirts and a pair of shorts, scarf tied on her head and face void of makeup. She had never looked so beautiful to him. His heart leapt. He walked over and kissed both her and the baby as he sat beside them.

"What was that for?" she asked suspiciously.

Toby put his arm around her and whispered, "I want a baby."

"Yeah, right," she snickered.

"I'm serious, Ron. I want us to have a baby."

She lifted Day onto her shoulder and began patting her softly on the back. "Clearly you have lost your mind. You'd better stop spraying that air freshener because it's messing with your brain cells."

"No, it's not. I don't understand why my wanting us to have a baby is so crazy," he replied.

"I'm not having a baby, Toby. I'm still in grad school, and—"

"I don't mean right now, Roni. I'm talking about after we're married."

"I'm not having one then, either. I don't want to have a baby."

He was taken aback by her statement. He had just assumed that they would have a child someday. Roni was always babysitting or shopping for Day and he knew she loved it. He thought she was practicing for when she had her own baby, which he had also assumed would be some time soon after they were married. He didn't know how to react. Luckily, Day picked that very moment to throw up on Roni's shoulder, so he didn't have to.

Roni quickly passed him the baby as she grabbed the nearby towel and began cleaning up. "Can you put her to sleep while I take a shower and get dressed?"

"Sure." He sighed and watched in silence, still holding the baby, as Roni placed three outfits on the bed, deciding which one to wear. This was her usual morning ritual and he was used to it.

"Which one do you like, Toby?" she asked like always.

"All of 'em," he said, reaching on the nightstand for Day's pacifier.

"What's wrong, Toby? I know you're not tripping because I don't want a baby, are you?" she turned and asked, noticing his change in attitude.

"I just thought we would have children."

"Children?" She seemed appalled at the thought.

"Well, at least a child. I like kids, and I wanted at least one of my own." He rocked Day as he talked. Her big brown eyes were looking into his. She looked just like her mother and aunt. *Something about those Hopkins women,* he thought.

"I'm sorry, baby. I'm just not the maternal type. I have too many other things I want to do in life, and having a baby isn't one of them." She shrugged and walked into the bathroom.

Toby's gaze returned to Day, who was drifting off to sleep. He slowly laid her on the bed and pulled the blanket over her. He was tempted to walk into the bathroom and talk to Roni some more about having a child, but decided against it. It didn't seem like the time to discuss it anyway. He lay back next to the baby and flipped through the channels, closed his eyes and drifted off to sleep.

He woke to the feel of Roni's lips on his. His eyes fluttered open and she grinned at him.

"Okay, sleepyhead, I'm gone to work. Kayla will be here to pick Day up around ten. You don't have to worry about dressing her. There are two bottles in the fridge and one by the bed. Are you sure you can handle this?"

"Yes, Ron. You act like I haven't watched her before."

"Well, after your panic attack this morning when she pooped, I was beginning to wonder, Mr. I-want-a-baby."

"Whatever," was his only comment.

"Oh, I forgot to tell you. I have a conference out of town next week. I'm pulling out Wednesday and will be back Sunday night."

"You're going by yourself?" he asked as he began drifting back to sleep.

"Yep. All by my lonesome." She looked at her watch and noticed the time. "I gotta get outta here. I love you. Call me if you or Day needs me."

"How's your dad?" Toby asked.

Kayla had arrived to pick up Day and was double-checking to make sure she hadn't left anything. She looked tired and he almost asked if she wanted him to watch Day a little while longer while she got some rest.

"Better. He's out of the coma and he's alert. If he continues to improve, they'll release him by the middle of next week."

"That's great. I'm glad to hear that," he told her.

"I really appreciate you and Roni doing this for me," Kayla said as she took Day from his arms. "You don't realize how much of a help it's been for me and Geno."

"It's not a problem. You know I love spending time with my beautiful goddaughter." He kissed Day's fingers.

"You'd better not let your brother hear you say that. He'll be ready to knock you out." Kayla laughed.

"Yeah, you know how his jealous ass is," Toby told her as he picked up the bag that held the port-a-crib and Day's diaper bag.

"It's about to get bigger too."

"Bigger? I doubt if that can happen."

"Believe me, it can. I got word that he was about to be promoted on the job. The announcement comes out today. Terrell Sims will be the new department supervisor," Kayla said matter-of-factly.

"Shut up! I didn't know. I can't believe he hasn't said anything to me. "Supervisor?" he repeated to make sure he heard her correctly.

"Supervisor. Can you believe I'll be working for Terrell?" she asked as they headed out the door. As soon as she got to the driveway, she stopped. He looked to see what the problem was and he saw Craig standing next to her car. "What the hell are you doing here? What? You following me now, Craig?"

"I wanna see my daughter. I been calling you for two weeks now."

"And? In case you didn't know, my father had a massive heart attack. I haven't had time to deal with you or your mess." Kayla hit the alarm on her key-chain and popped the trunk at the same time. She motioned for Toby to put the crib and bag in the back of the car as she fastened Day into her car seat.

"What's up, Toby?" he acknowledged, and Toby gave him a nod. "What mess? And I know all about your father being in the hospital. My mother called and offered to keep Day, but all of a sudden you don't want her to have nothing to do with the baby. But I bet you Geno's mom had her, didn't she? She can keep her whenever she wants."

"You know what, Craig? I don't have to explain anything to you about my child. It's none of your business. Now leave." She got behind the wheel and started the engine.

"What do you mean it's none of my business? Do you listen to yourself? That's my daughter you're talking about. I pay for her childcare and buy her clothes. I ain't one of these deadbeat niggas that ain't handling their business. I love my daughter. Even Toby can testify to that."

At the sound of his name, Toby slammed the trunk down. He had kept quiet because he didn't want to be involved. He knew that Craig did love Day. There was nothing he wouldn't do for her. He also knew that Craig had a wife who had recently moved in with Craig's parents along with their son, and that was the main reason Kayla didn't have anything to do with him or his family. Why Craig was questioning Kayla's actions when he knew all of this baffled Toby.

"I don't need Toby to cosign. His ass ain't no prayer book and his mouth ain't no Bible! No offense, Toby," she turned and said calmly. She returned her attention to Craig and her volume increased. "Again, what I do with my child is my business. You *and* your wife are full of games and I don't have time for that. You wanna play daddy? Go do it with your other child because this one doesn't need you." Kayla put the car in reverse, nearly hitting Craig and Toby as she barreled down the street.

"You know what, Toby? That girl is crazy," Craig turned and told him.

"I don't think she's crazy, Craig. She's just going through a lot right now," Toby replied. He could see the frustration in Craig's face and felt for the brother. Craig did try to be a good father in his own way. He made sure that Day was well taken care of, but Kayla was right; the brother played too many games. He had told so many lies that no one believed a word he said.

"I don't give a damn what she's going through. That doesn't have nothing to do wit' me seeing my daughter. She don't have no problem wit' me paying that daycare bill every month or buying clothes and toys, does she?" Craig asked. "Now, that's not fair."

Toby just shrugged. "I feel you, bro. Just keep taking care of your responsibilities and she'll come around, believe me. It's just a lot going on in her life right now."

"Oh, I'ma take care of some things. Believe that," he said. Toby didn't even want to know what he meant by it, so he didn't ask. "I'm outta here, Toby."

"A'ight, Craig." Toby watched him drive off then went back inside.

Looking at the issues that Craig and Kayla were having made him appreciate the fact that he didn't have kids yet. *And now it seems I may never have any*, he thought, remembering what his fiancée had told him earlier. He now understood why she was adamant about him wearing a condom whenever they were together. Even after he had shown her his clean bill of health from his doctor, she still insisted. There was another reason for the condoms. *She doesn't want kids, ever.*

50

"I'd like to propose a toast. To my little—"

"Younger," Terry corrected before Toby could go on.

"Younger brother Terry. He finally gets to be a *big dog* on the job." Toby raised his glass and his friends followed his lead. They were sitting in their favorite sports bar watching the basketball playoffs. The place was crowded and cheers were coming from the Lakers' and Pacers' fans throughout the bar as they enjoyed their teams.

Toby had called Terrell and they agreed that the beef they had in the parking lot was stupid. He invited his brother out for drinks to celebrate his new promotion. Jermaine agreed to tag along.

"So, what's up for the night, fellas?" Jermaine asked.

"It's your night, Terry. What are you trying to do?"

"I'm down for whatever," Terrell told his friend. "As long as you guys remember a brotha gotta be at work by nine in the morning."

"Man, please. You're trying to be home before Nicole gets home from work. Don't even try it," Toby joked.

Terrell looked at him and replied, "Don't even try it. The only reason you called me was because Roni is out of town."

"Ha! That's true. I been trying to get you to hang out since I moved back, and if you not working at the club, you're up under Roni." Jermaine nodded.

"Forget both of y'all. Don't hate because I'm 'bout to be happily married."

"We ain't hating because you're 'bout to be married. We're joking because your ass is sprung!" Terrell nudged Jermaine's arm. At that moment, his cell began ringing. Noticing the time, he knew it was Nicole calling on her break, and he had to answer. He raised his eyebrow at Jermaine and Toby as he slipped it out of his pocket and answered.

"Hey, baby."

"Aw," the men groaned in unison as he walked away from the table.

"Looks like Toby ain't the only one sprung!" Jermaine yelled.

Terrell ignored them, knowing that they would probably joke him the remainder of the evening. Any other time, he would have let the voice mail pick up, but he had been gradually making a change and was determined to remain focused on making his relationship with Nicole work, especially when he realized that there was a possibility he could lose her.

"Hey. You enjoying hanging with your boys?" she asked him.

"Not as much as hanging with you."

"I'll bet," she laughed. "What time are you going home?"

"We're not hanging out late. You know I have to get to work early."

"Okay. Um, Terry, I have something to ask you."

"What is it?"

"I don't want you to get mad or upset. I just want you to know."

His heart began pounding as he tried to think of what it could be. He knew he hadn't done anything in the past few weeks to cause suspicion, but there were so many other things she could have found out about.

"What's up?" he asked.

"Gary came by tonight to talk to me."

"And?" he asked. He tensed up, thinking about how much her brother irritated him. Since finding out about Nicole's pregnancy, Gary had become even more of a pain in the neck. He was always at her house, and when Terrell was there, he would purposely do things to irritate him, like talk about her old boyfriends or some guy he knew that wanted to holler at her. On more than one occasion, Terrell had been tempted to throw a punch, but he just ignored him.

"He's got a new girlfriend. He seems to like her a lot," she said. "He wants me to meet her."

"And?" Terrell asked, wondering what this had to do with him. He could care less whether Gary's short ass had a girlfriend.

"I told him we would go to dinner," she sighed.

"What? Nicole, come on, baby. Be real. You know your brother and I can't stand each other. It's no secret that he don't like me and I don't like him."

"Terrell, this is important to me. I know you and Gary don't see eye to eye at times, but you're both gonna have to get over it. I'm not going to be put in a position where I have to choose between both of you," she snapped.

"I'm not asking you to choose, Nicole. I just don't think us going to dinner is a good idea, sweetheart, that's all." He forced himself to remain calm as he stood in the small area near the pool tables, watching people play.

"Can you please just think about it, Terrell?"

"I'll think about it."

"I mean think about it with an open mind, Terrell. Gary is the uncle of your child, and might be your brother-in-law one day," she added.

He shuddered at the thought. If that was the case, that meant he would have to get used to the idea of Gary being around, and he definitely wasn't ready for that.

"I said I'd think about it."

"Thank you. You know I love you for that, right? It may seem like—"

The phone went dead in the middle of Nicole's sentence. He looked at his phone and saw that his battery was gone. He looked up and saw Jermaine headed toward the restrooms. He waved toward him. "Jermaine! Yo, let me hold your phone."

Jermaine walked over to him. "What's wrong with your cell?"

"My battery went out in the middle of talking to Nicole."

"And that's why you're shouting my name out like that?"

"Shut up and give me the phone." He snatched the phone and redialed Nicole's desk number. "Weren't you headed to the restroom?"

"Sorry. I'll give you some privacy, lover boy." Jermaine laughed and walked away.

"Labor and delivery," Nicole answered.

"Hey, it's me. My battery went dead," he told her.

"I thought you hung up on me. Guess there's no need to leave the nasty message I was going to, huh?"

"Oh, so it's like that?" He laughed, glad that the mood of their conversation had changed. There was a beep and he looked at the phone. He blinked twice to make sure he was reading it correctly, "Yo, Jermaine got another call. I'll be home when you get off. Call me."

"Love you," he heard her say just as he hit the button.

"Yo," he said, answering the other line.

"Jermaine?"

"Naw, he's busy right now. Who's this?"

"None of your business, Terrell. What is he doing and why do you have his phone?"

"I'm saying. What's up, Anjelica? Long time no hear from. I see why I haven't now," he said. He thought that the reason Anjelica hadn't called him was because she was caught up with her family. Now he saw otherwise.

"I got your messages. Thanks a lot. I've been meaning to call you, but you know a lot has been going on," she told him. "I really haven't had time to talk."

"You got time to talk to Jermaine, though, huh?"

"Why Terrell, is that a hint of jealousy I detect in your voice? I do believe it is."

"Don't even try it. I'm saying, I thought we were cool."

"We are cool, Terrell. I can't thank you enough for being there for me and my family. I appreciate it, and you know that. Please don't trip about this."

As she talked, Terrell watched the door of the men's restroom open. Jermaine walked out. As he passed a group of females standing nearby, they all stopped and stared at him, one of them even making a comment about how fine he was. Jermaine just thanked her with a smile and kept walking.

"I ain't tripping. I was just saying that all of a sudden you find time to call Jermaine but not me."

"And how are Nicole and the baby?" she asked sarcastically.

"They're fine. Here comes Mr. Wonderful right now," he replied, passing Jermaine the phone. "You got a call, bro."

"Hello," Jermaine said. "Hey, sweetie. How's it going?"

Terrell shook his head and returned to the table to join his brother.

"What's wrong with you?" Toby frowned. "Where's Jermaine?"

"On the phone. And get this—you'll never believe who he's talking to," Terrell told him.

"Who?" Toby asked, suddenly curious.

"Anjelica."

"Get the hell outta here!"

"I'm dead serious."

"You gave him the number?"

"Hell no. She called him."

"On the cell?"

Terrell was beginning to get irritated. "Naw, at home. Yeah, on the cell. You know she ain't call him here at the bar!"

Jermaine returned to the table with a smile on his face. He ordered another round of drinks and sat down. "What's the score?"

"What's up with that?" Toby asked.

"What? Y'all don't want another round?" He looked at the two brothers, both looking back at him like he had stolen something.

"That's not what he's talking about," Terrell told him.

"What are y'all talking about, man?" Jermaine asked innocently.

"Man, don't play dumb. What's up with your girl hitting you up on the cell and you coming back to the table grinning like a kid on Christmas morning?"

Jermaine cut his eyes at Terrell. "Damn, just blow up my spot, why don't you?"

"Whatever," Terrell said and focused on the big screen television against the wall. The fine waitress brought their drinks, smiling and flirting with him. It took all he could not to flirt back and get her number, but he had to check out her thick behind as she walked away from the table.

"Anjelica is cool people," Jermaine told them. "I started calling to check on her pops then we just started talking on the phone. I like her. She's funny."

He wasn't saying anything Terrell didn't already know. "So, it's just a phone thing. That's cool. For a minute I thought you were gonna say you were trying to holler at her."

"I am. I got tickets for us to go check out Maxwell next month," Jermaine said, raising one eyebrow, his signature gesture.

"What?" Terrell asked before he could stop himself. He tried to play it off when both Toby and Jermaine looked at him.

"What's the problem?" Jermaine asked.

"Man, that girl is nothing but trouble. She causes trouble if nothing else," Toby said, taking a deep swallow of beer. "Tell him, Terry."

"She must not be that bad. Terry was hanging with her. That's how we met, remember? She was dropping you to get your car. Now, according to her, y'all weren't kicking it. Tell me now if it's anything different and I'll step off."

"Man, you know Terry wasn't kicking it with her like that. Were you?" Toby now turned and asked his little brother, wondering himself.

Terrell didn't know how to answer. Granted, he hadn't really kicked it with Anjelica, but they were friends. And they had slept together, even if it was only once. For some reason, the chance of her being with Jermaine bothered him, and he didn't want it to happen. For once, he had the upper hand in the competition and he didn't want to lose it. He thought for a minute then told them, "I'm just saying you need to think twice before you get caught up. She's cool and everything, but I ain't gonna lie; I hit it and I know someone else who did."

"Are you saying she's a ho? She doesn't come off like a ho, Terry. Is she out there like that, Toby?" he turned and asked.

Toby just shrugged, wondering why his brother was saying that about Anjelica. He didn't think she slept around the way Terry was making it seem.

"I ain't say she was a ho, Jermaine. I'm just telling you what *I* did with her. I didn't know you were into my *leftovers*," he said arrogantly. He hoped that would aggravate Jermaine to the point where he would leave Anjelica alone. "You always wanted fresh meat, remember?"

Jermaine picked up his half-empty bottle of beer and swallowed the remainder in one gulp, staring at Terry the entire time. When he was finished, he slowly told him, "Leftovers, huh? I don't think Anjelica would be called a leftover, Terry. I think you may have just been the *appetizer* before the main course. And I've had a few appetizers myself."

"What the hell are you talking about, Jermaine? Who?"

"That's not important, Terry. And don't front like you ain't had a few *appetizers* yourself. The difference is I ain't trying to put nobody's business out there like you are. I like the girl. She's good people, and as her friend, I don't think she would appreciate you trying to call her out like that. I want you and her to remain friends, so the fact that you did that will remain at this table unless you bring it up to her." Jermaine leaned back in his chair.

Terrell stood up and looked over at Toby, who hadn't said a word. "Man, I can't talk to him. You try and talk to him."

"I don't know the girl, Terry. You said yourself that I ain't know her for real. I only know what you and other people have told me."

"Fine. You can't say I ain't warn you." He was about to walk away when he heard someone calling his name.

"Terrell, what's up, man?"

He turned to see his friend, Theo, headed toward the table. "What's up, Theo?"

Theo worked for the same company as Terrell. He was also a manager, but he worked in the finance department rather than customer relations, where Terrell and Kayla worked.

"Nothing. Came here to check out the game." Theo spotted Toby sitting at the table. "DJ Terror, how you been, man? You set that date yet?"

Toby stood and the two men gave each other dap. Toby told him, "Naw, not yet. I'm waiting for you and Tia to set yours first."

"Man, the way she's talking about everything she wants for the wedding, it's gonna take about two years to save for it. At least two years." Theo laughed.

"Wait. You're getting married too?" Jermaine asked.

"Yeah, got engaged back in December," Theo told him.

Toby invited Theo to join them. "You remember," he told Jermaine. You met Theo and his fiancée at Jasper's the night of the proposal.

"Oh, yeah. Tia, the fitness instructor." Jermaine nodded. "She came to the hospital the other week when we were there."

"Oh, you're the *friend* who was with Anjelica when her dad got sick?" Theo's eyes widened as he took a seat beside Jermaine. Terrell decided to sit back down and stay a little while longer.

"That's me, I guess." Jermaine smiled.

"So you own the security camera business, right?" Theo asked.

"Yeah, We Secure U."

"A friend of mine's brother just bought a crib and was looking for someone to install some equipment. You got a card?" Theo asked.

"Yeah, here you go." Jermaine reached into his pocket and passed Theo a business card. "Tell him to give me a call."

"Must be a pretty big crib if he needs security cameras," Terrell commented. He had remained quiet, still heated from the conversation earlier.

"Yeah, it is. It's over in Wheatland Heights." Theo nodded.

"Damn, Wheatland Heights. What does he do?" Toby whistled. Wheatland Heights was prime real estate property with homes starting in the half-million-dollar range.

"He's a pharmacist . . . I mean a real pharmacist in a drugstore, not a street pharmacist," he told them after he saw the way they were looking at him.

"Yeah, that brother's paid for real," Toby agreed.

"Your brother ain't doing so bad, either," Theo told him. "You know I was happy for you when they told me you got the promotion."

"You know I was surprised as hell when they told me. But it's cool," Terrell replied, once again fighting the urge to go after the waitress who kept asking him if there was anything else he'd like. He assured her he was fine, and she looked disappointed.

"I think she wanted you to ask for something else," Jermaine teased. "I can't believe I'm sitting here with three PWBs."

"What? You're crazy!" Terrell blurted across the table.

"Never that, son!" Toby added.

"I definitely don't fall into that category." Theo shook his head.

"There's nothing wrong with being pussy-whipped, my brothers. I mean, you should be glad. Some of us are still on that quest to find that special someone. More for me to choose from. Where did that waitress go again?"

The men continued joking as they watched the game. After watching the Lakers make it one step closer to the NBA championship, they said good-bye and got ready to head out, making sure they were all sober enough to drive. Terrell noticed Toby staring at an empty table in the back corner and tapped him on the shoulder.

"You a'ight?"

"Yeah, just got some stuff on my mind, I guess," his brother told him. "You going to Nicole's?"

"Naw, I think I'm just gonna head home," Terrell answered. "I don't feel like making that drive tonight, especially since the crib is only five minutes away."

"I feel you on that one." Toby sighed.

"You sure you're okay to drive?"

"Yeah, I'm cool. Let's go."

Terrell was concerned about his brother. Toby had seemed distant all night, as if he was deep in thought. He wondered if it had something to do with Roni, but he didn't ask. They were almost out of the bar when they noticed a group of women walking in. Terrell spotted a familiar face among them.

"Leaving so soon, fellas?"

"What's up, Meeko?" He walked over and gave her a hug. He was glad that even after all he had put her through, she was able to forgive him and they were friends. Meeko was a good person and he liked her. She told her friends she would join them in a moment and they walked away.

"Hey, Toby." She smiled. Terrell noticed her eyes brighten as she recognized Jermaine. "Well, well, well. I heard you were back in town. How are things going?"

"They're going good. What's up with you?" Jermaine stepped up and gave her a hug.

"Same old, same old. Working hard and still broke." She laughed, and Terrell noticed Jermaine's eyes lingering on her breasts a little longer than necessary.

"Aren't we all?"

"You guys aren't leaving, are you? Stay a little while and hang with us."

"Sounds good to me. You guys wanna hang out a little while longer?" Jermaine asked.

"I don't think so, Meeko. Thanks, though," Toby replied.

"Naw, I gotta be at work early," Theo said, checking out Meeko's friends. "Looks like I'd be in good company if I did hang around, though."

"Man, let's go," Terrell responded. He thought about Anjelica's claims that Theo was trying to hook up with one of her girls and wondered if there was any truth to what she was saying.

"You guys must be getting old or something. I remember a time when you would party all night, go get some breakfast, and the only reason you went home was to shower and change clothes, not even taking a nap." She smirked.

"Naw, they ain't old, Meeko. It's something else." Jermaine grinned. "But you go right ahead, fellas. Like I said earlier, more for me."

Terrell watched as Jermaine put his arm around Meeko and they joined her friends at the table. The women all greeted him with hugs and smiles and he turned around briefly to wink at Terrell. Terrell followed Theo and his brother out of the bar and into the parking lot.

"Man, back in the day I woulda been right in there with all them fine-ass women." Theo sighed.

"All of us would, man. All of us would. I'll check you guys later," Toby said and gave them each a pound with his fist.

As Terrell sat in his car, he looked through the window of the club. Jermaine was laughing with the waitress who had previously flirted with him. He tried to fight off the pangs of jealousy that were creeping in. He knew the waitress meant nothing to either of them. He also told himself that he was doing the right thing by leaving, especially since he already told Nicole he would not be out late, but there was something still bothering him. He couldn't put his finger on it. It was as if there was a building irritation deep within and Jermaine was the cause of it. *He was just messing with me. There's no way he was wit' anybody I was sleeping with.* He looked up and saw Meeko hugging Jermaine once again. *No way. There's no way he would go there, and neither would she.* He knew he was tripping. *I've had a few appetizers myself.* Jermaine's voice echoed in his head.

51

"Man, I appreciate you helping me out," Jermaine told Toby as he climbed into his truck. "This is a big job and it's kinda last minute."

"Yeah, yeah, yeah. You'd better be glad you're my boy," Toby replied, settling into the butter-soft leather. He was tired, even though it was 1:00 in the afternoon. He usually slept until 2:00 or 3:00 on Saturdays. Jermaine had called him at 11:00 this morning and asked him if he could help him out. He realized this meant a lot to his friend and agreed. "Where are we going, anyway?"

"To Wheatland Heights. Your boy came through. The guy called me late last night and asked if I could come out and give him an estimate this afternoon. He was upset and determined to have me get his house done as soon as possible. Told me money was not an object. You know I told him I'd be there first thing this morning. I just need you to help me measure stuff out, that's about it," Jermaine told him. "No manual labor required."

"Whatever. You still paying me regardless. Like you said, this is a big job."

"No doubt. You know I got you."

Toby felt his eyes getting heavy as they got on the Interstate. The weekend traffic was backed up, and he drifted to sleep, knowing it would be at least a thirty-minute drive out into the suburbs. When he woke, they were entering the sprawling neighborhood bearing the sign WELCOME TO WHEATLAND HEIGHTS, HOME OF PRESTIGE. He was amazed by the huge houses sitting on impeccable lawns which seemed to reach for miles. Some of them were surrounded by huge iron gates and circular driveways. *Some day, Roni and I will be living like this*. He smiled to himself as he admired the landscape.

"Man," he said as Jermaine turned into the driveway of the house at the far end of a cul-de-sac. There was a BMW, a Lexus, an Expedition, and a Camry parked in front.

"Told you this was a big job. The guy said there's a lot of new construction in this area and people are looking for security system installation. This may be just the break I been praying for."

"Then you may be able to hire me part-time and I can get a piece of the action," Toby said as he got out of the truck.

Jermaine reached into the back and removed a briefcase and small tool bag. They made their way to the front of the house, careful not to step on the landscaped lawn, still damp from the sprinkler located in the center.

Jermaine rang the doorbell then began whistling lightly. Toby smiled slyly, remembering that his best friend always whistled when he was nervous.

"It's gonna be a'ight, son. This is what you've been praying for, remember? You got this." He nudged his shoulder.

"I know, but it doesn't make my nerves any easier." Jermaine laughed.

The door opened and a younger guy wearing glasses greeted them. He was dressed in a plaid shirt, khaki shorts, and leather sandals. *He looks like a pharmacist,* Toby thought.

"Hello. Jermaine?" He looked at them hesitantly.

"How ya doing, Mr. Winston?" Jermaine extended his hand.

"Please, call me Stanley. Come on in. Glad you could find the place." He led them inside the massive marble-floored foyer. Sunlight was streaming into the connected living area through the skylights in the vaulted ceiling.

"This is my partner, Tobias Sims." Jermaine gestured toward Toby.

"Mr. Sims." The man shook his hand. He was a fair-skinned gentleman with a slight pot belly. Toby could tell he was quite jovial because he kept smiling at them the entire time he talked.

"Call me Toby. This is a beautiful home," Toby commented.

"Thanks. I'm still trying to furnish it. I've only been here about three months. Between work and teaching, I really haven't had time," Stanley told them.

"So you teach too?" Jermaine asked.

"Yes, I teach chemistry part-time at the university."

"Wow, you are busy," Toby told him.

Stanley gave them a tour of the home, telling them he needed the surveillance and security system installed immediately, and he wanted the top of the line, most extensive system on the market. "Cost is not an issue. I just need it done and done quick."

Toby looked at Jermaine and smiled. They had to be thinking the same thing.

"Stanley, can I ask you a question? I understand you wanting to protect your home, but you don't seem like the type of person that would need what you're asking for. That system is for politicians or even some rap stars."

"I know what you're thinking: What is up with this guy? And I feel comfortable enough to share this with you." The small man looked at them bashfully and said, "This may be hard to believe, but I really don't meet a lot of women."

"Really?" Jermaine looked at him like he was surprised by Stanley's revelation. It took all it could for Toby not to laugh.

"Yeah, believe it or not. A brother is paid, but he can get lonely. I think a lot of women are intimidated by my intelligence."

"I can see that happening," Toby agreed.

"Well, in my spare time, I began chatting online to various partners of the opposite sex. Just innocent conversations at first, but some of them actually began to develop into something more. Recently, I took a chance and invited a certain interest to my home to meet face to face."

"To meet for the first time?" Jermaine asked.

"Stan. You know you're always supposed to meet in a public place first. You're smarter than that, man." Toby shook his head.

"I know, I know. But what can I say, fellas? She had me wide open and there was a lapse in judgment, I guess. Call it temporary mental insanity. Needless to say, when she arrived, I noticed there was something strange about her."

"Was she ugly, Stan?"

"Naw, she was gorgeous. Beautiful, smart, funny. Everything she seemed to be online, but you know I'm in the medical field, and I pick up on some things. And when I realized what it was, I had to ask him to leave."

"What!"

"Naw, Stan. Tell me you're playing!"

"Seriously, guys, I couldn't believe it myself. Well, he didn't take it very well, and things around here have been crazy. It's to the point that I'm being stalked. I gotta get it done. When can you start?"

Jermaine looked at Toby, who gave him a nod. "I'll order the equipment tonight. We can start getting measurements right now."

"Fine with me." Toby shrugged. He should have known that he would be roped into helping Jermaine with the installation. He really didn't mind because he could use the extra loot.

"Thanks. I really appreciate it. Come on back to my office and I'll get you a check," Stanley gushed.

They followed him down the hallway leading toward the back of the home, where they entered a large office. They could hear music and laughter coming from outside, along with water splashing.

"You got a pool?" Toby asked, walking to the window and looking out.

"Yeah, my rowdy brother is here visiting for the weekend. He and his girl must be back there," Stanley answered, reaching into the large mahogany desk and taking out a checkbook. He sat down and began writing.

Toby saw a man dive into the swimming pool. He came up beside a sexy, bikini-clad woman, sitting poolside, tanning. Her back was toward the house. The guy soon swam nearby and came up from under the water, splashing some on her. She screamed and jumped up, running over to the nearby table and grabbing a towel. She wiped her face then began threatening the culprit. Toby's heart began pounding as he watched from inside. The Isley Brothers singing "Summer Breeze" faded from the sur-round-sound speakers.

"I told you I didn't wanna get my hair wet! You play too much!" she screamed.

"Aw, I ain't thinking about your hair," the guy said, walking over and putting his arms around her.

"Get off me! You're getting me wet!"

"I'm sorry, baby. Do you forgive me?" he asked playfully. The woman turned around and faced him, looking at him tenderly, then kissed him softly on the lips. Toby blinked, wanting it to be a bad dream he was caught in.

"Toby! Man, did you hear anything I just said?"

Jermaine was speaking to him, but Toby couldn't move. He continued to watch as the couple returned to the pool and sat on the side. The guy was muscular, the same light complexion as Stanley, dressed in a pair of black trunks.

"What's your brother's name?" Toby finally spoke.

"Sean. You know him?" Stanley asked, looking up.

"Naw, I was just wondering," Toby said solemnly. He finally turned and walked away from the window. Jermaine was staring at him.

"What's going on, T?"

"Nothing," Toby answered. He was still flabbergasted by what he had just witnessed. He was about to sit down but then walked back over and looked out the window again. Anger began to creep within him as he continued to watch the couple. Her legs were wrapped around his body and they were grinning at each other.

He was so caught up that he didn't realize Jermaine was standing next to him, observing as well. "What the—? You gonna go handle this?"

"Handle what?" Stanley asked.

"The measurements," Toby quickly answered. "Naw, we can get them later. You know we got that other thing to take care of and it's getting late."

"Right, right. So, we'll get started Monday. Is that cool, Stan?" Jermaine asked, picking up his briefcase.

"Sure, Monday's fine. I appreciate you guys coming out here, especially on a Saturday. But like I said, things have gotten crazy, and it's imperative that I get it taken care of," Stanley said as he walked them out.

"Well, see you Monday morning. Will your brother be here?" Toby asked, looking over at Jermaine.

"No. He's flying out at six o'clock tomorrow."

"All right then, it was nice meeting you," Jermaine said.

"Nice meeting you. I look forward to doing business with both of you."

Neither man said anything as they got inside the truck. Jermaine drove in silence for a good fifteen minutes before asking, "You a'ight?"

"Yeah, I'm good."

"You sure? Because we can go back and handle it if you want."

"Naw, I'm good. It's cool," he answered. His head was throbbing, but the pain was nothing compared to the hurt he felt in his heart. He continued to sit in silence and stare out of the window. It seemed to take forever for them to get to his condo.

"You want me to come in for a while, man?"

"I need some time alone to think. Thanks for offering," he said when they pulled in front of his townhouse.

The phone was ringing as he walked inside.

"Hello."

"Hey, baby. What are you doing?"

"Just walking in the door," he said, going into the kitchen. He opened the refrigerator door, not knowing what he was looking for. He scanned the shelves, suddenly realizing that he was hungry.

"I thought you'd still be 'sleep."

"Nope, I did some running around with Jermaine. I'm just getting back." He tried to think of how he would handle this situation without losing his cool. "How's the conference?"

"It's going good. Do you miss me?"

"Of course I do. What time are you coming back?" His voice cracked and he cleared his throat, hoping she didn't catch it.

"Probably around three. Can you meet me at the car rental place?"

"Sure. Which one?" he asked. He located a frozen pizza and popped it in the microwave.

"The one by the mall. What time are you going to work?"

"I'll be leaving here around eight thirty, I guess. Same time."

"Then I'll call you around eight. I have another seminar about to begin, baby. I'll talk to you later. I love you."

"Love you too," he said then hung up the phone. He stared at the floor, still thinking about what he had seen earlier. He felt the anger that had subsided beginning to return. The sound of the microwave beeping brought him back to reality.

He took his food out and placed it on the kitchen table, grabbed a beer out of the fridge and sat down to eat. As he closed his eyes and lowered his head to pray, the image of the guy and girl at the pool interrupted him. He shook his head in an effort to extinguish the mental image. *God, help me. I don't even know how to handle this*, he prayed then picked up a slice. He tried to eat, but the appetite he had just moments earlier was gone. He wrapped the food up and put it back in the fridge then poured the untouched beer down the sink. He decided that he was more tired than anything and went to the bedroom. He took off his shoes and climbed into the huge bed and fell into a deep slumber.

52

"That's not player." Terrell frowned at Nicole. She was holding a yellow-and-white sleeper with a matching hat. They were in the mall and had been shopping all afternoon. He had been ready to go for a while.

"I'm not worried about it being player, Terrell. I'm worried about it fitting the baby." She sighed and rolled her eyes at him.

"I want it to fit *and* be player. I can't have my son around here sporting yellow footie pajamas."

"Who said you were having a son? That hasn't been determined yet, remember?" she asked, putting the outfit back. He laughed as he looked at her belly, which was beginning to poke under her shirt.

"I wouldn't even want my daughter wearing that." He laughed, taking her by the hand and leading her out of the store. "Come on, let's go. I'm hungry."

"We just ate a little while ago. And I thought I was the pregnant one," she teased. They left the mall and headed to the car, both carrying large shopping bags. Terrell popped open the trunk and placed the bags inside.

"Better job, more money. Must be nice."

Terrell looked up and saw Geno and Kayla walking toward his car. Geno was pushing Day in the stroller. Nicole got out of the car when she saw them.

"Aw, don't you all look like the perfect family? How's your dad?" He hugged Kayla and greeted Geno with a pound. Day was chewing on a toy and he began teasing her with it.

"Released this morning. He's home, thank God. We just left there and decided to walk the mall this afternoon. We're not buying up everything like you all, though," Kayla told them.

"Girl, please. You know I'm not buying anything, unlike your buddy here." Nicole laughed.

"Don't even try it. If y'all think all those bags in there belong to me, then you're—"

"Exactly right." Nicole finished the sentence for him. They laughed because there was no doubt in anyone's mind that the majority of the bags belonged to Terrell. "I'm not even complaining, though. I'm just gonna let him get his shop on now because in a few months the only thing he'll be shopping for is diapers and formula."

"I know that's right." Geno nodded. "Where are you all headed to now?"

"To eat, of course," Nicole told them.

"Y'all wanna roll?" Terrell asked.

Kayla looked at Geno, who nodded. "Yeah. Where y'all trying to go?"

They decided on a restaurant and agreed to meet there in an hour. Terrell and Nicole arrived first and gave their name at the door. The hostess advised them that there would be a twenty minute wait, which they expected. Kayla, Geno, and the baby soon arrived and they sat on the benches outside, enjoying the evening air. Terrell told them all about his new job and his new supervisor, CJ.

"I can't stand her," Kayla told him. "She talks to me like I'm dumb. She talks to any female that isn't a manager like she's dumb, matter of fact."

"Aw, she's not that bad. I don't have any problems with her, myself," he told her. That was true. People, mostly women, complained about CJ being arrogant, nasty, and short-tempered. Terrell had never seen that side of her, and he had come in contact with her on several occasions.

"I bet you don't. I mean, you are a man. She doesn't have a problem with men. Now, let that have been me that got the position, then it would be an entirely different story." Kayla smirked.

"Oh, so it's like that, Kayla? He didn't tell me it was like that," Nicole uttered.

"Mm-hmm." Kayla nodded in a gesture of sisterhood.

"Both of y'all need to quit." Terrell shook his head at them. "It's not like that. You know Kayla's gonna *exaggerate* everything."

"Oh, so now I'm *exaggerating*?" Kayla gasped dramatically.

"See, DQ in full effect," he responded and they all laughed.

Their name was announced over the loudspeaker, so they proceeded inside to be seated. Terrell was holding the door open when he felt his phone vibrating in his pocket. He lingered behind and took it out. Recognizing the number, he told Nicole he would return momentarily. He went out and stood in front of the restaurant, redialing the number that had just appeared on his caller ID.

"Hey, Terrell, I got your message. What's up?"

"Nothing. I was just calling to check on you. What's going on with you? Kayla told me your dad was released today."

"Yeah, he's home and doing good. When did you talk to her?"

"We're actually at dinner right now. You should too," he told her.

"Yeah, right. Family crisis is over, she's back to hating me, so no thanks. Anyway, I have plans already," Anjelica told him.

"What plans?"

"None of your business." She laughed into the phone. "You are a funny dude, you know that?"

"Naw, I ain't funny. I know you don't have plans with Jermaine, do you?"

"What difference does it make? Did I ask who you were out with? No, because it's none of my business."

"It's not even like that. I'm telling you that he's no good for you and I'm telling you because you're my friend." He began pacing up and down the sidewalk.

"No, you're telling me that because you don't want to even think about the possibility of your boy sleeping with me. That's what it is."

He could hear the agitation in her voice and met it with his own. "The fact that we slept together has nothing to do with it. I'm telling you so you won't get hurt. I know Jermaine; he's my boy, and I know how he is. I saw that nigga the other night at the bar hollering at another friend of ours. What does that tell you, Anjelica?"

"It tells me that maybe you need to check yourself, putting someone that's supposed to be *your boy* on blast like that, telling me all of his business. Now, I don't know what's going on with you these days, but you need to chill. I have to go. Like I said, I got plans." She hung up in his ear.

He stood speechless for a minute, trying to figure out what had just happened. Not only had he pissed Anjelica off, but he had put Jermaine out there like he was trying to play her, which he hadn't intended to do.

"So, how long you been fucking her?"

The hairs on Terrell's neck stood up as he realized someone was standing right behind him. He put his phone back in his pocket, trying to think of something to say. He slowly inhaled as he turned around.

"Damn," was all he could say.

"Answer me. How long have you been sleeping with her?"

"It's not like that."

"Not like what? Oh, don't tell me. That was another Anjelica you were talking to on the phone, right?"

"Hold up for a minute. Please just let me—"

"Let you what? Explain? What is there to explain? There's no need. You know what? This kind of explains a lot of things. I thought it was kinda funny that you and she arrived at the hospital together, but I thought that had something to do with her maybe hooking up with Jermaine. But it was you she was with, and Jermaine was covering for you two. Damn, I can't believe this." Tears began streaming down her face and Terrell realized how hurt she was. He hadn't meant for her to find out this way.

"Kayla, wait." He reached for her arm but she snatched away from him.

"Don't touch me!"

People entering and exiting the restaurant stopped to look at them. He took a step back, not wanting to appear like he was hurting her.

"Kayla, I need for you to listen to me. It's not like that, for real."

"You were my friend—my best friend, at that. And this entire time you been screwing my sister! Now I know why you defended her every time I said something. I guess you all sit back and have a good ol' laugh about me, huh?"

"Kayla, chill. Listen."

"No, you listen. I never want to see or talk to you again! Leave me alone, and I mean that." Kayla wiped her eyes with the palm of her hand and took a deep breath. She scowled at Terrell as she walked past him and re-entered the restaurant, snatching the door.

Terrell waited a few moments before going in. When he arrived at the table, Geno was putting Day back into the stroller.

"What? You guys leaving?" he asked, avoiding looking at Kayla.

"Yeah, Kay has a migraine and she forgot her medicine. She went to the car to get it, but it wasn't there," Geno told him. "Guess we'll have to take a rain check."

"Yeah, we'll have to do that." He watched Kayla grab her purse and the diaper bag. She paused and looked at Nicole. His heart began pounding, wondering what she was about to say.

She looked over at Terrell then said, "Nicole, give me a call later."

"Sure thing, girl. I know how those migraines can be. Take care of yourself." Nicole stood and gave her a hug and watched them as they left.

"You still wanna eat?"

"Yeah, I'm still hungry," she assured him. "I wonder what happened to Kayla, though. She seemed fine when they first got here. She went to the car, and then when she came back to the table, she was like, 'Let's go!'"

"I don't know." Terrell seemed to be engrossed in the menu.

"Well, she's been under a lot of stress these past few weeks, so she's probably just tired."

"Yeah, probably."

Nicole's phone rang and she took it off the side of her purse. "It's Gary. He's probably with Arianna."

"Who? Who the hell is Arianna?"

"Gary's girlfriend. She's a nurse too. Can you believe that?" she said and began chatting into the phone to her brother.

"No, I find that hard to believe," Terrell muttered. Gary was probably lying to Nicole. His girlfriend being a nurse would require her having some level of intelligence, which obviously she didn't have if she was with his dumb ass. He had more important things to deal with than Gary and his fake-nurse girlfriend. He had to smooth things over with Kayla, Anjelica, and possibly even Jermaine if Anjelica told him what he had said. *I can't believe I've messed up all the way around. Tonight just ain't my night.*

"They're right around the corner. I told them they could join us. Is that cool?"

"Whatever," he said, not really paying attention to what she was saying. He told her he'd be right back, got up and walked over to the bar, ordering a Tanqueray and orange juice. He contemplated calling Toby, but thought about the warning Toby gave him when he found out Terrell was messing with Anjelica. He paid for his drink and returned to the table.

"They're on their way," Nicole told him when he sat down. "Please be nice—well, at least be civil."

"What are you talking about?"

"To Gary and his girlfriend," she replied.

"What about them?"

"I just told you they were eating with us. Matter of fact, here they come now."

Terrell turned around to see Gary walking toward them, decked out in a two-piece linen suit with matching gator shoes. *This guy really thinks he's a pimp,* Terrell thought as Gary threw up a peace sign and waved. Then, Terrell felt as if he was in a Quentin Tarrantino movie and things began moving in slow motion. Gary turned and reached back for someone, and his date appeared by his side. She was beautiful; an attractive blonde who reminded him of one of the girls from the TV show *Friends*. He had seen her once before, and never in a million years had he thought he would ever see her again—definitely not with Gary, of all people.

"What's up, peeps?" Gary smiled at them.

"Hey there, you!" Nicole gave her brother a big hug. She faced the girl and said, "You must be Arianna. It's nice to finally meet you."

"Nice to meet you too," the woman replied.

Terrell wanted to run before she saw him. He wondered if she would recognize him. If she did, would she remember from where?

"Gary has told me so much about you. This is my boyfriend, Terrell." Nicole took Terrell by the hand and pulled him to her side.

"How are you?" He extended his hand toward her nervously.

She took it into hers and their eyes met. He saw her eyebrows rise, and a look of surprise crossed her face. He knew that she remembered him. She blinked then took a step back. "Nice to meet you."

"Uh, sweetheart, I need to go to the restroom. I'll be right back," Terrell said to Nicole. "Please excuse me."

Terrell walked into the bathroom and stood over the sink. He turned the water on and let it run while he closed his eyes and tried to calm down. There was no way his life could be turning out this way. Stuff like this didn't happen to him. Shit was beginning to crumble left and right. *Tonight ain't my night. It just ain't my night.*

53

Toby turned into the parking lot of the car rental company. He spotted Roni getting out of a gold Camry, waving at him. He pulled behind her and got out. She ran over and threw her arms around his neck. He inhaled her sweet scent as he kissed her.

"I missed you, baby," she whispered into his ear.

"I missed you too." He cupped her face in his hands and looked at her intensely. She kissed him fully on the mouth and he held her tight. After a few moments, they pulled away.

"I'm going inside and take care of the paperwork. It should only take a few moments," she told him.

A young guy wearing a uniform came out and began checking the car. Toby had loaded Roni's things into his truck and was about to get in when the guy yelled for him.

"Yeah?" Toby walked over, thinking maybe Roni had scratched the car or something. "Found this under the seat. You know this guy?" he asked, handing the small piece of plastic to Toby.

He looked at the driver's license and smiled at it, thanking the guy. "Yeah, that's her brother. I'll give it to him. He'll be glad you found this."

"No problem. Have a good day," the guy said.

He drove to the front door and waited for Roni to come out. She finally did, and he walked around to open the door for her to get in.

"Thank you, sweetie," she said and gave him another kiss.

"You going to my crib or yours?" he asked.

"Mine. I need to unpack and get ready for the week."

"But what about spending time with me? I thought we'd go to dinner or something this evening. I want to have you in my bed tonight."

"I know you do, but I'm tired, sweetie. It's been a long trip. I'll make it up to you." She reached over and began playing with the back of his neck.

"Promise?" he looked over at her.

"I promise. Besides, soon you're gonna have to start kicking me out of your bed because I'll be over there so much."

He asked her to fill him in on her trip and the seminars she attended. She told him about the speakers that attended and the different topics covered, talking all the way to her house. He took her things inside as she checked her mail.

"You want me to go grab you something to eat?" he offered, pulling her into his arms. "Or is there something you'd like for me to eat before I leave?"

"Hmm, that's an offer I'll definitely be taking you up on later," she said as she kissed him. He walked her over to the sofa, both of them falling down onto it. She groaned as his hands crept along her thighs and worked their way up. She was wearing a short jean skirt and tank top. He went to reach under, knowing that she was wearing a thong, but she grabbed his hand.

"What's wrong?" he asked.

"I'm just tired, that's all, babe. I'm sorry."

"I understand," he told her, easing up. He stood and reached to help her up. He took a deep breath and said, "I guess I'ma leave. You go ahead and get some rest. I'll call you later."

"Okay."

He opened the door then snapped his fingers. "Man, I almost forgot. The guy found this under the seat of the rental car."

He reached into his pocket and handed her the license. She took it and looked at it. He waited for her reaction.

"Oh, wow, this is a guy that was at the conference with us. I gave him a ride to his hotel one afternoon." She laughed nervously. "I know he must be looking for it. He's not gonna be able to get on the plane without his ID."

"Good thing you found it, huh? Maybe you should call him. You got his number?" He folded his arms.

"I sure don't."

"He had to catch a plane? Where's he from?"

"I don't even remember. Philly, I think. Yeah, Philly."

"It's right on the license. What's his name? Dean?"

"Sean," she corrected.

"That's right, Sean. And you're sure you don't have his number?"

"No, I just gave him a ride that one night." Roni looked at him innocently. He almost believed her.

"Roni, you're not lying to me, are you? You met this guy at the seminar and you gave him a ride back to your hotel?"

"His hotel! And what's with the third degree, Toby? I told you what happened. It's no big deal. I'll drop the license in the mail to him tomorrow when I leave school. Damn, why are you tripping all of a sudden?"

"Why am I tripping? Did I tell you where Jermaine and I went Saturday?"

"You told me you ran some errands or something." She walked past him. He grabbed her by the arm and looked her in the face. "What is wrong with you?"

"Jermaine got a huge contract Saturday for a house in Wheatland Heights." He watched her face become clouded with confusion and held onto her arm as he spoke. "That's right, Wheatland Heights. It's a nice neighborhood. As I was driving through, I was thinking, man, Roni and I will have a house like one of these someday. Have you ever been there?"

"No," she said quietly.

"Don't lie to me. Please don't lie to me, Veronica." He looked at her, eyes wide with shock. He still had a grip on her arm and was determined not to let go. She stared back at him, saying nothing. "Tell me who Sean is."

"I told you," she whispered.

"I saw you, Roni! I was there at Stanley's house when you were frolicking in the backyard by the pool! 'Don't wet my hair!' Remember? Isley Brothers blasting from the surround-sound. You were having a ball. You and Sean."

"Toby, please."

"Please what? Oh, now you wanna talk? Well, I don't wanna hear it. You been with this nigga since last week, Roni? You spent the weekend with him. I wonder how many other seminars you've been to with Sean, huh? Correction—no, I don't wanna know how many other ones. Seminar, my ass!" he yelled. She flinched and he released her arm. He walked out, and she chased behind him.

"Toby, I need to talk to you. Don't leave like this, baby. Please."

He got into his truck and drove off. He was tempted to look back but didn't. He couldn't believe that she had tried to play him. He had pondered all weekend about how he would approach the subject with her. He knew she would deny it initially; that was why he gave her the opportunity to come clean. But she didn't, and that disappointed him. He was more hurt by the fact that she tried to lie about the situation than he was about catching her with another man.

He drove around aimlessly for an hour, eventually winding up at Jasper's. There were a few cars in the parking lot, although it was only 6:00. He didn't understand why he was torturing himself by thinking about the last time he was here, the night he proposed. His emotions were sending him into a combined state of confusion and devastation. For most of his adult life, Jasper's was the comfort zone he could go to whenever his life was filled with turmoil. He could hear soft jazz playing as he walked in and headed straight for the bar.

"Tobias, man, what a nice surprise," Uncle Jay called from behind the bar.

"Hey, Uncle Jay. What's going on?"

"Nothing much. What'll it be? The usual?"

"I don't even know, Uncle Jay," Toby said, looking at the bottles of liquor on the glass shelves behind the bar. "I may need something a little stronger today."

"What? It can't be that bad." The older man looked at Toby with his face full of concern. Monica, one of the regular waitresses, walked up and put in a drink order. She made small talk with Toby while Uncle Jay prepared the beverages.

"Uncle Jay, why are you tending the bar?"

"We're short-staffed tonight. Well, actually, we're short-staffed every Sunday since business picked up. Word got out about the kitchen being open at five. I guess that's a good thing, huh? So, I fill in back here."

"It's gonna be really busy tonight because we're short-staffed in the kitchen too," the waitress said, picking up the tray of drinks. "Nice seeing you again, Toby."

"Uncle Jay, why didn't you tell me you needed help? I'll work the bar for you tonight," Toby stood up and told him.

"You don't have to do that, Tobias. You came in here to drink yourself. Seems to me like you already got enough on your mind." Uncle Jay leaned on the bar. "Now, tell me what the problem is."

"I don't have a problem, Uncle Jay. Go ahead and work the kitchen. I got this out here," he told him. When his uncle hesitated, he assured him, "I want to do it, Uncle Jay."

"Well, once the evening crowd is served then I can come back out here. I appreciate this, Tobias. I really do." Uncle Jay removed his apron and Toby made his way to the back of the bar. "You sure you know what you're doing?"

"I learned from the best, Uncle Jay. You taught me well." Toby smiled.

People began coming in the door, and soon Toby was hard at work. The wait staff was patient and friendly as he racked his brain in an effort to remember how to mix drinks and cocktails. Monica teased him, but she helped out a lot. *Uncle Jay is right; this place is the spot on Sundays.*

Toby was in the middle of making a round of Harvey Wallbangers for a rowdy bunch when someone yelled, "Can a brother get some service?"

"Coming right up," he called and carefully handed the loaded tray of drinks to the server. He looked up to see his brother sitting with his back to the bar, checking out the scene. "What the hell are you doing here?"

"What are you doing behind the bar?"

"Helping Uncle Jay out."

"I feel you. This place is really jumping, huh? I heard them talking about it at work."

"Yeah, I think it has a lot to do with Liquid," he said, pointing to the band that was setting up. "What are you drinking?"

"Ginger Ale."

"You came all the way to Jasper's for a ginger ale?"

"That and the atmosphere, of course." He gestured toward a table full of females, laughing and talking. One woman waved for Terrell to come over, but he shook his head and waved back, surprising Toby. *Maybe he is changing his ways*, he thought.

The two men made small talk as Toby continued to work the bar. He noticed Terrell seemed distant, but he was too preoccupied with his own drama to even ask what was wrong.

"Get this," the waitress said as she walked up to the counter. She had to yell in order to be heard over the band. "This chick ordered something called a Slow Screwball or something. I told her you wouldn't know what it was."

"A what?"

"Maybe it was a Screwball with Sloe gin." She tilted her head to the side.

"Go make sure what she wants," Toby told her and began filling other orders. Soon she popped back at the bar, smiling at him. "Did you find out what she wanted?"

"Yeah. A slow, comfy screw."

He leaned closer to make sure he understood what she was saying. "What did you say?"

"A Slow Comfortable Screw." The voice came over Monica's shoulder, causing Toby to damn near drop the bottle of Courvoisier he was holding. His eyes met hers and they stared at each other for what seemed like a lifetime. Her hair was cut short, yet it did nothing but enhance her deep-set, keen eyes, and broad cheekbones. Her face was exquisite, and he thought that even if she had shaved her head bald, it would only make her more beautiful than she already was.

"Yeah, that's it." Monica smiled. "A Slow Comfortable Screw."

"Damn, Isis, you look good as hell." Terrell stood up and walked over to her. She gave him a hug, but her eyes never left Toby's.

"You're not looking so bad yourself, Terrell. Hi, Toby."

"What's up, Isis?"

"You wanna just sit here at the bar instead of your table?" Monica asked. "I already put your food order in to the kitchen."

"Sure, that's fine," Isis told her. "If these two gentlemen don't mind me joining them."

"Heck naw. Besides, Toby's the bartender anyway. He doesn't count." Terrell grinned as Isis took a seat next to him. "Where the hell you been? I mean, you showed up at the proposal and graced us with a song, and the next thing I knew, you were ghost and we ain't seen you since. What's up with that?"

"I was only in town for one night. It was a beautiful proposal. I have to admit I was impressed." She looked over at Toby. "You two looked very happy together."

Toby thanked her and began mixing her drink. He concentrated on mixing the exact amounts of Sloe gin, Southern Comfort, vodka and Galliano, but instead of orange juice, he used pineapple, topping it off with two cherries, the way he knew she liked it. It had to be perfect.

"So, you're visiting again?" Terrell asked.

"Yeah, for a minute. You know how I do," she answered.

"Meeko was pissed that you came to town and didn't holler at her. I thought she was your girl."

"She is. I called her and explained what happened."

"We saw her at the club a few weeks ago. When was that, Toby?"

"About a month ago," Toby said, placing the drink in front of her.

"Why thank you, Isaac—I mean Toby." She winked.

"Oh, you got jokes, huh?" He grinned. Her smile met his and she picked up the glass. "Should we toast?"

"I think we should." Terrell held his glass up as well.

"Toby, you're not joining us?" Isis asked.

He grabbed a glass and filled it with soda, lifting it to theirs. "To old friends."

"To old friends," they repeated. He watched Isis take a long swallow of her drink.

"Perfect," she told him.

The bar got busy and Toby got back to work. He eavesdropped as Terrell began filling Isis in on the latest gossip and caught her up on the people they knew. She tossed her head back in laughter; it sounded like music to Toby's ears.

"Your food should be out in just a few minutes," Monica said as she walked up to the bar with another order of drinks for Toby to fill.

"Thanks," Isis replied. She looked up and caught Toby staring at her again. He smiled, knowing he was straight busted.

"Uh, hello. Can my customers get their drink on, please?" Monica snapped her fingers at Toby. He snapped back to reality and had Monica repeat the order.

"Hey, check it out. Why don't I take over for a little while, Toby? You and Isis can talk," Terrell suggested. Toby didn't know how to respond. He looked over at his brother, who was already headed behind the bar.

"What are you doing?" he whispered as Terrell pulled on a white apron emblazoned with the Jasper's logo.

"Helping out." Terrell raised his eyebrows as he answered. "There's no point in you staring at each other all night and her sitting at the bar acting like I'm doing standup. Go sit down and talk. Well, never mind. It's too late. She's already gone."

Toby turned to see that the space where Isis had been sitting was now empty. He looked around the club, but she was nowhere to be found. There was no way to hide the disappointment he felt. *Stop tripping. You didn't have no business sweating her like that anyway. Her leaving is a good thing. You are engaged, remember?*

"Yeah, you're right," he told himself aloud.

"Right about what?" Terrell asked.

"Nothing." He stood in silence, still scanning the crowd, hoping to find her. The faces of people laughing and enjoying themselves were too much for him.

It had been a hell of a day and he decided it was time for him to leave. "I gotta go talk to Uncle Jay. I'll be right back."

Terry nodded and began talking with some female patrons who were now sitting at the bar. Toby set off to find his uncle. He was about to enter the kitchen when the door swung open. Monica walked out carrying a tray of food. He held it open for her.

"Thanks. Tell your friend I'll bring her food to her as soon as I take care of this other table."

"Don't bother. She dipped."

"What?"

"She left. I'm leaving too. Terry's gonna work the bar. Where's Uncle Jay?"

"Back there." She nodded, looking at him strangely. "I can't believe she left."

"Believe it. She's known for pulling disappearing stunts like that. Not the first time, won't be the last," he replied.

He found Uncle Jay piling plates with his famous fried catfish and potato salad. "Uncle Jay, I'm leaving."

"So soon? I thought you were gonna help me close up," his uncle said jokingly. "Thanks for pitching in tonight, Toby. I guess I can get outta this hot kitchen now. Especially since the cook finally showed up."

"Terry took over the bar, so you can relax for a little while, Uncle Jay."

"Terry? When did he get here?"

"About an hour ago. He's got everything under control out there. You know him."

"Yeah, he's probably out there giving out drinks in exchange for telephone numbers." Uncle Jay laughed. "I sure appreciate you boys. Can you believe how busy this place has gotten? That band packs a house, I tell you."

"Yeah, Uncle Jay." Toby sighed.

"Something wrong, Tobias? What's on your mind?" Uncle Jay continued piling plates as he talked, peering at Toby over his wire-rimmed glasses.

Toby inhaled deeply, not knowing where to start. He didn't want to put his and Roni's business out there, but he needed to talk to someone. Uncle Jay had always been the father they never had.

"Toby, you are such a liar!"

Toby frowned at Monica as she walked past him, reaching for the trays of food.

"What are talking about, ghetto girl?"

"That girl is sitting right in the back, waiting on you.

"Where?"

"What girl?"

Toby and Uncle Jay spoke at the same time.

"Some girl he and Terry were talking to," Monica answered. "She's at the table in the far left corner."

"Is that her food?" Toby asked.

"Yep."

"Show me where she is." He turned to Uncle Jay. "Can I get a plate?"

"Humph. I thought you were leaving," Uncle Jay said suspiciously. "Who's out there?"

"Isis."

"The singing girl?" Uncle Jay's eyes lit up and Toby couldn't help smiling. "I ain't even gonna ask."

"Please don't," he replied. His uncle fixed him a plate and placed it on the tray next to the plate for Isis. "Thanks, Uncle Jay."

He followed Monica out of the kitchen. She pointed to a secluded table located in the far corner of the restaurant. He thanked her and made his way through the crowd, balancing the tray. The saxophone player was playing a killer rendition of "For the Love of You" by the Isley Brothers. Isis was bobbing to the beat of the music and her eyes were closed. She was zoning, and he was tempted not to disturb her.

She looked up and saw him standing there. "So, you're the waiter too?"

"Don't hate because I'm multitalented," he replied, putting her plate in front of her.

"I was beginning to wonder if you had decided not to join me. I know you're an engaged man, Toby. I ain't trying to start no stuff."

"You're good," he said, taking the seat next to hers. "So, what's been up with you? You just dip and no one has seen or heard from you in damn near two years."

"I did a little bit of traveling. Stayed with some family out west for a bit, and now I guess I've made my way back here."

"You could've called and let someone know you were okay. I mean, I thought we were cool. Hell, I thought we were better than cool."

"You're right, Toby, and I'm sorry. But my head was all messed up, and I just needed to get away from everything and everybody. We were more than cool, and we always will be. You know that." She reached across the table and covered his hand with hers.

Toby looked at Isis and shook his head. "I guess it's just good to know that you're okay. And yeah, we'll always be cool."

She gave him a relieved smile and asked, "Anyway, where is your fiancée?"

Roni was the last thing Toby wanted to talk about right now, especially after the conversation he had with her earlier. He could feel his previous anger growing and pushed it down further. His only response to Isis's question was to shake his head as he began picking at his food. He still could not believe he caught Roni cheating.

"Toby, what's wrong? I know I've been gone for a minute, but I'm still me. If you wanna talk, I can listen." Isis picked a piece of fish off her plate and bit into it. "Mmm, good."

He raised his eyes from the plate and looked up at her. "I just found out some things that are making me question my decision to get married right now."

"Big things or little things?"

"Both."

"Things about her, things about you, or things about marriage?"

He thought about that question long and hard. There was the fact that Roni didn't want children, how she questioned his decisions and challenged him constantly, and now the fact that he had just caught her cheating. These were just a few of the things that were causing him to be doubtful that they were ready for marriage.

"Okay, no answer. Well, let me ask you this: Have you talked to her about it?"

"Not yet."

"Then maybe that's where you should start."

"Simple as that, huh?"

"Yep, simple as that. No point in speculating without communicating. Talking is the most important part of the relationship. How long have you two been together?"

"A year in July."

"A year?" she looked surprised.

"What?"

"Nothing. I just thought you had been with her longer," she shrugged.

"Nope, only a year."

"She's a pretty special girl."

"What makes you say that?" he asked, knowing that they had never met.

"She got you to turn in your player's card and commit to her. Only an exceptional woman can do that. She got you to marry her," she said matter-of-factly.

"I turned my card in the day I met you, but you didn't want me, so I had to get it back. And I haven't married her—*yet*."

"You will. You love her. I could see it in your eyes the way you looked at her. Now, when you think about the way you felt the night you proposed, any doubts you may be having about getting married should vanish. Think about the love you felt at that moment." She looked at him so intensely that he could feel the words as they escaped her lips. She had a way of reading him like no other woman could.

Before he could react, Uncle Jay appeared at the table. "You two need anything?"

"No thanks, Uncle Jay. You remember Isis, don't you?" Toby asked.

"How could I ever forget someone so beautiful— and talented, at that?" Uncle Jay smiled. "How are you? Is the food okay?"

"Yes, everything is fine," she told him. People began to applause as the band announced they were taking a five-minute break. Toby could tell his uncle was up to something. He watched, curiously, wondering what it was.

"Isis, since the band is here tonight and you did such a wonderful job the last time," Uncle Jay began, "do you think you can sing another song for us?"

"Huh? I . . . uh . . . I really didn't plan on singing, Mr . . ."

"Sims," Toby told her.

"Uncle Jay," he corrected.

"You didn't plan on singing that night either, did you? But you got up there." Toby winked.

"That was a gift." She gave him an evil look, which was obviously a fake one.

"Go on up there and sing, girl. Unless you're scared," Toby challenged.

"She ain't scared. I know you ain't scared, are you?" Uncle Jay asked.

"No, Uncle Jay, I'm not sacred, and Toby knows it," Isis told them. She shook her head at Toby and Uncle Jay. "I'll be right back."

Toby's eyes followed her as she stood and walked toward the door leading backstage. The silk dress she wore fit the contours of her body just right, and he forced himself not to think about what was underneath.

"I like her," Uncle Jay said as he sat in the chair Isis had just vacated.

"Forget it, Uncle Jay. She's too young for you," Toby joked.

"Believe me, your uncle ain't as old as you think he is. I still got a lot of hang time in me."

"All right, Uncle Jay," Toby told him as he began eating his food.

"I'm serious, Tobias. You can ask—"

"I believe you!" Toby quickly interrupted before his uncle began calling names. He had no desire to know who his uncle was having relations with.

A few moments later, the band came back on the stage, followed by Isis. The saxophone player placed a stool in the middle of the stage in front of the microphone. "Ladies and gentlemen, Liquid is pleased to present the vocal style of Miss Isis Adams."

There was a thunder of applause and a hush fell over the crowd as she took her place. She didn't say anything as she sat on the stool. The band began playing a few chords and she began singing "Feel the Fire" by Peabo Bryson. Her eyes remained closed, as if she was afraid to open them. She was in her own world, and her voice exuded power.

As he watched her sing, Toby recalled the first time he saw her and how this woman had turned his world upside down. Feelings he thought were long gone and buried began to rise, and he knew that he had to leave now for fear he would act upon them. He whispered good-bye to Uncle Jay as he stood up and headed for the exit. Toby looked back once more, locking his eyes to hers. He gave her a small nod of his head and he knew she understood why he couldn't stay.

54

"I need to talk to you. I'm at Jasper's, working the bar," Terrell said into his cell phone after he heard the voice mail pick up. "Meet me up here."

Chills ran down his spine as Isis's voice floated through the club. The girl had a voice that would make Patti LaBelle do a double take. He looked over at his brother, who seemed to be in awe as he watched her perform. There had always been a connection between Toby and Isis, yet nothing ever jumped off between them, and he always wondered why they never hooked up. Too late for that now, because Roni had staked her claim and he had no doubt in his mind that his brother was in love.

"They must really be desperate for help."

Terrell turned around to see Meeko standing near the bar. "No, they needed a skilled brother like myself for a change."

"Skilled brother like *me*," Meeko corrected. She pointed to Isis and asked, "How long has she been on stage?"

"She just got up there. Tearing it up, as usual."

"I see," she replied. They stood watching Isis pour her heart and soul into the song. "Damn, that girl can sing."

"No doubt about that. Did she know you were coming?" he asked as he looked her up and down. She was still the baddest redbone he had ever met.

"Yeah, I told her I'd meet her up here and check out the band. She didn't mention you'd be here, though," she said, sitting on an empty stool. He made an apple martini and placed in front of her. "Thanks."

"So, where your man at?" He couldn't resist asking.

She cut her eyes at him. "What are you talking about, Terry?"

"Your man. Where's he at?"

"I'm gonna ignore that question. Especially coming from you."

"Why's that?"

"Don't you have a woman?"

"Yeah, I got a woman. That's not the issue. The question I asked you was where's *your* man at?" He grinned.

"I don't have a man. Unlike your lockdown ass, I'm a free agent."

Terrell scowled at her as she killed herself laughing. He decided not to give her a rebuttal. Isis was completing her song and people were on their feet clapping. He saw Toby ease out the door without even saying good-bye. *Roni must've called and told him to come home,* he thought. Good thing, too, because the heat between him and Isis was obvious enough for Stevie Wonder to see.

"Was that Toby?"

"Yep," he replied, leaning past her to take an order from Monica.

"What's wrong with him? He didn't even speak. Did Isis see him?"

"They were sitting together before he left," Monica volunteered. Terry shot her an angry look and she shrugged. "Oh, sorry."

"They were sitting together?" Meeko asked. "Uh, I know this is none of my business, but where's his fiancée?"

"You're right; it's none of your business," Terrell warned, passing the tray of drinks to Monica.

"Whatever," Meeko told him, finishing off her martini and requesting another. "So, you seen Jermaine?"

"Haven't talked to him." He refilled her drink. "Were you expecting him?"

"Not really, but I did mention that Isis and I were gonna come check out the band this evening," she commented.

"And you think that because you told him you were coming through he would automatically be here?" he asked, wondering just how often they had been talking. "Sorry to disappoint you, but looks like your date's a no show."

"He's not my date," she said, sucking her teeth. She waved at Isis, who was coming through the stage door. People were on her like bees to honey. *Probably paying her compliments. That girl is a true talent.*

"I'm saying, you trying to kick it with him now?"

"No, and why are you acting like a jerk, Terry? What's going on with you?"

Terrell knew he was being a total asshole, but he had a lot on his mind already, and the fact that Meeko was asking about Jermaine of all people didn't help his mood. He was about to apologize when he saw Jermaine enter the club. "There's your boy now."

Meeko shifted around then turned back to Terrell. "Guess my date showed up, huh?"

He watched her walk over to Jermaine and hug him. Isis soon joined them and pointed over to Terrell. Jermaine was all smiles as he sauntered over to the bar, a beautiful woman on each arm.

"What's up, Terry? What are you doing behind the bar?" he asked. "I thought you were a big exec now."

"Aw, man, you never know where you'll find me when it comes to Jasper's. This is home. You know that." Terrell reached out and gave him a pound. "What you drinking? Long Island?"

"Naw, I'm taking it easy tonight. I got a new job to start on in the morning."

"Really? Where?" Meeko asked, sitting a bit too close for Terrell's liking.

"Over in Wheatland Heights." Jermaine beamed.

"Must be a pretty big job," Isis commented. Terrell followed her eyes to the table where she and Toby had been sitting, and he saw the sadness in her eyes.

"Isis, girl, you should really think about hitting a studio and laying down some tracks. That was beautiful," he told her.

"Thank you, Terry. I appreciate that, but I don't think so." Isis sighed. "Singing is just a hobby."

"I can't believe I missed you singing," Jermaine told her.

"She blew the roof off, too, Jermaine." Meeko nodded. "Didn't she, Terry? Toby was here but he left."

"How long ago did he leave? I need to talk to him, Jermaine quickly asked, looking at Terrell.

"I'm surprised you didn't see him in the parking lot before you walked in. He just left right before you got here," Terrell told him. He wondered why Jermaine looked worried all of a sudden, especially since Toby had been so distant earlier. Something was going on, and he wanted to know what it was. "What's up?"

"Uh, nothing," Jermaine said, glancing at Isis then back to Terrell. "He's supposed to be helping me out tomorrow and I need to get with him about the logistics of what we need to take care of, that's all."

Terrell didn't believe him for some reason. Maybe it was the bullshit way Jermaine answered or the obviously bogus excuse he quickly came up with. Helping Uncle Jay out at the club was one thing, but moonlighting for Jermaine was something else. He gave Jermaine a look to let him know he wasn't buying it and to come clean. Jermaine just stared back at him like he didn't know what was going on.

"Let's get a table, Jermaine," Meeko said after they talked with Terrell for a while longer.

"Cool. It's an empty one over there," Jermaine told her, taking her by the arm. "I'll holler at you later."

"You coming, Isis?" Meeko asked her girlfriend, who wasn't moving.

"I think I'm gonna get out of here soon. You guys go ahead and enjoy yourselves," she told them.

"They look cozy, huh?" Terrell asked Isis after they had gone.

"Yeah, maybe Jermaine will be the next one popping the question," Isis replied.

"I knew something was up with them," Terrell hissed.

"What is your problem, Terry?" Isis asked, realizing he was serious. "You can't possibly think that something is going on between the two of them. You know Meeko is probably trying to get him to give her the hookup on a security system or something."

"Or she's trying to hook up with him."

"So what if she is? You didn't want her, so why can't someone else have her?"

"Because he's supposed to be one of my best friends and she's my ex. That ain't even cool."

"If you say so, but believe me, there's nothing going on there. I'm leaving." She leaned over and kissed him on the cheek as she said good-bye. When she was gone, he couldn't help looking over at Meeko and Jermaine sitting at their table, laughing. Suddenly, he heard his name being called from across the club. He looked up to see his manager, CJ, walking toward the bar.

"Hey there, CJ, what's going on?"

She smiled. Terrell couldn't help noticing how nice she looked in the red sundress she was wearing.

"When they told me you were over here at the bar, I thought they meant you were having a drink. I had no idea that you were the bartender. Do we not pay you enough at your day job?"

"No, that's why I have to tend bar on the weekends. You think you can talk to someone and handle getting me a raise?"

"Depends on how good my drink is," she said seductively, leaning on the bar in a manner that left no question about whether she was wearing a bra.

"So, that's the determining factor?"

"That's the determining factor. You can show me just how good your job performance is." She nodded.

"Well, I hate to brag, but my performance has always exceeded expectations. What's your pleasure?"

"Um, let's see. How about a Long Island Iced Tea?"

"That's it?" he asked. "I'm about to be paid."

"We'll see," she said. She continued flirting with him as he made her drink and he wondered if she was serious.

"Here you go. I think you'll find it's well beyond your liking."

"We'll see," she said, taking a sip. "Brother, you're about to get a raise."

"Told you. I'm a man of many talents."

"So I see. You'll have to display more of them to me one day. It was nice seeing you, Mr. Sims." She paid him and waved good-bye.

"No, what she should've said was you're a man of much bull."

Terrell didn't even see Anjelica until she spoke. He had actually forgotten that he had called and left the message for her to come up there. Now he was wishing that he hadn't, especially when he remembered that Jermaine and Meeko were having drinks at a table a few feet away. He wasn't sure what type of relationship Jermaine and Anjelica had, but he was pretty certain that his boy wouldn't feel comfortable being seen at a table with another female.

"What's up, girl? Took you long enough to get here."

"I just knew you were lying about being the bartender. I would think such a job is beneath you, Terrell. I hope you notice that I didn't bring a purse, so my drinks will have to be on the house," Anjelica remarked, looking good in jeans and a crop top. Her long hair was in a mess of curls, surrounding her pretty face.

"No job is beneath me when it comes to Jasper's. If Uncle Jay needs me to clean the toilets, I would," he told her.

"Well, it's nice to see you can be loyal to something."

"What's that supposed to mean? You know what? Never mind. What do you want to drink? And you only get one on the house, so if you want more than that, I suggest you use the ATM located in the lobby."

She ordered a Tequila Sunrise and sat down. "So, talk."

He decided to talk as long as possible in order to distract her from looking around the club and seeing Jermaine. He told her about having dinner with Nicole and Gary and his girlfriend, whom he happened to be familiar with. Instead of being concerned, Anjelica found the entire situation funny. She nearly choked on her drink when he told her.

"What the hell is funny about that?"

"I mean, the fact that your future brother-in-law's girlfriend is the nurse from the abortion clinic you took your booty call to. If that ain't hilarious, I don't know what is."

"First of all, she was the receptionist, which is another thing. I think she told Gary and Nicole that she was a nurse, not a receptionist."

"Then there you have it. She was probably just as uncomfortable as you were. You know her dirt and she knows yours. Did she say anything?"

"Nope, not a word. We acted like we didn't even know each other. She didn't mention it to me and I didn't mention it to her. We had dinner, that's it."

"Then what makes you even think that she remembers you?"

"I can tell she remembered me. I'm not that forgettable, and it wasn't that long ago that we were there. She remembers. I don't know what I'm gonna do." He sighed. He was glad he had finally told someone about the situation he found himself in. He wanted to talk to his brother about it, but Toby seemed to have a lot on his mind, so Terry didn't bother him with it.

"I say be like the Army—don't ask, don't tell. If she doesn't bring it up, then you don't bring it up."

"I guess that's one way of looking at it, but there's something else that happened Saturday night."

"Damn, something else happened? You had a rough weekend, huh? Is this as funny as the other thing? If so, let me put my drink down before you tell me." Anjelica smiled.

"No, this one isn't that comical," Terrell told her, his voice full of tension. He had also been thinking of how to tell her about the other situation he found himself in.

"What is it?" she asked, noticing his grim face.

"Kayla . . ."

"Mr. Sims, I'm about to leave. I just wanted to say good-bye and thank you for a wonderful drink. We will talk about those other talents really soon," CJ called over the bar as she headed for the exit. He turned toward her and noticed Meeko and Jermaine standing right behind her. He prayed that Anjelica wouldn't turn around and see them, but CJ's yelling was hard to ignore. Anjelica swiveled around on the stool and got a full view of the couple. The look on her face confirmed just what he suspected; she was obviously not pleased with seeing them together.

"Okay, CJ, we'll do that. Drive safely," Terrell called to her and turned his back to Anjelica. He pretended to be busy washing glasses and putting away bottles of liquor, waiting for her to speak before he did. When she didn't, he turned back to see why she was so quiet. He was flabbergasted to find her chair empty. She was talking with Meeko and Jermaine. He stood, waiting for the catfight to break out between the two women, but it didn't. Neither one looked angry or even uncomfortable as they stood and talked. Soon, she resumed to her seat and Meeko and Jermaine walked out the door.

"You really are funny," Anjelica snapped. "I can't believe you did this."

"What are you talking about? I didn't do anything."

"I guess you called me up here to catch Jermaine with another woman, huh? Was that your little master plan? You thought I would clown and get all ghetto and show my behind like some crazy, jealous person? You must have me confused with . . . what's Craig's ghetto wife from New York's name?"

"Avis," he replied, thinking Craig really did have his hands full with both his deranged wife and Kayla as his daughter's mother.

"Yeah, Avis. Sorry, that's not how I roll. I may be a bitch some-times, Terrell, but I do have class. Jermaine's not my man. I told you before, I am a free agent."

Before Terrell had a chance to respond, Jermaine strutted up to the bar and put his arms around her. "What's up, sweetheart? You want another drink?"

"No, I'm good. I thought you were gone."

"Do you think I would have left without spending some time with you?" Jermaine asked. "Terry, have Monica send another round to the table, man. Okay?"

"No problem," Terrell told him.

Something about the way Jermaine ordered the drinks let Terrell know that his friend was a bit pissed, and he wondered if Jermaine also thought he had set this entire thing up. He wasn't about to hang around to find out.

55

Toby had been tossing and turning in his bed for thirty minutes, trying to fall asleep. He had turned the ringers off all the phones in his house and ignored the beep of the answering machine, letting him know that he had messages waiting. His cell phone remained in the glove compartment of his truck, where he had placed it before he even went into Jasper's.

He knew he had to have been dreaming when he felt someone climb into his bed. The warm body snuggled closer to him; he felt its nakedness and the familiar scent of Victoria's Secret Pink filled the air, letting him know that indeed Roni was there beside him.

"Baby?" she whispered in his ear.

"What do you want?" Toby groaned, refusing to roll over. He'd avoided her calls all evening and thought she would get the hint that he needed some time to deal with this situation. Considering the mood he was in right now, it definitely was not the time.

"I am so sorry, Toby. You have got to know that," she told him, her voice trembling.

"I don't wanna deal with this right now, Ron. I think you should just leave. Seriously, I need some time."

"I love you, Toby. We need to talk about this. Please, baby." He felt her drape her arms across him and his back remained to her as she rubbed across his chest. "Toby, please talk to me."

"Who the fuck is he, Roni?" he heard his mouth say. He had told himself to remain quiet, not to say anything, but that was one question he wanted to know the answer to.

"He's not you, Toby. That's all that needs to be said. Who he is isn't important. You are the most important person in my life, and I don't wanna lose you. I need for you to understand how sorry I am. It was a mistake and it will never happen again. I love you, that's all. Tell me you forgive me, Toby. Please." She caressed him as she talked, wrapping her legs around his.

Her soft feet ran up and down his calves. He could feel her breasts pressing on his back as she continued to whisper, pleading for his forgiveness. His mind told his body not to respond, but he felt himself getting hard, his physical wants ignoring his mental commands. She had aroused him and he was ready. He turned over to face her, and wasn't surprised to see the tears running down her cheeks. Her eyes were swollen and he could tell she had been crying for a while. She blinked as if she was surprised that he had turned over so soon. He didn't say a word as he pulled her mouth to his, kissing her fiercely, positioning his body on top of hers. He reached between her legs, touching the wetness that welcomed his fingers. Her response was to meet his touch while stroking his stiffness, making sure he was as eager as she was.

He entered her with such intensity that he felt her body tense in surprise. His eyes remained open because he wanted to watch her facial expressions as he made love to her. Her eyes were shut tight and he wondered if it was from the roughness of their lovemaking or because she was thinking of her other lover, the one she was with just hours before, the one that she had her legs wrapped around just yesterday in the swimming pool. *Did she make the same face as she is now when she was fucking him? Did she call his name out and beg him not to stop as she's calling out to me?* He could feel her muscles contracting as he drove in and out, and hear the sounds of his body meeting hers as she screamed in ecstasy. Flashes of red and blue collided with the darkness as he shut his eyes tightly. His passion was mounting and he could no longer hold back. Faster and faster, harder and harder, until he couldn't take it anymore. Once again, her muscles tightened against his and he felt her nails scrape across his back as he came deep inside of her. It was a much needed release. The tension he had been holding in for the last two days seemed to subside.

"Baby, are you all right?" she finally asked him.

Toby remained silent as he eased off her and sat on the side of his bed, reaching on the nightstand to turn on the lamp. He walked into the bathroom and washed himself. He realized that this was the first time they had ever made love without a condom, and couldn't help but wonder if she had done so in an effort to prove her sudden loyalty to him. He stared at his reflection in the mirror and became angry at the tears that he saw in his eyes. *Get yourself together, T,* he told himself, taking a deep breath.

"Toby, please talk to me," she said once again as he came out of the bathroom. He didn't even look over at her. Instead, he walked over to the dresser where he noticed her purse. He opened it, taking out her keys. He went through the ring, searching until he found the one he wanted. She sat up in the middle of the bed, not bothering to cover her nakedness. "What are you doing?"

Silently, he removed the key and climbed back into bed. He turned the lamp off again then lay back down with his back to her.

"Toby, please say something. Don't you dare lay there and ignore me like I'm nothing!"

"Lock the door when you leave," he told her.

"When I what? Oh, so you want me to leave? You just gonna sleep with me and then kick me out? Is that how you wanna end this, Toby? You know what? Fine then, I'll leave. But if I walk out that door . . ."

"Lock it behind you," he repeated. He had told himself that he wasn't going to argue, fuss or fight with Roni. The less he said, the easier it would be. He remained quiet as she continued to rant and rave about him being unreasonable about the situation. Finally, he listened as she gathered her things, took the keys off the dresser and descended the steps.

The door slammed behind her and he waited. With Roni, there was no telling if something was gonna come through the window or his car alarm would start blaring, letting him know that she had taken her frustration out on something he possessed rather than on him. She had done it before, and he prayed that she wouldn't do it again. But there was no sound of breaking glass or piercing alarms. Just the sound of her car as she drove away. Then, and only then, did Toby drift into a deep slumber.

"You sure you're up to this, man?"

"I told you I was. Now, will you quit asking me dumb questions? I told you, I'm cool," Toby replied. Jermaine had been asking him if he was okay for the past fifteen minutes. He had to admit, he had even surprised himself when he got out of bed and called his best friend to ask if he still needed help this morning. He didn't know whether it was because he didn't feel like moping around the house all day and was looking for something to take his mind off Roni or that he wanted to return to the place where he actually caught his fiancée cheating on him. There was no doubt in is mind that once they got to Stanley's house he would have to relive the images he witnessed the last time they were there. And somehow, he wondered if in the back of his mind he really hoped to run into Stanley's brother and talk to him. Either way, he had called, Jermaine picked him up, and they were well on their way.

"I know you're cool. I know you got a lot on your mind, that's all. Did you talk to her about what happened?"

"Yeah, she tried to deny it until I told her I saw her," he told him.

"No, I know she ain't try the 'It wasn't me' line. Please don't tell me that. I don't think I can take it."

"No, but only because she realized she was busted. I couldn't believe it myself, especially when I gave her the opportunity to be honest with me. I think that's what hurt me the most, the fact that she just straight-up lied to me about him. Come on, J. Roni was just as big a player as I was before we hooked up. I know that. It was one of the things that attracted me to her . . . Well, that plus she's fine as hell." He tried to laugh, but it came out like a pitiful sigh. "But when I told her it was all about her, I left everyone else alone. I just assumed she did the same thing. All she had to do was be honest wit' me when I asked her about him. I would've been pissed, but I would've respected the fact that she was honest."

"I feel you on that one. Let me ask you something. You said you left everyone else alone, but I hear you was up in Jasper's last night with Isis. How do you explain that one?"

Toby explained how he wound up working the bar and Isis happened to come to the club. He assured his friend that he left long before she did and he went home and went to bed. Jermaine was stunned when he told him of how he and Roni made love and then he took his key from her. "I told her to lock the door behind her when she left."

"And then what did she do?" Jermaine asked, focusing on both Toby and the morning traffic.

"She was pissed, but she left."

"And then what did she do?" Jermaine repeated the question as if Toby didn't hear him correctly the first time.

"I told you. She left. She locked the door and left."

"She keyed your truck?"

"Nope."

"She ain't slash your tires?"

"No, none of that. Nothing thrown, no broken glass, no property damage. I'm telling you, she locked the door and left."

"She's planning something big, then. Either she's gonna burn all your shit while you ain't home or she's plotting to kill your ass," Jermaine told him assuredly. Toby looked over at him like he was as crazy as what he just said. "I'm telling you, she's planning the big payback. You screwed her, didn't say anything to her, took your key off her key ring and then told her to lock the door when she left? She's gonna hire someone to kill you, for real." They turned into Wheatland Heights and onto Stanley's street.

"Are you listening to yourself? You sound so retarded."

"Are you listening to yourself? This is Veronica Black we're talking about. Has Roni ever taken anything that calm before? Don't worry. I got this new system we can install in your place later."

"Shut up, Jermaine. I already got a security system that works fine. You're blowing this way out of proportion. Roni couldn't overreact because she was wrong. Not only was she wrong, but she was caught. You can't act crazy if you're the one who's busted. Her tearing stuff up like she normally does, that would've just added fuel to an already lit fire," Toby replied, opening his door and getting out.

"And I'm telling you, you better pray your joint ain't a bed of ashes by the time we make it back this afternoon." Jermaine laughed, passing Toby a large tool bag out of the back of the truck.

56

"Is this one of your accounts?" Terrell walked up to Kayla's desk and asked. He knew it was; he was just using it as an excuse to talk to her. He had put off calling her, trying to give her some time to cool off. This was the first time they had ever had a falling out of sorts and he felt bad, mostly because it was his fault.

"Does it have my name on it?" She didn't even look up from her computer.

"Yes, but I don't understand the notes on it. Can you explain them to me?"

Kayla rolled her eyes as she took the file from his hand. She frowned, trying to figure out what he was talking about. After turning a few pages, she told him, "You were the last person to notate this account. I notated it three months ago. I don't understand the notes either."

"Can I see you in my office?"

"I'm busy," Kayla snapped, turning back around to her computer.

"Kayla, come on. Stop tripping. Come to my office so we can talk."

"I told you I'm busy. Call Anjelica. I'm sure she would have no problem talking to you. You need her number? Oh, my bad. You already know it."

"Fine then, Kayla. Be stubborn. You aren't even giving me a chance to explain myself," he hissed, making sure he spoke low enough that no one could hear them over the small cubicles.

"There's nothing to explain. You're a grown-ass man, Terrell. I ain't your woman or one of your hoes. You don't owe me an explanation for nothing you do," she told him.

He turned around to see CJ standing nearby. She waved at him and asked, "Is everything all right, Mr. Sims?"

"Yeah, CJ. I'm just going over something with Ms. Hopkins here."

"Well, don't forget we have that meeting coming up soon. I'll be stopping by your office later." She gave him a knowing look.

"I'll bet she will," Kayla said sarcastically.

"What's that supposed to mean, Kay?"

"That she'll be coming to your office later, Terrell—I mean Mr. Sims." She continued, "You know I can't stand her. I advise you to deter her from coming over here because if she does, there's nothing you can do to stop me from cussing her out. Today is not the day, and I am not in the mood."

"She ain't coming over here. Just come into my office so we can talk. I need for you to understand what went down," he told her.

"Is there a problem? Can I help with something?"

Terrell felt the hand on his shoulder and turned around. CJ was looking over him at Kayla's computer.

Her hand made its way to the center of his back as she moved closer. He tried to move a little in case someone happened to notice her obvious gesture of affection.

"No, we're fine, CJ. I was just going over some notes with Kayla in regards to an account. Everything's under control," he assured her. Kayla continued typing, not even acknowledging CJ's presence, which was probably a good thing.

"Really? Ms. Hopkins, do we need to retrain you in notating accounts?" CJ asked.

Kayla's fingers stopped immediately. She stood up and turned toward them. Terrell began praying that she wouldn't start talking without thinking, which she had been known to do on more than one occasion. The look she gave CJ said everything without anything coming out of her mouth as her eyes traveled from the top of CJ's head to her feet then back up again. Other employees nearby sat frozen, waiting for whatever was going to happen next.

"I believe it was a mistake that Mr. Sims made on the account that needs to be corrected. I'm sure you'll have no problem retraining him, since he's the one having difficulties. Excuse me. It's my break," she said with a smile.

Snickering could be heard from the onlookers and CJ turned around, giving them a threatening look. They quickly went back to work and Terrell excused himself as well. When he returned to his office, Kayla was there waiting.

"Look, Kay—" he started, but she cut him off.

"I didn't come in here to talk. I came for you to listen. Nicole is a nice woman with a lot going for herself, despite the fact that she is with you. We all make mistakes. That being said, you need to get your shit together. I know Nicole well enough to know that she's not stupid enough to be waiting in the wings for you. But even still, she loves your unfaithful, noncommittal ass for some strange reason, and I don't want her to be hurt or look stupid." The words came out of her mouth so fast that he doubted she had even taken time to breathe.

"What are you talking about, Kayla? I'm telling you that your sister and I were together one time and that's it. We're just cool. It's not even like that."

"I'm talking about you being with everybody, Terrell. Anjelica, Darla, CJ . . ."

"CJ! You really are out of your mind, Kayla. I'm telling you I'm not like that anymore. I've changed. I know I gotta get my shit together if I want things to work with Nicole, and I am. Part of the reason I know that is because your sister Anjelica pointed out a lot of stuff to me and I know I was wrong."

"Oh, so now you're taking advice from a whore? Well, I am so glad that she is being so helpful to you and has given you such great advice when it comes to your love life," she said, standing up. "I can see that I've done nothing here but waste your time."

She opened the door to his office. Terrell quickly ran over and pushed the door closed. "Kayla, wait a minute. Anjelica didn't say anything to me that you haven't said in the past. The reason I pointed that out was to show you that she's not this monstrosity that you make her out to be. I know you believe she's this evil sex fiend of a woman who tries to sleep with any man she comes in contact with, but you're wrong."

"I don't have to listen to this. I've known my sister all of my life and you've known her what, two hours? Please, spare me."

"Spare you what, the truth? Why should I? You come in here all condescending like you're holier than thou, without even giving me the chance to talk. I'll be the first to admit that I've done some trifling stuff over the past few months, but I've changed. I love Nicole and I'm not gonna do anything to jeopardize what we have. She's invested a lot into me and our relationship, and I respect that.

"Believe me, Kayla, even that night with Anjelica was a one time thing. It was the last time I even did anything that stupid. But your sister is a good person, just like you are. Maybe that's why she and I became cool, because you are somewhat alike. You never talked to her to give you the chance to see that side of her," Terrell told her.

He released his arm from the door and walked behind his desk, sitting in the soft leather chair. The initial tension that had embraced him when he first entered his office was subsiding. Kayla stared at him then opened the door. She turned and left without saying a word. He didn't expect her to, because he knew she needed time to absorb everything they had just shared with each other. That was how their relationship was. He was her backbone and she was his conscience. They were each other's strengths when the other was weak. She was his best friend and he loved her. But Anjelica had become his friend, too, and it hurt him to see the two beautiful, intelligent sisters hating one another.

Kayla's silence was good enough for him because he knew he had caused her to think. He would call her later and they would talk some more and by the end of the week, they would be having lunch together like old times. *Maybe she can help me figure out this Arianna dilemma that's been haunting me*, he thought as he sorted through the pile of work that he was supposed to have completed by the end of the day.

He was in the middle of working on a report when he heard a knock at the door. He looked at the clock and saw that it was after 5:00. *Kayla must be stopping by before she leaves*. He was surprised when it wasn't Kayla but CJ who walked in and took a seat on the edge of his desk. Her skirt began rising on her thick thighs, and he saw that a garter belt was holding up her black silk stockings.

"Are you busy?" She smiled, not even pulling the skirt down. He could've sworn that she maneuvered her body so that it rose up even more.

"Finishing up this report for the meeting tomorrow. You on your way out?"

"Yep, I'm all finished. I just stopped by to see if I could interest you in a bite to eat." She leaned over his desk and picked up a picture of him, Jermaine and Toby from his desk. It was one of his favorite pictures of the three of them, taken one summer after he had graduated from high school. They were posed on a set of rocks on the beach and looked like they had it going on, dressed in denim overalls, Cross Colors shirts, and black Doc Martens. She giggled as she looked at it.

"Okay, what's with the sunglasses? You all look like body doubles for Jodeci."

"Boyz 2 Men," he corrected. "And back then, you couldn't tell us that we weren't."

"Don't tell me you all were a group."

"Triple Threat. We won the talent shows every year. Shoot, you're laughing, but we were the bomb. We had backup dancers and everything."

"Is that a curl, Terrell? Did you have a curl?" she shrieked.

He snatched the picture out of her hands. "No, I didn't have a curl. Those are dreads."

"Let me see. That is a curl! I can't believe you had a curl." CJ reached for the frame, but he held it out of her reach and she wound up nearly falling off the desk. He reached out and she landed in his arms. They both ended up across the desk. He found himself staring at her cleavage then back into her dark eyes. CJ licked her lips at him and at that moment, the door opened.

"I brought you a picture of Day—oh, shit. Sorry."

Terrell quickly stood up, knowing what this must've looked like to Kayla when she walked in.

"Have you ever hear of knocking?" CJ barked as she readjusted her clothes.

Kayla looked at Terrell and shook her head at him. He tried to catch her before she got out of his office, but she was out the door before he knew it. Rushing into the hallway, he called out to her. "Kayla, Kayla!"

He made it to the end of the corridor just as the elevator chimed. He pressed the button in an effort to stop the doors from closing, but saw that Kayla was pressing just as hard on the inside to make them close. He looked over at the door leading to the steps and was tempted to beat her to the parking lot, but he knew that it wouldn't matter. There was no way she would believe anything he said at this point. He sulked back to his office.

"So, where shall we dine?"

"Huh?"

"Hello, dinner? Where do you want to eat? We were deciding when we were so rudely interrupted." CJ stood up and strolled over to him. She began playing with the knot of his tie. "Let's see if we can't straighten this a little. Now, that's better."

"Uh, thanks," he said, quickly moving from within her reach. He took his seat behind his desk and leaned back, groaning as he exhaled. His life was falling apart at the seams and there was nothing he could do about it.

"Maybe a massage would help. You seem a little stressed," CJ suggested. "I give a pretty mean one. Want me to demonstrate?"

"That's okay. I don't think that would be a good idea. I don't think our going to dinner would be a good idea either," Terrell told her.

"So, what do you think is a good idea, Mr. Sims?" she asked suggestively.

"I think my going home would be a good idea, Ms. Ware. That's a good idea."

"Does our sudden eagerness to run off have anything to do with that hussy rudely interrupting us? She's nothing but trouble anyway. She thinks she knows everything."

Terrell ignored her comments regarding Kayla and grabbed his jacket off the back of his chair. "No, that doesn't have anything to do with it at all. I just think that picking up some Mexican food and going home to rub my pregnant fiancée's feet is the best idea for me right now. I'll see you tomorrow, CJ." He left her sitting stunned in his office, closing the door behind him.

57

Toby pushed the button on his answering machine. He kept his hand on the delete button, knowing that most of the messages weren't worth saving anyway. Just as he thought, they were mostly sales calls, but a few were requests for him to deejay at weddings or parties. He even had an offer from a woman who wanted him at her family reunion.

"Money is no object. Just let me know how much," she said into the machine. This one was definitely worth keeping. He skipped to the next message.

"Toby, it's me. I know you said that you needed time to deal with this, but I need you to at least call me and tell me you're dealing with it. I love you so much and I—" He hit delete at the sound of Roni's voice. She probably thought he would have called by now, but he hadn't, although he was tempted. It was especially hard late at night when he rolled over to pull her warm body close to his and it wasn't there beside him.

The day had been long, but enjoyable. Working with Jermaine had provided just the diversion he needed. Not only did he learn a lot about the business, but his friend kept him amused, all the while putting a few extra bucks in his pocket. Out of all the jobs they had done that week, working at Stanley's had been the most strenuous. Not because of the manual labor, but because of the mental capacity it took for Toby to do it. The entire time they were working, he continually had flashbacks of Roni in Sean's arms by the pool. He paused to look at pictures Stanley had throughout the house of family members, especially the ones containing Sean.

"I see you checking out the horrible family photos," Stanley commented.

"Yeah," Toby answered, embarrassed that he had been caught looking.

"My brother keeps telling me to take them down, but I won't. These pictures of us are my prized possessions. Besides, I may need them one day to blackmail him," Stan laughed.

"I swear I think I know him from somewhere," Toby lied. "Does he live here in town?"

"No, he moved to Atlanta after he finished school. He comes to town every now and then to visit and spend time with his on again/off again girlfriend."

"Oh, yeah, the girl he was with the other day. So, she lives here and he comes to see her. Must be serious."

"With those two, you never can tell. Like I said, it's an on again/off again thing that's been going on for years. Well, I'm outta here. You guys are doing an awesome job and I really appreciate it."

"Thanks, Stan. You stay cool, man." Toby pounded his fist on Stan's and went back to work, still thinking about Sean, Roni, and the insight that Stan had given him. It took some effort, but they completed the job and Jermaine told him he had mad respect for him.

It had been a while since he had worked out at the gym, but he was full of energy and it seemed like a good idea. Grabbing his duffle bag out of the closet, he changed into some sweats and set out to get his workout on. He noticed that the regular crowd was there in full effect as he walked to the locker room. Vinny, the manager, greeted him with a smile.

"Hey, Toby. Where you been? We missed you." The short, young guy gave him a handshake.

"What's up, Vinny? I know it's been a minute, huh?"

"Well, I know you got engaged and I figured that had something to do with it. Where is your beautiful wife-to-be, anyway?"

It was the first time anyone had asked him about Roni, and Toby felt a twinge of discomfort. He thought about telling Vinny that they had broken up, but technically that wasn't true because Roni still had his ring. He didn't ask for it back and she didn't offer to give it. They really hadn't said that the wedding was off; he just took his key back.

"She's not here. I'm rolling solo today, Vin," Toby told him.

"Well, tell her I said hello." Vinny smiled. "Good to see you, Toby."

Toby began stretching, trying to decide whether to start with free weights or the exercise machines. The machines were almost all taken by other fitness gurus, so he opted for the free weights. He lifted, bench pressed, pushed and pulled for an hour, until his black We Secure U T-shirt was soaked and clinging to his body.

He was tired, but somehow convinced himself that thirty minutes on the elliptical machine was the perfect finish for his workout. By now, people had gotten off from work and the gym was packed. Somehow, he located and empty machine and rushed over to it before someone else snagged it. He was so busy trying to find some Janet Jackson on his mp3 player that he didn't notice the woman smiling at him on the machine next to his.

"So, how long are you gonna ignore me, Toby?" she asked. He looked up and saw that it was Isis. Her arms and legs were moving rhythmically like she was cross-country skiing. She made the machine look like a breeze, which he knew it wasn't.

"What's going on, Ms. Adams? I see how you stay looking fine; you work at it."

"And I thought those rippling muscles you have came from spinning and mixing records. I see I was wrong."

"Since when did you start coming here? I've never seen you here before," he said, getting on and setting the timer.

"Hmph. I've been here every day almost since I joined a month ago. What does that tell you? I think someone has been slacking on their workouts." She grinned.

"Well, I have to admit it's been a minute since I've been in here. So, you joined the gym. Does that mean you'll be here for a while?" he asked, trying to convince himself that the only reason he asked was to make general conversation. But he knew he really wanted to know the answer. He didn't even bother putting his headphones on.

"For a while. How are things going with you?"

"All right, I guess. You going back to your old job?"

"No way. You know I hated it when I was working there. I'm not cut out for that kind of work. I was on my feet all day, every day, dealing with dumb customers that think they have ten dollars in their accounts so they can talk to me any kind of way. I don't think so. Besides, nothing good ever came to me at that job." She huffed as she talked, her arms and legs moving faster and faster.

"That's not true," he said, smiling at her. "What about me? I came to you there."

She shook her head, blushing, which surprised him.

He remembered the first time he saw her. He had just gotten his first check from the club, and he went into the bank. He wasn't really paying attention. He was busy two-waying this girl he had been trying to get with for a week, and she had finally agreed to go out with him. He moved up in line and walked to the window with no one standing in front of it.

"Excuse me, but I'm closed," she had said.

"Huh? Oh, my bad. I didn't even see the sign." He smiled.

"Well, it's right there in front. See." She pointed at the small sign that indeed read CLOSED, SEE NEXT AVAILABLE TELLER.

He looked around and saw that all of the other tellers had customers and by now, the line was longer than when he first walked through the door. There was no way he was going to stand in it again. "I'm saying, you can't just help me out? I just need to cash this check right quick. It won't even take that long. Come on. Please?"

"Sorry. I'm closed," she said icily. She looked down at his check. "Besides, you have to have an account here to cash a check from another institution. Do you even have an account?"

"No, but I'm saying, can't you just open one up for me real quick?" he asked.

"Like I said, I'm closed. See the manager," she said abruptly then turned and walked away. He was livid. He was about to call her out about her nasty attitude when he noticed the sign on a nearby door directing him to new accounts. He figured he would go ahead and open the new account since he was there. There was a small white man in the glass office, and Toby softly knocked on the door.

"Can I help you?" the man asked, looking up from the newspaper he was reading.

"Yes, sir. Are you the person I see about opening a new account?"

"Yes, I am. Come on in and we can take care of you." He welcomed Toby and told him to have a seat. Fifteen minutes later, Toby was the newest member of their financial institution, complete with checking and savings accounts and the Christmas club. "Welcome, Mr. Sims. If you step right over here, Ms. Adams will be happy to take care of your accounts for you."

Toby looked at the window where the sign still sat. "I think she's still closed."

"Closed? She shouldn't be. I can get her for you and she can get you squared away." He pushed a few buttons and walked through a large wooden door, coming out on the other side of the teller windows. "Here she is. Miss Adams, this is Mr. Sims, our newest customer. I'm putting him in your hands, and I've assured him that you'll take good care of him. Nice meeting you, Mr. Sims." He nodded to Toby.

"It's a pleasure doing business with you, sir," Toby told him. He smiled at Ms. Adams, who did not seem so pleased to see him. "I guess you're open now, Ms. Adams?"

"How can I help you?" she asked, her face and voice void of any emotion.

"I need to make a deposit into my checking and savings accounts, but I want to get two hundred back in cash." Toby signed the back of his check and passed it to her. His two-way began beeping, and he reached into his pocket and took it out. He quickly scanned the message and began typing a response. His date was acting like she was going to cancel on him, and he was pissed.

"I need a deposit slip and a photo ID." She sighed.

He looked at her like she was crazy. "I just opened my account. The branch manager just introduced me to you. You know who I am."

"Can I see a photo ID, please? *And* a deposit slip."

Toby reached into his back pocket and pulled out his new checkbook along with his wallet. He snatched out a deposit slip and flashed his driver's license in front of her. She peered closely at it and thanked him. He watched her as she quickly took care of his transaction, meticulously counting his money. Her nails were neatly groomed, and he could tell they were real, not those acrylic things women usually wore. His gaze drifted to her face. Her eyes were frowned with intensity, yet she was gently biting her bottom lip as she flipped through the bills. She paused and looked up at him.

"Damn, you're beautiful." The words slipped out of his mouth before he could stop them. She went back to counting and he smiled. *She's funny. A straight, first class—*

She interrupted him before he could complete the thought. "Here you are. Twenty, forty, sixty, eighty, one. Twenty, forty, sixty, eighty, two. Here's your receipt. Have a nice day," she said. He tried to search her face for any signs of kindness, but there were none.

"You too, Ms. Adams. See you next week," he made sure to tell her. He looked at her once more before turning to leave. Indeed, she was gorgeous, and for some reason, her stank attitude made her even more attractive to him.

For weeks, Toby continued coming in to the bank, refusing to go to anyone's window but hers. On the days he would walk in and see that she was working the drive-through, he would go back and get into his truck. He knew he irritated her, and it became a game to him.

Then one night, she strolled into Dominic's with her girlfriend. Terry, who happened to be in the booth with him, pointed the two women out as they sat at a table near the back of the club.

"Man, look at the two hotties over there. They are fine," Terrell announced. Toby looked over at them and shook his head.

"That's shorty from the bank, the mean one I pick with. She thinks she's all that."

"Which one? The redbone one or the other one in the skirt? She looks mixed. Is she mixed?" Terrell was stretching his neck to get a better view. "They both look good."

"The other one. And I don't know if she's mixed or not. I think she is," Toby told him. He often wondered that about her. She had thick, wavy hair and keen eyes along with her satin toffee skin, which led him to believe that she was not one hundred percent African American. Her looks were what he considered a combination of Janet Jackson and Amiel Lareaux, with a touch of Kimora Lee. He said her name aloud to no one. "Ms. Adams."

"If it's the other one, then she is all that. And since you got dibs on her, I'm about to go holler at the red-bone. I'll tell her you said hello," Terrell said as he headed down the steps.

"I ain't got dibs on nobody. I told you I just mess with her because she always has an attitude. And you'd better hope and pray that she doesn't cuss you out when you tell her you know me." Toby laughed.

The crowd was kind of thin since it was a rainy Thursday in March, but he tried his best to entertain them. It took some coaxing, but soon a few people were actually on the dance floor, including Terry and the female who was with Ms. Adams. Noticing his prey standing at the bar alone, he popped in a slow mix CD and took it upon himself to join her.

"Slow Comfortable Screw, please," she told the bartender.

"Why, Ms. Adams, I would be honored, but don't you think we should go on a few dates first?" he asked her, grinning.

"Oh God. What are you doing here?" She rolled her eyes at him and asked, "Am I giving off a vibe attracting wannabe smooth operators or something?"

"Don't even try it. You know I work here. I've invited you several times and you read my paychecks every week when I bring them to the bank. It's okay to admit that you came to check me out."

She turned away from him, reaching for the drink the bartender handed to her.

"Believe me, checking you out is the last thing I want to do. The only reason I'm here is because Meeko dragged me. She told me she heard this was the spot. And by the look of the crowd, obviously it's not. There's no one even here."

"Come on. It's cold and raining outside. Most people are at home hugged up in front of the fireplace with their boo, getting their groove on. Those people that have a boo, that is. The only people that come to the clubs on a night like this are those who are *looking* for a boo to get their groove on with."

"Well, that definitely isn't me," she told him.

Another woman who had been giving him the eye all night walked up and spoke to him. She introduced herself as Darla and offered to buy him a drink. He kindly declined, telling her he'd take a rain check, but to come by the booth and he would hook her up with a CD.

"See. On the prowl," he said. "What'd I tell you?"

"She's desperate."

"Now that's cold," he laughed. He leaned closer and asked her, "Why you always gotta look so mean?"

"How do you know how I always look?" she asked then swiveled back around to the bar. Damn, she looked good.

"I'm saying, though, it makes it difficult for a man to approach you. That evil look could easily intimidate a brother, discourage him from coming over here and talking to you."

"Good," she replied with attitude. "I don't wanna be bothered with a man without balls anyway."

Before he could respond, she grabbed her drink off the bar and walked away. Toby was right on her heels as she returned to her table.

"This is much nicer. Now we can have some privacy." He laughed, startling her as he sat down. "So, what's been going on?"

"Don't you have some records to spin or some shout-outs to make over the mike or something?"

"You know, this stuck-up attitude is getting real old, Ms. Adams. Here I am trying to be the nice guy that I am, and you still got this hardcore, queen bee, I-am-me-and-I-don't-need-you attitude, which, by the way, isn't cute."

"You can just leave me alone. I didn't ask for you to come over here, so you can go right back to being DJ Terror, hooking up with these *boo prowlers* out here buying you drinks and blowing up your two-way. And you're right; I don't need you!"

A big grin spread across his face and suddenly Toby was laughing. He couldn't believe that from the first day he walked into the bank, she had been playing him. It became so funny to him that he was crying. He saw that the corners of her mouth were actually starting to curl up, and although he could tell she was fighting it, soon she was laughing with him.

"Can someone tell me the joke?" a deep voice asked. They both looked up to see a man standing over them. He was average height and build, dressed in grey slacks and a conservative shirt. Toby wondered why he was interrupting them.

"Oh my goodness, Jeff! What are you doing here? When did you get in town? I thought you were gonna be gone another month. How'd you know I was here?" she asked all in one breath.

"I called Meeko's house after you weren't home, and her sister told me you all were coming here. I wanted to surprise you, which I see I did," he said, motioning toward Toby.

"Oh, Mr. Sims, this is Jeff, uh, my—"

"Fiancé." Jeff finished her sentence for her and reached out for Toby's hand. "How you doing Mr. . . . . Sims, was it?"

"Toby, man, and I'm good." Toby stood up.

"Mr.—uh, Toby is one of my customers at the bank," she explained.

"Oh. Well, it's nice to meet you. Isis usually complains about her customers, so you must be one of the few she likes. I'm gonna grab a drink. You guys want anything?"

Isis. Her name is Isis. It's perfect for her.

"I'm fine," she told him quickly.

"Naw, I'm good," Toby said. "I gotta get back up in the booth anyway."

"I'll be right back," Jeff said and walked off, leaving Isis and Toby alone again.

"Why didn't you tell me you had a man?"

She shrugged and replied, "I didn't think it was any of your business."

"You're right; it's not. Well, you have fun and enjoy the rest of your evening," Toby told her, turning to leave.

"Toby, wait!" she said unexpectedly. He did an about face and she rose to her feet, her eyes meeting his. The chemistry between them was so strong that the hairs stood up on the back of his neck. Without warning, he reached out and touched her cheek. She closed her eyes then they quickly fluttered open and she took a step back, away from his reach. "I'm sorry."

"No need to apologize." He smiled at her. "I'll see you later."

For the rest of the night, he fought urges to look over in her direction, knowing she would be staring back at him. He let his music speak for both of them as he chose the last song of the evening. He began packing up as couples took advantage of their final opportunity to dance, including Isis and Jeff. It was the first time they had gotten on the dance floor. As the music played, his eyes drifted to them and he locked eyes with her.

Erykah Badu put his feelings into words as she sang about seeing him next lifetime. He wound up taking Darla up on her rain check that night.

Strangely enough, Toby and Isis continued the cat and mouse game when he came to the bank. He continued to go only to her teller window, and she continued to give him the cold shoulder. But now, there was a look in her eyes that told him that there was more to it than she was letting on.

After Meeko and Terrell started dating, he often asked about her. Meeko volunteered information on Jeffery, Isis's fiancé, telling him that they hadn't been together that long and he was a merchant seaman, often out of town for months at a time.

"And when he is in town, he's such a cornball that she wishes he was gone. I don't know why she's marrying him," Meeko told him. "But that's my girl, and if she's happy, then I'm happy."

One evening while leaving the 7-Eleven, he noticed a woman parked to the side, struggling to change a flat tire. He pulled his truck over and hopped out, offering to help, then smiled when he recognized Isis.

"No, I got it," she said, not even looking up. He waited for a few minutes then watched as she threw the tire iron down in a fit of frustration.

"Let me help you out, Ms. Adams," he told her. She sucked her teeth when she saw that he had been standing there looking at her struggle.

"I should've known it was you. I don't think I have the right tire iron. I can't get my rim off."

He picked the iron off the ground and walked over to her Honda Accord. He placed the end on the edge of what she was calling a rim and popped it off, revealing what really were the lug nuts of the tire, "You don't have *rims*, boo. You have hubcaps."

Isis tossed her head back in a fit of laughter. "No wonder."

"Women. I swear . . ." He sighed and quickly changed the tire for her.

"Thanks, Mr. Sims. How much do I owe you?"

"Let's start with you calling me Toby. Then let me take you out to dinner tonight." He already knew from Meeko that Jeff was gone, and he had been waiting for the perfect opportunity to ask her out.

She began biting on her bottom lip, instantly turning him on without even knowing it. "I don't think that's a good idea. Besides, I already have plans for tonight."

"Come on, Isis. It's just dinner, nothing else. I wanna take you out, get to know you, and I know you want the same thing. Tonight is Tuesday, and I don't have to work."

"I told you I have plans."

"What plans? Who has plans on a Tuesday?"

"I do! Meeko and I are going to karaoke," she answered.

"Karaoke? You've gotta be kidding." From the look on her face, he knew she wasn't. "Fine, then Terry and I will go with you. Tell me where and what time."

"You and Terry are going with us to karaoke? I don't think so. You two don't know how to act and I am not gonna be embarrassed."

"I promise we won't embarrass you," he assured her.

She stared at him for a few moments then told him to meet her at Floyd's, a small bar downtown, at 7:30. He agreed. After pleading with his brother, who wasn't too keen on the idea of going to karaoke, they arrived to find the two women already seated inside.

Toby knew that after a few drinks, most people actually believed they could dance in the club, but this gave him the opportunity to see firsthand that alcohol had the same effect on their belief that they could sing too. Surprisingly, they had a blast, laughing at most people and applauding others.

"What are you gonna sing tonight, Ice?" Meeko asked.

Isis gave her a look of horror. "Nothing! I'm not singing."

"That's right. I heard you can blow, Isis. What's up with that? You not gonna demonstrate your skills for us?" Terry asked.

"I didn't know you sang," Toby leaned and whispered into her ear. As he got closer, he could smell the scent of jasmine. He looked at her full lips and wondered what her mouth tasted like.

"I don't," she told him.

"She does so. Ask the emcee. She sings every week." Meeko nodded.

"Come on, sing for me," he told her. She cut her eyes at Meeko then said she'd be right back.

A few moments later, the emcee appeared on stage.

"Okay, we have a real treat for you, ladies and gentlemen. One of our regulars, Ms. Isis Adams."

The room fell silent and Isis stepped forward. She gave a perfect rendition of "Inseparable," and Toby knew at that moment that it would always be their song.

They began spending more time together, just talking and going on 'unofficial' dates, as he called them. There was no denying their attraction to each other, but he was enjoying living the single life and his newfound status of being the area's hottest deejay. There was also the small problem of her engagement, which caused him not to think about becoming involved with her, no matter how much he wanted to.

He often questioned her uncertainty about Jeff, but she said that it was time for her to be married. Toby became content with their friendship. There were times when the urge to pull her close and savor the feel of her soft lips on his was almost too much for him. He knew that she was just as much aware of how much he wanted her, but they never acted upon any of their desires, physical or emotional. Toby wondered if it was just as hard for her as it was for him.

Now here they were, nearly three years and several lifetimes later, talking and working out in the gym like no time had passed between them.

"So, what is it that you do now?" he asked.

"I work at a day spa called Tasteful Tranquilities. I'm a masseuse," she said proudly.

"Tasteful Tranquilities? Sounds like a cemetery. So, can a brother get more than a massage?"

"Shut up. It's a day spa, not a brothel. See, that's how men think."

"I'm saying. I figured I would ask, just in case."

"Just in case what?"

"Just in case I could get a hand job—I mean a manicure," he laughed.

She stopped the machine and got off, wiping her face with a towel. "You are so trifling. Good-bye."

"Wait a minute, Isis," he said, getting off the machine and walking beside her. "I was just playing. There you go being all sensitive and stuff. Hey, I'm about to leave. How about we go get a smoothie or something from the juice bar?"

"A smoothie?" she frowned.

"Hell, I don't know. Isn't that what people go get after they work out?"

"How about we just go outside and talk, Toby?" she said. "I'll meet you out front. Just give me enough time to jump in the shower and change."

He agreed and was waiting for her when she walked out of the locker room twenty minutes later.

"I thought we were gonna meet out front."

"I was talking to Vinny and decided to catch you in here instead. You ready?"

They each grabbed a bottle of water and walked outside the gym. Sure enough, there were small tables outside the juice bar in the same shopping center, and they took a seat there.

"You sure you don't want a smoothie?"

"I'm sure." She laughed. "This water is fine. So, tell me what's going on? Did you and your wife-to-be talk the other night?"

"Uh, I saw her, but we didn't talk," he admitted.

"Say no more. I don't even wanna know what you all did. Things will work out for you." Isis took the cap off her water and took a long swallow. Toby could see that her hair was still wet from the shower, her curls glistening from the dampness.

"I don't think so. She has some major issues that I'm not up to dealing with right about now."

"Toby, this is what marriage is all about, working through those issues. It's not a walk in the park."

"I don't expect it to be a walk in the park, but there are some things I expect from the woman I marry, and right now, Roni isn't willing to do those things." He was trying to go about this conversation without giving Isis details, but she wasn't making it easy for him. It wasn't that she was trying to get in his business intentionally; Isis would never do that. After all they had been through, he considered her a friend.

"I know you don't expect her to quit her job, cook, clean, and stay home to take care of you. Please don't tell me that's what this is about."

"No, not at all. But I do expect her to be faithful!" There, he said it. He had admitted that his fiancée was cheating on him. And now that the words had come from his mouth, the numbness he had been feeling for the past few days instantly turned into pain. He needed to be alone to deal with it. He stood and told her, "I'll talk to you later."

"Wait a minute!" Isis jumped up. "I mean damn, I'm sorry, Toby. I just . . . I thought you guys were having problems over dumb stuff like wedding colors. I definitely wouldn't have pushed the issue if I would've known it was like that."

"It's all good. You were just trying to help and I appreciate that." Toby was grateful for her sincerity. He pulled her to him and hugged her tight. "Thanks. I'm out of here."

He was crossing the street into the parking lot when he heard her calling his name. He turned to see her jogging toward him, carrying his gym bag. "You might wanna take your funky clothes with you, Mr. Sims."

"Thank you, Ms. Adams. But I know if I left them with you, they would be in good hands."

"Yeah, right into the trash can over there." She grinned. "Just kidding. Here you go. And Toby, know that I'm here for you if you need me. Don't forget; Man's rejection is God's protection."

"Thanks."

"Everything happens for a reason."

"I know."

"If He brings you to it, He'll bring you through it."

"Yep."

"Weeping may endure for a night, but joy cometh in the morning."

"That's right."

"If you love someone, set them free."

"How many more of these do you have, Isis?"

"After all the heartache I've been through, I can quote 'em all, Toby." She sighed. "You sure you're gonna be okay? Because I have some more if you need them."

"No, you've given me enough for today."

"All right, then. Bye, Toby. Take care." They embraced once again and he opened the door of his truck, tossing the gym bag in the back seat.

"Ice!"

"Yeah?"

"Same time tomorrow?" he said sheepishly. "Wash those funky clothes before you put them on. I'll meet you on the treadmill."

58

Nicole looked like she had swallowed a beach ball; other than that, you could hardly tell that she was six months pregnant. Terrell couldn't believe that it was June already. It had been a struggle, but for the past three months, he had been the loving, faithful boyfriend that he knew Nicole wanted and deserved. He no longer hung out in the clubs or had females blowing up his cell phone. Outside of the occasional conversation he had with Anjelica, there weren't even any females that he talked with on a social level. And now it seemed that she was so caught up in Jermaine, even that didn't happen all that often.

And then there was CJ. He had been avoiding her as often as possible since that evening in his office when she asked him to dinner and he declined. That was also the last time he had talked to Kayla. She let him know in no uncertain terms that she didn't have anything to say to him outside of business, and he respected that. Their sudden distance did draw some attention from people, though, including Nicole.

"Babe, why don't we invite Kayla and Geno over tomorrow and cook out on the grill?" Nicole asked, climbing beside him on the couch. This was one of the rare weekends she had obliged him to stay at his place rather than him at hers, and he was enjoying it.

"I thought we were gonna go pick the crib and stuff up this weekend. I was gonna finish the nursery," he told her. She leaned back in his lap and he wrapped his arms around her belly.

"You've been saying that every weekend since Easter and it hasn't happened yet," she laughed. "Seriously, Kayla hasn't hung out over here in a while and she really hasn't called. Is something going on between you?"

Terrell knew this conversation was coming, and he had thought long and hard about what he was going to tell Nicole when she brought up the subject. He was prepared to answer.

"She thinks I have something to do with her sister hooking up with Jermaine. She's mad."

"Why would she be mad about that? And how did you hook her sister and Jermaine up? I thought Anjelica was bad news."

"I didn't have anything to do with that. That's the thing. Jermaine met Anjelica at the club one night."

"If they met at the club, I'm surprised you didn't have anything to do with it. Heck, I'm surprised you didn't try to hook up with her." Nicole laughed.

"Girl, please. I keep trying to tell you that I went to the club to hang out with Toby, that's all. I didn't go there to meet women. For what? I have the best woman in the world right here." He kissed her on the side of her neck and she giggled.

"Please, Terrell, save it. You are full of it. And I still don't understand how Kayla could be mad about something as simple as that. I'm going to call her and see what the real deal is. It probably has something to do with the job and that CJ woman."

"What?" Terrell sat up, nearly knocking Nicole off the sofa. "Oh, sorry, boo. What are you talking about? What does this have to do with CJ?"

"She said that she couldn't stand CJ from the jump. Then you get the promotion as CJ's right hand man, then you don't have any time for Kayla anymore. I'm sure she feels frustrated, especially when you're her best friend."

"That's crazy. I have time for her."

"I just told you to invite them to a barbecue and you gave another excuse. That's okay. I'm going to invite her to my baby shower. I still love Kayla and have time for her."

"I had no doubt in my mind that she would be coming to your shower. And I still love Kayla too."

The phone rang, ending their debate over who loved Kayla more. Nicole reached over and grabbed the cordless. "Hello. Who's calling? One moment please."

"Who is it?" he asked, wondering if letting her answer his phone was a bad idea.

"Somebody named Meeko." She shrugged.

Terrell took the phone out of her hand. "Yeah," he said nonchalantly.

"Terry, It's me. I didn't think a female would be answering your phone. My bad," Meeko told him.

"It's all good. What's up?" He couldn't imagine what Meeko wanted with him, especially on a Friday night.

"I need to ask you a question, Terrell, and I need for you to be very honest with me," she told him.

"Okay, I'm listening."

"Did you know Jermaine got engaged?"

"Huh?" Terrell asked, confused by what she was saying and who she was saying it about.

"Jermaine. He got engaged."

He didn't know how to answer. There was no way that Jermaine could be engaged. Who would he even be engaged to?

"Wait a minute, Meeko. First of all, where is all of this coming from? How do you figure Jermaine's engaged?"

"Who is that?" Nicole asked. "And why is she calling you asking about Jermaine?"

"Shhhhh!" Terrell told her, covering the mouthpiece with his hand. He knew that if Meeko heard Nicole getting loud, she would get louder.

"You remember my cousin Leslie? Well, she works at Weinstein's," Meeko told him.

"How the hell did she get a job at Weinstein's?" Terrell asked, remembering Meeko's crazy cousin. "Does she get a discount?"

"Yeah, you know if you go in there she'll hook you up, Terry. But that's not what we're talking about right now. Wait a minute. Don't tell me you're about to get married too," she shrieked into the phone.

"Calm down, Meeko. Who told you Jermaine was engaged?" Terrell demanded.

"Oh, well Leslie said Jermaine and this girl came in the other tonight and they were trying on rings. He was asking her which one she liked. Well, when she got to work today, she saw a receipt for two thousand-something dollars with his name on it."

"Get the hell outta here! Yo, I'ma call you back," Terrell told her.

"Are you saying you didn't know anything about this, Terrell?" Meeko asked.

"I'm telling you I don't, but I'm about to find out," he answered. Nicole maneuvered herself off the sofa and he sat up. "I'll call you back later."

"Okay," he heard Meeko say before she hung up.

"What was that all about?" Nicole asked.

Terrell didn't answer. He was too busy dialing Jermaine's cell number.

"Thank you for calling We Secure U security installations service. Unfortunately, we are unable to take your call right now—"

Terrell hung up without leaving a message. He dialed Jermaine's home number and there was no answer there, either. *He's probably at Dominic's with Toby. I'll go up there and see what Meeko is talking about.*

"I'll be back," he told Nicole.

"Where are you going, Terrell? I know you're not going to the club, are you?"

"I'll only be gone an hour at the most, baby. I promise. I just need to talk to Jermaine and see what's going on, that's all," he assured her as he put his Timbs on. "It's not even that late."

"I don't care how late it is, Terrell. I'm saying, what difference does it make if Jermaine got engaged? What's wrong with that?" She stood at his bedroom door.

"It's who he may be engaged to that's the problem. He's barely even known this girl more than a month. I just need to go holler at him right quick. Go ahead and get in the bed. By the time you finish watching *Law & Order* I'll be right there beside you."

"Whatever," she said and disappeared in the room. He heard her fussing, but he left anyway. Just as he made it to the bottom of the steps, he heard the phone ringing. Thinking it could be Meeko or even someone worse, he ran back upstairs to answer it himself. He quickly unlocked the door and dove for the phone.

"Hello," he panted.

"Damn, T. What, you running a marathon or something?" Jermaine laughed. "Imagine that, your big behind running."

"Forget you, Negro. Yo, where you at?"

"At the crib, chilling."

"I need to talk to you. I'm 'bout to roll over there."

"Naw, son, don't do that. I got company."

"Who? Your fiancée that I heard you got now?" Terrell blurted out.

"What? You're tripping. I ain't saying she's all that."

"Oh, I ain't all that now? You weren't saying that a few minutes ago." Terrell recognized Anjelica's voice in the background. "Who are you talking to anyway?" he heard her ask.

"Terry. He was about to come over here, but I told him that was a bad idea."

"Your coming over here is definitely out of the question, Terrell," she yelled to him. "I'm going to see what I can find in this empty fridge to eat."

"For real, Terry. What's up? Something wrong?"

"Naw, I just heard that wedding bells were in your near future and I wanted to make sure you hadn't done anything dumb like asking her to marry you without telling us. That would be like thinking with your little head instead of the big one. Know what I mean?" Terrell chuckled.

"Maybe yours is small, but that ain't my business. But who told you some stuff like that?"

"I just heard you made a major jewelry purchase for her, man, and I was just checking, that's all," Terrell said, very much relieved.

"And if I did, why would I have to tell you? You think that because you hit that three or four months ago that you still got dibs on it? Be for real, man. I told you I'm feeling this girl. You said yourself that she's good people. But what she and I do within our relationship is between us. I don't care who she's been with in the past; I care about her being with me now. Believe that."

"I hear you," he replied.

"So you can call Meeko and tell her that ain't nobody engaged, because I know that's who told you about the whole thing. Her girl probably couldn't wait for us to leave out the damn jewelry store before she called and told her that I was in there looking at rings with some girl."

"Okay, you got me."

"Look what I found. Some Popsicles," Anjelica sang in the background. "Wanna lick?"

"Gotta go. Bye!" Jermaine told him. Terry thought he heard a click in the background before the sound of the dial tone filled his ear.

He got up and looked toward the bedroom door where Nicole was, but only heard the television. *She's probably already asleep.* He went into the living room and sat down, flipping through the channels. He tried to be content just being there, but temptation got the best of him. *I'll just run by the club for a minute.* He prayed Nicole didn't hear the door closing behind him as he sneaked out of the house.

The line to get into Dominic's was wrapped around the building. Terrell parked his car and walked past the anxious patrons, straight to the front door. He was greeted by the security guard, who let him in without even doing a search. He was making his way through the crowd to the deejay booth to see Toby when he heard his name being called. He turned to find Roni heading toward him.

"What's up, Ron?" He met her halfway. He hadn't really seen her in a while, and Toby told him they were taking a break. She still had the ring on her finger, though, and she still looked fine as hell.

"Nothing much. What's going on with you? How's Nicole?"

"She's good." He nodded.

"Getting big? You know if it's a boy or girl yet?"

"No, not yet. We're supposed to find out next week. But I ain't betting no money on it. Remember Kayla was supposedly having a boy when big-headed Day came popping out." He laughed. They walked over to the VIP section and the bouncer lifted the rope, allowing both of them access.

"So, who you here wit'?" he asked, thinking maybe Kayla or Yvonne was with her. Roni rarely frequented the club by herself.

"Rolling solo tonight, believe it or not."

"Wow. Where's your crew?" He held the chair out for her to sit down. He caught her looking over at the booth where Toby was mixing a slamming old school combination of Doug E. Fresh and Dana Dane that had everyone who wasn't on the dance floor nodding their heads.

"They all have lives, I guess. Tia has Theo, Kay has Geno, Von has Darrell. I am the remaining member of the Lonely Hearts Club," she told him.

"Aw, come on. You're not lonely, Roni. You got Toby."

"No, I don't. I messed up, Terrell. And no matter what, I can't fix it. He won't talk to me. I've tried and tried for the past three months, but he still won't talk to me." Roni sighed.

She looked so sad and Terrell felt bad for her. Toby didn't give him the details of what went down, but he knew it had to be pretty big for his brother to act the way he had been acting lately. Toby always pulled himself into a shell when things got to him, shutting everyone out, and lately, he had been keeping to himself. Terrell couldn't remember the last time his brother had hung out and had fun. It was killing him not to ask what happened, but he didn't.

"I know, Roni. Just give him some more time. I'm sure he'll come around," he told her, though he knew that his brother could shut people out for months at a time. If it had been three months, Roni must've hurt him pretty badly. "Look at it this way; you still got the ring, right? That must mean something. Believe me, if he wasn't gonna come around, he would have asked for the ring back."

Roni looked down at the ring, which was on her right hand, and began twisting it. She looked up at Terrell and smiled. "I hope you're right, Terrell."

"He loves you. He just takes his time dealing with things. Uncle Jay calls him a thinker. He thinks things through before reacting to them." He bobbed his head to "Ownlee Eue" by Kwame. He glanced over to the dance floor, wanting to be out there in the middle doing the Whop with everyone else.

"But how long does it take to think about things?" she asked.

"Did he ever tell you about the time I got a ticket and gave the cops his social security number?"

"You what?" she laughed.

"I told the policeman I was Tobias Sims and I got a ticket."

"Now that's just wrong, Terry."

"No, the wrong part was that I never paid the ticket and his license got suspended. I never told him about it."

"So, how did he find out?"

"He got pulled over on a traffic violation."

"No."

"And he was driving with a suspended license, so they arrested him and towed his truck," Terrell admitted.

"I betcha he whooped your ass when he got out!"

"Naw, but he was pissed, I'll tell you that much. He didn't speak to me for a year, not even when he came to my college graduation. Just gave me a hug and a card and then he left."

"So, when did he start speaking to you?"

"A year later. We had just gotten back on good terms right before that night when we all came to Dominic's for the first time. You remember that?"

"And Kayla and Janice were about to fight." Roni laughed. "Man that night was crazy. We had such a good time. I miss those days."

"Me too," he agreed. He thought about that night and all that happened after. "How is Kayla?"

"She's good. I guess she's a lot like your brother. They just need time to deal with things. I heard about what you and Anjelica did."

Terrell looked at her. "It's not what you think. It just happened. We did it and it was nothing, really."

"But why her, Terrell? Of all people."

"Kayla and Anjelica are alike in more ways than just looks. They are both loving, intelligent women with magnetic personalities. And they are both headstrong about making people believe what they want them to."

"So, are you saying that Anjelica is misunderstood because of Kayla?"

"Could be," he shrugged. "But let her know I asked about her and give Day a big kiss for me. I'm gonna go holler at Toby and then go home to curl up beside my baby."

"That is so sweet, Terrell. I'll deliver your message. Take care." Roni stood up and gave him a big hug.

He walked over to the booth and joined his brother, who was flipping through albums. He had the headphones wrapped around his neck and beads of sweat appeared on his forehead.

"What's up, Tobe? You a'ight?" he asked and gave him a grip.

"Yeah, man. This place is jumping tonight, huh?"

"You putting it down, man. That's for sure. You are in rare form tonight, kid. Does that have something to do with your girl being here?" He gestured over to Roni, who was still sitting in the VIP section, rocking to the music.

Toby looked over at her and shook his head at Terrell. "Nope, not at all." He pushed Terrell aside and put the headphones back over his ears.

"So, are you even gonna talk to her?" He tapped Toby on the shoulder. His brother paused long enough to look at him then went back to spinning music. Terrell took this as his cue to leave. "I'll check you out later."

Toby nodded. "I'll hit you up over the weekend, Terry."

"Cool," he replied. He waved at Roni, who was now holding a drink. He hoped that everything would be cool between them, because she was a good woman and he knew how much his brother loved her.

Terrell stopped at 7-Eleven on the way home and picked up a Slurpee for Nicole. He figured he was saving himself a trip because she was sure to send him out at 3:00 in the morning because she was craving one. He wasn't mad, though. He liked doing things for her and his unborn child, and he was looking forward to them being a family in the near future. In a few months, he would be a father, a dad, a pop. He didn't have a relationship with his father. He died when Terrell was only two years old and Toby was three. Now, he would have the chance to do all the things with his child that he and his dad never had the opportunity to experience, and he was excited.

Being extra quiet as he unlocked his door, he walked into his pitch black bedroom. He leaned across the bed, reached out for his sleeping girlfriend and whispered, "Baby, I brought you a Slurpee. Cherry, of course."

There was no answer and to his surprise, no sleeping Nicole. He checked the bathroom to see if she was there, but she wasn't. She wasn't anywhere in the apartment. He walked out to the parking lot to see if her car was there, but it was gone. He hadn't noticed it before when he first got home. He rushed back inside and dialed her home number, but she didn't answer. She didn't answer her cell number either. He called the hospital to make sure that she wasn't admitted, and was relieved when they told him she wasn't. He waited another thirty minutes before jumping in his car and searching for her. He drove around trying to think of places she could be, but eventually wound up back at home.

Something was wrong and he knew it. Nicole would never just leave without calling his cell and telling him something or at least leaving a note saying good-bye. He checked the caller

ID to make sure she hadn't called. The last call had come in at 11:34, while he was still at the club. The number belonged to an A. Moore, but he didn't recognize it. Not caring that it was after 1:00 in the morning, he called the number.

"Hi, this is Arianna. I'm sorry I can't take your call, but leave me a message and I'll call you back. If this is an emergency, feel free to call 911. Peace."

Arianna. What does she want and why is she calling my house? He leaned back on the couch and rubbed his tired eyes. He sat up quickly when he answered his own question. *She must've talked to Nicole.* He tried to convince himself that maybe Gary used Arianna's phone or something and he was panicking for no reason.

He tried calling Nicole once again and still got no answer. Hours later, he didn't even realize he had fallen asleep until he woke up to the sun shining through his window. After still not being able to reach Nicole at home or on her cell, he called Arianna's number again.

"Hello," she answered. There was still a hint of sleep in her voice.

"Arianna, its Terrell. Have you talked to Nicole?"

"Huh?"

"Did you call here and talk to Nicole last night?" he questioned, trying not to sound frustrated.

"What time is it, Terrell?" she asked.

"Eight thirty," he answered, looking at the time on the cable box. He knew it was too early to be calling someone on a Saturday morning, but at that moment, it didn't matter. "I see on the caller ID that you called here last night. What did you want? How did you even get my number?"

"Nicole called here from that number and I called her back. Is that okay?" she whined. "Now, I need to call you back, Terrell. It's too early in the morning for this."

"I don't give a damn how early it is. I need to find my girl. When I left here last night, she was asleep. I come home an hour later and she's gone. She's not at home, not answering her cell, and you're the last number on the caller ID. Now, I need to know number one, was Nicole here when you called? Number two, if she was, did you talk to her? Three, do you know where the hell she is?"

"Look, Terrell, I don't have to deal with your attitude. I really don't have to deal with you, period. But out of the kindness of my heart, I will tell you that I talked to Nicole last night and you don't need to worry. She's fine."

"What the hell do you mean you don't have to deal with me? You call my house and talk to my girl and then she ups and leaves without saying anything to me? What did she say? Where is she?"

"I don't know where she is."

"You're lying. You know she's okay, but you don't know where she is? That's bullshit and you know it! What did you talk about? What did you say to her?"

"None of your business. I tried being nice and telling you that she's fine, but it didn't work, so now I'm hanging up. And don't call back," she said.

"I will come over there and—" The sound of the dial tone in his ear stopped Terrell from finishing his threat. He redialed the number, but the voice mail picked up immediately. There was no point in calling back because she had obviously turned her phone off. He had no idea where she lived. Deciding he couldn't just sit there, he grabbed his keys and hurried to his car.

Terrell hoped that by the time he made the fifteen-minute drive to Nicole's place, her car would be parked in front and she would be home. To his disappointment, neither of those things happened. He became desperate and went to the only other place he thought she could possibly be. He prayed all the way there, asking God to help him. *Lord, I need you to be there with me and help me remain calm as I do this. I love her. Make her see that.*

He turned down the street and pulled in front of the house. His stomach was a bundle of nerves as he got out of the car and knocked on the door. He didn't know what he was going to say to her or what to anticipate.

"What the hell do you want?" Gary growled when he opened the door.

Terrell took a deep breath before answering. "I don't want no trouble, Gary. I just wanna talk to Nicole."

"And?"

"Don't play games with me. I just wanna talk to her."

"Nigga, ain't nobody playing. Obviously you did something wrong to think that she's over here! Where the hell is my sister? What did you do to her?" Gary stepped out the door toward Terrell.

Taking a step back in case Gary tried to swing on him, he replied, "When I came home last night she was gone. The last person she talked to was Arianna, so I figured she was over here, that's all. Now, is she here?"

"No, she ain't. Wait right here while I go call my girl and find out what the hell is going on." Gary turned and went back inside his house. Terrell looked around, peeking inside the storm door. He noticed that even though it was small, it was nice. There wasn't a lot of furniture, just a small grey sofa with a matching chair, a coffee table and a television. Everything was in its place. He didn't know why, but he expected Gary's place to be on the junky side.

A few moments later, Gary came back outside. "Well, looks like my sister finally came to her senses. Seems like your little secret has been found out and she's got firsthand knowledge that you are the loser I told her you were."

"Gary, you've got to believe that I never did anything to hurt Nicole. I swear. I love her. That was one of the reasons I did it!"

"You are crazy! You did something as trifling as that out of love? What the hell was that supposed to prove? How is that love? That's selfishness. And you never thought Nicole would find out about it, but she did and she's hurt. I don't blame her."

"I don't blame her either. And I'm sorry she had to find out about it the way that she did. I didn't want Arianna to be the one to tell her. I should have. And yes, I did it out of love—love for Nicole. There was no way that I could have a baby with that girl. I thought that I was doing the right thing by taking her to get rid of it. Especially since Nicole was carrying our child."

"What the hell are you talking about? Arianna ain't tell Nicole nothing. Nicole overheard you talking to your boy on the phone before you went to the club, and y'all was talking about some girl you boned three months ago. If that shit wasn't foul enough, now you standing here talking about some girl you took the clinic for a vacuum job? Nigga, you is foul!" Gary hollered.

Nicole must've been listening on the other end, Terrell thought. His heart began pounding in his chest as he realized what was about to happen. With a swiftness, Gary's right arm came out of nowhere and caught him in the face. In an attempt at self-defense, Terrell blocked his next shot and recovered with one of his own to Gary's abdomen. His opponent doubled over in pain but was determined not to be defeated. He raised himself up and charged at Terrell, knocking both of them to the ground. They rolled across the front of the lawn, ending up near the edge of the driveway. Neither of them noticed the green Toyota pulling up as they fought.

"Oh my God! What are you doing?"

"Stop it! Stop it!"

The two men continued to wrestle on the ground, ignoring the screams. Terrell had pinned Gary when he felt someone tackle him from behind. He fell to the side, landing next to Gary. He looked up just as Arianna pounced on him. It was then that he recognized Nicole's screams.

"Please, please, all of you! Stop it right now!" she cried as tears rolled down her face.

Terrell rolled over, pushing Arianna off of him and rushed over to her side. "Nicole, baby. It's okay."

He tried to grab her, but she pushed him away. "What are you doing here? What is your problem?"

"I came here to find you. When I came home last night, I was worried to death." His face was drenched with sweat and the taste of blood was in his mouth. He wiped it with the palm of his hand, checking to see if he was actually bleeding.

"Ari, are you okay?" Nicole walked over to the woman who was still sitting on the ground. Gary rolled over and led beside her as well, scowling at Terrell.

"I'm fine," she replied, checking her arms and legs for war wounds.

"I'm sorry," Terrell told them.

"You need to leave." Nicole shot him a look of hatred, which made him feel worse than he already did.

"I will, but I need to talk to you first," Terrell told her. She stood up and walked over to him, her round belly leading the way.

"There's nothing I have to say to you, especially right now. You know my brother is on probation, and you come over here and fight him in front of his house? Just leave right now, Terrell."

He reached for her once again, thinking that maybe if he could just touch her face and look into her eyes she would feel how much he loved and needed her. She stepped back from him and shook her head.

Gary jumped up and stood in front of his sister. "You'd better do what she says before I whoop your ass again!"

"You ain't whoop my ass the first time. Your girlfriend saved you," Terrell hissed. Gary charged at him again, but this time Terrell was ready for his attack. He stood firm and pushed him to the ground in one quick movement.

"What are you doing?" Nicole screamed at him. "Leave!"

A look of horror came over her face and she grabbed her stomach. Arianna rushed over, putting her arms around her. "Nicole!"

"Aaaaaaaaauuuuugh!" Nicole grimaced. Terrell caught her right before she collapsed.

"Call 911!" Arianna shouted to Gary. Before he even made it off the ground, Terrell had already lifted Nicole and was headed to his car. He hit the alarm and Arianna opened the door for him.

"Wha . . . shouldn't we . . . where . . ." Gary started mumbling.

"Shut the hell up and get in the car!" Terrell told him. He glanced over at Nicole, whose face was filled with pain, and told her, "Hold on, baby. I'm right here."

As he sped off to the hospital, he wasn't the only one praying this time.

59

"So, did you talk to her?" Isis asked as they got to the stationary bikes in the center of the gym.

"Yeah, I did," Toby answered.

"Good. That's a start." She straddled the bike and set the timer. "Thirty minutes?"

"Forty-five," he told her, "and we didn't really talk that long."

"But you talked to her. That's all that matters. I mean, let you tell it, you were never talking to her again. That means you're healing."

"No, that means she cornered me at my truck as I was leaving the club." He began pedaling.

He and Isis had been working out every weekday for a while now, and he looked forward to the two hours he spent with her each day. It was therapeutic for him, and it was easy for him to open up to her. "But you're right; for some reason, I talked to her."

"Because you're no longer bitter toward her. I told you time heals all wounds." She smiled at him. He couldn't help laughing. Her 'Isisms,' as he called them, had become a part of their daily workout. Each day she had a quote, scripture or line from a movie that somehow suited whatever situation they were discussing.

"Okay, Ice, okay."

"What did you all talk about?"

"Like I said, nothing really. She asked me about Fourth of July and if I was having my annual backyard bash and I told her no." He shrugged.

"Why not? I heard that's become like a must attend event around here. People have already started looking for outfits," she told him. "What's wrong?"

"I'm just not in the partying mood, I guess. And I've only had two, so it can't be that big of an event."

"I heard the one last year didn't end until two days later."

"That's not true; it lasted two days," he corrected her.

"Well, what are you gonna do to celebrate the Fourth? It's next month, you know. And what are the masses gonna do without a DJ Terror backyard bash to celebrate?"

"That's not my problem," he said, panting. The bike was on uphill mode, and he adjusted his pace. "Like I told Roni, I'm not hosting it this year. She suggested we go away for the weekend."

"That's a nice idea. It would give you two the chance to spend some quality time together. You should go." Isis pedaled with ease. Toby looked over at her bike to see what setting she was on. He did a double take when he saw that she was also on uphill.

"I don't think so. I'm taking things nice and slow. I have to admit she looked good. I was glad to see that," he said.

"You guys will work things out. You just need time. I've been telling you that. I haven't been wrong yet, have I?"

"No, you haven't," he answered, "but I don't think we'll be getting back together. I don't trust her. Even after I got home last night, I was wondering if she went to see him after she left the club."

"I thought you said he lived out of town." She looked over at him.

"He does, but you know what I mean. I always wonder how many other times she lied about where she was and who she was with. It's gotten a lot better, because I was tripping after I first found out," he told her. "But you already know that."

Isis just laughed and continued pedaling. He knew she understood what he was talking about. Toby had been on an emotional roller coaster. Some days his mood was dark and depressing, and others he was full of rage. The only people in his life that he found it necessary to talk to were Isis and Jermaine, who he now worked with regularly.

Both of them seemed to understand what he was going through in their own way. Jermaine was always reminding him that he had his back with whatever he needed him to do, including using his business contacts to seek Sean out and beat him down. Isis was there for him every day to encourage him, and he found himself confiding in her more and more. That also added to the attraction he had for her. But when he mentioned it, she told him that what they both needed in their lives was a true friend, and that's what they would remain to each other, nothing more. He agreed and never brought it up again.

"Is she still wearing your ring?"

"Huh?" he asked, slowing his pace.

"You heard me. Is she still wearing your ring?"

"Yeah," he said slowly. It was a hearty laugh that escaped her this time, and he looked over at her like she was crazy. "What?"

"You'll get back together."

"Why?"

"She's still wearing the ring. Let me ask you this: have you ever asked for it back?"

"No. I wouldn't ever do that. I bought that for her. She can keep it. I know most guys would've took it off her finger the day they walked up on her and another dude, but it was a gift, and that would just be petty. You know what I mean?"

"No, but I can tell you what I think. I think that you're hurt and mad, but you're still in love with her. And she's still in love with you, because she is still faithfully wearing that ring and reaching out for you. It's only been three months. I say that by the end of July, you all will be back on the road to romance."

"Why are you pushing this, Isis? I mean, you push this harder than Roni does. Is she putting you up to this?" He reached for his towel lying across the front of the bike and wiped his face.

"I'm trying to stop you from making the mistake of throwing away happiness, that's all. You deserve to be happy."

"What about you?" he frowned.

Her legs worked faster and faster on the pedals. Her sports bra was wet with perspiration, drops of it running down her back into the basketball shorts she was wearing. He could see the muscles in her calves as he admired her smooth, shapely legs. He knew she was ignoring him because she refused to look at him.

"Don't ignore me. What about you, Isis?"

Her legs stopped and the bike slowed down. She hopped off the seat and snatched her towel off the back of the bike. Toby knew he had struck a nerve with her, but he was tired of being the only one sharing his issues and Isis keeping all of hers inside. He stopped his bike and stood up as well. He touched her arm, forcing her to look at him.

"What about me?" she asked, placing the towel around her neck.

"Don't you deserve to be happy? What about your true love?" He stared at her. He could see the rising of her chest as she inhaled and wondered if it was from the workout or anger at his question. "What about you?"

"I lost my chance at happiness that night, remember? I don't deserve true love," she answered. He was speechless as she turned and walked away from him, leaving him standing alone.

A chill went down his spine as he thought about the night she was speaking of. It was a night that played in his head a million times, like a dream etched into his memory. For him, it was one of the greatest moments of his life, but he knew that for her, it only reminded her of the worst moment of hers.

That night, both couples had decided to hang out together, Meeko and Terry along with Isis and Toby. They went to check out Rickey Smiley at the comedy club then went down to the waterfront to have dinner. They had a ball, and were finishing up dessert when Terry suggested they walk along the pier.

They all looked at Isis, who knew she was outnumbered. She shrugged her shoulders and sighed. "I don't care."

The tab was paid and the two couples exited through the back door of the restaurant, leading directly to the pier. It was a nice fall night, with just a hint of a breeze. Terry and Meeko walked ahead of them, hand in hand. Toby strolled beside Isis, close enough to notice the small chill bumps that were beginning to form on her arms and shoulders.

"You cold?" he asked, taking off his blazer and wrapping it around her.

"Not really." She smiled and thanked him. "It actually feels nice."

"Then what's up with the goose bumps?"

"I don't know."

"Don't worry. I have that effect on women sometimes." He smiled.

"Don't flatter yourself." Isis rolled her eyes at him.

He couldn't resist stepping behind her and putting his arms around her waist. She squealed and tried to get away from his grasp.

"What are you doing?" she shrieked, turning toward him.

He looked down into her big brown eyes and got lost in them for a moment. She looked so funny standing with her hands on her hips and her head cocked to one side, waiting for his answer.

"What? I was trying to keep you warm, that's all. I'm not trying to attack you. You got people looking at us about to call 911." He gestured toward an older couple who was staring at them, cell phone in hand.

"Oh, sorry. I'm fine." Isis waved at them. They nodded and turned away.

"See, that's how innocent black men get locked up," Toby told her, sitting on a nearby bench.

She paused, looking ahead and asked, "Where did Meeko and Terry sneak off to?"

"Do you really want me to answer that question?"

"I guess it was kind of dumb of me to ask." She took a seat beside him. Her pager began beeping and she looked at it.

"You need to use my cell phone?"

"No, I know who it is. It can wait." She sighed, placing it back in her purse.

He noticed her sudden somberness in attitude and asked her what was wrong. She shook her head and looked out into the darkness. He could hear the sounds of the waves breaking against the nearby shore and embraced the silence between Isis and himself. After a few quiet moments, he finally spoke.

"So, what's the deal between us, Isis? I mean really."

"What are you talking about, Toby? There is no deal. Has it totally slipped your mind that I'm engaged to be married in a few months?"

"I know that's what you and everyone else keeps telling me, but I've never seen you wearing your ring, and you really don't act like you're excited about your upcoming nuptials. I'm beginning to wonder if you're even in love."

From the way she reacted, he knew he struck a nerve. "First of all, you don't know me, so how would you know how I act? I don't have to explain to you why I don't wear my ring and I . . . I . . . " She stopped mid-sentence.

Toby rubbed her back as he noticed the tears falling from her eyes. "It's okay, Isis. It's going to be all right. You can talk to me."

"I don't know what's wrong with me. Jeff is a good man, he has a good job, and he cares enough to wanna marry me. He doesn't hang out at the club, I don't have to worry about him beating on me. Why shouldn't I marry him? He's a good man."

"But you're not in love with him. What about love, Isis?"

"What about it? My father loved my mother, but when he found out she was pregnant, he left her high and dry because she was black and he was Japanese, and the reality of bringing her and a half-black child home was enough to make him forget all about her," she said in one breath. "So what makes me so much better than her? Jeff is a good man. We've been together for five years. When my mother died and I had nothing or no one, he was there. I had no family. My mother's people acted like I was a throwaway doll, and my father's family didn't even know that I existed. But Jeff was there for me. The fact that I'm biracial never mattered to him."

"You're crazy. I can't believe that someone as beautiful and intelligent as you has such low self-esteem that you think you have to marry the first man that asks you. You're making a mistake, Isis." He turned to face her. "The world is full of good men that don't give a damn if you're polka dotted. I'm a good man, Isis. At least you can say that you're in love with me. I understand that he was there for you, but you're with him out of obligation, not love. I love you."

He watched her shoulders slump in frustration, and he held her in his arms as she wept. There was no denying that she was caught between a rock and a hard place, and he wasn't making it any easier for her, but he was tired of denying his feelings—feelings that he had never held for anyone else. He was just as much in love with her as she was with him. He knew that.

"What do you want from me, Toby? You want me to just tell him that it's over? After all we've been through and all that he's done, you want me to just throw all of that away? That's not even fair to him."

"I know. But it's not fair to you to marry a man you know you don't love. Is that how you want to spend the rest of your life?"

Isis looked into his face then kissed him tenderly on the mouth. It was what he had been waiting for the entire night. Her lips felt so soft and warm on his, and her taste was all that he imagined it would be.

She finally pulled away from him and said, "I can't risk throwing away a sure thing for a *what if*, Toby."

"Hey, you guys ready to roll?" Terrell called from the darkness. Soon, he and Meeko strolled into the light, walking hand in hand, looking very much like the happy couple they were.

"Yeah." Isis stood. They walked back to Terrell's car in silence, which continued until they pulled in front of Toby's condominium.

"I'll check you guys later," Toby said, climbing out of the back seat. He had made it to the front door when he heard someone behind him. He quickly spun around, ready to swing on the prowler he thought was there. Instead of a robber, he found Isis holding the suit jacket he had loaned her. "Oh, thanks. You could've left it with Terry and I would've gotten it later."

"No, I wanted to talk to you anyway, Toby. I don't like the way things ended between us. Terry and Meeko said they'd wait for me."

"Yeah, we can talk. Come on in." He opened the door and led her inside.

Isis blew out a long whistle as she looked around his den. "Oh my God. How many of these do you have?"

She was speaking of the walls of CDs he had in the room. There were hundreds of them that he had collected over the years. He smiled. "I don't know. I think I stopped counting at four hundred thirty-three. Anything in particular you wanna hear?"

"No. Besides, I should really be going." She sighed.

"You don't have to leave. I can take you home. I don't mind."

"No. I should be going, really."

"Have a seat," he said and picked up the phone. "Yo, Terry. Y'all go ahead and roll. Isis is gonna chill for a while and I'll take her home. What? Meeko, don't go there. What? Okay, okay, hold on."

He passed the phone to Isis. "Yeah. Yeah. Uh-huh. I know. It's cool. I will. Girl, please. I don't think so. Definitely not. Okay, I'll call you when I get in. Bye."

"Did you convince your girl that you were safe?" he asked, taking the phone from her.

"Don't get mad because your reputation precedes you, Toby. She just wanted to make sure that you hadn't put nothing in my drink to make me stay." She sat back on the soft cushions of his sofa.

"Would you like something to drink?" he asked.

"No, I'm good. I thought you were gonna play me some music."

"I got you. Let's see . . ." He tried to think of what she would like. He walked over and kneeled toward the bottom case, finding what he was looking for. He placed the CD in the stereo and hit play. She tossed her head back in laughter when UTFO began singing. They talked and laughed about old times, and she even relaxed enough to dance a little bit.

"Hold up, hold up. I got something for you."

"Is it Klyymaxx? You know those were my girls." She nodded and then sang, "Don't you know the men all pause when I walk into the room?"

"No, it's not Klyymaxx. You probably only liked them because they had the Japanese-looking chick!"

"You are such a bum!" Isis reached out and punched him in the arm. "You know they could throw down."

"Check it out. What about this one?" he asked her.

Music played through the speakers and she closed her eyes, rocking. She started singing, and then he was right behind her. His arms came around her body and they started dancing, his front to her back. He sang into her ear and she leaned her head against his shoulder. She smelled so inviting, as if she had just stepped out of the shower. The feel of having her in his arms made him smile. There was no doubt this was indeed love.

The song faded and another one of his favorites, "Fairy Tale Lover" came on. This time, as he sang, she turned to face him. He brushed her thick, long hair from her shoulders and noticed a small mark on her collarbone. He rubbed his fingers across it.

"A mole," she told him.

"No, a beauty mark," he corrected her, then leaned down and licked it. He could feel her tense up in his arms, so he stopped.

They continued to dance, Toby holding her close in his arms. They made their way to the sofa, where she sat down and he kneeled before her.

"Toby, this is crazy," she whispered and shook her head at him. Her face was illuminated by the glow of the light coming from the small lamp in the corner of the room.

"The only thing crazy is the way I feel about you," he told her. "Now, just chill and relax."

As if on cue, "Let's Chill" by Guy began to play, and they began laughing. Unable to control his desire to have her mouth on his again, he kissed her with a passion. He felt her hands reaching under his shirt, and helped her by pulling it over his head. He began unbuttoning the dress she was wearing, slowly revealing the black lace bra she wore underneath.

"This is crazy. This isn't supposed to be happening. I'm engaged," she told him.

He looked deep into her eyes and told her, "But you're in love with me. You can't marry him."

"If I do this, something bad is going to happen. I know it is," she said, removing his belt and licking his earlobe.

"No, it won't. I promise. I am just as much a good man as he is. And you know that. Let me show you," he told her, pulling her onto the floor with him.

By the time Isis was naked, Toby was performing a full pelvic examination with his tongue. She called out his name over and over, making him want to fulfill her every desire. He raised himself over her and felt her fingers around his swollen hardness.

"No way! There's no way you're putting that big thing in me." She tried to sit up.

"Don't even try it. It's not even that big." He couldn't help grinning at her.

"Maybe if you plan on being a porn star."

"Just relax and let me take care of everything, Isis."

She leaned up once again and asked him about protection. He reached over into his pants pocket and pulled out a condom.

"Do you do this very often? Because you certainly are prepared." She giggled.

He could feel her legs shaking under him and he kissed her again, telling her to relax, everything would be okay. He began to slowly make love to her, wanting it to last forever. He wanted her to feel how much he wanted her and wanted to be with her. And as he felt her legs around him and looked into her face, she called out to him, letting him know that she felt the same way. It was as if they were meant for each other, and after it was over, they lay on the floor, holding each other tight. She lay against his chest, and he kissed the top of her head.

Their perfect moment was interrupted by a knock at the door.

"Who the hell—?" he asked, reaching for his pants. Isis scrambled for her clothes, and he showed her to the bathroom. He rushed back to the door, peeping to see who it was. Meeko stood shivering on his doorstep.

"What's wrong? Where's Terrell?" he asked when he opened the door.

"Where's Isis? I need to talk to her," she blurted out. "I've been paging her, but she hasn't called me back. Where is she?"

"She's in the bathroom. She'll be out in a minute. Where's my brother? Did something happen?"

"He's at home. He doesn't even know I'm here. I came right over here to get Isis."

"I'm here, Meeko. What's wrong?" Isis came out of the bathroom looking like the last hour with Toby had never even happened.

"We've gotta go. You gotta get home!" Meeko began pulling at her arm.

"Meeko, you're scaring me. I'm not going anywhere until you tell me what the hell is going on," Isis insisted.

Toby stood waiting for Meeko to answer her friend.

"Isis, there's been an accident. Jeff and some guys were on the road headed back when an eighteen wheeler came into their lane."

"Jeff isn't supposed to come home until next month." Isis shook her head as if she didn't want to believe what Meeko was saying.

"His mom said he wanted to surprise you, so he told you it was next month," Meeko explained, tears streaming. Toby could see in her face that this was not going to be good news, and that she had even more to tell.

"Well, where were they? I have to get to him. Where's Jeff?"

"Isis, he died about an hour ago on the operating table. I'm so sorry," Meeko whispered.

Isis stood in shock. Toby reached out for her, but she snatched away.

She looked at him and told him, "I told you something bad was going to happen. I killed him. This is all my fault!"

Isis left his house that night with Meeko, and it was the last time Toby had seen her until the night he proposed to Roni. He knew that she blamed herself for Jeff's death, and Meeko told them that she left to deal with her grief. Toby dealt with his own grief for several months, then he found himself back in the swing of things, being the player he was before Isis Adams had even entered his life.

60

"How is she?" Terrell asked as Dr. Fisher came out into the waiting room. They had been waiting over an hour for someone to come and tell them something.

"Is she gonna be a'ight?" Gary brushed past Terrell and asked.

"And who might you be?" Dr. Fisher questioned.

"This is Nicole's brother, Gary, and his girlfriend, Arianna." Terrell introduced them out of respect for Dr. Fisher.

"Yes, Nicole has told me about you. Well, we were able to stop the contractions, so that's a good thing. But we are going to monitor her for the next day or so. After that, if all goes well, she'll be released, but she is to remain on bed rest for the remainder of her pregnancy. That means the only reason she is to get out of bed is to go to the bathroom, nothing more."

"I understand, Dr. Fisher. Can we see her?" Terrell asked.

"Right now, she's resting. Give her a little while. Her blood pressure was extremely high, and our goal is to keep her as peaceful as possible. Stress is what caused her to go into premature labor, and we don't want that happening again," the doctor warned.

"You don't have to worry about *nobody* stressing her out, Doc. I'ma see to that." Gary glared at Terrell.

"You don't have to see to nothing. I can take care of Nicole."

"You ain't taking care of shit! My sister don't wanna have nothing to do with your trifling ass! You'd better stay—"

"Gentlemen, gentlemen, gentlemen! This is a hospital. Now is not the time or place for this. I just told you how sensitive this situation is." Dr Fisher's voice boomed.

Terrell was immediately embarrassed. Usually he was the voice of reason in a time like this, and here he was being one of the causes.

"I apologize, Dr. Fisher," he quickly told him.

"You can come back when you've calmed down, but for now, you both need to leave." Dr. Fisher turned and left them.

Arianna, who had been quiet this entire time, finally spoke. "You two are so stupid! I am so embarrassed. Both of you are acting like children. Now, listen. This is how this is gonna go down. I'm staying here until Nicole wakes up. Terrell, you need to take Gary to get my car from his house. When you get back, if Nicole wants to see you, then fine. If not, then you'll have to deal with it."

Gary began to smile at him surreptitiously. "Don't worry. She won't wanna see you."

"Shut up, Gary, because you aren't gonna make matters worse by telling Nicole anything either. Neither am I. What goes on in that clinic is nobody's business but the people involved, and that doesn't include you, me, or Nicole. So get over that too, Gary, and I mean it. If I find out Nicole knows anything and Terrell didn't tell it, you're gonna regret it."

Terrell was amazed at the spunk and attitude that was coming out of this white girl. She always seemed so timid to him, but he now knew that was merely his perception of her. He now had a newfound respect for her, and he could see that she was demanding all of this because she had Nicole's best interests at heart.

The two men agreed and somehow made it back to Gary's house without killing each other. As his future brother-in-law got out, Terrell looked at his face, still swollen from their early morning rumble. He could see that he was worried.

"Gary."

"What?" Gary turned around and frowned.

"Nicole and the baby are gonna be fine. I know they are."

"Yeah," was all that he mumbled, looking down.

"You also have to believe me when I say that I love your sister. I swear I ain't gonna do nothing to hurt her."

Gary looked at him and replied, "Terrell, you'd damn well better show me better than you tell me."

Terrell nodded and pulled off. He went home, took a quick shower and raced back to the hospital. He stopped at the gift shop and picked up some flowers, a card and a big teddy bear wearing a yellow ribbon. Gary was in the waiting room when he got there.

"Any word yet?" Terrell asked him, setting all the gifts in the middle of the table.

"Ari is back there with her now. She should be out here in a minute," he replied.

Terrell took a seat and picked up a magazine from the table. There was a cute little girl on the cover, smiling with only two teeth at the bottom of her mouth. She was the cutest thing, and he wondered if he had a daughter, what she would look like. He sat back and closed his eyes.

"What's up? How is she?" he heard Gary ask. He looked around, realizing he had fallen asleep.

"She's good. She not too thrilled about being on bed rest, but she understands what has to be done," Arianna told them.

"I'm going back to see her." Terrell stood up.

"Hold on, Terrell. She's not ready to see you right now. I told her you were out here, but she doesn't care. I'm sorry, but you can't go back."

"What about when she comes home? Who's gonna take care of her? She's gonna need help," he told her.

"Don't worry about her. I'm quite capable of taking care of my sister. She'll be in good hands," Gary said.

"No way. You don't—"

"I'm gonna stay with Nicole while she's home, Terrell. I don't work at the clinic anymore, and it won't be a problem. I've already talked with Nicole about it. Don't worry. I'll keep you updated on her progress daily, and I promise if anything happens, you'll be the first person I'll call," Arianna told him. She must've noticed the distress in his face because she added, "Just give her a little time. I'm sure that she'll be calling you soon. I know she loves you, but her hormones are a little out of whack, and there's no reasoning with her right now. I'll give her the stuff you bought and tell her you're waiting for her call."

Terrell reluctantly took the items off the table and passed them to her. Gary was even giving him a look of sympathy. There was nothing left for him to do or say. He slowly turned and left.

He sat behind the wheel of his car in the parking lot, not knowing where to go or what to do. For the first time in his life, he felt alone. He cursed himself for letting his ego and sexual desires get the best of him. Trying to be a player had cost him his best friend and now his girlfriend, and now the one who always had the answers for everyone else didn't have any words of wisdom for himself.

Terrell threw himself into his work. He went in early and stayed late working on special projects and developing new procedures for the company. He became a mover and a shaker, causing management to take notice of his skills and abilities. He was offered positions on executive committees and staff councils by managers and department heads left and right. At work, he was the man.

His home life was a different story. He didn't hang out any-more. His social life consisted of calling Arianna and checking on Nicole. Once a week, he would go to the grocery store and buy everything he thought she would need make her stay in bed more comfortable. He bought her DVDs, novels, puzzle books, and he even bought her a laptop and computer games. He purchased things for the baby in her favorite color, yellow. She still hadn't told him whether it was a girl or boy, and he didn't know if she knew or not, because he hadn't talked to her. When he questioned Arianna about the baby's sex, she would say she didn't know.

He was still determined to be faithful to her and a good father to his child, no matter what it took. Working with CJ made it a challenge for him. She was constantly in his office, leaning on his desk, propositioning him every chance she got. He was going over some notes one afternoon when she walked in without knocking.

"What are you doing, sweetheart? Working on something new to wow the powers that be?" She walked around his desk, looking at his computer.

He frowned at her, wondering what she was up to. "What can I do for you, CJ?"

"I tried calling you, but your voice mail kept picking up, so I came to see what you were doing." Her eyes scanned the computer screen. He was tempted to turn it off while she was standing there being nosy, but didn't.

"Just going over some notes, that's all. I must've forgotten to turn my voice mail off when we got back from the meeting earlier, that's all. You act like I'm in here sending out company secrets or something."

"You never can tell these days, and the way you've been moving up the corporate ladder, I'm trying to learn some secrets from you." She turned and looked out his window, which gave a full view of the parking lot. "So, do you have big plans for next weekend? I heard your brother has a huge party that is off the chain. Think I can tag along?"

"He's not having one this year, so no, I'm not doing anything special."

"We could always have our own private party. You could come over and I could throw some steaks on the grill, open a bottle of Dom P." She winked at him.

"I don't think so. I have to finish decorating my baby's room, which I've been putting off for a while."

"How is your girlfriend? I saw an invitation to her baby shower on Kayla's desk."

He didn't even know when her shower was. No one had even mentioned it to him—not even Kayla. Even though they weren't speaking beyond a polite hello when they passed in the hallway, he knew that she was aware of his and Nicole's situation.

"She's fine. Doing great. We're excited about the baby." He nodded.

"Speaking of Kayla, looks like she's got some excitement of her own in the parking lot." CJ laughed.

Terrell got up to see what she was talking about. He looked out the window to see Kayla screaming angrily at Craig, who was standing nearby. He hurried out of his office and down the staircase, praying he got there before anyone else saw them.

"Yo, what's going on peeps?" he called to them as he rushed out the door.

"Get the hell away from me, Craig. If you don't, I'm calling the police to come and haul your ass away from here, and you know your dope dealing behind is already skating on thin ice!" Kayla yelled.

"Call them. I don't give a damn! I don't understand why you're tripping. All I want to do is spend time with my daughter. Is that too much to ask?"

"Nope, it sure isn't. You can come by the house and see her whenever you want to. I told you that."

"See how unreasonable she's being, Terrell? I'm paying day-care and taking damn good care of my daughter, but I can only see her at the house."

Terrell looked over at Kayla, who was daring him to say something. He decided to take the neutral approach. "Where is it that you want to take Day, Craig? I mean, why can't you see her at the house?"

"Man, next weekend is my family reunion. I want her to meet my people, which is her people, since she is my child."

"She's not even a year old! How the hell is she gonna meet somebody, Craig? No, I'm not letting my child go with you, and that's the end of that. Now, leave!"

Terrell still didn't understand what was going on, so he quietly asked, "Kayla, why can't she go? It's only his family reunion."

Kayla looked at him like he was speaking some language she didn't understand. "How about because his *wife* is a fucking retard? Do you know how often she calls my house at two and three o'clock in the morning talking about how she hates me, and her son will always be the king of the family? Do you know how many messages she leaves talking about how I got her fired from her job and had food taken from her son's mouth? How about how she called and asked me why I didn't let Day call her son and wish him a happy birthday or send him a card? Day can't talk! And you know what? I really don't care about her son's birthday!"

Terrell pulled Kayla away from Craig and told her, "You're wrong, Kayla."

"What?"

"You're wrong. I love you and you're my dawg, but you're wrong. Despite what went down between you and Avis, and no matter how stupid and psycho she may be, that boy is still Day's brother."

"Half-brother," she corrected him.

"Whatever. They still come from the same father. You should let her go and be with her people some time. Craig takes care of her. He should be allowed time to spend with her."

"Whose side are you on, Terrell? Mine or Craig's?" she snapped.

"Day's," he told her. "I take it you don't want to go to the reunion?"

"Hell no! Avis' fat ghetto behind will be there!"

"Okay, okay. Are you still cool with his parents?"

"I don't have a problem with them. It's her psycho self."

"I don't have nothing to do with her. All I do is take care of my son the same way I take care of my daughter. I don't hear you complaining about that."

"Do I need to call security?" They turned around to see CJ standing in the doorway.

"Does it look like we need security?" Kayla snapped.

"Well, being that this is a place of business and not the parking lot of the projects . . ." CJ began.

"No, we don't need security, CJ. We're just out here talking. You can go back inside," Terrell told her. She hesitated, kissed her teeth then went back inside.

"She makes me sick. Who does she think she's talking to? Old Amazonian-looking hussy."

"Let it go, Kayla." Terrell thought for a minute and then yelled, "Craig!"

"Yeah?"

"Kayla's gonna let Day come to the family reunion," Terrell informed him.

"Word?" Craig looked at Kayla to see if she was in agreement, which she obviously was not.

She started to object, but Terrell stopped her.

"But she's gonna be with your parents. And you'd better keep your ignorant wife—"

"Ex-wife," Craig corrected.

"You ain't filed no divorce papers, so she's still your wife. I don't care what you wanna call her, but you'd better keep her away from my goddaughter. If I hear about her even breathing on her, I'm coming after you. And I mean that. We may be cool and all, but I don't play when it comes to Day."

"That's my daughter, Terrell, man. I'ma make sure don't nothing happen to her. Is it all right if I come by later and see her, Kayla?" Craig asked.

"I don't care, Craig."

"Thanks, Terrell. I 'preciate it, man." He shook Terrell's hand and went to hug Kayla, but she rolled her eyes at him. "I'll call before I come."

"Whatever," she said, and watched as he got into his black Honda and drove off. "I guess I should thank you for coming out here and mediating?"

"You don't owe me an apology. I was just trying to stop things from getting out of hand, that's all. It's all good." He turned and walked toward the building.

"Terrell, wait a minute. I'm sorry. Look, thanks anyway. I'm glad you came out here when you did. You know how emotional I can get." She smiled and gave him a hug.

"Naw, for real? Not you, Kayla Hopkins."

"Shut up. I haven't forgotten that I'm not talking to you. Don't push it."

"A'ight, a'ight. But seriously, Kayla, you've got to start thinking about things. You're blessed enough to have a man that takes responsibility for his child. You know how many women out here would kill for a guy to *want* to take their child to a family reunion? That's a good thing."

"I know, Terrell, but I still don't feel comfortable with my child being around Avis," she told him.

"That girl may act crazy, but she's not stupid. She knows that she'd better not lay a finger on that baby to harm her, and she won't. She'll have to answer to you, Craig, me, *and* Geno!" He laughed.

"You're right about that," she told him. "I know I should have told you this a while ago, but I am really proud of the way you're doing things around here. You are really making a change and handling your business in the office."

"Thanks, Kayla. Coming from you, that means a lot. I know how you hate to give compliments."

"Yeah, I really had to struggle to get that one out."

"So, Nicole is having a baby shower? Can you tell me when?"

"The fifth of July, that Saturday. I heard what went on between you two, and I'm sorry. But what you're doing is a good thing, and it doesn't go unnoticed."

"She still ain't talking to a brother, though. Think you can sneak me in to see her?"

"Past Arianna the warden? That's gonna be a hard one. I had to convince her I wasn't going to talk loudly in the room before she let me in."

"I can believe you. When I drop stuff off for Nicole, I only get as far as the doorway, and that's on a good day. Most of the time she meets me in the parking lot of Nicole's building when I pull up."

"I like her, though. The fact that she's so cool took me by surprise. And she don't play, either."

"Terrell, Mr. Phillips needs to see you in his office," CJ walked up and announced.

Kayla scowled and opened her car door. "I'll talk to you later, Terrell."

"Do that, and please give Day a kiss for me. Oh, and tell Geno I said what's up. He ain't hung out with me in a minute."

"That's probably why we're still together. The only person he needs to be hanging out with is me." She laughed as she got in. She waved good-bye and cut her eyes at CJ as she pulled away, honking her horn.

"What does Mr. Phillips need to see me for?" Terrell asked as they re-entered his office.

"He doesn't want you for real. I just decided to rescue you from the likes of her. You all had been out there talking for a while, and I thought you needed an excuse to get away."

He couldn't believe the nerve of her. He could see now why the females disliked her so much. She was catty, and in a matter of a few seconds, she seemed less attractive to him.

"I didn't need you to do that. Kayla is my best friend, not to mention the mother of my godchild. There was nothing to rescue me from."

"Well, I don't like her. She's disrespectful to me and thinks she's all that. When we do the department cutbacks next month, hers is gonna be one of the top names on the list." CJ sat down and crossed her legs. She began examining her nails as if she was pondering what color she should polish them next.

"What are you talking about, CJ? Kayla is one of the best reps we have at this company, not to mention one of the brightest."

"That may be one of her problems. She's too smart for her own good. And you see what almost happened in the parking lot. You and I work too hard around here disproving stereotypes and breaking through glass ceilings for our people, and here she comes like she knows every damn thing and someone owes her something."

"Kayla's not like that at all. I will admit she has the tendency to get dramatic every now and then, but when it comes to intelligence and hard work, I would put her up against you and myself any day of the week. And I'm not just saying that because she's my friend, either. You have no reason to fire her." Terrell was furious. To think that CJ was actually considering letting Kayla go because she was intimidated by her was unthinkable.

"Well, I'll say this because she *is* your *friend* . . . Looks like you just found a reason to make my Fourth of July a little bit hotter." CJ stood up and smoothed down her skirt.

"What are you saying, CJ?" he asked, trying to control his tone. Never in his life had a female given him an ultimatum, and he wasn't about to take one from CJ, of all people. He didn't care how fine she was.

This trick has lost her damn mind. I know she's not about to do what I think she is.

"I'm saying that if you want—your goddaughter, is it?—to continue to have benefits with this company, you'll make our little rendezvous on the Fourth happen. It's not that difficult, Terrell. What's the big deal? It's only one date."

Terrell knew she was serious. He had been putting her off for several weeks, and now she had the leverage she needed to do whatever she wanted. She was the puppet master and he was damn Pinocchio. *And the strings are tied around my balls.*

61

"So, you mean to tell me that we ain't doing nothing for the Fourth of July?" Jermaine asked Toby as they installed the security camera. This was the sixth job they had done together, and another one based on a referral from Stanley, their favorite customer.

"I mean, we can throw something on the grill and have some drinks in the backyard, but no, I'm not having a huge cookout."

"Damn, man. Anjelica and I were hyped up about it and everything. We went to the mall last week and got our outfits."

Toby stopped what he was doing and looked at his best friend.

"I was gonna be clean, too. We were gonna wear all white. That was gon' be fly." Jermaine actually sounded disappointed and Toby shook his head.

"Tell me you're playing, right?"

"Naw, I ain't playing. You can call her and ask. And I told Meeko I was chillin' over here when she called wanting to do something for Isis's birthday."

"Isis's birthday? When is her birthday and why didn't Meeko call me?"

"Her birthday is on the fourth. And duh, why would she call you if I already told her I was coming to your bash? By the way, she is mad that you didn't invite her. Pass me those wire cutters."

Toby passed him the tool and said, "How am I gonna invite her to a party that I'm not even having? I can't believe I forgot about Isis's birthday."

"That's messed up, Toby. And you see her every day, too. I can't believe I bought new gear and you're not having a cookout," Jermaine said through clenched teeth holding the wire he was cutting. "Are we at least gonna go to a club or something?"

"No. If I step into a club, they're gonna be calling for me to come into that booth. I definitely ain't going to a club," Toby told him. "Tell you what. I'll call Meeko and we can have a small get together at the crib. That way we can celebrate Isis's birthday and all hang out."

"That's cool with me. Anjelica and I can wear our new gear," he winked.

"You're about as bad as a woman. And the operative word is *small*—you, Anjelica, Meeko, me, and maybe Terrell. That's all."

"What about Isis? I mean it is her birthday, after all."

"You're not funny. And Isis."

They finished up the installation and were loading up the truck when an Infiniti SUV pulled behind them.

"Hey there, fellas! I see you guys are working hard today," Stanley called from the driver's side.

"What's up, Stan? Looks like you're the one that's been working hard. I like your new ride," Toby said as they walked over to him.

"See, Toby, I told you we were in the wrong line of business. The drug game is definitely where it's at." Jermaine nudged him and they all laughed.

"I bet you get all the ladies with this, huh, Stan?" Toby joked. "Don't lie, either."

"Aw, come on, guys." Stan shook his head bashfully and pushed his glasses up on his nose. "It's not even like that. I got this for tax purposes. Besides, I've been too busy to get with the women these days."

"Come on, Stan. You always gotta make time for the ladies. All work and no play makes life dull," Jermaine said. "Look, I have someone you might be interested in. What are you doing next Friday?"

"Next Friday, that's Independence Day, right?" Stan asked.

"Yeah. You got plans?"

Toby looked at Jermaine, wondering where he was going with this inquisition and who he was talking about.

"No. I was gonna hang out by the pool and catch up on some reading. That's about it." Stan shrugged.

Jermaine raised his eyebrows at Toby then looked back at Stan. "Well, Toby is having a get together Friday evening and she'll be there. Why don't you drop by? Toby and I will introduce you."

"Really? That would be great. I mean, what's she like? Is she cute? Not that it matters. Is she smart? Now, that matters more than her looks. Well, as long as she can hold up her end of a conversation. What does—"

"Just show up Friday and you'll see for yourself. Now, we're not promising that you're gonna marry this girl, just that we'll introduce you. That's it, nothing more," Jermaine clarified.

"That's all I need. I really appreciate this, you guys. Man, I heard about your parties, Toby, and now I'll get to be at one. I gotta go find something to wear. I'll see you guys Friday." Stanley jumped into his SUV and started it up. He was about to drive off when he slammed on the brakes, startling them. "Hey, you guys didn't tell me what time to be there."

Jermaine looked at Toby, who was still confused by what his boy was doing. "What time you kicking things off, T?"

"Five o'clock," Toby said, slowly shaking his head at Jermaine.

"Five it is. You need me to bring anything? I'll bring something anyway. Thanks again," he yelled and took off.

"Jermaine, man, what are you doing? Didn't I say a *small* get together? Here you go inviting people already. And how the hell are you gonna hook Stanley up with Isis? She ain't gonna be interested in him," Toby said.

"What are you talking about? Stan is only one person, and he's our best customer. That's why I invited him to hang out. You know he's cool. I didn't think you'd mind. It ain't like I told him to bring his brother. And I plan on introducing him to Meeko, not Isis."

"Meeko?" Toby asked, surprised. He started laughing when he thought about Meeko and Stanley. "Meeko. Terrell thinks Meeko is trying to get with you."

"Please, Meeko is trying to get me to hook her up with any single man that owns a house out here. That's the only reason she's been on my back these past few months. Besides, she knows I'm with Anjelica."

"Meeko and Stanley. That's hilarious." Toby was laughing so hard that he was crying. "She is gonna curse you out next Friday. This get together may not be so bad after all."

Since Jermaine was the one who thought having a party was such a great idea, Toby made him come over early Friday morning to help get everything prepared. They went to Sam's and bought plenty of food, drinks, and a birthday cake for Isis, then went to Party City and picked up balloons, decorations, and paper products for the event.

"You didn't invite anyone else, did you?" he made sure to ask Jermaine while they were unpacking everything.

"I haven't told a soul, Toby. I swear. The only person I'm responsible for is me, Anjelica, and Stanley. That's it. You talked to Meeko, Terry, and Isis, right?"

"Yeah."

"So they're *your* guests."

By 2:30 they had everything ready and Jermaine left to get dressed and pick up Anjelica. Toby lay across his bed, thinking he would get some rest before everyone arrived. The phone rang, preventing that from happening.

"Hello."

"Hey, Toby, were you 'sleep?" Roni asked.

"Not really. What's up, Ron?" He rolled over onto his back, not really wanting to talk to her. Their last few conversations had led to arguments, and he wasn't in the mood to argue today.

"I just wanted to wish you a happy anniversary, that's all," she said with a sigh.

"Huh?"

"We met a year ago today, at your house."

"That's right. Happy anniversary to you too. You hanging out today?"

"Not really. My mother is having a little something over at her shop. That's why I'm calling. She wants you to come. You feel like rolling over there with me?"

"Sounds like fun, but I can't. I already have plans. I'm sorry. Tell her I'll be there next time."

"Plans? What are you doing today?" Roni asked.

"Jermaine and Anjelica are coming over in a while." He regretted telling her the moment the words came from his mouth. He started to lie and tell her he had to work, but didn't feel the need to.

"I thought you said you weren't having a party, Toby," she retorted. He knew she was mad. *I should've just lied*, he thought.

"I'm not having a party, Veronica, just Jermaine and Anjelica."

"I can't believe he's still dating that girl."

He really wasn't up to having this conversation with her, so he told her, "Give your mom and everyone my love and tell everyone I said hello. I'll talk to you later."

"Fine, I will. And Toby?"

"Yo?"

"I love you."

He tried to think of a correct response, not wanting her to read into anything. "You too, Roni."

His answer must have satisfied her because she hung up the phone. He sat up on the side of the bed, trying to get his thoughts together. He was so confused. He loved Roni, no doubt about that, but he still didn't feel ready to pick up where they left off like she wanted to do. There was something still preventing him from making that move.

And then there was Isis. He smiled at the thought of her. She was so special to him, always had been. There were times when they were together he wanted her so bad he could taste it. But it wasn't going to happen. He had accepted the fact that they would be no more than friends—good friends, special friends, but friends nonetheless. And for right now, he was cool with that. *For right now.*

He decided to get up and get dressed. There were some last minute details he needed to take care of.

He was in the backyard making sure his bar was stocked when he heard his doorbell ring. He looked at his watch and saw that it was only 4:30. He hurried to the door and opened it.

"Uncle Jay?"

"What's up, Toby? Am I the first one here?" His uncle brushed past him. He was dressed in a pair of white shorts and tank top, a pair of white sandals on his feet and a white hat. He was carrying a plastic bag in each hand.

"Uh, yeah. What are you doing here, Uncle Jay?"

"I came for the cookout. What do you think I'm doing here? I got some fresh catfish for you to fry. I already battered it up. You want it in the kitchen or the backyard?"

"I, uh, you . . . put it in the kitchen." Toby closed the door and followed him into the kitchen.

"This all the food you got, Toby? I know you got more food than this," Uncle Jay said, looking into the refrigerator.

"That's all the food I'm gonna need. I'm not having a big party this year. Just a little get together."

"So, I bought a new outfit for nothing. You like it, though? I look nice, huh?" He started dancing like he was a long lost member of the Temptations.

"You look good, Uncle Jay." Toby laughed. The doorbell rang again and he told his uncle to hang out in the backyard while he went to answer it. Jermaine and Anjelica were kissing on the doorstep.

"Uh, y'all might wanna get a room instead of coming here," he told them.

"Don't hate because I got the flyest female in town on my arm tonight, Toby. Ain't that right, boo?"

"No, I have the finest brother by my side," she told him. "But you come in as a close second, Toby."

"Come on in before the flies start buzzing with all that crap both of you are talking." Toby laughed. They made a great couple and they looked good dressed in their white attire. He didn't know whether Jermaine brought out a different side of Anjelica or maybe he had just never noticed it before, but Terrell was right. She was as funny and down to earth as her sister, and he liked her.

"You start the grill yet?" Jermaine asked.

"No, not yet. I was about to when Uncle Jay showed up."

"Uncle Jay? He's here?"

"In the backyard. Go on back. I'm gonna put some music on."

"Please don't let it be Bobby Womack. You know how your uncle is."

The doorbell rang again. "Shut up and go in the backyard. This is probably Meeko and Isis."

It wasn't. Decked out in an all-white linen suit, complete with a derby on his head, was Stanley. He was even carrying a huge bouquet of white roses and a bottle of champagne.

"Hey, Toby. Is she here?"

"Naw, Stan. She's not here yet. Come on in. You got clean for this one, huh?" Toby couldn't help laughing.

Stanley brushed the front of his shirt and adjusted the flowers. "I wanted to make a good first impression. You think she'll like the flowers?"

Toby thought about Meeko and nodded. "I'm sure she'll be impressed. Come on out to the back."

Toby took the flowers and champagne from him and directed him to the backyard. He was introducing Stanley to everyone when once again the doorbell beckoned him.

"I'll get it," Jermaine told him. "It's probably your date, Stanley. You ready?"

Stanley looked at Toby, who gave him a pat on the back. "Let them in, Jermaine. He's ready."

Jermaine went back into the house and Toby lit the grill. He was about to get the meat that was marinating in the fridge when Jermaine came back out. Instead of Isis and Meeko, he was followed by Tia, Theo, Kayla, and Geno.

"What's up, Toby? Hey, DJ Terror. Player, player, where's the food?" they all greeted him.

Jermaine rushed over and told him, "I didn't know what to do. I couldn't just turn them away. I swear I didn't invite them."

"Then why are they all wearing white?"

"I don't know." He shrugged.

Before Toby could respond, Isis and Meeko came through the side gate and entered the yard. He walked over and hugged both of them. Isis looked stunning in an all-white strapless halter dress with silver accessories. Her hair was beginning to grow back, and was held off her face by a silver studded headband. Her partner in crime, Meeko, was also decked out in the color of the evening.

"You look beautiful," Toby whispered into Isis's ear as he held her close to him. "Happy birthday."

"You don't look so bad yourself, and thank you." She hugged him back.

"Ahem." Meeko interrupted their moment. "Why is everyone dressed in all white but you? Aren't you the host of the party?"

"No one told me there was a theme, I guess," he answered, looking down at the yellow Nautica shirt he was wearing along with his jean shorts and yellow-and-white Air Force Ones. "And

I didn't know I was having a party until all these people showed up."

"Oh." Meeko looked over at Jermaine, who was serving drinks at the bar. "Well, Jermaine told us he was wearing all white like we were all supposed to. Let me go curse him out right quick."

"Wait!" Toby stopped her, remembering her date was already present. "There's someone here that's been waiting to meet you. Sit over there at the umbrella table and I'll bring him over."

"For real? Don't play with me, Toby. Where is he?"

"Just go sit down and I'll bring him over. Isis, you want something to drink?" he asked. "How about a Slow Comfortable Screw?"

"How about a bottle of water? We'll discuss the other thing later." She winked at him. He smiled at her, hoping that she wasn't talking about the drink. He rushed off to get her water and find Stanley.

He found him near the back of the yard, talking to Uncle Jay, who had started frying fish in the deep fryer.

"I found this here deep fryer in the kitchen closet. Good thing I remembered to bring some cooking oil," Uncle Jay told him. "And I see you done stole some of my Jasper's aprons, too."

"Yeah, Uncle Jay," Toby admitted. "Hey, Stanley, there's someone looking for you."

"Uh, okay, Toby. Where?" he asked nervously.

"Right over there, sitting at the table with the umbrella. I told her you would come over."

"God, she's beautiful. She looks like Janet Jackson! You guys didn't tell me she was *fine*! Not that I care," he added. "Oh God, I can't wait to meet her. What did you do with the flowers?"

"Hold up, man. I think you're looking at the wrong one. The one sitting at the table across from Janet is the one waiting to meet you. Let's go into the kitchen and get the flowers." He gestured toward the house. *And pray that we can scrounge up some more food for these people,* he thought, looking around at the crowd of people that was now in his backyard.

62

Terrell sat on the side of the bed, rubbing his throbbing temples. He looked over at his clock and saw that it was close to 6:00. He was supposed to pick her up an hour ago, but he didn't care that he was late. His head was pounding and he didn't want to go pick her up at all.

"So, what are you going to do?" Anjelica had asked when he told her what CJ had threatened. "I don't know. I really don't have a choice. If I don't take her out, your sister is gonna lose her job."

"Can't you just report her to human resources or something? There has to be something you can do. That's sexual harassment."

"I know, but I'm just gonna bring her to Toby's house, stay for about an hour, then tell her I have to leave."

"Okay, I can go in the house for a minute then come back out and say you have an emergency phone call. You go to the phone then pretend that you have to leave."

It sounded like a damn good plan when Anjelica said it, and he agreed that it was foolproof. But even with a plan, he still didn't want to go. Unfortunately, he had no choice, so when CJ called his cell phone for the ninety-ninth time, instead of letting his voice mail pick up, he answered it.

"Where the hell are you? You were supposed to be here an hour ago," she yelled in his ear, making his head hurt worse.

"Man, stop yelling. I had a headache and laid across my bed. I fell asleep. Damn, you act like we gotta be there at five. It's a cookout, not the job. We can be late."

"When you tell me you're gonna pick me up at a certain time, I expect that. Now, what time do you think that'll be, because it definitely ain't gonna be at five now, is it?"

"I'll be there in thirty minutes."

"You'd better be," she said and hung up the phone in his ear. He looked over at the white shorts set hanging in the doorway of his closet along with his brand new white Classics. For the first time that day, he smiled.

"You're wearing all white to a cookout?" she asked when she opened the door to her townhouse.

"You know how I do," was his only response. She leaned over and gave him a kiss on the cheek. He recognized the strong scent of Fendi, which she usually wore. He was beginning to hate it.

"Come on in. You want me to make you a drink?" she smiled. He smiled back when he noticed she was wearing an all-red Capri set and red sandals. Her micro-braided hair was hanging to the middle of her back.

"No thanks. We'd better get going," he told her.

"I thought you said there was no rush. You can come in for a minute. I have to get my purse anyway." She pulled him inside.

He looked around in her nicely decorated living room while he waited. She had a lot of African paintings and statues. There was also a bookshelf full of books, mostly about Black history, and also quite a few books on beauty and makeup. Her furniture was red, and the room accented with black lacquer tables.

"Nice place," he called out.

"Thanks. I haven't really done what I wanted to do with it, but it's home," she replied. "You ready?"

"Yep, let's be out."

Their conversation in the car was mostly about music and movies. Terrell tried to keep the topics light, anything not to add to his stress level. He was surprised at the number of cars parked in front of his brother's house when they got there. Toby assured him that this was going to be a small barbecue, no more than ten people. There were at least ten cars parked outside the house.

"I thought you told me that he wasn't having his usual big party this year." CJ looked at him.

He shrugged in reply and said, "He told me he wasn't. And believe me, if he was, we wouldn't even be able to turn down the street it would be so crowded."

They got out and walked inside without knocking.

"Wow, he has a lot of CDs!" CJ commented as they walked past Toby's living room. "This place is nice."

"Yeah," Terrell said and continued to the kitchen. He was surprised to see Uncle Jay inside making potato salad. "Uncle Jay, what are you doing here?"

"What does it look like I'm doing? Your brother got all these people that just showed up, and we're trying to figure out how to feed them all. You know the club is closed tonight, so I rode over there and got some stuff out the freezer."

"It's that many people here, Unc?"

"You'll see when you get out there. How you doing there? I'm James Jasper Sims, Terrell's uncle. But you can call me JJ." He wiped his hands on his apron and held one out for CJ.

"I'm Cora Ware, Terrell's coworker, but you can call me CJ." She laughed.

"Come on, CJ. Let's see if Uncle Jay is exaggerating as usual," Terrell said, opening the back door. He noticed that his uncle had a strange look on his face as he went back to stirring the big bowl of salad.

Uncle Jay wasn't exaggerating. The yard was full of people. Some were dancing; others were at the bar where Terrell noticed Jermaine was mixing drinks. He spotted Toby behind the grill, decked out in yellow, unlike all the rest of his guests who were dressed in all white—with the exception of CJ, of course.

"Everyone has on white," she hissed. "This is an all-white party and you didn't tell me."

"I didn't know. And Toby doesn't even have on white; he has on yellow."

"I am so embarrassed. I can't believe this." She grabbed his arm and squeezed it.

Hoping this was his way out, he offered, "You want to just go ahead and leave? We can go."

She looked around and saw the good time everyone was having and hurriedly told him, "No, I'm fine. Just get me a drink."

Terrell directed CJ to a seat he spotted at an empty table toward the back of the yard, and told her he would bring her drink to her. He didn't even ask what she wanted, thinking that if she was thirsty enough, she would drink whatever.

"What's up, Terry?" Jermaine greeted him. "I see you brought your date from work."

"Your girlfriend has a big mouth," Terrell responded.

"Hey, don't talk about my woman. You wouldn't want me to say anything about yours now, would you, Anita Hill?" He cracked up and then noticed Terrell wasn't laughing. "Just kidding, bro. What can I get ya?"

"Man, I don't care. As long as her ass can drink it and she won't be thirsty no more."

"How about a Margarita?"

"Fine. Just hurry up before she comes over here and someone sees her."

"Man, you can't miss her. How tall is she, 'bout six feet? And she got on all red. How could you not see her?" Jermaine passed him the drink.

"Thanks, Jermaine. If I wasn't already feeling bad about this situation, I definitely would be feeling that way now," he told him as he turned to walk away.

"No problem, Terry." Jermaine snickered.

Terrell had just made it back to the table when he saw Kayla dancing with Geno. Toby had thrown on one of his line dance CDs and everyone was up doing the Bus Stop to a mix of Teddy Pendergrass's "Get Down" and Michael Jackson's "Don't Stop 'til you Get Enough". Even Meeko was dancing with some corny-looking dude wearing glasses.

"Come on, Terrell, let's dance!" CJ pulled at his arm.

There's no way I'm dancing with her so everyone can see us, he thought.

"I hate line dances," he lied. "They remind me of square dancing we had to do in high school."

CJ finished her drink and stood up. "Well, I'm going out there and join them. You sit here and be a spoil sport all you want. You've had a stank attitude all day. If I were you, I'd change it. After all, your girl's job depends on it. Isn't that her over there? I think I'll go and speak."

It took all he could not to curse CJ out right then and there. He took a few deep breaths and told her, "Wait. You want to dance, we can dance."

They joined the bunch dancing in the middle of the yard and began sliding with the music. Terrell started to relax and told himself that he needed to loosen up if he wanted the evening to go off smoothly. After a while, the crowd of dancers thinned out as people went to eat the food that Uncle Jay was spreading on the table. It wasn't Toby's usual smorgasbord, but they had hooked it up the best they could.

Terrell told CJ he was hungry, and they went to stand in line to make their plates. He was trying to make eye contact with Anjelica to give her the signal, but she was too busy yapping with Isis. He excused himself and scurried over to where they were talking near the bar.

"Uh, are we gonna do this or what?" he asked her.

"Do what?" Isis looked at him like he was crazy.

"Not you. I'm not talking to you."

"I don't know what you're talking about either." Anjelica smirked.

"Come on, Anjelica. Don't play with me."

"All right, all right. Calm down. You ready for me to do it now?" she asked. Isis looked at both of them, trying to figure out what scheme they were about to perform.

"Not right now. We're about to eat. But as soon as you see me taking our plates, you come and get me. Okay?"

"Okay." She nodded.

"What's going on here?" Isis squinted her eyes at him.

"She'll fill you in later. I gotta go," he said, noticing CJ had started fixing her plate. Terrell was on his way back to her side when the goofy guy Meeko was dancing with earlier started screaming. He was standing right in front of CJ.

"What the hell are you doing here? Someone call the cops! Now! Toby! Jermaine, call the police!"

Toby came flying from behind the grill and Jermaine from behind the bar.

"What's going on?" Jermaine yelled.

"Stan, calm down!" Toby told him.

"I told you he was stalking me! How did you know I was going to be here? You'd better get away from here! I have a restraining order against you!" Stanley yelled.

"I had no idea you were going to be here. Terrell brought me here as his date. I suggest you leave if there's a problem. I am an invited guest, the same as you." CJ popped her neck and put her hands on her hips. As much as she talked about Kayla acting ghetto in the parking lot that day, she was doing a good job herself, Terrell observed.

"Stanley, she's my brother's date. She came with him," Toby explained calmly.

"Do you know who that is? That's the guy that's been stalking me for the past six months."

"Oh, hell!" Jermaine's eyes widened. "This is *him*?"

"What are you talking about, *him*?" Terrell asked, confused by everything they were saying. "What the hell is going on, CJ? What the fuck is he talking about?"

"I am very much a woman, Terrell. I don't know what they're talking about," CJ responded. "This man is obviously crazy, and I can't believe you're asking me this, especially in front of these people."

"Tell her to prove it!" Anjelica yelled from where she was standing.

He turned and looked at CJ. She had a pleading look in her eyes, and he didn't know if it was from the embarrassment of the situation or because she knew Stanley was telling the truth. "Prove it, CJ."

"I will do no such thing. How dare you!"

"She can't prove it. She's a pre-operative transsexual. A man, living as a woman, who plans on having the surgery one day. A man who fools people into believing he's a real woman," Stanley announced, cutting his eyes at CJ.

"I don't have to take this from you. I'm leaving." She ran out the gate leaving everyone at the party stunned.

"I knew it! I knew there was something about her! I told you, Terrell! A man!" Kayla laughed out loud. Terrell looked at her, his eyes filled with anger.

"Chill, Kay. This ain't funny right about now." Geno told her. "It may be later, but right now, it's not."

"Damn, Terry. I know you ain't one of those DL brothers, are you?" someone cried out.

"You never can tell these days. Maybe that's why he tries so hard to be a mack anyway," another guy said, laughing.

"Fuck all of y'all!" Terrell yelled, still baffled by what had just happened.

His brother patted him on the back then called out, "What happened to the music? And Uncle Jay, we need some more fish. Y'all wanted me to have a party, so hell, let's party."

"I ain't even realize the music stopped," Terrell looked over and told Toby.

"The music always stops when the drama goes down. You know that, baby brother. But the party always starts up again. Always remember that."

"Now you giving out words of wisdom?" Terrell laughed.

"I learned from the best," his brother told him, looking over at Isis, who was talking to Uncle Jay. She looked over at the two brothers and blew them a kiss. "Was that for you or me?"

"I think that one was for me, Toby. She knows I need some feminine affection right about now. I can't believe CJ is a dude. I knew she was tall, but she ain't even look like a dude. Am I losing my ability to screen them out? Am I giving out a signal or something?"

"No, man. It was just one of those things that just happened. It has nothing to do with your manhood. And don't let this mess with your head, either," he told him. "I gotta get back to this grill before Geno burns my crib down. You gonna be all right? I need to call Nicole and get her over here so you can feel better?"

Terrell laughed. "I wish she could, then I wouldn't be in this mess, for real. I miss her."

"I know you do, but time heals all wounds. Believe me, I know."

"More words of wisdom?"

"I got plenty if you need them. I'll check on you in a minute." Toby rushed back to the grill where it looked like Geno had started a small fire. "Geno, man, what are you doing to my meat? Don't you know this is steak?"

Terrell sat at the table, still in a state of disbelief.

"You mind if I talk to you for a second?" Stanley asked.

"Naw, have a seat," he sighed.

Stanley sat across from him and took off the white derby he had been sporting all evening. "I think that I'm the only one out here that can relate to what just happened, and I feel the need to tell you that it's not your fault. That was the first issue I had to deal with myself when he did the same thing to me. Just because you didn't know, or even the fact that you were attracted to her, doesn't make you a punk—or shall I say a homosexual? These guys nowadays look just as good if not better than most of the females out here.

"But what they're doing is deceitful, and they don't understand that they could easily wind up hurt. I commend you for not snapping on her and taking a swing," Stanley laughed.

"I ain't the one to talk about anyone's lifestyle," he continued, "but when you try to infringe on mine and be deceitful about it, that's just wrong. That's all I wanted to tell you."

"I appreciate that, Stanley. I really do."

"Now, I have a new lady I'm trying to impress myself, so I'd better get back over there before someone scoops her up from under me." He stood and put his hat back on.

Terrell gave him a handshake, and as Stanley walked away he told him, "Hey, Stanley, the lady you're trying to impress, she loves poetry. Oh, and walks on the pier."

"Thanks, man. Good looking out."

The vibration of his cell phone caught him off guard and Terrell nearly jumped out of his skin. He didn't recognize the number and hesitated as he answered it, thinking it might be CJ stalking him now. "Hello."

"Terrell Sims?"

"Uh, who's calling?"

"This is Leah. I'm a nurse in labor and delivery over at County Hospital. Your girlfriend has just been admitted and she wanted us to call you," a snotty voice told him.

"Very funny, Anjelica. You know I ain't in a playing mood," he uttered.

"I'm sorry, sir. This isn't a joke," the woman replied.

He looked over at the bar and saw Anjelica feeding watermelon to Jermaine. She looked over at him and waved.

"Uh, I . . . I'm on my way!" He closed the phone and rushed out, ignoring his brother and Kayla, who were calling behind him. *I've got to get to my wife and my child,* was all he could think about as he raced to his car. As he turned the corner, he saw CJ climbing into the back seat of a cab. *Please, God,* he thought, *no more drama.*

63

"He should have never invited her over here to begin with," Kayla told her friends as she grabbed a Pepsi from the cooler. "I told Terrell a long time ago that there was something wrong with that woman—I mean man. Well, whatever it is. But he didn't want to listen to me. He's gonna mess around and Nicole is gonna leave him for good if he doesn't get his act together."

"I can't believe she found out about him and your sister. And she has the nerve to be here all up in Jermaine's face," Yvonne added.

Toby was still flipping burgers and hot dogs on the grill, glad that they hadn't mentioned his name. But when he saw Anjelica standing behind them, he knew it was about to get ugly and the music was about to stop again.

"That's right. I'm here all in his face because he is *my* man. And you know what? He ain't got no complaints. You barely got a man yourself, Yvonne. And you, Ms. Hopkins, let me tell you a thing or two. The reason Terrell brought CJ was because she threatened to fire you if he didn't. So to save your ass—again—he did what he had to do."

"What?" The two sisters stood face to face.

"She was going to fire you when they did the departmental cut backs next month. Now, you know and I know that you haven't done anything to be fired because Ma and Daddy would kick your behind. But you were about to be let go, sweetie, until your boy stepped in. So, while you're talking about him behind his back, you need to be thanking him."

Anjelica turned, walked over to Jermaine and placed a passionate kiss on his lips. She smiled and called out, "Sweetie, I think you know all about my past and what went down with a few people here tonight, don't you? There are no secrets between us."

"You're right." Jermaine nodded then gave Geno a wave. Yvonne and Kayla looked appalled.

"Now, since he doesn't have a problem with it, that's all that matters. Anybody got any questions?"

No one made a sound as she looked around. Satisfied, she called out, "What happened to the music? Y'all wanted to have a party, so hell, let's party!"

The music came on again, and people began dancing. Meeko beckoned for Toby to come inside, and he followed her. Uncle Jay was placing candles on the birthday cake.

"I know you got a lighter somewhere around here, Tobias."

"Should be one in this drawer right here. Here it is." He passed his uncle the lighter then said to Meeko, "I see you and Stanley looking cozy over there. What's up?"

"I mean, he's cool. A little corny, but he's a sweetheart." Meeko smiled and sniffed her roses, which were sitting on the counter.

"I bet you he is. Brought all them flowers like it was a funeral or something," Toby teased.

"Don't hate because he's a romantic. There's nothing wrong with that, is there, Uncle Jay?"

"Nothing at all. Matter of fact, I can get real romantic myself. Get some candles and some baby oil . . ."

"Okay, Uncle Jay. We get the idea. Let's take the cake out. The candles are melting." Toby opened the door and held it while his uncle and Meeko walked out. Everyone started singing, and he grabbed the microphone next to the stereo.

"Happy birthday, Isis. I know you thought we forgot, but we didn't. We love you," he told her. She looked at him and he saw the tears in her eyes. Meeko ran to her side and gave her a big hug. "Now, may I have this dance, birthday girl?"

She nodded and met him in the part of the yard that was the designated dance floor. He took her hand in his and held her close. The music began to play, and he looked down to see her reaction. People had to be wondering why he chose that song, but he knew why and so did she. They smiled at each other as they rocked to Klyymaxx singing "I'd Still Say Yes." It was the one CD that he didn't have in his collection, but he searched on Amazon and had it rushed out to him so he would have it in time for this night. It was the best idea he'd had in a long time.

"Thank you," she whispered to him.

"For what?" he asked.

"Just being you." She laid her head on his shoulder.

He had no doubt that her friends were watching, but he didn't care. Isis was his friend, and she deserved everything he was doing and more. She had been there for him when he was at his lowest and taught him a lot about himself.

The song went off and they began jamming to "The Men All Pause." Everyone was having a ball, and Uncle Jay began putting away the food.

"Having fun at your party?" Toby asked.

She looked up at him and smiled. "Don't even try it. This isn't *my* party. This is your annual bash. It's just a coincidence that my birthday is today. But I am having fun. Is it always this excitement-filled?"

"Yeah, it is," he admitted. "Let me go help Uncle Jay before he calls me out. After all, it is *my* house."

"I'll help out too. After all, it is *my* party," she hit him playfully on his chest.

They began carrying trays of leftover food into the kitchen to put away. It had gotten dark and Toby said they needed to hurry because the fireworks were about to start.

"I think I've seen enough fireworks for tonight," Uncle Jay told them. "I knew something wasn't right about that woman when she shook my hand. I tried to give Terry the look, but he didn't see it, I guess."

Isis cracked up. "What look is that, Uncle Jay?"

"You know; the look." Uncle Jay's eyes widened and he gestured with his head as he grimaced, demonstrating the look he gave Terrell.

"How was he supposed to know what that meant, Uncle Jay? You just made the same face when you wanted me to open the fridge for you." Toby shook his head. Isis laughed even harder.

"That was this look, not that one. And he should have known something was up when I made it. Shut up and hand me that foil!" Uncle Jay snatched the box out of his hand.

They finished just as the fireworks began. Toby grabbed Isis by the hand; she grabbed Uncle Jay, and they returned to the backyard. Toby put on some mellow music then sat close to Isis on a picnic table, away from the rest of the crowd.

"I thought you said you weren't having a party."

Toby turned and was shocked to see Roni standing behind them.

"Hey, Roni. Believe it or not, I didn't plan on having a party. All of these folks just showed up. I think it was a set up, though, because as you can see, they're all dressed in white." He jumped off the table and stood up. He looked at Isis, who excused herself. He reached out his hand and helped her off the table.

"She didn't have to leave. Obviously she was an invited guest, unlike me. I can't believe this. I'm walking around here wearing your ring and you have a party, don't invite me, and when I do show up, I catch you hugged up with some chick." Roni folded her arms in disgust.

"Hold up. I told you I ain't plan to have a party. You know you would've been invited if I did. And I wasn't hugged up wit' nobody. Don't even come here with that bull. We've had enough drama for the night," he warned. She looked at him and he saw the look on her face soften. He couldn't help smiling at her. "You want something to drink? We got strawberry daiquiris."

"With whipped cream?"

"Always a diva, huh? But I think we can make that happen. How was your mom's?" They strolled over to the bar where Jermaine was holding Anjelica in his arms.

"It would have been better if all of my friends had shown up there instead of here."

"Well, they're right over there. Go over and I'll bring your drink to you." He pointed toward Kayla and the rest of the crew. She swept past him to join her girls, ready to hear about everything she missed.

He walked over to the bar and began fixing her drink. He looked up and saw Isis standing next to Uncle Jay. Her head was tilted up to the sky and he could tell that she was laughing. As if she could sense him staring, she turned around and waved. He gave her a nod and took Roni her drink.

"Thank you, baby." Roni put her arm through his and leaned on him. "So, who is the girl you were with?"

"That's my friend, Isis."

"Your friend? Wasn't she the girl that sang that night at Jasper's?"

"Yeah," he answered.

"I've never met her before. How long have you known her?"

"About three years. And she just moved back in town. That's why you've never met her." Toby began to be irritated by Roni's line of questioning. "What's with the third degree?"

"Don't get loud out here, Tobias."

"I'm not loud. You are, Veronica."

Toby had struck a nerve and he knew it. People around them turned and stared. Roni's face turned red and she looked as if she wanted to kill him. "Can I see you inside for a moment?"

He wasted no time following her into the house. They climbed the steps and went into his bedroom. He sat down on his bed, not even in the mood to argue. His day, although filled with unexpected events, had been pretty good until she showed up and started grilling him about Isis.

"What's going on with you, Toby? Even if you didn't plan to have a party, when people started coming, you could have called me. But it's obvious that you're not happy to see me anyway. I get no kiss, no hug, no affection period."

Toby listened to what she was saying, wanting to answer her, but couldn't. It was true, he loved Roni.

She hurt him, but he was healing. And there was still the possibility that they would wind up together. That's why he didn't mind that she wore his ring. He did still love her.

"I love you, Roni, but you are the one that got caught wit' another dude. Or has that incident slipped your mind? And now you're here making an issue over nothing. I ain't even trying to hear that."

"I know, but isn't part of loving someone forgiving them? I've apologized time and time again. I love you, Toby, but I feel like you're going to let this hang over my head forever. Do you love me enough to forgive me? If so, then we've got to move past this. If not, take your ring back and let me go on with my life. I can't keep living in limbo like this," she cried.

He hated seeing her like this. He reached out and held her close. "Don't do this to me, Roni. Please, don't. I love you, I do." Not knowing what else to do, he grabbed her and kissed her passionately on the mouth. His mouth explored hers for several minutes until he pulled away.

"I missed you so much," she told him as she ran her fingers along his back.

"We need to get back downstairs." He turned and opened the door.

"I told Mama that I would help clean up after everyone left. You want me to come back when I finish?" she offered when they made it down the steps. Toby was hesitant in his answer, so she added, "We still need to talk.

"It's cool. I'll be here." He kissed her once again as she got in her car. *It's just to talk, that's it,* he reminded himself.

People began leaving, and Tobias was glad that the bash he didn't even know he was hosting was over. Instead of going inside the house, he walked back into the yard to make sure everything was put away and in order. He picked up two bags of trash and took them to the large garbage can located on the side of the house. When he got inside, he was surprised to find Isis washing the remaining dishes.

"Where's Meeko?"

"She left with Stanley. He offered to give her a ride in his truck. I'm taking her car home. Everybody else gone?" she asked.

"Yeah, the party is over. I think everyone had a good time, though. Anybody heard from Terrell?"

"No, he rushed outta here without saying a word to anyone. Pass me that dishtowel."

"You know you don't have to do this, right? I could have finished all of this myself." He handed her the towel. "I'm glad you did, though."

"So, you and Roni made up? That's good," she smiled at him.

"How do you know that?" Toby leaned against the counter.

"Okay, I need to be honest with you." She folded the towel and laid it on the side of the sink. Toby's heart began to beat rapidly as he prepared himself for what she was about to tell him. "I didn't stay here just to wash the dishes. I stayed for something else."

She walked up to him and seductively ran her hands under his shirt.

"What's that?" he asked. She looked up at him and licked her lips. *This can't be happening to me. I've wanted this woman for months and she rejected me. Now that I've reconciled with Roni, she's coming on to me. What am I supposed to do?*

"I stayed to tell you . . ." Her hands moved to his back and she ran her fingers along his spine. He shifted his weight so she could reach farther.

"Tell me what, Ice?" he whispered.

"I told you so! I knew you were gonna get back with her!" she laughed. "I knew you were getting back together, especially when she walked up and saw me with you. That was it right there."

"You're crazy. If I didn't know it then, I definitely know it now. Why you playing with me like that?" He snatched her arms from around him, laughing.

"What did you think I was gonna say, Toby?" She raised her eyebrows at him.

"I thought you were gonna discuss your Slow Comfortable Screw that you didn't get earlier," he confessed.

"You can give it to Roni when she comes back. She is coming back later, isn't she? And don't lie."

Toby looked at her. He couldn't lie. "Yeah, she says she's coming back."

"I guess I'd better get outta here, then. I ain't trying to get you in no trouble."

"Wait a minute, Isis. I got something to give you before you leave." He rushed up the steps and into his room. He opened the drawer and took out the small box. He was glad that he had left it in the bottom of his drawer instead of on top of his dresser where it had lain all week. Jermaine had ordered it for him from an exclusive jeweler he had done some work for in the mall. He hoped Isis would like it.

She was waiting at the bottom of the steps when he got there. "This is for you. Happy birthday."

"Toby, you didn't have to do this. The party was enough." She hugged him. "Thank you."

"Come over here and open it." He pulled her to the sofa.

She slowly unwrapped it then looked up, her eyes filled with tears. "It's beautiful, but I can't accept this."

"Yes, you can. Let me put it on you. You know I had to get some ice for my Ice." He reached into the box and removed the platinum necklace holding the heavy platinum charm. It read *True Love*, and was encrusted with diamonds.

He reached around her neck and fastened it. "It's perfect. This is the one true love you have to be willing to accept. You are such a special woman, and deserve everything your heart desires, but you've got to stop pushing people away and let them in. Part of learning to love is learning to trust."

"Now look who's the one giving advice on love. You've been back with Roni how long, thirty minutes, and now you're giving out Tobyisms? Thank you, Toby. I'm glad that you've found your way back to that person that you believe in and trust enough to love unconditionally."

She stood up and walked to the door. "Does this mean I have to find another workout partner?"

"Be there Monday, same time. Meet you at the treadmills." He hugged her, enjoying the feel of having her in his arms. She was the most beautiful, intelligent, humorous, talented person he knew. *Whoever winds up with her is damn lucky, and I'll be the first to admit it.* Isis Adams was truly a gem, and he knew it.

64

Terrell made the forty-minute ride to the hospital in twenty minutes flat. He didn't care that it was a holiday weekend and state troopers were on the lookout. All he cared about was making it to Nicole's side. He skipped taking the slow elevator and climbed the five flights of steps to labor and delivery. He could barely talk when he got to the nurses' station.

"I'm loo . . . looking for . . . my girlfriend. Some . . . someone called and . . . told me she was . . . here," he managed to say as he struggled to catch his breath.

"Are you okay? Calm down. Breathe. Do we need to get you some oxygen?" the nurse asked him. He shook his head at her. She was a young girl and her nametag read PEACHES. "Okay, now, what's your girlfriend's name?"

"Nicole. Nicole Matthews."

Peaches' fingers ran quickly along the keyboard and she told him, "We don't have a Nicole Matthews, sir. Are you sure she's here at County?"

"Yeah, I'm sure. That's who called me. Some nurse named Leah called and said she was in labor!"

"Calm down. Let me page Leah and we'll see what's going on. She could have been here and we released her."

"That was less than forty minutes ago. I don't understand why she came to County anyway."

"Well, this is a county hospital. Does she have insurance? If she doesn't, we would be where she would come." Peaches picked up the phone and paged Leah to the reception area.

"She works at Mercy Memorial in labor and delivery. This is crazy!" He exhaled loudly. His nerves were already shot from the entire CJ fiasco, and now someone was playing games on his phone. He took his phone out of his pocket and was about to call Arianna when a short, plump brunette came through the doors.

He could hear screams coming from one of the rooms and he shuddered.

"Hey, Peaches, you paged me?" she asked.

"Yeah, did you call this gentleman about his girlfriend?" Peaches asked.

"I called quite a few gentlemen this evening. Did you look her up? What's your girlfriend's name?" Leah questioned him.

"Nicole Matthews," Terrell answered. "She looked but couldn't find her."

"We don't have any Nicole or Matthews, I don't think. What's your name?"

"Terrell Sims."

"Oh, okay. I remember calling you. You got here fast. Come on back. You're just in time." She smiled.

He looked back at Peaches, who just shrugged at him, then he followed Leah through the doors. As they walked down the hall, the screaming became louder. They entered the room where the howls originated and as he realized what was going on, the blood rushed from his head. His worst nightmare was coming true right before his eyes. Instead of Nicole, the love of his life, lying with her legs in the stirrups, there was Darla. Her hands were gripping the sides of the bed, and she was shaking her head back and forth like she was possessed, her hair standing on top of her head. A masked doctor was posted between her legs, ready to catch whatever was about to come out.

"What the hell is going on? Is this some kind of a joke? It has to be!" Terrell growled.

Darla's eyes grew wide and she reached for him. "Oh, Terrell, you're here, baby. I knew you would make it!"

"You need to get over there and hold her hand so we can coach her through this, sir. She's been refusing to push until you got here," the doctor told him.

"I'm not holding her hand. You've lost your damn mind, and so has she!" he snapped.

"Mr. Sims, if you're not going to help the situation, then you need to leave. You can have a seat in the waiting room and we'll come and get you when your baby is born. You would think you would be a little more concerned and sensitive at a time like this," Leah huffed at him. She pointed to the door and he turned to leave.

"No, Terrell! Please don't leave me! I need you here! This is our baby and you should be in here. Just stay in here, please!" Darla howled.

"She's crowning. Okay, we're gonna need you to push, Darla. Come on."

"Just stay right there, please!" She begged him.

Terrell looked over at the doctor and the nurse, who was trying to calm her down and get her to cooperate.

"Can you just stand over there in the corner where she can see you?" Leah asked.

He quietly walked over to the corner of the room farthest away from the action.

This has got to be some kind of set up. I can't believe I am in here while she's over there having a kid—my kid, which I already paid for her to get rid of. She hasn't called, come by, wrote me a note to tell me shit, but she wants me to be here to hold her hand. There's no way.

Why, God? I've started living right, I don't hang out, I don't party, I work hard. I even started going back to church. All I wanted to do was marry Nicole, be a good father, a good employee, and a good person. Now here it is I got transvestites on the job harassing me, the woman I'm in love with won't even see me, and now a girl I can't stand the sight of is about to deliver my baby. Life can't get any worse.

At that very thought, Terrell's phone began ringing.

"You need to cut that off in here!" Leah yelled so she could be heard over Darla's squelches.

He looked at his caller ID and saw Nicole's number. He looked from his phone to what was going on in the room then back at his phone. It soon stopped and the screen read 1 Missed Call. Just as he was about to turn it off, it began ringing again.

"Turn it off!" the doctor yelled.

Instead of turning it off, he walked into the hallway and answered it.

"Terrell, its Arianna."

"What's up, Ari? How's Nicole?" he whispered. The door was closed, but Darla's screams could still be heard. He saw a sign for the waiting room and he headed toward it.

"Her water broke and her contractions are steady. We're leaving for the hospital in about fifteen minutes," she said.

If ever Terrell wanted to crawl in a hole and hide from the rest of the world, it was at that very moment. He hated the fact that God had a sense of humor and had proven his last thought untrue. He tried not to panic, and to focus on what had to be done.

"Is she okay? Does she need anything?"

"She's in labor, Terrell. She doesn't have the flu," Arianna replied. "I don't know where the hell Gary is. I can't find him anywhere. I need for you to get here!"

"I can't," he confessed weakly.

"What do you mean, you can't? Where are you, and what's all that crying in the background?"

Terrell thought quickly. *God, I know what I'm about to ask you is wrong, but please help me come up with a lie and make it a good one,* he prayed.

"I'm across town at County. One of my friends had a little mishap, and I came to try to help out," he blurted.

"Oh, okay. Well, get to the hospital as soon as you can," Arianna told him.

"I will," he assured her.

"And Terrell?"

"Yeah?"

"She's asking for you. Please hurry up."

"I'll be there in twenty minutes," he told her and put his phone back in his pocket. Leah was coming out of the room when he walked back down the hallway.

"Well, it's a boy. Nine pounds, four ounces," she announced.

"A boy," he said to himself. *I have a son.* "Can I see him?"

"Sure," she said with a confused look on her face. "I didn't think you'd wanna come back inside."

They walked into the room where the doctor was still with Darla. She was no longer screaming, but she was still moaning something terrible. Terrell focused his attention away from her and on the tiny creature lying on the warming bed, wrapped in a blanket. Terrell just stared, waiting to see if he would feel that instant bond he had heard so many fathers brag about when they tell of the first time they laid eyes on their children. There was none for him. No tingling sensations, no overwhelming emotions; all he saw was a kid he didn't want.

"Wanna hold him?" Leah asked, picking up the small bundle.

"No, that's okay. I gotta go. Nine pounds. That's pretty big for a preemie, huh?" He looked at Leah.

"Preemie? This kid definitely isn't a preemie. As a matter of fact, she was two weeks past her due date."

Terrell began to calculate. He counted months and days, and remembered the two times he had slept with Darla. Both times were in early December, before he was committed to Nicole. There was no way that this baby was his. As a matter of fact, she had to already be pregnant while she was sleeping with him.

She set him up. It took all the strength he had not to walk over to her and push her fat, yellow behind out of the bed. Instead, he looked up at the ceiling and gave God thumbs up. Without saying anything, he walked out of the room and never looked back.

65

Toby had just stepped out of the shower when he heard the doorbell. Hoping it was Roni, who never showed up the night before, he threw on a pair of shorts and went to open the door. He prepared himself for the pitiful excuse he knew she'd have. But instead of his fiancée, Stanley was standing in his doorway.

"Oh, I'm sorry, Toby. I thought you'd be up by now. I left my hat and I came back to get it. I guess I should've called," he said, clearly embarrassed.

"No, it's no problem, Stanley. Come on in. Where did you leave it?"

"It was on the bar. That was the last place I had it. I can get it later, really."

Toby unlocked the back door and cut on the porch light. He looked down at his feet and told him, "You go ahead."

"Okay," Stanley said and walked outside. "I don't see it. You think someone picked it up?" Toby went to the hall closet and slipped on a pair of old K-Swiss he wore whenever he cut grass. He joined his friend in the backyard in an effort to find his missing hat. While they were searching, Stan's phone rang.

"Must be Meeko. I told her to call me when she got up." He smiled and flipped the state of the art device open. "Hello."

Toby walked away to give him some privacy and continued the search. He reached behind some tables that were stacked near the bar and found that what he thought was a paper plate was Stanley's hat. He tried to smooth it out as best he could. "Yo, Stan. I found it, but it's a little messed up."

Stanley was sitting on one of the picnic tables, rocking back and forth. Toby eased up to him, noticing something was very wrong.

"You okay, Stan? What did Meeko say?" he asked.

"It wasn't Meeko. It was the police. Someone set my house on fire," Stan mumbled.

"What? When?" Toby was stunned.

"A little while ago. I have to get to the hospital."

"The hospital? For what?"

"My brother was inside when the fire was set. He's pretty messed up." Stan continued to rock. Toby could see that he was in shock and in no condition to drive. He pulled him up and led him to his car, which was parked behind Toby's.

"Where are your keys?" Toby asked him.

"On your kitchen counter."

Toby ran to the door and turned the knob. It was locked. He ran around to the back of the house and went through the door that was still slightly ajar. While inside, he grabbed a We Secure U T-shirt and threw it on. He found the keys and rushed back outside. Stanley was leaning up against the truck. He unlocked the doors and commanded him to get in.

"What hospital, Stan?"

"Mercy."

Toby kicked the truck into gear and high-tailed it to Mercy Memorial.

"My brother is all I got in this world, Toby. You know that? We don't have any parents. It's just me and him. If he dies, what am I gonna do?" Stanley asked.

Toby's heart went out to him. He knew exactly how Stan felt. With the exception of Uncle Jay, Terry was all Toby had for family. He couldn't imagine life without his younger brother. "Don't worry, Stan. Your brother is going to be all right. You have to stay positive, though."

Stanley wasn't in any better shape when they made it to the emergency room. Toby had to ask for Sean, because Stan couldn't even say his name, he was so broke down. The nurse had to practically carry him to the back so he could see Sean. Toby told him he would be waiting for him when he came out.

He was leaving a message for Roni, letting her know that he had an emergency and wouldn't be home if she stopped by, when another call came in. Recognizing the number, he answered.

"Yo. You a'ight? I was worried about you," Toby said as he paced down the hall.

"I'm cool, man, but have I got some stuff to tell you. I had a hell of a night," Terrell replied.

"Naw, I bet it don't compare to what I gotta tell you. You're not gonna believe where I'm at."

"You ain't gonna believe where I'm at. Nicole has been in labor since last night. We're at the hospital now."

"Stop playing. I'm at the hospital too!"

Toby heard Nicole let out a yell for Terrell to get off the phone before she threw it across the room, and his brother told him he had to go.

"Let me know what happens. And Terry?"

"Yeah?"

"I love you, bro. Congrats."

"Love you too, Uncle T."

"You're talking to Toby? I'm dying over here and you're talking to Toby of all people?" he heard Nicole squeal.

"I had to call him and tell him we were at the hospital, baby."

The phone went dead and Toby walked back down to the waiting area. He had just taken a seat when he saw Ms. Ernestine coming in, wiping tears from her eyes.

"Ms. Ernestine," he called to her.

"Oh, Toby," she cried as she embraced him. "I'm so glad you made it. I knew you'd be here soon enough. I just knew it."

"Ms. Ernestine, what's wrong? What are you doing here?" He was confused.

"What do you mean what am I doing here? This is where they brought Roni."

"Roni? What happened? Where is she?" Toby was distraught.

"She was in an accident, Toby. No one called you? I'm so sorry." Ms. Ernestine began crying harder.

"Accident? Where?" Tears began to form in his eyes now. He knew she was upset, but he needed to know what happened.

A few moments later, Kayla, Geno, Tia, and Yvonne all arrived. They began to comfort Ms. Ernestine and he slipped out to the receptionist to see if he could find out some more information.

"Excuse me. I'm Veronica Black's fiancé. Is there anyone that can give me an idea of what happened to her and how she is?" he asked.

The nurse recognized him from earlier and nodded. She told him to stand there and wait a few moments while she found someone to talk to him. He stood, expecting a doctor rather than the police officer who approached him.

"You're here for Veronica Black?" the man asked.

"Yes, I am. I'm Tobias Sims, her fiancé. I understand she was in an accident, but no one is giving me any information. Where was she driving?"

"Driving? She wasn't driving. Your fiancée was in a fire in a home located in Wheatland Heights. She's received some serious burns and she's in stable condition. All in all, she's lucky to be alive. So is the friend she was with."

"Roni?" Toby called her name softly. She looked so fragile, lying in bed with all the tubes and monitors attached to her. He walked a little closer. "Roni?"

There was a nurse at the foot of her bed, writing something on her chart. She looked at Toby and told him, "She's pretty out of it because of the drugs, but she can hear you. Just talk to her."

"Ron, can you hear me? It's me, baby. Open your eyes for me."

Her face was dark and bruised. The doctors said that she had suffered several first- and second-degree burns, but she would be fine. He had spent all day at the hospital along with every-one else, waiting to see her. Her mother told him he could go in first, alone. He thought seeing her would be hard, but it wasn't. He needed to see her; he wanted her to be awake so she could explain why she was inside Stanley's house, asleep with Sean when the fire was set. There had to be a reasonable explanation for it. Just hours before, she had assured him that she loved him and he could trust her.

God, just let her wake up and tell me something, anything to make me understand how she could do this to me. Could she really betray me like this again?

"Can I kiss her?" he asked the nurse.

"Gently, just on her forehead."

He leaned over and kissed her lightly, whispering her name again. "Roni, I love you."

Her eyes fluttered open and she blinked. He smiled at her, elated that she was finally conscious. The feeling of anger with her seemed to subside when he saw that she was alive.

"Hey, sweetie." He grinned. An overwhelming feeling of love came over him as the fear of losing her gripped his heart.

"Sean?" was the name that escaped from her lips. Her eyes closed once again and she drifted back to sleep.

Devastated, Toby looked down at her hand, which he was holding. As he slipped the ring off her finger, a tear rolled down his cheek.

66

Tyler Alexander Sims was born at five minutes after 7:00 on the fifth day of the seventh month. He only weighed five pounds, seven ounces, and although he was born premature, he was healthy. For that reason, his father felt he should be named Seven Cinque Sims, which would be a tight name should his son want to embark on a future career in hip-hop. His mother, who already had plans for her son to be either a biochemist or a heart surgeon, instinctively said no to such a ridiculous name. They did, however, agree that he was the most adorable baby they had ever seen.

Not only was Terrell present for the delivery, he even cut the cord. And when he looked into his son's eyes for the first time, he wept like he had never done before. He looked over at Nicole, who was crying as well, and told her, "Thank you. You have always been a remarkable woman, but this is the most remarkable thing I have ever seen. Thank you for letting me be here with you."

"You were there with me the entire time, Terrell. I love and appreciate everything you've done over the past few months. Now you're ready to be a father *and* my husband."

He took his son into his arms and carried him over to his mother. He had never felt so complete in all of his life. He was glad that he had made the changes he did, because having Nicole and his son in his life made it well worth it.

The nurse came in and said that she was going to take Tyler and let Nicole get some rest. Terrell kissed Nicole and told her he would be back by the time she woke up, then followed his son, making sure he got to the nursery safely.

"You did good, Terrell," Arianna said as she walked up to him.

"You did good too, Ari. You held it down for my girl, and we have a healthy son. I don't know how I can ever repay you." He hugged her.

"Oh, I'm sure you'll think of something. How about something big and expensive, like oh, let's say a Benz?" she laughed.

"Sure. After my son's first album goes platinum, I got you." He nodded. "Where's Gary? I'm surprised he hasn't shown up yet to regulate."

"Well, you know we're not together since he can't regulate what time to come home at night. He thought that just because I was staying with Nicole he could go out and do whatever."

"Take it from someone that knows firsthand, that's the easiest way to lose your woman," Terrell told her.

She went inside to see Nicole and he went off to find Toby, who hadn't shown up yet.

As he was headed to his car, Terrell found his brother sitting outside the front of the hospital.

"What are you doing out here, Toby? I thought you would've been up to check out your new nephew."

Toby nodded. There was something about the way he looked that worried Terrell.

He walked over and sat beside Toby on the curb. "What's going on?" he asked.

"Too much to tell. Where do I even begin?" Toby shrugged and looked down.

"You been here all day?"

"Yep." Toby nodded. He picked up a pebble that was next to his foot and threw it.

"Come on. You can treat me to breakfast and tell me all about what happened."

Terrell held his hand out. Toby looked at him then grabbed it, pulling himself up. They went into the hospital cafeteria and each got a cup of coffee. Finding a table in the far corner, they sat and Terrell listened as his brother recounted everything that happened after he left the cookout. At the end of his story, he reached into his beat up sneaker and pulled out the ring he took back from Roni. It was then that Terrell truly saw how hurt his brother was.

"I'm sorry about all of this, Toby. I'll be the first one to tell you that what happened last night was messed up. I mean, I never would've thought that Roni would even cheat on you."

"Join the club. But she did—not only once, but twice, and with the same guy, at that. I guess I must be real stupid, huh? I wonder what he had that I ain't have."

"Don't be stupid. That's Roni's loss, not yours. You have a lot. She just threw it away. Just like I did with Nicole, but I was blessed enough to get it back, and I am not losing it again. I think when you lose it, it makes you appreciate it more, because then you realize how you really fucked up after it's too late. And then, if you're ever given that second chance, you'll do whatever you can to make it even better than when you first got it, if it's true love."

"Terry, what the hell are you talking about?" Toby asked with a frown.

"Man, who cares? All I know is that I been up all night, my girl took me back, I got a new son, and life is good. Yesterday my life was at the worst possible point I thought it could be, but today it's at its best. What a difference a day makes, huh? Come on. Let's go buy some *It's a Boy* stuff for little Seven."

"You named him Seven?"

"No, Nicole made me name him Tyler Alexander Sims, but Seven would've been a tight name, huh?"

"You gave him my middle name?" Toby beamed.

"Yeah, I wanted the middle name to be Cinque, but let me explain why . . ." Terrell put his arm around his brother as they walked out of the cafeteria and he explained the method to his madness.

67

Toby stepped out of his truck and looked at the mirrored glass building. He looked down at the card and made sure he was at the right address. The sign on the front door confirmed that he was. It looked more like a finely decorated doctor's office than the atmosphere he expected. There were several women sitting in the lobby, chatting softly as they waited.

"Can I help you?" a beautiful Puerto Rican woman asked him. She was dressed in what he thought was a lab coat, but he could see she had on a dress underneath.

"Um, yes. I'd like to get a massage," he told her.

She stared at him with a look that let him know that a massage would be all that he was getting. "Full body?"

"Uh, yes." He nodded.

"Let me see if we have anything available. Weekends are always busy, and it's the holiday weekend, which makes it even worse." She looked down at her schedule. "I think I can squeeze you in. Marguerite can take you if you can wait twenty minutes."

"No, I want Isis to do it," he said quickly.

"Excuse me?" She frowned.

"I prefer Isis. That's who I need an appointment with."

"I'm sorry, sir. Isis is our busiest masseuse. She's been booked up for months. I can get you in with Marguerite today, and then let you have Isis's next available, which is two weeks from Thursday. How about that?"

"That won't work. I need to see her today. I'll pay double."

She gave Toby a startled look. The women who were waiting became silent as he waited for her answer.

"That's very generous of you, sir, but I'm sorry. There's nothing I can do. She's really booked up."

"Please, ma'am. I have had the worst night of my life. I am tense to the point that if I don't get a massage by the best in the business, I am going to snap. There has to be something that can be done." Toby threw his hands up in exasperation.

"Lisa, let him have my appointment with Isis and I'll go to Marguerite," a woman approached and said.

"Why, Mrs. Taylor, that's very generous of you," she said. "You should thank her, sir."

"Thank you, Mrs. Taylor. I appreciate it." Toby nodded.

"You're welcome." The woman went back and took her seat.

"Let's see. That one hour with Isis, that'll be $300."

"What?" he shrieked.

"You said you'd pay double, and you know we're gonna have to compensate Mrs. Taylor, as well."

Toby took out his credit card and passed it to her. After giving him his receipt, she told him to follow her, and led him further into the office.

There was soothing jazz playing and the aroma of lavender in the air. He found himself relaxing with each step. She opened a door and gave him a robe, a towel and some slippers, telling him to get undressed and lie on the table. "Isis will be here momentarily."

He obliged, and after fighting the sudden wave of sleep that overcame him when he lay face down on the table, he heard the door open. He buried his head into his arms, which were crossed in front of him.

"Hello, I'm Isis. I heard you requested me personally. I'm flattered. Did someone recommend me?" she asked him softly. He could hear her moving around.

"Yes. A friend of mine," he said without lifting his head.

"Well, you be sure to thank your friend for me. Is this your first time?"

"Yes," he told her. He moaned as her hands began to knead into his back.

"Then I'll have to keep that in mind and be gentle." Isis laughed, and he giggled along with her.

She remained fairly quiet as she pushed and rubbed his shoulders and then his legs. Her stroke was strong yet her touch was light, and he thoroughly enjoyed it. He was grateful that his tattoo was on the front of his chest and she couldn't see it.

"It's okay if you fall asleep. That happens quite a bit. But I can always wake you up with a hand job—I mean a manicure."

He lifted his head and looked at her. "You knew it was me!"

"Of course! How could I not? You think guys come in here every day and pay three hundred dollars for me?" She slapped him on his shoulder.

"I would've paid more, believe that," he confessed, noticing that she was still wearing the chain and charm he gave her.

"What are you doing here?"

"Meeko told me you had to work all day, and I had to see you. Your cell isn't on."

"Because I'm at work." She sighed.

"So, I figured I'd buy an hour of your time. Didn't know it would be three hundred dollars, though."

"You would've paid more, though. What's going on, Toby?"

He sat up and told her about Stanley and his house being burned down, and Roni getting caught in the blaze with Sean. She climbed on the table next to him and laid her head on his shoulder as he confided everything.

"You're gonna be okay," she told him when he finished. "I know you will. You're a strong man."

"Ice, please don't. Just let me say something before you go off on one of these encouraging tangents, please. I know that I'm gonna be fine. I found true love and someone I can love unconditionally. I didn't know that before, but I have."

"I know what I said earlier, but Toby, don't be stupid. I mean, unless she has a really good excuse, which I'm not saying she can't have, then I think it's time to let it go. I like Roni and all, but—"

"I'm not talking about Roni, Ice. I'm talking about you. I love you. You are my true love."

"Toby, you're talking out of hurt and anger because of what happened."

"No, I'm not. I'm talking out of frustration of being in love with you, but you won't forgive yourself for what happened that night and just allow me to love you. Loving someone is not beating yourself up over something you had no control over. You've got to love yourself enough, Ice, to let someone love you. And that someone is me, baby."

Toby didn't stop the tears from falling, and this time there was more than one. He stood up and looked at Isis so she could see that he was serious and this was real. He reached into his pocket and pulled out the ring.

"I know that's not what I think it is, Toby."

"What is that?" He smiled through the tears.

"You took the ring back?"

"I took it back. Now I can pawn it and pay off my three hundred dollar credit card bill for this massage that I'm not even getting."

He pulled her to him and kissed her on the mouth. As her tongue met his, he thought this was what perfection must feel like. She stroked his back, and he felt himself getting aroused. When they separated, they looked down at the towel he was wearing. "Looks like I need a manicure, huh?"

"You'll get it when I get the drink I never got at the party," she teased and kissed him again.

"Let me ask you this question," he said then paused. "How do you feel about having kids?"

"Depends on if I'm having them with a man who loves me enough to make some." She winked and his heart leapt.

68

T'was the night before Christmas, and the church was standing room only as everyone prepared for the entrance of the bride. The bridal party was fairly small, consisting of two bridesmaids and two best men. The maid of honor, Meeko, who had recently become engaged to Stanley, proceeded down the aisle first. The matron of honor, Kayla, who had wed a month before, was next. The bride was escorted by her father, who beamed with pride as he walked down the aisle with a daughter on his arm for the second time. And as happy as he was that both his daughters were now married, he knew he would still be working for a long time to pay off the debt of their weddings.

The bride looked lovingly at her husband-to-be, who now, with the help of his partner and best friend, owned one of the fastest growing security installation firms in the state. The groom looked over at his best men, knowing that this day would not be complete without them.

As the couple took their place at the altar, Toby, along with his fiancée, Isis, came before them and performed "The Closer I Get to You." Before they even finished, there wasn't a dry eye in the church. The wedding went off without a hitch.

Uncle Jay hosted the reception at Jasper's. While everyone ate, drank, and partied to "This Christmas" by the Temptations, he passed out cigars.

"What's this for, Uncle Jay? Anjelica, is there something you and Jermaine need to tell us?" Toby asked.

"He's passing out cigars, I'm not." Jermaine laughed.

"And you won't be passing any out until after we buy that house in Wheatland Heights, either." Anjelica kissed him on the nose.

"You all ain't hear?" Uncle Jay asked. "I found out I'm a father. Got the call on Friday."

"What? When did you have a baby?" Isis laughed.

"Well, the baby was born Fourth of July, but the mama just moved back into town last week and called me. You all may remember her. Darla. Yes sir, got me a big old fine boy!"

Everyone groaned as he began singing along with the Temptations, happy with the news he'd just shared.

After toasting the new couple, Terrell went and sat next to his best friend who was now his supervisor. Cora Ware had been convicted of first-degree arson and sentenced to thirteen years in prison. Kayla now had her job and was doing fine.

"What's up, DQ?"

"Not anymore, Terrell, not anymore. I haven't had any drama in a while, so you have to find a new name for me." She smiled.

"I have to find something else to call you since you've relinquished your title as the queen of drama. You're growing up. You were there for Anjelica on her big day, and I'm proud of you," he told her.

"I mean, she is my sister. Nothing can ever change that. You can't pick your family."

"You're right about that," Terrell looked over at Uncle Jay, "but you can always pick your friends."

"I'm glad I picked you," she told him.

"What are you talking about? I picked you."

"You did not Terrell. I remember that day we were in the break room and you came in sitting by yourself. I invited you over there to sit at our table!" Kayla yelled.

They went back and forth with each other until he noticed a couple walking in. She looked over and stopped mid-sentence. All eyes seemed to be on Roni and Sean as they walked into the room, hand in hand.

"I'm going over there before something jumps off," she told him.

"And I thought you said there wouldn't be no more drama." He stood. "Man, this stuff is just getting started."